Past Preserve Us

by

Carol Nickles

The Wild Rose Press, Inc.
PO Box 708
Adams Basin, NY 14410-0708
Visit us at www.thewildrosepress.com

Publishing History
First Edition, 2025
Trade Paperback ISBN 978-1-5092-6126-0
Digital ISBN 978-1-5092-6127-7

Published in the United States of America

Dedication

To my forever love, Gerard Peter "Boom Boom" Nickles, Jr. You inspire me to be a better human.

Prologue

Drawing the tips of her ice-cold fingers over her nose, Jeannie Parks blew tepid breaths into her tented hands. In a dream-like state, she shuffled toward the living room bay window overlooking the school district parking lot. Towering lights eclipsed a blue-black, predawn murkiness and illuminated crystalline snowflakes frosting rows of warming school buses.

Across the street, at the home of Widow Anderson, a bedraggled string of holiday lights loitered two weeks past the Feast of the Epiphany.

Jeannie pressed her nose against the window and squinted. Passing headlights revealed the yard adjacent to Mrs. Anderson's. She gasped. Yesterday and every day since their oldest son deployed to Vietnam, a red-white-and-blue swag festooned the anterior porch of Enrico and Maria Fernandez's stone house. The symbol of tribute and hope endured the day-to-day and month-to-month rains, winds, heat, frost, snow, and ice. Now, their veranda stood bare.

Cinching the ties of her corduroy bathrobe, Jeannie gritted her jaw.

The phone sounded. She reached the kitchen on the ninth shrill ring and plucked the receiver from the wall.

"Jeannie, have you heard?"

The raspy voice of her mother-in-law grated against her left ear. Clenching the phone, Jeannie fought the inclination to corkscrew into a fetal position. "Virginia, what's wrong?"

"President Nixon signed a ceasefire agreement late yesterday. Every American troop is recalled. Our boys are finally coming home." Virginia cried.

Loosening her grip on the phone, Jeannie pressed her spine to the kitchen door and slithered to a hunched position. Sobs racked her chest.

"Frank…" Virginia whispered.

Would be coming home, too. Jeannie squeezed shut her eyes. She opened them. *But he's not.*

Above the fish bowl, a winter scene of white-tailed deer foraging among Eastern white pines marked the calendar page of January 1968.

The refrigerator hummed.

From her bedroom, the clock radio played "Puff the Magic Dragon."

"Love you, honey. Dad and I will visit soon."

"Love you, too, Mom." Jeannie pulled a wadded tissue from her bathrobe pocket. She snugged the phone into its cradle and dabbed the tissue over her eyes and cheeks. She walked into her bedroom and closed the door. Collecting a photo of Private First Class Frank Parks from her dresser, she sat on the edge of her one-side-dented double mattress. The picture had been taken in Fort Benning, Georgia, where Frank completed basic training. Jeannie studied the American flag in the background and the globe on an axis in the foreground. She licked a finger and then manipulated the end to smooth the severe expression on his youthful face. She trailed her finger over the crisp Army cap with the jutting brim trimmed in parallel rows of white soutache trim and gold rivets covering his clean-shaven head.

She traced his strong chin, football-player neck, and broad shoulders decorated with a platoon leader's regalia. She fingered the striped bars on his breast pocket and followed each gold button down the middle of his chest. And then, for the millionth time, Jeannie pressed a kiss over the glass-shielded protected mouth, clutched the picture against her breast, and hung her head.

As thousands of yard ornament American flags waved in jubilation, Jeannie let her tears fall for Frank, the other men and women who chose courage and honor over selfishness and apathy, and the ones left to plod through life without them. Jeannie cried for Virginia and Pete, who lost their only son, for five-year-old Joey, who lost his father, and for herself, who lost her youth, her happiness, and the only man she ever loved.

Chapter 1

Great Lakes University
Winter Term, 1968

Jeannie Parks yanked a hard left on the steering wheel, flattened her right foot on the gas pedal, and swerved into the last available Home Economics Department staff parking space. She glanced at her watch for the twelfth time since she'd left a sulking Joey waving goodbye. Mopping spilled apple juice, chasing a runaway puppy, and coaxing Joey out of dinosaur-printed pajamas and into his school clothes had put her behind schedule.

Despite the forty-five-degree outside temperature, perspiration shimmered on her forehead and threatened the matronly hairdo she had hastily knotted at the nape of her neck.

The likelihood of facing the sour side of the dean's assistant, Marie, grew with each hindered minute. Jeannie grabbed her briefcase and darted around the dormant football stadium to the paved path leading to the Home Economics building.

Atop Beaumont Tower, on West Circle Drive, forty-nine carillon bells chimed and announced the hour.

Jeannie quickened her pace. *Only four more days until Spring Break. Tina will leave with her roommates*

4

for a sunny getaway, and there goes my college work-study helper. The timing is terrible. I am so behind on cataloging, and dang, why did I agree to serve on the time-guzzling, mind-numbing Museum Faculty Selections Committee?

Sunlight streamed over the shadowy depths of the Red Cedar River and reflected off fourteen stories of the mirrored-glass south wing of the Graduate School library. Bursts of golden forsythia and glossy myrtle softened the starkness of the stone bridge spanning the waterway.

Jeannie's navy, thin-leather heels boasted expensive quality. But the footwear hadn't been designed with haste or muddy Michigan conditions in mind. She speed-walked, continuing in the center of the cement walkway. Collisions were possible if you strayed. Passers to the left, bikes to the right, and slow walkers in the middle, where a campus of eighty-thousand plus faculty, administrators, students, support personnel, and seasoned visitors adhered to the recognized traffic flow.

Rhythmic panting sounds advanced.

Sole-smacking concrete vibrations loomed.

A sweat-soaked runner bounded in front of her. Tight gray shorts clung to his muscled backside. Her breath caught. She stalled her steps. *What a perfect butt.*

He stepped widely to the right.

"Hey," Jeannie screamed.

A ten-speed bicycle, a student, and an overstuffed backpack bounced off the errant jogger like tennis balls ricocheting off a brick wall.

The bike spokes twirled wildly as intensely as the pounding of her heart. The accident occurred within inches of her. *I can't step off the path. My heels will sink into the ground.* Jeannie clutched her briefcase and planted her feet. *Breathe. Just breathe.*

"So sorry." The student scrabbled to his knees and leveled his palms on the ground.

The errant runner planted his feet and pulled the biker to a standing position in one easy tug. "No harm done." He smiled and set his fists on either side of his beveled waist. Then, he jumped his gaze to Jeannie.

She pursed her lips and scowled.

The quickly downed bacon-and-egg scramble that had brought morning pep jolted upward and blasted a malevolent taste. Jeannie crisscrossed an arm over her abdomen.

"So sorry." The student brushed his sleeves and pants and threaded the backpack straps over his arms. Then he shrugged the load to settle in the middle of his back, balanced himself on his bike, and rode toward the Student Union.

The jogger resumed running. Then, he glanced back, grinned, and snapped a right-handed salute.

"Look where you're going," Jeannie muttered. *Humph. What a knucklehead. Can't he run somewhere else? Good grief. Several running tracks and a great big field house are within easy access. That idiot is responsible for this mishap.*

His chiseled physique jeopardized the morning commuters as he continued on his unpredictable path. Still staring, Jeannie stood riveted to the sidewalk. *His calves are so cut. His thighs are rock-solid.* Diminutive tremors zinged throughout her chest. Recalling the unmasked intensity of his gaze and the combination of morning calamities, she accelerated her steps. Reaching the wide-cut steps of a cavernous Gothic-style building, she darted up the stairs, grasped a brass door handle on a ten-foot-tall oak door, and pulled. Then, thrusting her slim hip against the door's interior, she stepped into the hallway.

Classrooms flanked either side of the corridor.

Whirring sounds radiated from the Sewing Lab.

Jeannie shoved open a floor-to-ceiling door. Gold letters stamped on the inset window spelled *Department of Home Economics*.

Shifting between the registration counter and the closed entry to the boss's suite, Marie patrolled like a Doberman Pinscher behind a chain-link fence. A leopard-print top bubbled over her generous curves. Her piled-high hair was shellacked into a style that should have been abandoned ten years prior. Reading glasses edged in glistening red sequins pinched the point of no return on the slope of her flared nostrils. Marie peered over them and tapped one crimson fingernail on the form facing the book-laden student on the opposite side of the counter. "It states here on line twenty-three that all transcripts submitted for consideration must bear the granting institution's official seal. So, the copies you have will not suffice."

Jeannie clenched her teeth. Marie's accent further damned the copies by voicing them in a high nasal *cop eez*.

"But Mrs. Wilson," the unsuspecting student began.

Marie's piercing glare scored a double play. First, the glower silenced the student's lament. Secondly, the scowl stalled Jeannie as she entered the office.

Glancing at the industrial clock over the door,

Marie swerved her gaze to Jeannie and arched her eyebrows.

Jeannie cinched her shoulders. *No one is immune to Marie's ironclad definition of punctuality, not the dean or faculty, and God help the students.* "*Bonjour,* Marie." *Speaking in Marie's native tongue is one possible neutralizer of her temper.* Jeannie gritted her teeth and smiled wanly.

"*Bonjour, Madame.*" Marie amplified her eyes and scowled. "Your teacher's assistant, Tina, is sitting outside the Collections Room." She folded her arms over her curvy chest. "For more than ten minutes."

Jeannie cringed. "Thanks, Marie. Any messages?"

"Eve from the American Costume Society called to see if you'd like to present at the next conference in Chicago." Marie pushed her glasses higher on her nose.

"I'll call her today." Reaching around Marie, Jeannie retrieved several message slips and interoffice envelopes from her staff mailbox.

"Oh, Jeannie. There's a package in the Collections Room from the manager of the Carburetors."

"As in Detroit Basketball Carburetors?"

"The very same." Marie smirched. "Maybe they sent you game tickets. There are a lot of handsome, single men on that team." She winked.

Jeannie froze. *Hmmm… Well, I'll be. Marie has a saucy side.*

****

With the tip of her shoe, Jeannie wedged open the office door. Then, she walked past classroom scenes of handsomely tailored and painstakingly coiffed faculty writing on chalkboards or poised regally at the helm of their domains. *Compared to Mathematics, Biology,*

History, Languages, oh, heck, any other department, this department of Clothing and Textiles, we can claim the best dressed and most professional appearances. Jeannie smirked.

Hunched at a desk outside the Historic Textiles and Costumes Repository, graduate assistant Tina gripped a yellow highlighter pen in her right hand. In sharp contrast to faculty garb, Tina wore the university student uniform—long straight hair parted down the middle, hip-hugger frayed blue jeans, tennis shoes, and a slogan T-shirt.

Norton's Anthology of British Literature lay open on the desktop.

"Hi, Tina. Sorry I'm late." Jeannie juggled her briefcase and office keys to unlock the Collections Room door.

"No problem. I always have reading to do. What's on our agenda today?"

"First, check the faculty requests on the class schedules for artifact displays. Then, hopefully, you'll get to the dusting, and working together, we will reroll the quilts." Jeannie stepped inside the dimmed, climate-controlled room.

The Historic Textiles Collection at Great Lakes University was housed in an area equivalent in size to a mom-and-pop bookshop and paneled in musky-redolent, moth-repellant cedar. Floor-to-ceiling cabinets stored hanging garments and boxed accessories. In addition, glass-fronted cabinets contained textile tools, manuscripts, catalogs, and fashion magazines.

Jeannie paused in front of an open closet. A silk jacquard vest dating back to the 1700s and likely worn by a French nobleman hung on a padded hanger. *Was the owner spared the guillotine?* Jeannie shivered.

A bank of western-exposure windows allowed the only natural light in the room. Jeannie dropped her briefcase alongside a scarred oak desk below the casements and sat in a sturdy Windsor chair. She had insisted on bringing the family heirloom, regardless of the university promising comfortable seating furniture. Jeannie stroked the silky-smooth wraparound arm and settled her butt into the carved-out saddle seat. *If only this chair could talk.* Thanks to Grandmother's passion for family lore, Jeannie knew a bit of what this family keepsake had endured. Crafted in 1880 from red maple by Polish immigrant and skilled master cooper, George Worchok, the chair survived the Great Thumb Fire of 1881, Michigan's most devastating natural disaster.

On their wedding day, George gifted the chair to fire survivors, her great-great-grandparents Peter and Ginny Nickles. Four generations of her family had rested their weary backs on the slanted slats of this chair, and now, it was hers.

Sewing from before she started school and familiar with a tape measure and sharp shears, Jeannie clerked weekends and after school at her family's retail fabric store, Andreae Fashion Fabrics. As a college student at Michigan State University, she earned a Bachelor of Arts in Clothing and Textiles and a Master of Science degree in Clothing and Textiles with an emphasis on physical sciences and historic preservation. Sighing, Jeannie turned her attention to the phone communication slips, each painstakingly written in Marie's vertically rigid, French-flourished penmanship.

From: Museum Director's Office. Interview Meeting Reminder. All Search Committee Members and

Museum Directors, Mammalogy candidate Dr. Nicholas Randall presents today at noon in the Grand Parlor, Second Floor of the Exhibits Museum. Jeannie shook her head. *Maybe I'll learn something about Michigan mammals I can share with Joey tonight.* Her breathing slowed, and she smiled.

From: Sharon. Call me regarding Widow Care Fall Schedule. The Joey-inspired smile leveled to a sober lip-biting. She pocketed the yellow slip of paper. *I'll call her right before I go to bed.*

From: Dr. Eve Creekmore, American Costume Society. Your doctoral dissertation on the history of the Yale, Michigan woolen mill has been accepted as a workshop presentation. Jeannie clapped a hand over her mouth. *What an honor. It will take work to polish my lecture, but I have all summer to do that.*

"Should I pull the 1830s day dress and the velvet Balenciaga gown?" Tina called from the doorway.

"Are you prepping for Dr. Hally's class?" Jeannie plucked a pencil from a vase on her desk.

"Yes, I checked the syllabus, and today's lecture and class presentation are textures. I thought the day dress would challenge students because of the nubby silk. Besides, it's plaid. The Balenciaga original has such a plush pile."

Screech.

Tina dragged a metal dress form into the tiny office. As she straightened and adjusted her lopsided load, she stretched a logo with ghoulish skulls, art deco roses, and what looked to be hallucinogenic mushrooms over her chest.

Jeannie grimaced. She rolled a pencil between her thumb and index finger. "Both the dress and gown are good choices."

"By the way, we're running low on acid-free paper. When I stuff those big leg-of-mutton, day dress sleeves, I will empty another box."

"Noted." Jeannie scribbled *acid-free paper* on a notepad on the right side of her desk.

"Are you attending the Brown Bag Lunch Series at the museum today? I will earn extra credit in my biology class if I do." Tina straddled the mannequin, crumpled a sheet of paper, and thrust it into a sleeve cavern.

"So, you're interested in the mammal population on Isle Royale?"

"Well…not especially." Tina grinned. "I'm going because my friend Ashley says Dr. Randall, the speaker, is quite the hunk."

"Does attending a candidate job talk of a hunk get you extra credit?" Jeannie arched an eyebrow. "I think your prof sees the value of Dr. Randall exposing you and your fellow students to reputable field research. As a Search Committee member, I'm expected to be there."

"Are you going to open that package?" Tina's gaze jumped to the box appropriating three square feet of floor space. "I'm dying to see."

"I'm curious, too." Jeannie chewed her lip. "Okay, we've got fifteen minutes." Pulling a letter opener from her desktop, the curator bent over the box and tore the taped edges.

Rip.

Ramming a hand into the cardboard box, Jeannie gasped. "Is this what I think it is?"

Tina shoved the mannequin aside. "What?"

"Oh, my. Now, this artifact will be prized forever." Jeannie flopped a tennis shoe on her desk.

Tina dropped her jaw.

"Grab that tape measure."

Standing close to the desk, Tina pinched one end of the tape with an index finger and thumb and held the flexible measuring tool over the center front of the artifact. Then, laying the tape taut around the remaining perimeter of the shoe, she turned her head and with eyes as open as a waiting basketball net, she gazed at Jeannie. "Oh, my gosh. This sneaker is twenty-two inches long. Hey, there's a note inside."

"What's it say?" Jeannie clasped her hands.

"Shoes worn by Detroit Carburetor Captain, Bill 'Big Foot' Bunyan in the National Championship Game, March 14, 1966." Tina squealed. "My boyfriend will be so jealous. I got to touch Bill 'Big Foot's' monster-sized basketball shoes." She sighed. "Just one more?"

"All right. All right. But, please, let's not lose the shoe box. We don't have any shoe containers large enough to store these." Stretching her hand, Jeannie delved stealthily into the package. She extracted a wadded gray textile. With both hands, she held the object aloft.

"A pair of shorts." Tina screamed. "A pair of Carburetor workout shorts."

Jeannie's face flamed. She dropped the garment as if it burned her fingertips. The image of a flippant jogger with brown curly hair and butt-hugging gray shorts scorched her brain. Swallowing, she grabbed the garment and dropped it on top of the shoes. She rubbed her hands together. "Now, get those classroom requests down the hall, and I'll finish reviewing the candidate vita. See you in the Grand Parlor."

"Are you okay? Your face is flushed."

Jeannie moved her hands as if she were sweeping the floor. "I'm fine. Go on."

Tina dragged the mannequin through the entry and shut the door.

Taking a sheaf of papers, Jeannie scanned the pages. Then, she lowered herself into the Windsor chair, removed her glasses, and chewed on the end of one sidebar.

Nicholas Randall, Ph.D. Candidate for Combined Position: Museum Field Mammologist and Associate Professor. He certainly has all the qualifications. He's spent much time conducting research in extreme weather conditions. Jeannie pressed her lips together and rubbed her palms over the edge of her desk. *What kind of man has the passion and energy to devote his life to animals in such climates?* She sat straight. *Maybe he prefers the company of four-legged creatures? How will he work on an exhibit team? Or any team, for that matter? How he interacts with students will be a crucial factor. Well, I'll know soon enough.* She grabbed her handbag and strolled downstairs to the ladies' room. Jeannie smoothed her hair and reapplied dewdrop pink lipstick, her only concession to makeup. *Who am I kidding? I'm curious if Dr. Randall, the job candidate, is a hunk.*

Chapter 2

Nicholas Randall shrugged from his sweaty athletic wear and dropped onto a soft cloud of luxurious hotel bedding. He closed his eyes and splayed his fingers over his bare chest. Images of a petite, trench-coat-wrapped spitfire tapping her foot on campus concrete and scolding him with her blazing blue eyes played behind his eyelids. He grinned. *The chances of running into her again are as slim as her nicely turned ankles.* He sighed. *Why am I here? Elizabeth. I'm here because of Elizabeth.* Initially, he had no interest in applying for the joint Mammalogy Professor-Field Director of Exhibits position at Great Lakes University.

But Elizabeth had urged him to seek what she deemed a great opportunity. "You would work with two of the world's most renowned field scientists."

I'll let her figure out the career moves. Her strategizing allows me time to do what I'm passionate about—preserving endangered animals.

He had promised to call her after breakfast. Sighing, he lifted the phone receiver from the nightstand. He dialed zero for the front desk and recited the outside number to the hotel operator.

"Harcourt Residence," the maid answered on the second buzz.

"Is Elizabeth there?" Nick massaged his forehead.

"May I ask who is calling?"

"Nick, Nick Randall."

"Just a moment, Dr. Randall."

Click.

"Nick. Darling. How was your flight?"

Elizabeth's sultry voice streamed through the phone. Nick smoothed his calf muscles over the silky sheets. *God, she's sexy.* "A bit bumpy and long." Nick shimmied his backside against the ultra-cushioned bed. He sighed. "A guy on leave from Eielson Air Force Base in Fairbanks sat beside me and made the ride home more interesting. He's a proud member of the fifty-tenth Combat Support Group."

"Nick, you know I don't want to hear anything associated with the military."

Elizabeth switched the tone of her voice from kitten purr to cougar snarl. Nick squeezed shut his eyes. *Nor does anyone in your circle of friends.*

"How did the study go?" She breathed slow, drawn-out huffs.

"We gathered enough data for the grant submission. I think Alaska Fishery and Wildlife appreciate me. Well, listen, I have to go. A committee member picks me up and drives me to the museum within the hour." Opening his eyes, Nick scanned the room's dresser and closet.

"You're wearing the camel hair jacket and the blue oxford shirt?"

"Yes, thanks for shipping them to the hotel."

"I asked for them to be pressed and ready. Nick, wear the repp tie today. That's the one with the diagonal stripe. I also sent the tasseled loafers. You should have navy-blue socks. And, darling, I selected the silky boxers you prefer."

Nick rolled his eyes. She meant the silky boxers *she* preferred. He couldn't care less what kind they were. He was happy to have clean ones. So many times in the field, he had none at all. "I will be coordinated neck to toe by you. Thanks again."

"Darling, call me tonight. I want to talk when I'm alone." Her voice vibrated.

Was she licking the mouthpiece? Oh, boy. She's coming on hot, and I need to keep my focus on an imminent interview. Yikes. He drew the receiver away from his ear, held it at arm's length, and exhaled. "No promises, but I'll try, Elizabeth." Pinching the receiver with the tips of his fingers, he dropped it back in its cradle.

Clunk.

****

Dang. Back-row seats are all taken. Jeannie shrunk her shoulders, wrapped her arms around her chest, and tiptoed to one of the vacant chairs at the front of the Grand Parlor. *I am keeping my coat on—darn old drafty buildings.*

A student from Audio-Visual Services fiddled with the overhead projector.

A man wearing a camel hair jacket with straight auburn hair brushing his collar stood beside him.

Brown paper lunch sacks dotted the tabletops. Vinegary dill pickles, sulfurous egg salad, ripe bananas, and tiny, tangy tangerines scented the air. A fifty-cup percolator emitted predictable burps, misty steam, and the acrid smell of roasted coffee.

Jeannie nodded to colleague and Search Committee member Steve Granger who sat among his entomology undergraduates.

Tina waved, then continued an animated discussion with two girls on either side. Her long hair swished in an arc as she turned from one to another.

Wearing a frayed-collar, tattersall shirt with a dark stain on a section where a classic tie could have easily hidden it, entomologist Steve Granger left his students and stepped to the podium. "As chair of the Search Committee, I am pleased to introduce Dr. Nicholas Randall."

Jeannie gasped. A fresh version of the zigzagging jogger who sent her heart into a bewildering twirl earlier that morning turned from his preoccupation with the audio-visual equipment and faced the crowd with a boyish grin.

Steve motioned as if he were herding a cluster of kindergartners. "C'mon up here, Dr. Randall."

Ashley's description was an honest appraisal. Nicholas Randall was a hunk. Jeannie's breath stuck in her throat. She shifted in her chair. *Oh, my God.*

Rocking the wooden podium with a shoe much in need of a polish, Steve beamed. "Dr. Randall received a bachelor's degree in biology from Bowling Green University and both master's and doctoral degrees in Zoology from Cornell. He has been a faculty member at Arizona State University and Michigan Tech. While in Marquette, Dr. Randall researched mammals at one of our country's national parks—the isolated and spectacular Isle Royale, an archipelago of wilderness in Lake Superior. And he's just returned from research at the Walrus Islands State Game Sanctuary in Alaska. Dr. Randall." Steve sidestepped and applauded.

"Thank you, Dr. Granger." Nick stepped forward, unbuttoned his jacket, spread the front open, and placed his hands on his hips. "I'm thrilled to be here and share my research. First, let me tell you I'd be delighted to continue my career at this university. Michigan has some exceptionally curious mammals here to study, for instance, party animals?"

Tina giggled.

Other students guffawed and slapped their thighs.

He's got the students in the palm of his hand. Jeannie shook her head. *For an incoming instructor, that is a good thing. Interest equates to filling classes and a healthy revenue stream for the department. But, oh, my God.*

****

Nick gripped the podium, bent his head, and turned slowly from side to side. When he straightened, he tucked his chin and met Jeannie's gaze. He chomped on his bottom lip and grinned. "Yesterday morning, I flew from Round Island in the Bering Sea on a twelve-seater floatplane. Next, I transferred to a commercial flight, collected a rental car, and checked into the University Inn—a magical structure with hot water and indoor plumbing. You can't praise those conveniences enough! So first thing this morning, I threw on a pair of shorts and tennis shoes and went for a run on this fine campus. I recognized I was back in civilization when: A. I was terrorized not by a bull walrus but by a student on a bicycle. B. I smelled popcorn rather than sled dog excrement, and C. Women wore pumps and pantyhose, not mukluks and seal parkas."

He leveled his gaze at Jeannie and flashed a smile. *She's checking me out just as much as I am examining her.* A tiny mole accentuated the left side of her face, just outside of the blue eyes that stared earnestly. She wore little makeup, but she didn't need it. Her expressive eyes reflected the blue depths of Lake Superior. He shifted his weight from one Italian leather-clad foot to another. *Bet she's as humble as a mouse. Why am I intrigued?*

****

Jeannie crossed and uncrossed her legs in her folding metal chair. Slipping her coat off, she perused the tie expertly knotted and snugged to the candidate's athletic neck. A coordinating tailored shirt sported a precisely pointed collar. His wool tweed trousers exhibited flawless construction, welt pockets, and cuffed hems with a perfectly executed European cut. His footwear was a stunning contrast to the sloppy tennis shoes he had worn earlier. *He must have a woman in his life. No animal researcher I've ever met has had such superb taste in clothing or the wherewithal to care for it. He might be a good-looking, charming, intelligent guy, but I still think he's a knucklehead. And according to all the Psychology of Dress research, first impressions count.*

Enthusiastic applause ripped through the room.

Breaking from her reverie, Jeannie clapped.

Steve Granger rose and walked to the podium. "Thanks for showing up, everyone. We're all more enlightened about the gray wolf, and we wish Dr. Randall well on his next venture. I'd like museum staff and members of the Search Committee to stay and meet our candidate."

Jeannie compressed her lips, slipped the strap of her handbag over her shoulder, and tucked her coat in the crook of her elbow. She walked to the milling group of Selection Committee members. As she paused to be introduced, she felt her pulse kicking into staccato.

"And this is Jeannie Parks, Curator of Historic Costumes and Textiles. She's a doctoral candidate in Home Economics, and, by the way, Jeannie's on the Search Committee." Steve crossed his arms over his chest.

Nick grasped her hand, held it, and firmly pressed it before he released it. "Jeannie, pleased to meet you. I better do my best to impress you."

As Nick's hand squeezed hers, Jeannie relived the vision of his squeezed buttocks. *Darn. This is awkward.* She slid her warmed hand down her side, jutted her chin, and inhaled deeply. "Dr. Randall, I now appreciate the International Wolf Center and the Timberwolf Alliance." She tucked her right ankle behind her left foot and straightened her spine. *Better put a quick end to this cat-and-mouse game.* "On behalf of this campus, I apologize for your morning mishap. The daybreak traffic can be pretty dangerous." Nicholas Randall's eye color dissolved from foreboding brown to perceptive amber.

"Jeannie, thank you for the compliment." He bowed slightly, scanned her from top to bottom, and grinned. "Regarding the latter, you could say I was just getting my land legs back." He stomped his feet and swooned his shoulders.

Stunned, she shook her head and attempted a scowl. Despite her first efforts, an involuntary smile lifted her cheeks. Her breath stalled and netted the scent of his woodsy aftershave. Her heart raced.

Standing beside Nick, Steve raised his eyebrows. "Have you two already met?"

Jeannie blushed.

Nick gummed his lips and nodded.

Steve placed a hand on Nick's shoulder. "C'mon. More introductions to make."

"Lead on." Nick adjusted his briefcase against his hip and stepped behind Steve.

"Good luck, Dr. Randall," Jeannie called.

He turned his head.

His gaze impaled her.

Then he curled his lips in a smirk and raised a hand in a salute.

Jeannie startled and narrowly avoided a collision with Chief Preparator Cal.

"Whoa. Slow down, Jeannie. Good presentation, wasn't it?" Cal drawled in his soft West Virginia accent and squeezed lightly on her upper arm.

"Oh, Cal. Yes, it was." Jeannie expelled a deep breath. She clasped Cal's elbow.

"Hey, do you have a few minutes? I'd like to show you the space dedicated to the Michigan Mammals Exhibit." Cal rested an arm over her shoulder.

"Sure. I always have time for you." Jeannie smiled and traipsed in tandem as they descended the wide granite stairs to the first floor. The afternoon sun filtered through the Carnegie-inspired, stained glass windows above, warming her head and shoulders.

As chief preparator, Cal's opinion of candidates was vital. During his thirty-year position, Cal had worked with the best archaeologists, paleontologists, ornithologists, anthropologists, and mammalogists. He had the patience of fall-planted bulbs and the enthusiasm of a Notre Dame cheerleader.

Three years ago, Cal took Jeannie aside following her introduction to the University Exhibits squad.

"Anything you need, dear, I'm sure I have it in my tool collection or up here." He had tapped the fringe of white hair between his freckled bald head and oversized ears.

Cal became more than a colleague. He was a dear friend and protector. He and his librarian wife, Loretta, often included Jeannie and Joey in their Sunday night family dinners featuring smoked ham and a recreated blue-ribbon-prize-winning, smoky-maple pecan pie.

"Jeannie?" Cal's voice lowered.

"Yes?"

"Are you all right? But, hey, is there a reason I shouldn't trust this Dr. Randall?" Cal sucked in his left cheek and puffed out the right. His glasses tilted precariously.

She waved a hand in front of her face. "Why would you think that?"

Cal gripped her shoulder. "Just a feeling."

"I know as much as you do. So, what have you been up to?"

"Well, glad you asked." Cal righted his spectacles, blew out a breath, and formed an elfish grin. "Let me show you."

Stopping in front of a bare area about twenty feet square, Cal gazed through the aslant, wire-rimmed glasses bridging his pitted nose, cocked his head, and fidgeted with a paintbrush sticking out of his chest pocket. "Well, I'm prepping this space for the otter exhibit, and I need some inspiration. I'm heading to Rose Lake to look for a beaver hut and take snapshots and measurements. You know, otters and beavers are amenable. So, a beaver home in an otter exhibit is akin to exhibiting life in the suburbs."

"Assuming the otters don't mind that crazy, smacking-beaver-tail echo." Jeannie laughed and patted Cal's back. A faint trace of paint thinner fumes filled her nose. She coughed.

Cal bent to tie a loose shoestring. "I'd be happy to take Joey along. And you, too, for that matter. How about Saturday?" He stretched to a stooped position and shoved his hands into his paint-and-glue-smeared scrub jacket.

"Sounds good. Joey enjoys tromping in the woods."

"Meet me in the west side parking lot at ten a.m. I'll have my old pickup truck. Now that's settled, how about the shindig tonight?" Cal stretched his neck and squinted his eyes.

"The candidate reception at Mac's? I will be there." Jeannie bit her bottom lip and readjusted her briefcase against her hip.

"I'm just glad you know attending a candidate reception at the home of the museum director, however annoying he and his wife are, is a very good idea. Mac can hold a grudge against personnel who fumble with social graces." Cal tapped an index finger against the point of his nose.

Jeannie sighed.

A group of elementary school students and adult chaperones meandered around them, creating a cacophony of excited children—the symphony of museum educators.

"Mom, Mom, Mom, look. I saw one of those in our backyard." A chunky boy, his hair flopping on his brow, pulled the hand of a petite ponytailed woman.

Two uniformed girls, matching right down to their

cuffed white socks, held hands as they pressed their noses against the glass fronting the white-tailed deer exhibit.

"Look, under that bush. There's a fawn!" A student wedged his way between them.

"Jeannie?" Cal lowered his chin and raised his untamed, wiry eyebrows.

"Cal, I know I'm expected to attend. It's one of the social duties of the Search Committee." Jeannie slipped her trench coat over her blazer, tossed a scarf around her neck, and pulled her purse strap over her shoulder.

"I know you're more comfortable in the quiet isolation of your Collections Room, but moderate mingling is good for you."

Oh, sweet, sweet man, I know you always want the best for me. "I'll commit to staying thirty minutes." She furrowed her brow and turned away. *And then I'm making a fast getaway.*

"Well, that's something."

It is a big something. Mr. Sweaty-Gray-Pants, Dr. Repp Tie, Italian Loafers will be there. Jeannie shuddered.

Chapter 3

Twinkling lights woven through thick arborvitae cast a welcoming glow along the brick pavers leading to the McIvors' front door. Jeannie parked her car next to the carriage-style garage and stepped into a cloudless, balmy evening. Fecund smells of thawing earth and decayed autumn leaves permeated the walkway.

Jeannie clamped her lips and sucked air. *Ah, nature, primal and intoxicating. Nicholas Randall is a man of the wilderness, rugged and raw. He's inside.* She stiffened her spine and maneuvered through the entrance.

"Let me take your coat." A uniformed maid held out her hands.

Slipping her coat from her shoulders, Jeannie stepped over the doormat and passed the garment to the maid. Then, she sauntered into the house and paused in front of an open fieldstone hearth housing a crackling fire. Aromatic cedar perfumed the air.

Grouped as wall art, African artifacts, including an Aboriginal mask and a horned animal mount, embellished the adjacent bricked wall.

"So, does the textile complement the mammal?"

Jeannie spun. Her breath gummed in her throat. Nicholas's fire-backed silhouette, the musky scent lingering about his collar, the proximity to the remains of a wild animal, and the thrumming of reggae music piped through the home's stereo system generated an overwhelming primal reaction. She nodded and motioned with her index finger. "I think the mask's texture mimics both the spiral horns and the bristly fur. What do you conclude?"

"I think Mac enjoys the thrill of the hunt." Nicholas scratched the back of his neck. "To your knowledge, has Mac ever been to Africa?"

"Several times. He gushes about his experiences there."

"Well, the mammal we see here is a red hartebeest." Nick pointed. "Prized for his pronged, spiral horns." He dropped his head to his right shoulder. "He sure is a good-looking fellow. Look at that noble face and the distinguishing black strip from his eyes to his snout."

"This probably doesn't sit well with you, as your mission is to preserve animals rather than hunt for sport and wall decoration." Jeannie peered at his face.

Nick flicked his head back and forth, darted his gaze, and wrinkled his nose. "Am I that transparent?"

"I think it's no secret how passionate you are about animal welfare." Jeannie licked her lips.

"You certainly have the first part right." He bent his knees and lowered his head level to hers.

Jeannie collapsed her shoulders. *Did he imply something racy?* She turned toward the front entrance. "Cal, Loretta, it's good to see you."

Cal and wife epitomized the law of opposites attract.

Usually holding residence on the back of his office door, Cal's garment mimicked the shape of a protruding hook along the back collar line. Errant hair sprouted from his ears and the back of his neck and grazed the hook line silhouetted on his back. Waist pockets sagged due to the strain of carrying carving tools and bubblegum balls.

Jeannie repressed a giggle.

Petite with shiny black hair fashioned in a French roll, Loretta smelled of lilacs. She sauntered like a boarding school student practicing proper posture while balancing a dictionary atop her head.

After introductions, Cal grasped his hands behind his back and rocked on the heels of his shoes. "Dr. Randall, could you see yourself as a Great Lakes University Sailor?"

"I could relate more easily to a sailor than a wolverine, a mythical figure in this state."

Clever one, Nick. You have done your homework. Looks like you've got quite a few folks under your charm. Me, I'm not so sure.

"Hah, hah." Cal shook his finger under Nick's nose. "No, we wouldn't want you to champion the Sailor's biggest rival."

A group of students approached Nick and engaged him in conversation.

Jeannie trailed Cal and Loretta to the hors d'oeuvres table. She chose a plate and a meager selection of carrot and celery sticks, radish roses, spinach dip, and bite-sized chunks of rye bread. Then, she made obligatory greetings to her hosts and to her colleagues. With those courtesies bestowed, the curator nibbled the crunchy vegetables, spread the spinach mixture over the seeded bread, and gulped the pieces. Then, reclaiming her coat, Jeannie aimed for escape.

A tap came on her shoulder.

Stalling her steps, she turned.

"Jeannie?" Nick teetered on the balls of his feet an arm's length behind her.

"Yes?"

"I seem to have offended you."

Nick's intense gaze reigned over the decibels of chatter, the clink of glasses, the rhythmic drumming flowing through the house speakers, and the patterns and colors of suits and dresses, stuffed mounts, oriental rugs, and a tribal mask. She struggled to answer the implied question. Unwavering and sober, his gaze remained constant.

"No, no..." she replied in a voice barely audible. Before he could make a stronger advance, she unfastened the door and strode through the doorway. "Best wishes, Dr. Randall."

With her parting message flung through the closing storm door, Jeannie Parks dashed to the refuge of her car. *Why the heck are you trying so hard to impress me, Dr. Nick Randall?*

Chapter 4

Saturday morning dawned in a thick haze of wet, hugging-the-earth clouds. Following a breakfast of cold cereal and sliced bananas, Jeannie and Joey met Cal in the Rose Lake Nature Center parking lot.

Unbroken snow lay in every compass direction. Uninterrupted opaque sky enveloped the tips of Michigan white pines and the naked branches of elms, birches, cherry, poplars, chestnuts, maples, oaks, and seasonally dormant shrubs and grasses and presented an artistic statement of variable texture—glossy fire bush, spiky hawthorn, and nubby spicebush. *Why would anyone want to leave Michigan in the winter?* Jeannie dropped to her knees, rolled onto her back, and brushed her arms and legs in arcs. "I made an angel!"

"Me, too, Mom." Joey curled his head to his chest, somersaulted on the ground, and splayed his arms and legs. After creating a smaller cherub, he came alongside Cal. "Do you think we'll see otters today, Cal?" A milk mustache etched atop Joey's upper lip like a tattoo. In the aftermath of ripping his pine-green cap from his head, a halo of static-cling, sandy-brown hair framed his thin face. His booted footsteps created crunching sounds as he jumped through the ice-glazed snow.

"Let's go toward the lake. Otters like water best. They have bodies that propel them into rivers, lakes, or streams like a torpedo shot out of a submarine." Cal crafted a whooshing noise and moved his arms as if he were pushing water.

Joey giggled, picked a stick from the ground, and plunged it into a labyrinth of weeds like a Tyrolean mountain climber.

Jeannie grinned.

"What do otters like to eat, Cal?" Joey pressed his lips together.

"They like turtles, crayfish, and just about any kind of fish."

"Do otters eat toads? I really, really like toads. Last summer, Mom and I made friends with a toad. He lived in our garden, and one time, he jumped right into our house. So I named him *Oadie Toadie*."

Cal scratched his head. "Well…"

Catching Cal's gaze, Jeannie clenched her lips, amplified her eyes, and shook her head.

"Naw, I think toads taste yucky." Cal spat.

A sudden gust blew the thin strands on Cal's pate. He reached to smooth his hair. Then, treading closer to a bunch of fallen white birches, he grasped Joey's shoulder and moved his hand in front of the boy's face. He pointed.

"Looks like someone's been cutting trees with their big choppers." Cal gave Joey a big gaping smile and clicked his teeth. "Looks like someone's been fixing their house. I would guess it's a beaver family. We might be getting close to a beaver lodge."

"I'm going to find it!" Joey ran ahead.

Powdered snow ascended in his wake.

"Joey sure is growing up." Cal trudged over a tangle of marsh weeds.

"Faster than I'm ready for." Jeannie snugged her

wool cap over her ears.

"Boy should have a man around. Not just an old guy like me."

"Cal…" *Oh, Cal, not again.*

"Jeannie, there are lots of good men out there. And it wouldn't be a bad thing for you, either."

"What?"

"To have a man in your life."

"It's just not that simple."

Glossy-black starlings landed en masse into a thicket of red pokeberry branches. A cacophony of trilling, chirping, and rattling ensued.

A thunderous boom resonated.

"Joey!" Jeannie screamed. Adrenaline and nausea coursed through her body. "The ice, The ice!"

Cal stumbled, slipped, and landed face-first into a track of three-toed turkey prints. Snow wadded his nostrils and packed between his glasses and his eyes.

Please, God. Please, God. Jeannie bolted toward the lake.

An eerie stillness broken only by the soft shushing of a patch of open water greeted her at the lake's edge.

There, three feet out, a scrap of green, the color of Joey's cap, floating on the surface. From behind, someone grabbed her mittened fingers. Jeannie turned.

"I found it. I found it!" Joey's cheeks glowed pink.

Collapsing to her knees, Jeannie buried her face into Joey's dry hat. She drew deep breaths and squeezed her eyes shut. *Just breathe. Cal!*

"Hey there, partner." Cal squinted through fogged glasses, pulled a handkerchief from his jacket, and wiped his nose. He extended a hand to Jeannie and tugged her upright.

"Hang on, Joey. I've got my tape measure and my camera right here in my pocket. I'm sure glad you're here to help."

Cal's disturbingly right. Joey's approaching full-blown boyhood, and pitfalls lie ahead.

****

Wednesday nights in the spring and fall, Jeannie logged volunteer hours in an organization that had resuscitated her. The Widowed Support Group met in the basement of the First Presbyterian Church not far from campus. Tonight, a new session began. Jeannie entered the cool lower level, approached the classroom tables arranged in a U-shape, and selected a seat beside a woman in a motorized wheelchair.

Veins protruded on the back of the woman's thin hands that folded over a worn Bible in her lap.

Additional sober-faced, slow-footed, and mostly silver-haired people arrived.

At seven p.m., a stout, gray-haired woman dressed in baggy slacks and a pilled sweater strode in. She grasped a mug of fragrant jasmine tea in one hand and a folder thick with paper in the other. Off the pinky finger, a box of tissue dangled. "Hello, everyone." She set down her tea, folder, and tissue box, pulled her snug-fitting top to thigh length, and scanned the group. "Welcome to a club none of us want to be a member of."

Mumbled sounds filtered through the room.

"Amen to that."

"*Right about that.*"

"Jeez, no Pete."

"This program will help you understand the grief process and provide a safe place to articulate your feelings. I'm Sharon DiNardo, and I've moderated this process for eight years. I've walked in your shoes. I'm so sorry for each of you and your loss. I hope sharing this journey will bring you some comfort. Tonight, we are going to…"

Creak.

The door opened.

With her arm linked with another woman's, and her hair towering over her head, Marie Wilson edged her way to vacant seats in the corner of the room.

Marie? Jeannie's heart plummeted.

"So tonight, we will go around the room and introduce ourselves. Say your name, your spouse's name, how long you were married, and how your spouse died. If you'd like to pass, that's okay." Sharon rotated her chin in notches as she gazed at each person present. "I'll start. My husband, Pat, and I were married for twelve years and had three children together. He died ten years ago following open-heart surgery when he was thirty-six years old. I recently married a fellow widower named Dean." Sharon nodded toward the widow on her right.

"Since I was a tiny girl, everyone has called me Bunny. My husband's name is, oh, I mean, was, oh…my husband, Bert, passed six months and eight days ago. Since fifth grade, he and I were sweethearts. We were Bert and Bunny—inseparable. He died of throat cancer and was sixty-eight years young. Oh, he suffered so much and never complained."

Jeannie pursed her lips.

Bunny turned the plain gold band on her ring finger several rounds and inhaled sharply. "I tell you what. I am so grateful his suffering ended. Seeing him struggle for breath was unbearable. He gasped his last one in my arms. I miss him so much."

A slim blonde with persimmon-colored lipstick splayed her fingers over her cheeks. "My husband, Mike, was my best friend. He rescued me from the despair of single parenthood and assumed my son, Daniel, as his own." She dabbed a soggy tissue to her eyes.

Someone coughed.

Someone rubbed their nose.

Outside the door, rock and roll blared on the janitor's portable boombox.

The odor of disinfectant ruptured under the door and into the room.

The blonde sighed and closed her eyes. "I thought we'd grow old together." She convulsed a sob.

Sharon yanked tissues from the box and passed them to the widow. "Thanks, Marjorie. We know how hard that was."

A square-jawed, whiskered man on Marjorie's left clicked and unclicked the plastic pen he held in his calloused hand. "My wife, Mary, died on Halloween night. She sat beside me on the couch, watching our favorite detective show. She had a massive heart attack and died in my arms. I always told her I'd take her to Hawaii—you know where the show is filmed. She didn't know it, but I had been saving to surprise her for our fiftieth anniversary. Now, well, where she is now is more beautiful than Hawaii. We were married forty-eight years, and we have four wonderful sons who have seen me through this."

"And your name?" Sharon asked.

"Jim." He moved the pen to his shirt and slid it

over a plastic pocket flap.

"Thanks, Jim."

"I'm Verna," offered the woman seated left of Jim. Clenching a pack of cigarettes, Verna blew out a short breath. "These killed my husband, Hank, and I'm just so damn mad. I pleaded with him since the first Surgeon General warnings in 1963. But like everything else, my words fell on deaf ears." She dropped the package into her lap and shook her head, giving motion to the excess skin under her chin. "I miss him. I don't have anyone to nag anymore." She sniffed loudly and curled her lips in a half-smile.

"Pass," a red-eyed widow whispered.

Marie patted the woman's hand. "My name is Marie Denue Wilson. I was a war bride in the Great War. My husband, Paul, was an Army Lieutenant stationed in Versailles. After the war ended, we moved here, and he worked in his family's auto parts business. We had a good life for twenty-one years. He died in 1965, but I'm really here for my neighbor, Jennifer. Her husband, Bill, died two months ago of cancer. They were married...how long, *Cherie*?" Marie rotated her shoulders.

"Thirty-one years. Not long enough." Jennifer shuttered her eyes. "That's all I want to say tonight."

"Anyway, I'm here to support Jennifer." Marie ran two fingers over her crash-proof hairstyle.

At the opposite end of the room, Jeannie jotted names in columns, widowed person, and spouse's name. This would be her homework. She would memorize them in pairs to personalize her interactions with this heartsick group. She would also keep track of wedding and death anniversaries, knowing those were the most challenging days for a widowed person to navigate.

The introductions meandered to her.

Whistling sounds mingled with the soulful Marvin Gaye lyrics sounding outside the door.

Jeannie cleared her throat. *Each time I voice this story, aching fills the room.* She blinked twice. "My husband, Frank, and I met at Western Michigan University. He enlisted in the Army and was killed in Vietnam. Frank never got to see his son, Joey, who is now in kindergarten. I'm here because it comforted me to be with others who understood grief the way I was experiencing it. So, now I volunteer with Sharon and hope my status as an experienced widow helps you. Let me add that I'm so sorry for your losses."

More people told their stories.

More tears were shed.

More hands were patted.

Jeannie knit her eyebrows and scanned the room.

The state of widowhood altered moods and emotions. *No wonder Marie's temperament is so mercurial.* Finally, she turned to Marie, caught her gaze, and nodded.

Sharon rose and gripped the tabletop. "Next week, we'll talk about how to be good to ourselves. In the meantime, make sure you exercise, eat healthily, talk to a friend at least once a day, and call me anytime, day or night."

****

The *tap-tap* of skinny heels skittering across the tiled floor of the Collections entry resonated. *It has to be Marie.* Jeannie tilted her head.

"Mrs. Parks? Good morning. I know it's very

early."

"I'm in the preparation area, Marie." Jeannie sat on a tall stool, a sharpened pencil lodged behind one ear, and a stack of basketball jerseys on the table fronting her.

Marie approached. "It was good to see you last night."

Jeannie nodded.

"I guess I don't know what goes on in here." Marie uprooted her glasses from the bridge of her nose, blew on the lenses, polished them on the hem of her blouse, and returned them to her face. She gazed at Jeannie. "Good golly. What will you do with those uniforms?"

Jeannie laughed. *Marie materializes genuinely starstruck.* "The first thing we do when we receive donations is put them in that chamber over there—to ensure no destructive insects are present that would infest the collections. After that process, we make a detailed description of the artifact. The aim is to compile a description that can minimize the need for a natural human touch. The less we handle the artifacts, the better their chances for preservation. And that is one of our goals, of course, to preserve the past for future researchers."

"The past will preserve us." Marie nodded.

"It does in many respects, doesn't it?" Jeannie laid down her pencil.

"Would you like to accompany me for a morning refreshment break? We could go next door to the Union if you'd like."

Plucking the pencil from her hair, Jeannie smiled. She rotated her shoulders and stretched her fingers. "I'll take you up on that invitation, Marie. I will see you in about an hour?"

"I'll meet you there."

Tapping noises echoed in the wake of Marie's *"Adieu."*

Jeannie sighed. *Marie, maybe your dispirited heart is as rigid as your hair?*

****

The Union corridors reverberated with the clamor of students passing through the campus hub. Within the perimeter of the historic building, quiet study rooms with comfortable chairs and library tables offered a safe place to compose a manuscript, edit a report, or read a thick textbook. A post office papered in seeking roommate signs, rides wanted messages, and flyers touting campus groups occupied a two-hundred-square-foot area at the south entrance.

Moving through the cafeteria line, Jeannie purchased a cup of hot chocolate.

Teetering on animal-print heels, Marie added a silver teapot, a china cup, and a saucer to the tray she slid across metal rails fronting steaming wells filled with bubbling oregano-scented lasagna, overcooked green beans, and red-pepper-flecked fried rice.

Jeannie selected a booth with a view of the intersection of Abbott and Grand River, where a steady stream of diesel buses and cars entered the west side of campus.

"So, we both have had our hearts broken in the worst possible way," Marie murmured.

"I am so sorry for your loss, Marie. The widowed care group does help."

"I'm glad I came with Jennifer last night." Marie dipped her tea bag and laid the soggy contents onto the saucer.

"Me, too. I remember thinking I would be over this sadness and life would magically feel better. But I know you never get over it." Jeannie enfolded her cup and smoothed her palms against the warm ceramic.

"That's true, *Cherie*, but time goes by, and you find a tiny bit of happiness one day and a bigger piece of happiness after that." With one finger, Marie elevated her glasses farther up her pointy nose. "Look out the window. See those tiny yellow flowers on the bush, what do you call it?"

"Forsythia."

"Yes, *forzithia.* They are giving us a tiny bit of happiness."

"Bunny said last night she thought she couldn't cry anymore." Jeannie looked up from her cocoa and attempted a smile. "How could I tell her I have cried every day for five years—every day since an Army chaplain traveled to Port Hope, Michigan, and knocked on my front door? Marie, I was six months pregnant."

Marie reached across the table and clasped Jeannie's right hand between her two. "*Encore moi.*"

With her free hand, Jeannie wiped tears from her cheeks. "We're a pair of sorry things, aren't we?"

"What do they say, one day at a time?"

"Yes." Marie made her eyes wide. "*Un jour à la fois.*"

"I like the French sound of that." Jeannie puffed her cheeks.

A blue-jeaned, hair-parted-down-the-center student walked past. "Oh, hi, Mrs. Parks. I enjoyed your guest lecture last week." She smiled at Jeannie, turned, and frowned at Marie.

Catching Jeannie's gaze, Marie rolled her eyes.

Jeannie made a moue with her lips. "Guess we better get back to work. That means cataloging for me. And for *Vous*, it means keeping the department clocks wound."

"Speaking of time, *Cherie*, maybe you have reached an hour when you might consider love again? You are such a fine, beautiful woman."

"Oh, Marie, I just don't know." Jeannie shrugged.

Marie sighed and gazed out the window. She turned and faced Jeannie. "Like the *forzithias*, start with a tiny bit of happiness. Keep your face in the sun. Love will find you."

But my love is in the shade. A bronze placard affixed to a granite stone catches sunlight that streams branches of gnarly barked pines and leads me to you.

Chapter 5

Daybreak sunlight poured through the slats on the east side of the rustic log cabin shelter, four-hundred-and-thirty crow-flight miles from the metropolis of windy Chicago. A canopy of broad-leaved, white-paper birch leaves infused in their lustrous green summer hue fluttered outside an iron-rimmed, four-paned window.

Nick rubbed his eyelids and brushed gritty sand aside.

The tremolo call of a loon echoed across Siskiwit Bay, less than two hundred human steps from his research campsite on the remote Isle Royale in Lake Superior.

Probably a lonely male announcing his presence. It's summer, and it's mating season, after all. Good luck, fella. Nicholas grinned, pushed the flannel sheet from his chest, swung his legs, and sat at the edge of his cot. Flexing his toes, he pressed the soles of his feet on the puncheon floor, and lifted a clipboard from the makeshift desk. Photographing the three identified otter sites, collecting scat, and taking print impressions highlighted the daily to-do list. Today, he would make his weekly trek to the island's combination general store, bait shop, and post office, which offered a public telephone. A month had passed since his interviews at Great Lakes University. Perhaps a response from the dean and the Selection Committee would be included in his mail. He scratched his chin. *Wonder how that textile curator is spending her summer.*

****

The Harcourt maid put him on hold.

"Oh, Nick, just getting in from a rousing game of racquetball. It gets my blood coursing," Elizabeth gushed into the phone.

From his far-flung location in the Isle Royale General Store, he envisioned her dabbing her forehead, neck, and collarbones with a thick monogrammed towel. The image stirred his body. "Elizabeth, I've been offered the job at Great Lakes University."

"That's wonderful, darling. How about taking Daddy's plane and coming down for the weekend? We should celebrate."

"I think that can work. Weather permitting, tomorrow afternoon would be an ideal time." Nick scratched the back of his sweaty neck and collected a layer of sloughed skin in the process. He wiped the flecks onto his shorts. *I better take a shower.*

"I'll get tickets for *The Exorcist*. It's showing at the Gateway Theatre."

"That demon, horror movie?" Nick scowled.

"It's the rage, Nick, a real cultural phenomenon."

One thing I can count on with Elizabeth is exposure to all things newfangled and almost always grossly expensive. He sighed. *What about a quiet night at home, a bowl of popcorn, and an absorbing chess game?* For the one hundredth time, he questioned himself. *Will Elizabeth be content living within the moderate finances I can provide?*

****

With its distinctive engine-cowling bulge, Doug

Harcourt's six-seater, private bush plane approached the landing strip in Tobin Harbor on the northeast end of Isle Royale.

Standing below, Nick raised his right hand and angled it like a ball cap visor.

The three-blade metal propeller whirled and stirred spindly, greenish-brown sedges rooted inches from the watery edges of Lake Superior.

Soothing humming sounds from the plane's machinery melded with the soft *splish-splash-splish* of swaying plants.

A flotilla of floating ring-neck ducks pointed their name-inducing, white-ringed bills and propelled themselves across the waterway to the safety and seclusion of the aqueous plants on the far side of the port.

Whirring above them, the mechanical bird sporting white wings, thirty-six feet from blade tip to blade tip, sloped at a forty-five-degree angle.

Mirrored sunglasses zapped lightning bolts from the pilot's face.

He raised a gloved finger and signaled a circular movement.

The plane soared overhead, paused, and then made a graceful descent.

The pilot shoved open the door.

Nick tossed his duffel bag into the cabin, dipped his head, and climbed into the co-pilot seat. He settled a microphoned headset over his ears, fastened the seatbelt across his chest, and buckled it across his lap. In contrast to the jarring motion of the aircraft, the beat of Nick's heart calmed. High-octane aviation fuel fumes filled his nostrils. Inhaling deeply, Nick leaned forward and turned toward the pilot. *Ah, this smell.*

Making a fist and thrusting up his thumb, the pilot grinned from chin strap to chin strap.

Nick mimicked the gesture.

The amphibious float plane lifted from the ground and gained elevation.

Below him, bowl-shaped duck nests fashioned from dense watery vegetation bobbed on the lake's surface. Whorls of watery blues and greens and brown-specked earth mounds capped the surface of the world's largest freshwater lake.

"Sure is pretty scenery from up here. I never get tired of looking at it." The pilot turned his head. "We'll hit a cruising speed of about one-hundred-and-sixty miles an hour, so we'll reach Chicago with plenty of time to spiff up before for cocktails." Grinning, the pilot gazed at the dashboard, flicked a switch, and depressed a button on his microphone. "Chicago approach, Floatplane 328GN. VFR request."

"Floatplane 328GN. Chicago approach. Go ahead," a voice answered.

"Floatplane 328GN, sixty miles north of Houghton County Memorial Airport, heading directly to Chicago. Request flight following." The pilot scanned the horizon.

A static noise crackled.

"Floatplane 328GN approved. Squash 0503. Chicago altimeter 30.03."

"Well, we got our flight pattern. And we got somebody tracking us. Enjoy the ride." The pilot curled a fist and thrust his thumb.

They broke through a low-level cumulous cloud. Nick eased his back into the cushioned seat, closed his eyes, and dropped his head into the pillowed support.

Long-legged Elizabeth and her insatiable sexual appetite lay ahead.

The grin on Nick's face climbed as the plane gained altitude.

****

As the butler opened the artisan-crafted door, Nick set his duffel bag inside the foyer. A visit with the Harcourts ensured a reprieve from the austere amenities Nick experienced during fieldwork. In addition to the butler, the home offered maids, a chef, and a chauffeur to attend to the family's and frequent guests' needs. Each of the seven bathrooms featured waterfall showerheads, imported European bidets, and whirlpool tubs that offered personal selections regarding speed, pressure, and direction of the underwater jet nozzles. Crisp five-hundred-thread-count cotton sheets, air-light down comforters, and eiderdown pillows dressed each bed in all seven bedrooms.

Nick knew to expect a private room, bath, and an iron-trellised balcony overlooking an Olympic-sized pool, landscaped with rows of fragrant Asiatic lilies.

And Elizabeth waited to warm his bed.

He opened the hotel-sized refrigerator and discovered a full array of delicacies—mountain-filtered water, goose pate, Belgian chocolates, and golden Muscat grapes harvested from a local Illinois vineyard. He plucked a cluster of grapes and bit into the icy-cold fruits of the vine. Sweet juice filled his mouth and quenched his thirst.

A crystal bowl engraved with water lilies set on a glass-topped table filled with fragrant gardenias, spicy freesia, and heady lilies scented the air. A note written in Elizabeth's script rested alongside.

Welcome, my darling. Cocktails downstairs at six-thirty. Love, Elizabeth.

He showered, shaved, and applied the Harbor Rum cologne setting atop a high-nap cotton towel in a wicker basket on a granite-topped vanity. Then, Nick donned the outfit Elizabeth had readied and descended the circular banister with five minutes to spare.

Elizabeth postured on the tiled floor below. She wore a lissome, black-velvet strapless dress. Her Rubenesque tits jutted over the tight bodice. Her pale-yellow hair swept from her dermatologist-pampered face in a graceful curvature. Crimson-red lipstick accentuated her flaxen skin and her chocolate-colored eyes.

Nick's heart thundered in his chest. He missed his footing, grabbed the banister, and suctioned a shaky breath. He met Elizabeth's gaze, chuckled, and descended slowly the remaining steps. Her embrace paired them eye to eye since Elizabeth in flat shoes matched his length.

"I thought you'd never get here." Elizabeth blanketed his chest with the warmth of her compressed breasts.

"Well, glad to be here." He laughed, returned her hug, and rested an arm around her shoulders.

"Dad will be eager to hear of your research on Isle Royale."

"And I'm eager to…" He pulled her tight and let the rest of the message trail into her soft ears.

"Well, Dr. Randall, I think that can be arranged. After dinner, we'll take a stroll to the lakefront cottage. There's no company this week, so we'll have it all to ourselves, and there are five cozy bedrooms. Maybe we'll use all of them." Elizabeth patted his shoulders, his back, and his upper arms.

"We wouldn't." He leered. Then, he tugged on her skirt.

"Oh yes. We would," she countered.

"Is there a dining room with an enormous flat table, perchance?"

"Oh, Dr. Randall, you know how to make a lady crave something besides dinner."

I've spent the last weeks in an isolated cabin with the company of loons, ladybugs and leaf hoppers. Bring it on, Elizabeth.

****

Holy Moly. How many brands of vodka are there? If I were a drinking man, I would be impressed as hell. But Nick Randall wasn't a drinking man. The sight of row after row of bottles labeled in Russian and German languages signaling expensive imports left an angry feeling in his stomach. So *much money wasted. How many shelter dogs could be vaccinated and rehomed with the dollars spent? How many families could keep their pets had they received free veterinary care?* Nick squeezed shut his eyes.

"What can I procure for you, sir?" A uniformed bartender broke Nick's reverie.

Setting an elbow on the wraparound bar, Nick opened his eyes and nodded. "Virgin Bloody Mary, a slice of lime, please."

"Nick." Mirrored in the gold-filigree-edged bar mirror, Elizabeth's father held a sweating, ice-clinking, old-fashioned tumbler aloft.

Taking up his glass, Nick turned. Doug Harcourt

gleamed like a floor-model, five-figure sports car. The cufflinks fastening the cuffs of his crisp white shirt glittered like flashy hubcaps.

Doug raised his glass and tapped Nick's drink with his tumbler. "Congratulations on your appointment at Great Lakes University, son. I put in a good word with Mac McIvor. He's an irritating old coot, but he knows his way around almost any horned mammal on seven continents."

Nick lifted his lime and tomato beverage. "Thanks for the recommendation, Doug. I'm sure your word tipped the scales in my favor." Flattening his lips, he teetered on his wingtip shoes. *God, I hate sucking up.* Doug smiled the sly smirk of a man accustomed to flattery.

"Glad it worked for you. So, Nick, what's the next step after spending a few years at Great Lakes University? I'd love to see you at the helm of the Global Wolf Center." Doug nudged Nick's elbow. He tucked his head and spoke in a tone suggesting a clandestine operation. "I've got a lot more influence in getting you named to that position." The magnate pressed his glass against Nick's chest. Then he gazed straight between Nick's eyeballs and flattened his lips.

"It's worth keeping in mind." Nick downed a sip of tomato juice and turned to observe an elegant couple walking toward them.

"Oh, Pearl, Harry, so wonderful to see you. Harry is my favorite big game partner. Kodiak bears, next, right?" Doug kissed Pearl on her sagging, rouged cheek.

How about a different hobby, Doug? Nick clenched his teeth.

Doug clasped Nick's upper arm. "Excuse me, son. Now, you be sure Elizabeth takes good care of you." He turned to the couple who enfolded him in an animated conversation.

Better than you'd imagine, sir.

They dined on red salmon topped with dill sauce, steamed green beans, a Caesar salad with crisp, garlicky croutons, and whipped herbed potatoes. *Nothing wrong with smoked white fish and buttermilk pancakes, but four weeks of little else sure makes a man appreciate a fine meal. And nothing against the seasonal Isle Royale restaurant cooks, but they could consider a condiment selection broader than salt and pepper.*

A maid served pecan tarts drizzled in caramel and topped with frothy cream.

A second maid offered demi cups of espresso and aperitifs.

Elizabeth imbibed in every round of alcohol—from the before-dinner cocktails to the after-dinner cordials. Then, downing the last drop of an amber-colored liqueur, she brushed her hair behind an ear. "Darling, I'll be right back."

Nick sauntered the glass-walled front room. Moonlight flooded Lake Michigan. Jazz music pulsed and throbbed. From behind, a pair of soft hands grazed Nick's earlobes and covered his eyes. "Guess who?" A sensual voice exhaling the scent of raspberry liqueur slurred in his ear. *Elizabeth.* He clasped her hands and rotated her to come face-to-face. He swung her into a dance embrace and tipped her as a throaty female voice sang.

"Come rain or shine."

"Have we made enough of an appearance?" Nick

gripped her to his chest. "I think that guest house is lonely."

"All five bedrooms. And a dining room with a lustrous table and a kitchen with a counter." Elizabeth laced her fingers into his and tugged him toward the door.

Beds, table, counter. Where shall we start?

Chapter 6

"I can see the lake, Mom!" Joey kicked the back of her car seat.

"*Pffft.*" Jeannie blew a hot breath over her top lip. The hair affixed to her face didn't shift. The temperature had to be more than ninety degrees, and the humidity level had to be at the top of the melting to the liquifying range. For an August weekend, the weather was typical for Michigan. She ran her fingers over her cheek and tweaked the tresses that mutinied from her ponytail.

Sitting on the passenger side of the car's front-seat bench, Jeannie's pal, Dee, removed an oversized straw hat, unleashed a springy mop of tightly kinked, copper-brunette curls, and stretched her neck out the window. "Someone's backing out. Put your blinker on."

"Thanks, and that's what best friends are for. You know, for being a second pair of eyes." Jeannie winked and maneuvered into a parking space between two convertibles. "Joey, hold on. Wait for me. We need everybody's help to get our gear to the beach."

"Okay, Mom. I'm happy Tammy came with us today. She's a good swimmer." Joey tugged the puffy life preserver surrounding his neck.

"Gee, thanks, Joey. I'm glad to be here, too. It's going to feel so great to get my hot feet into that cold lake." Teenage Tammy unfurled her tall, lean body, pushed the car door with her lifeguard physique, and vaulted onto the asphalt.

"Your mom and I are grateful for Tammy's presence, as well." Dee rolled up the car window, opened her purse, and pulled out a tube of sunscreen. "Gotta slather up. Redheads are a sun magnet."

"Tammy's the best babysitter in the world and bonus for us, she is also a certified lifeguard." Jeannie walked to the back of the car, opened the trunk, and extracted a wagon, folding chairs, beach towels, sand pails, and a cooler that sloshed with melting ice.

Reaching around her, Dee hefted the cooler into the wagon.

Tammy stowed the remaining gear between the cooler and the wagon sides.

People of all shapes, sporting foot fashion from bare to gladiator, crowded the parking lot, swarmed the manicured beach, and overflowed into the shallow, sandy-bottomed Capitol Lake.

Joey ran ahead.

"Jeannie, how about taking out a sailboat?" Dee grabbed the wagon tongue and pulled.

"Sure, that's what we brought Tammy, the best babysitter in the world, for, right?"

"Joey and I will be fine building sandcastles and catching minnows. You ladies should enjoy your day to the fullest." Tammy ogled a pair of sun-tanned, hairy-chested, athletic-built guys tossing a football along the water's edge. She winked. "Lots of fish in the sea, ladies."

Jeanie rolled her eyes. *We're not taking fishing gear.*

****

53

"It's a perfect day for floating free on the water." Jeannie closed her eyes and lifted her chin. She trailed her fingers in the refreshingly cool water as their fourteen-foot, single-mast sailboat cruised through the undulating waves topping Capitol Lake. *Ahhh…*

The odor of barbecued chicken and grilled hamburgers wafted from shore.

"Cute suit." Dee chirped.

Flashing open her eyelids, Jeannie smiled. "Thanks, I made it. Does the chevron placement give the illusion of a bigger bust?" Jeannie pulled her spine straight and her shoulders back as she tucked her toes under the opposite gunwales.

"Well, I understand the design concept, but I gotta tell you, I'm not seeing it." Dee chuckled. "So, are you ready for work to start in earnest again?"

"I am. Walking across campus during those first few weeks of the fall semester is always exhilarating. I love hearing the band practicing on the quad on a golden autumn day. It's the best. Oh, and there's a new member of the museum faculty. He's been invited to the picnic today."

"Whoa. Are you talking about Dr. Nick Randall—*the* Nick Randall, who disturbed your dreams and made you think of men again?"

Jeannie squirmed. "Yes. And I caution you. As my best friend, you are sworn to never divulge this information which, I will remind you, was extracted during a very vulnerable moment."

"I think you're referring to a moment that involved finishing a bottle of wine one dark and stormy night." Dee stuck out her tongue.

The boat lurched. Water sluiced over one side.

"Prepare to capsize!" Dee yelled.

The sail dipped and poleaxed parallel to the water. Surrendering to gravity, the boat expelled both occupants into the lake.

Panic lodged in her throat as Jeannie shut her eyes, blew air from her nostrils, and kicked her legs to put space between her body and the flipped boat.

Emerging from below the water's surface, Dee spat. She hooted. "Oh boy, now we've got to get this sucker right side up. I'll come to you, Jeannie." She swam around the boat.

"I've got a problem here." With her chin and fingers resting on the above-water edge, Jeannie treaded water.

"What?" Dee came alongside her.

Pointing toward the bottom of the translucent lake, Jeannie pouted.

"Oh, no. How did that happen?" Dee wrinkled her nose.

"This is terrible timing, but I just discovered that the elastic I sewed into my bottoms flunked." Jeannie swore under her breath.

"It's gotta be twenty feet down. There's no way to retrieve that sunken treasure. Good grief, how will I get this boat righted by myself? We can't have you jumping on the centerboard with all the world to see you mooning the shoreline." Dee shook the water from her hair.

"Sorry," Jeannie offered.

Dee gritted her teeth, gripped the gunwales, and impelled the top half of her body above the waterline. "Grah..." Guiding her feet, she slammed her weight against the centerboard.

The boat made a futile twenty-degree righting and flopped back like a surface-floating lily pad tethered to the sandy bottom. Lake water rippled around the bobbing boat.

Grunting, Dee wrenched on the guide ropes. "I'm gonna need some assistance."

Jeannie turned her head and scanned the lake.

A single occupant sat astern in a small approaching aluminum motorboat.

Putt-putt.

His large paw engulfed the thirty-horsepower engine's tiller. He wore a Hawaiian print shirt that rippled over his body and a coarsely woven Panama hat shading his face.

Dee flagged the driver. "Yoo-hoo?"

The boater pushed abruptly on the tiller and nosed the boat toward them. "Need any help?" He tipped his hat back and cut the engine.

Oh my God. It's Nick Randall. Heat suffused Jeannie's face. She bowed her head, gripped the boat edges, and aligned her chin with the boat.

"We need more weight to upright this thing," Dee yelled. "But a bigger problem is my friend lost her shorts. Do you happen to have an extra pair?"

Jeannie shielded her face from view. *What do I do if he recognizes me?* She froze.

Nick turned his upper body and reached for a duffel bag visible on the middle seat of the boat. "Here, hope these work for your...friend." He wadded the shorts into a ball and tossed them.

Dee held one hand above the water's surface and caught the pants. "Thanks, we'll see that you get these back. Where can we find you once we get to shore?"

"My name's Nick. I'm with a group at the pavilion by the merry-go-round. Are you sure you can manage to right the boat?"

Keeping her chin tucked, Jeannie motioned him away.

Nick raised his eyebrows, steered the boat toward shore, adjusted the speed to high, and left a wide wake in his retreat.

Jeannie grasped the shorts. The Hawaiian print trunks smelled faintly of coconut suntan oil and an old diesel-fuel-sucking truck. Holding onto the boat's side, she wiggled one leg at a time through the waistband. Finally, she hoisted the borrowed garment over her hips and snugged the drawstring, which wrapped almost twice around her waist. The pants ballooned around her frame. "Okay. Altogether, now." Curling her fingers over the gunwale, Jeannie jumped on the daggerboard.

"Argh." Dee gripped the side of the boat and kicked the fin-like board.

The little boat popped right side up. The vessel's sail shed liquid like a Portuguese water spaniel.

"I'll bet Joey and Tammy are ready for a couple of hot dogs." Dee tumbled on board.

Jeannie flopped into the boat and sat across from Dee. "I can tell you now that that was Nick."

"Nick?" Dee crinkled her nose. "Oh my gosh, you mean *that*, Nick. Oh, good grief." She giggled. "Well, how does it feel to be inside *that* Nick's pants?

"Dee, maybe it appears to be a beautiful sunny day. But for you, think of this as a dark and stormy night, and you want to remain my best friend. The first thing I'm doing once we get to shore is make a wardrobe change."

"Yes, Captain No-bottom," Dee cackled. Then, she seized the mainsail line.

Jeannie grabbed the tiller, coxswained for shore, and some awkward explanations.

****

Fronting a smoking charcoal grill in the closest pavilion to the Capitol Lake carousel, Dr. Mac McIvor held a spatula in one hand and a sweating longneck beer in the other. He wore plaid shorts, a white short-sleeved, tab-front shirt, canvas sneakers, and a college ball cap pulled tight over his springy white hair. A lanyard with folded sunglasses dangling from it hung from his neck. "Hey there, Jeannie. Glad you made it."

Museum shopkeeper Peg and her husband, Manny, stood in conversation with Entomologist and Search Committee Chairman Steve Granger and his wife, Iris.

Jeannie carried a bowl of coleslaw to the tables inside the sheltered pavilion's perimeter. Dishes of baked beans topped with strips of bacon, taco salad, potato salad, a gelatin salad with marshmallow icing, a tray of carrot and celery sticks, sweet gherkins, dill pickle slices, black olives, and radish roses set atop the wood-planked tables.

Nestled on an antique-looking crystal platter, a watermelon carved into a basket brimmed with cantaloupe balls, watermelon balls, grapes, blueberries, cherries, and pineapple chunks. *Someone is an overachiever here*. Next, she turned her attention to a glossy inflated bag. *And someone chose the easy way out by bringing a bag of chips*. She grinned. *Where's Joey?* "Joey, hey, come here, honey." Jeannie started after him as he hovered over the table, weighted with three tons of calories.

"Hey, Mom. Look, my favorite." He reached for a thickly iced chocolate cupcake.

"How about a hot dog or a hamburger first?" Jeannie sniffed the air. "They smell so delicious, don't they?"

"No way." Joey gripped the edge of the dessert table and jumped as if he were on his pogo stick.

"Son, let's get some grow food."

Joey furrowed his brows, pursed his lips, and shook his head.

From the other side of the pavilion, Nick Randall approached. He pulled a hand from behind his back. "Anybody here like baseball?" The pants angel rolled a ball between his palms, tossed it in the air, and caught it. "How about a game of catch?"

Joey flopped his head to his chin and back up.

"I'll take that as a yes." Nick smiled. "But first, you need some good grub to give you a better grip. So, line up here and get yourself a hamburger."

Joey picked up a paper plate and selected a burger. "I just want it plain, Mom. I'm going to sit with Tammy."

Jeannie sighed. She turned to Nick. *Thank you*, she mouthed.

"Sweet kid. I'll bet he's always too busy to eat."

"Unless there are treats involved. By the way, congratulations on your faculty appointment."

Nick gripped the baseball and ran it down his thigh as if he were polishing an apple. "I think I'm really going to enjoy working here. All the folks seem so friendly, but geesh, there are a lot of names to remember." He turned his head and scanned the group of people clustered in the pavilion's shade. "Will I be meeting your husband, too?"

"No, it's just Joey and me. Frank died." Jeannie sucked in a breath.

"Damn, I'm so sorry." Nick frowned.

"Me, too."

A fly buzzed between them.

Mac dropped burgers on the grill, and the fatty mounds sizzled.

"Do you remember these?" Jeannie flipped a bent elbow and extended her arm. She straightened her curled fingers. The balled tropical print pants expanded in her palm.

Nick widened his eyes and put his hands on his waist. "You?"

"Yes." Heat flamed her cheeks. She raised her shoulders to her ears and her cheeks to their highest crest.

"Well, talk about a coincidence." He made a funny face and laughed.

"A word to the wise, if there is elastic in your bathing suit, make sure it's sound." Jeannie fisted her fingers into two balls and tugged an imaginary length of elastic between them. "I've never seen it happen before today, but within five minutes of a thorough soaking, the waistband expanded to its pre-gathered, twice-my-waist measurements. And poof! My pants dropped to the bottom of the lake."

"No kidding?" Nick made his eyes big and smacked a hand on his forehead. Stepping forward, he reached for the shorts.

Jeannie gazed at her sandals and her pink-polished toenails. "I don't know what I would have done if you hadn't come along and if you didn't have a pair of shorts. Dee needed my help to right the boat. So, I owe you a great big thanks."

"You're welcome." He looked down at his feet and, with the smallest of movements, alternated his head from side to side. Looking up, he caught her gaze. "Can you imagine how perilous the fate of the downed sailboat would have been if our situation had been reversed?" Wrinkles formed on the side of his eyes. He grinned with all his teeth exposed.

Jeannie's heart thundered within her chest. Heat rippled up her neck and her cheeks like the gentle swales in Capitol Lake.

Peg stepped to Mac. "I'm taking this from you." She lifted his lanyard off his chest and over his cap. "And for good reason." She slipped it around her neck, wiped the whistle with her T-shirt, lifted it to her lips, and blew.

The shrill yelp pierced the air.

"Sheesh." Steve covered his ears.

"Hey, everybody." Peg held a plastic water pistol above her head. "Let the games begin. Anybody who wants a chance to win one of these, step up."

"I'm in." Manny stuck up a thumb.

"You don't know what you're starting here, Peg." Mac raised his spatula.

"Me, me." Joey shot both hands in the air and kept his shoulders tight to his ears.

"Manny, can you confiscate that whistle?" Steve complained.

"All right, let's form three teams. Nick, I'm starting with you. Say one."

Nick folded his arms across his chest. "One." He gazed at Jeannie.

61

Peg pointed to Manny standing to Nick's left. "Manny, say two."

Manny scratched his head. "Two."

"The rest of you get the idea. Keep counting off, one, two, three until you are in a group. All number ones over here." Peg lifted the whistle from her chest and toyed with it. "And you twos, over on this side. Threes, this is your spot."

Joey grabbed a cupcake from the table and licked the frosting.

Peg waved erratically. "Let me explain the rules, everyone. We're going to play a good old-fashioned game of dress-up." Reaching behind her, Peg dragged three stuffed laundry baskets to a grassy spot thirty feet from the pavilion's cement pad. "When I blow this whistle, the first team members run to their laundry basket and get dressed, using every item in their basket. Then, take everything off and put it back in the basket. Finally, hurry back to your team, and tag the next person in line. The first team to get everyone dressed and undressed wins!"

"And Steve." Peg shook her finger. "You do not get extra points by taking off more than you put on."

"Ah, gee." Steve hung his head.

Iris jabbed him in the ribs. "They do know you."

"Here we go, folks." Peg blew the whistle.

First out of the chute from Team One, Dee sprinted in the form of a high school runner.

Team Two front man Manny huffed along with his bowlegged gait.

Entomologist Steve, the inaugural runner for Team Three, moved like a pole vaulter. His gait propelled him to cover the distance in half the time Manny took.

"I think I'll include the task of light bulb changer to Steve's new contract," Mac hollered. "Look at that leg span."

Screams, guffaws, and claps ripped the air.

"Faster, faster, Dee."

"Come on, Manny. You can do it."

Steve reached a laundry basket first. He grabbed a yellow-and-orange floral skirt, threw it on the ground, stepped into it, and yanked it to his waist.

Beside him, Dee stretched a double-sized T-shirt over her head.

Manny plopped a beret on his head, hung a long strand of crystal beads around his neck, and stumbled as he tripped on a flowing skirt. Then, with one hand on the skirt, he wrestled with a stretchy, neon-green tube top. "Hey!" he yelled. "What the heck do I do with this?"

"Put it over your head and pull," Peg screamed.

Manny poked his head through the flat cylinder and tugged. The tube squashed the beret over his nose and lips and fashioned a silhouette that resembled a bulbous pickle.

"Whoo, whoo, Manny. I'm starting to see why Peg rushes home every night." Mac winked.

"Oh, he's a beauty, all right." Peg bent from her waist and chuckled.

Dee picked up a basket and upended it.

A flurry of clothing and accessories drifted to the ground.

"She can get dressed in three minutes flat. I am a witness," Jeannie shouted.

"Manny. Buddy, hurry!" someone yelled.

Dee made it back to tag Nick in Team One. "Go,

Nick. Go, Nick."

"What is this?" Nick held a flat rectangular piece of cotton with strings.

"It's a wrap skirt. Wrap it around you and tie it!" Jeannie acted out the motion.

Manny lumbered back to his team and tapped Joey's shoulder.

Joey darted toward the costume tub, stumbled, and sprawled face-first. He raised his head and sneezed dirt from his nostrils.

Jeannie's eyes watered. She clenched her teeth so hard her jaw ached.

With the ties of the wrap skirt trailing and in the midst of shimmying a lacy-knit tank top down his torso, Nick ran to Joey, saddled him on his broad shoulders, and galloped to Joey's team's clothes basket.

"Hey, cheating," a Line Two member shouted.

"No rules against helping a downed player." Nick swung Joey to the ground.

Giggling, Joey punched a high five on Nick's palm.

The shrill blast of a whistle punctuated the air.

Dropping the whistle from her lips, Peg clapped. "I determine Team Two the winners! Joey, you won this fair and square. Will you help me pass these prizes to your team?"

With shining eyes and sweaty hair, Joey distributed bright-red water pistols and high fives to all the adults on the winning team.

Jeannie approached Nick. "Thanks for saving the day, yet again. I need to get home. We have a puppy that needs walking."

"Goodbye, Nick. Thanks for helping me win." Joey

held aloft the gun prize.

"Next time, we can toss the ball around, okay?" Nick pulled the baseball from his pocket and palmed it.

Joey smiled. "See ya, Nick." Brushing up against Jeannie's side, Joey sighed. "He's a nice man, Mommy. His shoulders are fun to ride on. I like him."

Gazing at Nick's honed shoulders, neck, thighs, and calves, Jeannie's heart lurched. *He was a hero today. Dee, I'd like to answer your question again. Yes, I am happily anticipating my return to work.*

Chapter 7

The Tuesday following Labor Day marked the first official back-to-school day for the community. Yellow buses rolled. Neatly clothed and freshly groomed kids punched each other on driveway edges and kicked the dirt with their new sneakers.

For Nick Randall, like all first days, it was a day of excitement, second-guessing, and getting lost.

At ten a.m., Dr. McIvor escorted two students to Nick's new office. "Dr. Randall, I'd like you to meet this year's crop of doctoral interns assigned their field assignments with you. I think you've already talked to Donita Powell. She just completed a master's degree in physical anthropology and now works on a combined program with the Detroit Zoo, preparing specimens for exhibit. Donita will manage our dermestid site while she is here."

Nick nodded. "Donita, better you than me." He gritted his teeth, and stretched his cheeks into high mounds.

As she giggled, the sheeny natural Afro on Donita's head bobbled and her luminous-white teeth gleamed. "Incorporating dermestids is ingenious. Those meat-loving beetles clean bones better than chemicals, and the taxidermists love the results."

"Yeah, I just know always to check inside the work boots I leave here in the museum before I slide my feet in." Nick grinned.

"And now, Walter Ling, a dual biology and education major, who is planning a career in Museum Education. Walter is appointed as your teacher's assistant in Mammalogy 101. It's a big group since that class is a requirement for all biology majors." Mac tugged his wiry eyebrows.

"Walter, glad you're joining me. I'd like you to accompany me on an elementary school trip next week. I'll call you with the details." Extending his right hand, Nick winked. *Walter looks like a kid at heart.*

"I want to hit the ground running." Walter shook Nick's hand. "This sounds like a great opportunity. Thank you, Dr. Randall." The graduate assistant opened a notebook and wrote an entry.

Nick squeezed the skin between his lip and chin. *I'm a mentor now. Better watch my step. Damn.*

Shortly before one p.m., Nick climbed the marble stairs to the third floor of Morrill Hall Auditorium.

Sunlight poured through the domed skylights overhead. The sounds of shuffling feet and zippers unzipping filled the voluminous space.

From the glassed-in production booth, teacher's assistant Walter signaled with a thumbs-up motion.

Nick occupied the stage. He pulled notes from his briefcase and stowed the faculty carryall on the top shelf inside the lectern.

Illuminated by rafter-hung floodlights, the ceiling-to-floor proscenium curtain created a royal-like backdrop.

Gazing upward, Nick pointed his finger and nodded.

A large white screen lowered from the ceiling.

An image flashed onto the screen.

"Hello, Mammalogy 101. I am Dr. Nick Randall." Pointing to the slide, Nick grinned. "Here are my office number and hours and my campus phone number. Also included are the office number and hours of our fantastic TA, Walter Ling. Everybody turn around and wave to Walter. He's the guy next to the bright light in the black booth. Next slide, Walter."

"Here you see a salamander, a robin, and a black squirrel. Which of the three might be included in our study of mammals?" Nick pointed to a student with a raised hand in the middle of the front row.

"Black squirrel." The student grinned.

"Yup, you're in the right class. Why not the robin or the salamander?" Nick turned his head from side to side. Gripping the lectern, he twisted right and left. "Anybody? Yes, way in the back."

"A salamander is a reptile, and a robin is a bird. Neither one has fur or hair," a curly-haired student called.

"Great answer. Next slide, Walter."

Darkness enveloped the stage.

Click.

Light returned with the next screen display.

"Who would like to read aloud?" Nick indicated a student with their hand elevated.

"Factors that delineate a mammal: vertebrate, warm-blooded, four-chambered heart, pulmonary respiration, mammary glands for feeding their young, three middle ear bones, fur, or hair covering."

"Thank you. Last count, there are five thousand nine hundred and nine species of mammals on earth. For tomorrow's homework, I want you to memorize them."

Rumbling sounds reverberated.

Heads turned.

Nick laughed. "I promise I'll be easier than that. While Walter passes out the course syllabus, introduce yourself to someone you don't know. I encourage working as a team in this class. Collaborative research is a good model for expanding knowledge."

Tittering and chuckling noises ensued.

Smiles rippled.

"Back to the syllabus. You'll be graded on two components—quizzes, mid-term and final exams, and a semester-end project. I'd like you to start thinking of the latter and come with ideas to our next class. The semester-end project is an exciting opportunity to choose one Michigan mammal and make a poster presentation depicting that mammal's nocturnal activities. The posters will hang in the Main Exhibits Museum during the Michigan Nightlife Exhibit next spring." Nick smiled and smoothed the four-in-hand knot of his paisley tie.

Murmurs and grins permeated the auditorium.

"For the remaining time, I will turn our attention to some of the world's most extreme climate conditions and the mammals that exist there. Walter, I will signal slide changes. This will go pretty fast. Stay awake, everyone!"

Snickers flouted.

Nick scanned his class list. *All two hundred of you.*

Following class, Nick stopped in his office, filed his class notes, grabbed a folder labeled *Staff Meetings*, and jogged a circular staircase to the upstairs conference room. *Feels good stretching my legs after standing at a lectern for a full ninety minutes.* As he walked the long corridor, the numbers above the doors turned smaller. He stopped at Room 422 and pushed open the door. Only one other person preceded him— Jeannie Parks.

She sat at the far end of a conference table with her hands in her lap and her upper body bent over the tabletop.

As he moved the door farther, an irritating creaky noise rent the air.

Jeannie looked up, frowned, and then riveted her gaze on the calendar fronting her.

"Well, hello." Nick eased into a chair across from her. "So, how was the first day back to school?"

She didn't elevate her head. "Hello. Just fine." She scrunched her brows in a horizontal line. The line deepened into a furrow.

What gives? Why is she so irate, and why is she treating me like a pesky housefly? I've been a complete gentleman. I even loaned her a pair of pants for her bare butt.

Raising her hands, Jeannie flipped the top page calendar and laid it print-side down. She stretched her long fingers. A gold band with a single diamond circled the third finger of her left hand.

She told me her husband died. I don't remember seeing her wedding ring. Hmmm…people remove their bands before they go sailing or swimming. Why does she still wear the ring? Maybe that explains her discomfort with my attention. So back off, buddy. After all, marriage to Elizabeth seems pretty ordained. I better tone down the charm and stick to using this stint as a career. After all, I don't plan on making this job an everlasting, undeviating, till-retirement-do-us-part commitment. Nick loosened his collar. *It's so stuffy in here.*

Peg bustled in, lugging a carton of multi-shaped boxes.

Steve Granger rolled in a cart topped with an overhead projector.

Mac's drab but competent secretary, Wanda, carried two stainless steel carafes, set them on a credenza, and returned with a white bakery box, powdered cream, paper cups, sugar, and stirrers. She returned once more with a sheaf of papers, selected her place at the front of the table, produced her steno book, flipped it open to a blank page, and laid it on her top crossed knee.

Representatives from each of the university's six museums: Entomology, Paleontology, Textiles, Botany, Ornithology, and Mammalogy entered the room, discussing the football team, the most recent student demonstration, and the stringency of campus parking.

Tall and elegant with soft white hair and a thick snowy mustache, Mac filled the doorway as he arrived. He sat next to the Exhibit Museum's secretary. "Do I have a motion to approve the minutes from the June staff meeting?"

"Approved," Hector, an antisocial, squinty-eyed, world-renowned paleontologist who spent his days in a dimly lit lab scraping bones, responded.

"Seconded," Peg said.

Mac raised his head and scanned the room. "Any objections?" He cleared his throat and nodded. "No objections—unanimous approval." Mac transferred his eyeglasses from the top of his silver head to the bridge of his nose. "On to new business. Gift Shoppe. You're up, Peg."

Grabbing an assortment of boxes, Peg scattered them on the tabletop. "Here are samples of new items geared for school groups. First, I would like to thank Dr. Randall for suggesting the mammal skeleton kits." She directed a schoolgirl smile to the newest staff member and passed around wooden puzzle pieces that replicated the skeletal forms of a brown bear, a red fox, and a gray wolf.

"My eight-year-old nephew had a great time putting these together. I passed the idea to Peg this summer at the Capitol Lake staff get-together." Nick grinned and shrugged.

"Well, I think they're a great addition to the kids' novelties," Peg gushed. "Something to capture kids' interests and teach them simultaneously."

"Thanks, Peg, and speaking of Dr. Randall, he's next on the agenda. Once again, Nick, it's great to have you here. We're all looking forward to working with you." Mac fiddled with a puzzle piece.

"I'd like to thank everyone for a cordial welcome, dinner invitations, and directions. It's a big campus! I'm impressed with the caliber of graduate students I'll be directing." He paused and nodded toward the students seated in the corner. "I'm also pleased with the enthusiasm and curiosity of the undergraduates. I'm thankful to the Science Department for supplying me with a teaching assistant since my undergrad sections have two hundred students. That's the entire population of Falstaff, Alaska."

Steve slapped the table.

Peg giggled.

Jeannie pursed her lips.

"I'm happy to collaborate with Cal and Jeannie and others on the upcoming Michigan Nightlife Exhibit, and I'm developing a proposal for children's educational programs. That's about it for now."

"Sounds like you're off to a great and ambitious start, Nick." Mac curled a fist and thrust up the thumb.

Scanning the room, Nick reciprocated the smiles of his new colleagues.

"Your turn, Steve. What's going on in bugland?" Mac scratched his head.

"We've got literally ground-breaking, international collaboration ahead." Steve clutched a stack of transparencies and walked to the overhead projector. He slapped one sheet on the projector. "Peg, can you please hit the lights?"

"Last year, officials from the Mexican Agricultural Service contacted us." Steve moved to the table, extracted an object, and returned to the projector under cover of darkness. "This..." he said, holding the object in the projector's light beam. "is an ear of corn."

Jeannie set her elbow atop the table and linked her fingers together. She smiled.

There's that sense of humor. Nick slid lower in his chair.

Warmth poured through his body.

"Corn?" Chief Preparator Cal asked. "And, Steve, why?"

"Glad you asked. The United States is the number one importer of Mexican agricultural products, and corn is the chief Mexican export. Think globally. Forty percent of crop loss can be attributed to plant pests and diseases."

Mac cleared his throat. "Great Lakes University is a premier United States research institution specializing in crop science and entomology. Steve will work with our crop scientists and will lead this international project to prevent Mexican crop loss. Well done, Steve."

Clapping noises filled the windowless room.

"I've already registered for a Spanish immersion program, and I'm updating my passport and my vaccinations." Steve grinned.

"How about Botany? Martha?" Mac looked up from his clipboard.

Martha fingered a glass pendant from a delicate silver chain wrapped around her slender neck. "As most of you know, our specimen collection dates back almost as far as the origin of this university. We are in the planning stages with the Fine Arts College for students to render illustrations of indigenous plants to use in the Michigan Nightlife Exhibit. Our staff is working to identify those native plants that exhibit interesting nocturnal activity."

"That sounds pretty exotic." Peg made her eyes big. She blew out a low whistle.

"Glad to hear of student inclusion." Mac rotated his shoulders. "Hector, what's happening in Paleontology?

Drawing a white-linen handkerchief from his pants' pocket, the balding scientist wiped his nose. "Once again, we'll participate in the Cooperative Extension's summer school for middle school students. We'll be offering a class titled Digging for Dinosaurs. This past summer, we were able to accommodate one hundred students. More than one hundred kids were on the waitlist, so we are adding two more sections next summer. Other than that, it's rooting and digging as usual."

"Thanks, Hector."

"Hector, I did order another case of dust masks." Wanda pointed her pen in the air.

"Rooting and digging. Thanks." Hector shaped a slight smile.

"Bob, let's hear from Ornithology."

"I think I've got the easiest job of curating an exhibit for the Michigan Nightlife Exhibit." The bow-tie-wearing, big-belly-bird enthusiast smirked. "I mean, owls? This state is home to eleven species. There's the Short-Eared, the Long-Eared, Great Horned, Snowy, Barred, Northern Saw-Whet, the rare owls—Great Gray, Boreal, Northern Hawk, and Barn. And let's not forget my personal dramatic favorite—the Eastern Screech. *Screeeech.*"

Jeannie clapped both hands over her ears.

"Will you provide similar sound effects during the exhibit?" Cal lifted his brows.

Bob raised his right hand. "Wanda, please record that Ornithology will provide authentic bird sounds."

"That leaves Textiles." Mac tugged the ends of his mustache.

"Bob, let it be known the Textiles exhibit will utilize music. I'm keeping the details under wrap, but here's a clue. Think Detroit originals." Jeannie bounced her shoulders and hummed.

"Folk? Jazz? Rock? Girl Groups?" Steve bellowed each guess.

Pinching a thumb and index finger together, Jeannie brought them to her mouth, and tugged an imaginary latched gate over her lips.

"Her lips are sealed. Hah!" Cal smoothed his mustache and winked.

"In other news, we are the recipients of player-used Detroit Carburetor team apparel. We could do a great sports-themed exhibit sometime." Jeannie rested an elbow on the table and set her chin on her fist. "How much money do we have in the maintenance and utility fund?"

"Why?" Mac asked.

"We might need a new shelving unit. You would not believe the size of those shoes!"

Mac inhaled a wheezy breath. "Check with Wanda on that."

Wanda fashioned a finger and thumb into an okay sign.

"And check with Wanda regarding folks you wish to include on the special guest list for the Opening Night Party of the Michigan Nightlife Exhibit. Does anybody want to make a motion to adjourn?"

Cal raised his hand and wiggled the digits.

"And a second?" Mac clicked the end of his pen.

"Screech."

"I'm recording that Bob seconded the adjournment motion." Wanda smiled.

Stretching back in his chair, Mac chewed his bottom lip. "Any objections?" He turned his head right and then left. He grinned. "None noted. I call this meeting adjourned."

Blocked in a path to the door by Steve, who collected his slides, Nick drummed his knuckles on the table. *Jeannie is escaping. What's with the cold shoulder? With the rest of the group, she's functioning competently. But with me, she's acting like a wounded animal and imposing a protective barrier.* Nick was no stranger to wounded mammals. He had earned the trust of many an animal who had shied from him. Patience, consistency, and no false moves had won them over. Those tactics could work with Jeannie Parks, too. *And Jeannie Parks is worth winning.*

Chapter 8

Widow Care reconvened after a summer reprieve. *I wonder how everyone fared in their year of firsts wading through the first Mother's Day, Father's Day, Fourth of July, birthdays, and wedding anniversaries following the death of their spouse.* Jeannie held the door for old acquaintances and new widowed folks. *I wonder if anyone feels guilty for being attracted to someone new. Oh, geez.* Jeannie ground her teeth.

Hugging two overflowing paper sacks with his burly arms, Jim edged by Jeannie.

Earthy scents of dill and lavender permeated the cool, industrial-built hallway.

Gulping resonant sniffs, Jeannie grinned. "I think I know how you spent your summer, Jim."

"Gardening is a great distraction. I brought surplus tomatoes, zucchini, and herbs to share." Jim smiled.

"That's so thoughtful. Thanks! I so enjoy making zucchini bread." Jeannie patted his shoulder. She inhaled deeply. "Oh, fresh lavender. I'll put this whole bunch under my pillow tonight."

"I hope lavender brings you sweet dreams, Jeannie." Jim pressed his lips together and puffed his cheeks.

"Thanks, Jim, for the garden gifts and the wish." Jeannie nodded. "Looks like Sharon is ready to start."

"Welcome, newcomers, and welcome back, old

friends. I hope you had a good summer. We have a guest speaker scheduled tonight. Dr. Anna Young is an anthropologist who studies how different cultures are affected by grief and how they view the concept of an afterlife. She qualifies as one of us. Her husband died fifteen years ago."

"Let me pose a question. Raise your hand if you have felt…" Anna paused. She removed her square-framed glasses and polished them with the hem of a paisley shawl wrapped around her shoulders. She set the glasses back over her aquiline nose and rotated in a clockwise direction, her gaze meeting each person's contemplation. "Pressured to move on or get over it. Does anyone react to that?" Anna tucked a fist under her chin and tapped an index finger over her closed lips.

Throat clearings and hand liftings ensued.

Anna acknowledged Jennifer.

"My mother came over to my house when I was at work. She took it upon herself to go through our closet and pulled all of Mike's things." Jennifer squinted shut her eyes, gummed her lips, and drew a ragged breath. She opened her eyes and dropped her gaze. "I wanted to do that myself. Now, I can't go to the closet and bury my nose in Mike's bathrobe."

Marie reached and draped her arm over Jennifer's shoulders.

Verna darted her filmy eyes. "I absolutely, and I'm stressing absolutely, hate when people say, 'How are you?' Last week, one of our neighbors asked me, and I told her. I said, 'I'm mad as hell. I'm so lonely I've considered joining a gym. And I hate those smelly places. And more than that, I hate moving on with life without Hank." Verna's loose neck muscles wobbled.

"And Mrs. Goodbody said 'so sorry' and scuttled off with a quick retreat. I think she won't ask in the future unless she really wants to know."

"My kids just don't want me to keep talking about Nancy anymore. And all I want is to hear her name spoken." Jim shook his head.

"I guess that's the theme. Your life is not what it was, and no one should give you a timeline or demands on how to deal with this." Dr. Young wrinkled her brows and tilted her head. "The best insight I can offer is this. Grief isn't something you get over or has a final stage. Suffering will endure as long as you live. My research shows that is a universal phenomenon, no matter what culture you relate to."

Jeannie cinched shut her eyes. She curved her spine and rocked forward.

"Are any of you of Irish descent?" Anna craned her neck and scanned the rows of chairs.

"My grandparents emigrated from County Cork." Marjorie bobbed her head.

Opening her eyes, Jeannie gazed at the speaker. "Very distant relations from Galway."

"Donegal is where my family is from." From her hooded eyes to her chin, Verna beamed.

Anna smiled. "I have a special affinity for the manner in which the Irish grieve. They hold a big, boisterous party. And they include their departed in their daily lives. Allow me, please, to read this prayer. The message reverberated strongly with my children and me. The words are printed here, on the back of the memorial card passed out at my husband's and their father's funeral. *Death is nothing at all. I have only slipped away into the next room. Whatever we were to each other that we are still. Call me by my old familiar name. Speak to me as easily as you always did. Laugh as we always laughed at the little jokes we enjoyed together. Play. Smile. Think of me. Pray for me. Let my name be the household word that it always was. Let it be spoken without effort. Why should I be out of your mind because I am out of your sight?"* Anna set the paper in her lap. "I brought enough copies for everyone. Thanks, all. I'm turning the meeting back to Sharon now."

The next time I speak with Virginia, I'll share this meditation. And this just reinforces my commitment to Joey to never forget Frank. Jeannie clutched the edges of her chair.

"Thank you, Dr. Young, for reinforcing that grief's timetable is unique to everyone. And thanks for sharing that prayer. It's an excellent closing for this meeting. Dr. Young agreed to stay after and speak privately with anyone. For all of you, the assignment for our next session is to devise a plan for rituals you would like to establish to maintain the memory of your spouse. I'd also like you to prepare a response for your friends and family when they say, 'you have to move on,' or 'why are you still wearing your wedding band?' See you next time. Stay safe." Sharon gathered her tissue boxes and tea mug. "Oh, and don't forget to take garden surplus home. Thanks, Jim."

Grief is so dang hard. Some days, all I want is to numb my brain and pretend Frank's death is all a bad dream. Sighing, Jeannie gathered three zucchini plants, some lavender-shocks and walked silently from a band of heartbroken souls.

****

Lying in bed that evening, Jeannie wrestled the suppressive heat of an Indian summer September night, cotton sheets, and lingering thoughts regarding the widowed session. Most of her friends had long since stopped mentioning Frank's name. Instead, they seemed worried she hadn't "gotten over" him and hadn't "moved on." Rather, they felt their duty was to direct her to a lifestyle of shedding the past and diving into the future.

Joey, they said deserved a mother who embraced joy and had the emotional substance to plod through challenges.

Yet, Jeannie yearned for the partnership she and Frank had, someone to share the joys and challenges of her day, someone to review a movie with, someone to tweeze a sliver from, someone to lay on a blanket on a sticky-hot summer night and pick out the stars in the Cassiopeia constellation with. She missed Friday night football games in Port Hope, Ubly, Kinde, Pigeon, and Cass City and sharing a Penny Burger at the Pirate Cove Restaurant. She hated solo parenting. Some of her friends told her, "Joey needs a father. He's heading into those years when a father figure is so important." Jeannie knew that. And she was, at times, frantic about the future and parenting alone through Joey's teen years and beyond.

But don't ask me to abandon Frank. She turned and lifted her head. She stared at the face topped with a crisp Army cap for long moments. Shuddering, she reached and pulled the chain attached to the light on her nightstand. But with lights out, she saw the sun-shaded face of a boater at the till of an aluminum motorboat.

Chapter 9

"Come on, Mom." Joey tugged Jeannie's wrist.

He pulled her across the elementary school parking lot with the weight of his heaving fifty-seven pounds. Jeannie caught her reflection in the side-view mirror of a parked service truck. Sunshine echoed off the granny-style sunglasses cresting her cheeks. Her favorite shade of orange lipstick harmonized with the prominent stripe in her flannel shirt. The bottom of her English-style braid bounced over her left breast. She smiled. *I'm cute, and what a perfect October day for a field trip to Rose Lake—intense blue sky, pristine and puffy clouds, and a temperature in the high sixties.* "Okay. Okay." Jeannie chuckled. She hastened her pace to match the energy of her five-year-old.

"Teacher said we must be on time or the bus will leave without us."

"Easy, buddy. We're here. I see the bus, and I see Miss Cassidy. Let's find out what group we're in." Jeannie buttoned her jacket and slung her backpack on her right shoulder.

Parents milled about.

Kids jumped, swatted, swung, dodged, hopped, and tripped.

Some laughed.

Some pouted.

One sucked her thumb.

One picked his nose and wiped a booger on the seat of his pants.

The scene could have been filmed to promote abstinence in a high school health class. Jeannie smiled and shook her head.

"Oh, hi, Mrs. Parks. Hi, Joey." Holding a clipboard and a pencil in one hand and wearing a whistle around her neck, a short, lively, scaled-to-kindergarten-furniture brunette smiled. "You're in seats seventeen and eighteen. You'll be across the aisle from Erica and her dad."

"Yay! Erica is my very best friend in kindergarten, Mom." Joey jumped and spun in a circle.

The bus filled and rolled to a start. Once on the highway, the participants broke into song. "The wheels on the…"

A breeze hurled the scent of burning leaves and ruffled uncapped heads through the open windows.

Turning off the road, the bus driver parked in a grassy spot.

Rose Lake shone in full array.

Golden-leaved and silver-bark aspens, scarlet-bedecked maples, and royal-purple embellished oaks graced the perimeter of the blue-green basin.

Jeannie threaded her backpack over her shoulders and traipsed to the bus front. As she helped kids depart, she crouched in the aisle and gazed out the vista-view windshield.

Standing in the eclipse of a maple-leaf canopy, Nick raised a small, red-enameled tool and scraped the bark of a tree.

What are you doing here? Jeannie clutched the handrail. Her breath seized. Following the last person to leave the vehicle, she positioned herself before the rearview mirror. Gripping both sidebars of her glasses, she lifted the frames from her face. With a finger, she smoothed the puffy skin below her eyes. Then, she resettled the glasses and made a moue with her lips. *Okay.* Jeannie descended the steps and joined the fidgety crowd.

Miss Cassidy blew her whistle and motioned them to sit on the ground.

Standing beside the diminutive elementary teacher, Nick Randall loomed like a tall, buffed giant.

"Students, guest grownups, this is Dr. Nicholas Randall from Great Lakes University. Dr. Randall, we appreciate you taking time with our students."

"Sharing a day outside with kids is my favorite out-of-the-office excuse." Nick grinned.

"Dr. Randall is a mammalogist. Does anyone know what a mammalogist does?" Miss Cassidy turned her head from side to side and gazed at the seated children.

"Does he hunt possums and deer and elephants?" A redheaded, freckled-face boy pushed his way to the front of the crowd.

"Does he take care of sick animals?" an impish boy with missing front teeth asked.

"Well, a mammalogist is a scientist who studies animals to improve their lives." Nick folded his arms. "I brought along a friend today. This is Walter, and he studies animals, too. Walter likes being with kids, and I hear he plays a mean kickball game."

Graduate student Walter clasped his hands, raised them over the right side of his head, and shook them.

Seated cross-legged on a floor of crackling leaves, Jeannie jutted her chin and stretched her neck. She stared at Nick.

Nick caught her gaze and raised his eyebrows.

Jeannie pointed toward Joey.

Grinning, Nick scrutinized the crowd. "Curious kindergartners, let me ask you another question. What time of year do animals and birds build their nests?" The museum mammalogist squatted and teetered on his feet.

"Oh, I know. I know," a chorale of enthusiastic kindergarten voices burst.

"Springtime," the thumb sucker sputtered.

"Well, that's right." Nick opened his eyes wide.

Nice job, Nick Randall. You've captured these kids' interest. Jeannie smiled.

"Well, how about this question: What time of year do leaves fall off the trees?"

"I know, I know. In the fall," a gaggle of wiggling kids clamored.

Erica scooped a heap of leaves and sprinkled them over Joey's head.

"Hey!" Joey laughed and with both hands, brushed the crinkled foliage from his jacket.

Nick stood stock-still, removed his hat, and made a production of scratching his head. He turned to Miss Cassidy.

Jeannie suppressed a giggle.

"Miss Cassidy, you have a brilliant class here. All of them are on their way to becoming outstanding scientists."

The petite teacher beamed.

The grownups bumped their fists and high-fived the nearest child.

"What season are we in now?" Nick asked.

"Fall!"

"Of course. Fall is a perfect time to look for nests. There are three reasons why. One—they are already built. Two—most bird and animal nests are empty now. And three—the leaves are down, so the nests hidden in the spring and summer will be easier to find. I think Miss Cassidy has some papers for you. The papers have clues to help you today. I will tag along and see if I can use my scientist eyes to help your eyes make animal discoveries."

"Okay, everyone, come and get your instructions," Miss Cassidy called.

Pixie-eyed, frizzy-haired Erica and Joey ran hand-in-hand to their teacher.

"Ah, childhood," Erica's ponytailed dad said.

"Yes, such innocence, such energy." Jeannie tilted her nose to the sun.

The crisp air, the heartwarming, innocent friendship of two children, the camaraderie of other invested parents, and the enthusiasm of an intriguing man catapulted Jeannie's mood into a place of long-lost familiarity. The very air that filled her lungs imbued a sense of buoyancy. A slow-moving smile crept from her lips to the crest of her cheeks.

"Dad, we've got pictures of nests, and we must find them. Let's go." Erica waved a pile of black-and-white prints.

"I've got the crayons because we have to color them." Joey jammed the box into his jacket pocket.

"We're right behind you," Erica's dad called.

Nick crouched over a downed tree. He wore a buffalo-plaid, zip-front hooded jacket. Rag-wool gloves stuck out of the large side pockets. Faded lines etched his jeans in the places his joints had forced the fabric to bend countless times. A threadbare spot stretched over his left knee.

Jeannie gulped.

Surrounding Nick's scuffed boot-clad feet, a dozen pairs of tennis shoes, some with super hero masks embroidered on the edges, shuffled and dug into the earth.

Motioning the kids to move closer, Nick turned and put a rigid index finger to his lips.

Joey approached on tiptoe.

Clasping her hands over her mouth, Jeannie hid a smile.

The kids crowded behind Nick.

"I'm glad you're here to see this," he said. "What do you think my scientist eyes found?"

"Maybe a black bear baby?" a dainty, diminutive girl asked.

"Maybe a fox?" Erica tilted her head and lolled her tongue.

"How about a skunk?" Joey pinched his nose.

Cries of "P.U." skittered across the landscape.

Erica ran in a large circle, stopped behind her dad, and stretched the neckline of her sweater over her face.

Nick laughed. "Naw, I wouldn't do that." He laughed and tousled the hair on the head of the closest boy behind him. "One at a time, come close, and I'll show you." Patiently, he accommodated one child, one parent at a time, to point out what he discovered in roots surrounding a majestic white pine. He gave each child an opportunity to use his pocket ruler to measure the shallow depression lined with finely shredded grass, leaves, and fur.

"How many inches long is the cavity?" Nick asked a child with raggedy shoelaces.

"It says six inches."

"And how deep is the hole?" Nick leaned in and helped the child position the ruler.

The child pulled up the ruler and showed Nick. "Four inches."

"Great data collection here. Well, future scientists, what kind of animal do you think nested here?"

The children and their parents formed a huddle and pored over their fact sheets.

"I know. It's an eastern cottontail," Joey shouted.

Nick grinned. "Hi there, Joey. Nice to see you. Excellent answer. I want you on my fieldwork team. How about a high five?"

Jumping, Joey raised his right hand in the air.

Extending his palm, Nick connected with Joey's palm.

Smack.

"All right. Cool, man." Joey punched his fists in the air.

Nick caught up with Jeannie. "Well, hi there."

"Hi there, yourself." Her heart lodged in her throat.

"So, do you go on all the field trips?" Nick pulled a pair of sunglasses from his pocket and popped them over the bridge of his nose.

"I try to. I think being present is important." *You're such a natural with the kids. Do you plan on your own someday?* Jeannie slanted her head and viewed him from the side.

Miss Cassidy blew her whistle. "Lunchtime! Students and chaperones, let's eat."

Nick nudged her shoulder with his. "Do you mind

if I sit with your group?"

"That's fine." Jeannie dropped to the ground and sat in a crisscross-applesauce position. She pulled her backpack off her back, unzipped it, and extracted bag lunches for Joey and herself.

Nick squatted, pulled an apple from his backpack, burnished the fruit over his denim-coated thigh, and bit into the polished red orb.

Crunch.

The tangy aroma swirled under her nose. *Ah, fall.*

Lunch bags rustled.

"Anybody wanna trade raisins?" a child wearing a bandana hairband asked.

"I like raisins." A boy wearing a sports logo T-shirt reached toward the bandana wearer.

"Hey, sweetie. Finish your lunch." Jeannie cajoled a girl who threw her peanut-butter- and-jelly sandwich on the ground.

"Hey, partner. You, too." Nick retrieved a lunch bag another child attempted to discard.

The shrill of Miss Cassidy's whistle pierced the afternoon. "Before we board the bus, let's get some exercise. Students, gather here. Chaperones, you can stay where you are. I mean, all except Walter. We could use a good kicker!" Miss Cassidy executed a high-stepping Irish dance movement and concluded with a flourished bow and a jaunty grin.

No wonder the kids love her. She's so lighthearted. Jeannie clapped.

"Absolutely. Come on, kids. Let's move!" Walter sprang up and joined Miss Cassidy.

Erica turned. "C'mon, Dad. You can play, too."

"Do you two mind keeping an eye on all the gear?"

Erica's dad pressed a palm into the ground, flipped to his knees, brushed the fleshy parts of his hands together, and rose.

"Go on. Have fun." Jeannie smiled, stretched her legs, and crossed her ankles. She leaned back her head.

"Joey's a cute little guy, very inquisitive, and very respectful. And I bet he keeps you entertained." Nick scratched the back of his neck.

"Oh, there's no boredom in our life," Jeannie said. "This morning, he told me he didn't need a bath today. I asked him why. He looked me square in the eye and said, 'Mom, it rained yesterday.' "

Nick covered his mouth and, in the process, smushed the apple on his cheek. His shoulders shook. Tears ran down his face. He smiled and shook his head. "Awe. He's all boy—frogs, snails, and puppy dog tails, and likes to keep his distance from soap and water." Nick rotated the apple and sunk his teeth through the peel. Juice saturated his mustache.

Chitter-Chitter-Chitter.

Nick tossed his apple core to a raucous squirrel scrabbling through rusty-colored leaves. "Here you go, buddy."

"Was your husband as comedic as Joey?"

My husband? Jeannie twirled her wedding ring. A knot grew in her stomach. She licked her lips. She closed her eyes and dropped her head.

"Great run! Go. Go. Go." Walter's cheering soared above the shrieks of Joey's classmates.

A breeze lifted wispy hairs around her face and tickled Jeannie's ears. Shifting her butt in the trampled grass, she inhaled deeply. Jeannie swallowed a clotted stream of melancholy. She opened her eyes to Nick's steady gaze. *He's comfortable in talking about the dead. Wow.* Jeannie's heart leaped. "First of all, thanks for asking. That is so very kind."

Nick folded his fingers over her shoulder and applied gentle pressure. "You're welcome."

"Frank made me laugh." Jeannie chuckled. "He could be a prankster. One time, he filled a paper bag with dog poop, placed the seemingly innocent bag on the doormat of his parents' house, and set the paper on fire. Then he shouted, 'Dad, Dad.' His dad charged out the front door with his suspenders dangling below his hips and his face half-shaved. He ran to the bag and stomped the flames. Dog poop exploded on his shoes, his pants, and his remaining whiskers." Jeannie bent over her crossed legs and guffawed.

"No." Nick snorted.

"Oh, yes. Frank got in so much trouble."

"So, I guess Joey comes by his humor naturally. That's a great story to share with him."

Jeannie blew out a deep breath and bit her lower lip. She pressed her hands against her cheekbones. "So, you were saying something about puppy dogs…"

"What about puppy dogs?" Nick squinted one eye and tilted his head.

"We have one. And I admit freely. I'm out of my element. Gunther was an unexpected gift from Joey's grandparents."

Nick groaned.

"Oh, don't get me wrong. Joey loves Gunther. And I do, too…" Jeannie compressed her legs against the ground and bobbled her knees. "When he's not barking, chewing my best-loved leather pumps, or tearing into the garbage."

"Yikes."

Jeannie smiled. Then she contorted her expression, as if she were being directed by a photographer to make a silly face.

Leaning near, Nick gazed into her eyes. "Whoa. Hold still—absolutely still."

Jeannie froze.

"You've got two bees stalking your hair." Nick moved closer. And then he darted his hand as quickly as a cobra's tongue lashing its prey. With no trepidation, he clamped the bee and squashed it. He repeated the onslaught, and the second troublesome insect buzzed no more. "Are you allergic to bee stings?"

His voice held genuine concern.

"No," she whispered.

"Besides the possibility of an imminent emergency, I didn't want to see your nose swell like a party balloon."

The sun backlit his hair, gilding his mustache and the top of his ears.

Jeannie recognized quivers up and down her spine.

Michigan nature painted the landscape with her autumn palette—sugary orange maples, cool golden ash, and brilliant red fire bushes.

Nick reached curled fingers, grazed the side of her face, and tucked a stray lock of her hair behind her ear. "Now, you're even better—just perfect."

She swallowed, and the pooled liquid plummeted directly to a pleasure center.

"Hey, Mom, Miss Cassidy says it's time to go home," Joey yelled.

Jeannie rolled to her side and pushed against the

ground. She rose and brushed her hands on the seat of her pants.

Kids and adults kicked leaves and darted toward the bus.

Nick touched the small hollow of her back. "Are you okay?"

"Oh, yeah." *Could he see it in my eyes?*

Nick yanked his cap farther down his head and pulled his gloves from his pockets.

"Guess we better do as Miss Cassidy says. I'd hate to serve detention."

Jeannie laughed. "Well, see you back on campus."

"Sure."

Jeannie gathered with the other chaperones and the kids and lined up in a single file to board the bus.

Nick walked to his truck parked in the adjoining field.

He looked just as good moving in that direction. She already knew that, though. She met his backside long before she met his face.

On the bus ride home, the children were lulled to sleepiness.

Jeannie sprawled in a cracked leather seat.

Joey's slumbering heaviness weighed against her shoulder.

She smoothed the knit hat wadded above his ears. The afternoon sun cut through the paned windows and cast oblique slices of light and shadow across her face and over her lap. She stroked her cheek, mimicking the movements of Nick's rough fingers. He eradicated more than two menacing bees. The mammalogist's touch destroyed her defenses. *Now what?*

Chapter 10

Nick shuffled to the kitchen. He poured himself a glass of water. Yesterday, he tutored five-year-olds. Today, he faced young adults. He gripped the tumbler in his hand and sauntered to the picture window.

Outside, a thermometer tacked to the cedar shingles registered fifty-five degrees.

At the end of his property, luminous gray and icy-white clouds scudded over a shallow creek. He didn't sleep well. *Dammit.* Elizabeth telephoned and laid it on—thick. The woman was relentless. What started as a pleasant recapping-the-school-field-trip day, drifting-off-to-shut-eye evening had been interrupted and set off the rails by Elizabeth's indefatigable across-the-wire seduction.

The conversation kicked off benignly. "Nick, Dad wants to invite you to a private hunting party on Goose Island. You'll stay in a luxurious lodge. A private chef and hunting guides will be at your disposal. This is a great opportunity to mingle with influential men. Dad includes Senator Moss, Brad Ensign, and a few other celebrity-big-game hunters."

At the mention of hunting, he swallowed an acidic solution welling in his throat. *Elizabeth, why don't you understand how I feel about killing animals for trophies? Doesn't your dad have enough carcasses decorating his halls and walls? Gah.* After the dad news, she had bated him into mutual heavy breathing. *And I fell—hook, line, and sinker. Damn. I'm a sorry son of a bitch.*

****

Basking in the mid-afternoon sun, Nick scanned the silhouettes of the campus landscape. Four towering red-oak trees provided the sole barrier to Morrill Hall and the Home Economics Building. He readjusted the briefcase hanging from his right shoulder, thrust out his left arm, bent it at the elbow, and checked his watch. *Good chance Jeannie is sequestered in the Historic Costumes Collection. I've got thirty minutes until my office hours.*

As if wrapping the foremost oak in a diagonal stripe, a pair of eastern fox squirrels, fortified with the ability to swivel their clawed feet one-hundred-and-eighty degrees, chased each other head-first down the tree. Once on the ground, the pair scuttled underneath a building-hugging bank of fire bushes.

Nick's chest filled with an expansive feeling. *Jeannie will get a kick out of this story.*

Walter had prepared a sign-up sheet for the students to indicate which Michigan mammal they chose to feature in their poster project, with implicit instructions to avoid duplicating a confirmed choice.

Recollecting the aftermath, Nick laughed aloud.

As Walter's sheet circulated the auditorium, scowls, head-scratching, grumbling, and groans erupted from the student body. Pausing mid-sentence in his mammal digestion lecture, Nick flicked the overhead lights.

A quiet fell over the crowd.

"Could someone enlighten me in regard to the

ruckus?" Nick peered into a sea of somber students.

A mid-center-seated student raised a hand.

Nick acknowledged the gesture.

"Dr. Randall, I think I'm speaking for many of us. By the time this sheet got to me, all my choices were taken."

"Yah."

"Same here."

"That's frustrating."

Grasping the acanthus-leaf crown molding edging the mahogany lectern, Nick bowed his head. *Well, I wasn't expecting this reaction.* He raised his chin and scanned the crowd. Grinning, he shook his head. "Out of four thousand possibilities, you are challenged to select a unique mammal?" Two hundred pairs of blank eyes gazed back.

"So, how about a hoary bat—flies at night, features dark-brown hair tipped in white? Or a meadow-mouse, a critter capable of jumping eight feet? How about an ermine weasel, or a fisher weasel, or the water shrew, or the North American river otter? Tell you what, I'll give you all a reprieve. By next class, be prepared with a new selection. Like I said, many choices."

Mounting the cement steps to the building housing Jeannie's workplace, Nick smacked his lips. *Whoops, I forgot to mention the Eastern Fox Squirrel.* He found the office on the second floor and approached the counter.

"Can I help you?" A frowning, shrill-voiced, thin-lipped woman wearing caked makeup and a gaudy, floral-print shirt eyed him from her seated position. A wood-grained placard set at the top left edge of the woman's desk bore a name and title: *Mrs. Wilson,*

Assistant to the Dean.

"I'm looking for Jeannie Parks."

"And what is the nature of your *businezz?*" The woman rose, stiffened her spine, and folded her arms across two six-inch printed peonies.

"I'm Nick Randall, a new faculty member in Mammalogy. Jeannie and I collaborate in the Exhibits Museum."

"Mrs. Parks is in the Collections Room. It's private. I'll take you there."

He followed her billowing top and her beehive hairdo, all the while breathing what he knew to be expensive French perfume. She smelled like Elizabeth.

Stopping in front of a four-panel, unlabeled door, Mrs. Wilson extracted a key from her pocket and slipped it into an embedded metal lock.

Click.

Opening the door, the taciturn woman straddled the threshold. "Mrs. Parks? You have a visitor."

Soft shuffling sounds neared. "Thanks, Marie."

God. She's a knockout. Nick swallowed. *Did my tongue just swell?* A stretchy blue dress clung tightly to Jeannie's bust, waist, and hips. The armless Greek statue *Venus de Milo* surfaced in his memory viewer. He clamped his tongue. *Yup. It's swollen, all right.*

"Nick. Come in." Jeannie set aside a magnifying glass and removed a pair of cotton gloves.

Lifting her chin and raising her eyebrows, Marie cast a lingering glance, turned, and walked out.

"Wow. Who is that? Where did she get her interrogation training?" Nick skimmed his hand over his scalp. "Any chance she worked in the Resistance?"

Jeannie laughed. "That is our Marie, and she is

very protective and very punctual and very loved, regardless of all the prickliness. A word of advice. Try to stay on her good side."

"So noted." He puffed a breath and set his briefcase on her desk.

She wetted her lips with her tongue. "How's your class going?"

"I've got a funny story about today." After he related the tale of the sign-up sheet, he scratched his head and gazed into her watery-from-laughter eyes. "I'm trying to decide who is easier to teach—Miss Cassidy's kindergarten class or the Great Lake Sailor students."

"Stop it. My stomach can't handle this." Jeannie crossed her arms over her abdomen and guffawed. She pulled out a chair and sat at a desk. "So, you stopped by to test my funny bone?"

Nick laughed. "I thought about your puppy dilemma, and I do know a fair amount of what it takes to get a puppy under control. My Golden Retriever, Sam, put me through the paces, too. I could give you a few pointers. Next Monday, I've got some free time after I meet with the field biology team."

Jeannie's posture slacked. Her eyebrows flashed.

"Would that work for you?"

"Nick, that is so thoughtful." She leaned back, gripped the edge of the desk, and lengthened her spine. "Joey will be thrilled. I bet Gunther will be, too." She grabbed a piece of paper from her desktop, gripped a pencil, and scribbled on the paper. "I live off of Mt. Hope, on the south side of campus. Here is the address and our home phone number. The house is set back behind some really tall pine trees. Oh, and you'll see a fleet of school buses, too. Our property borders the district's bus garage." She handed the document to Nick.

"Monday night. Five-thirty."

"See you then."

With a boyish pep in his step, Nick retreated to the hallway and bounced down the granite steps. *My chance to shine. My chance to be the hero.*

****

Stepping on the porch, Jeannie shivered and pulled her shawl about her shoulders. *He's running late.*

The sun spread like runny eggs on the western skyline. Sugar maple trees, last week in full scarlet bloom, stretched their bare silhouettes in graceful arcs.

Across the yard, proud military dad Enrico Fernandez unfastened his mailbox, twisted out an assortment of envelopes, turned, and waved.

Jeannie returned the gesture.

A family in a wood-paneled station wagon passed through the gap in the tall pines bordering her property line.

Honk-honk.

Again, Jeannie waved.

At a slow speed, a small, red, two-door car with bug-eye headlights approached the end of her driveway and paused.

A sun-glassed man stuck his head close to the windshield and peered.

She lifted her arms, overlapped them, and spread them.

The driver manipulated the steering wheel and closed the gap.

Jeannie's heart raced. She alternated her weight

100

from one foot to another over the porch deck planks. *Nick.*

He thrust the stick shift into Park, turned off the ignition, pushed open the driver's door, and lengthened his left boot to the ground. He withdrew the sunglasses from his face and met her gaze. Gravel crunched under his feet.

A flock of crows beat their wings as they arranged themselves on a utility line.

The disappearing sun leaked enough light to illuminate a five o'clock stubble on Nick's chin.

Opening the front door, Jeannie ushered Nick inside. From the kitchen, savory scents of onion, beef, clove, garlic, and twelve ounces of Cal's home-brewed-high-yeast beer wafted from the stovetop pot of simmering braised short ribs.

Five feet from the porch, Nick paused and breathed deeply.

Did he just rise on his toes? Jeannie grinned. *The man can smell. I'm sure that is an essential attribute for an animal scientist.* She pulled the shawl from her shoulders and moved aside. "C'mon in. Joey's expecting you."

"Am I interrupting your dinner hour?" Nick furrowed his brows and bent his head.

"No, no. The stew needs time to cook." Jeannie stepped to the bottom of a staircase. "Joey, Nick is here. Bring Gunther."

Clomp-clomp-clomp.

Skitter-skitter-skitter.

A stocking-footed Joey bounded down the creaky wooden stairs.

The puppy vaulted past the boy, clattering his nails

over the hardwood flooring.

Nick winced.

Growling, Gunther retreated, circled between Jeannie's legs, and barked.

I've got my hackles up, too. With trembling fingers, Jeannie gripped Gunther's collar.

Nick knelt and extended a hand. He held the pose as if he were a statue.

Gunther lowered his ears and inched toward Nick. He sniffed the proffered hand.

Nick stroked the ridge between the dog's ears.

Gunther thumped his tail.

Bump-bump.

"There you go. Good boy."

Jeannie expelled a deep breath. *All is well*.

Joey knelt and scooted on his knees to Gunther. He petted the puppy on the crown of his head.

"Hi, Joe." Nick flashed a smile.

Gunther flopped onto his back and splayed his legs.

Nick laughed and stroked the dog's underside. "I'm getting acquainted with Gunther. He sure is a fine-looking dog."

Joey put a hand on Nick's shoulder. He reached and found an empty spot on Gunther's belly and scratched the puppy's skin. "Yah, he's a German Shepherd. My grandma and grandpa said my dad liked German Shepherds. Did you know my dad trained dogs in the war?"

Jeannie walked to the stove, sucked her breath, and stared out the window. *My innocent boy*.

"I didn't know that, Joey. That makes your dad a hero."

"Yeah, my dad, he's a hero. I wish I knew him."

Joey pursed his lips and smoothed Gunther's paw.

"I wish you did, too, Joe. But I bet your dad watches over you." Nick formed a dent in his pants with the edge of his thumbnail.

A pinhole of sadness winged Jeannie's heart. *Somehow, that didn't hurt so much. Maybe it's because we have a new friend who lets us talk about Frank.* Jeannie sighed. *This is so unexpected.* Picking up a wooden spoon, Jeannie lifted the cover off a pot.

A cloud of steam escaped.

"Ouch!" Jeannie shook her fingers. "Whew, that was hot."

"Be careful, Mom."

"Thank you, Joey. Son, will you please put food in Gunther's bowl? Check his water dish, too." She inserted the wooden spoon into the pot and stirred.

"Yes, Mom."

"Jeannie, do you mind if I help? I've got an idea here." Nick rose and scratched the back of his head.

"Sure, go ahead." She dipped the spoon, extracted some stew, and sampled the broth. *Needs salt.*

"Hey, Joe." Nick stretched his shoulders. "Let's teach Gunther a few commands before he eats dinner."

Joey clasped the doorknob and turned.

"Reach into his dog food and pull out a few pellets. Put them in your pocket. Come over here by me." Nick dipped his head and came eye to eye with Joey. "When you want Gunther to be where you are, you give him the command, *Gunther, come.* When he gets to you, take a piece of food from your pocket and treat him. Then, pet his head and say, 'Gunther, good boy.' Ready?"

Bobbing his head, Joey patted his bumpy pocket.

Nick grasped Gunther's collar and led him to the opposite side of the room. "Ready, Joey?"

"Gunther, come." Joey slapped his thigh.

The puppy bounded to the boy.

"Gunther, good boy!" Joey tucked his hand in his pocket and retrieved a dog food morsel. He flattened his palm and bounced the dried pellet.

Gunther licked the food from Joey's palm.

"Excellent," Nick called. "Let's try this again." He grasped Gunther's collar and returned to the opposite side of the room.

Jeannie smiled. *The trainer training the trainer is so patient*. Her heart clenched. As she wrung out a dishcloth and wiped the stovetop, she listened to the tutoring continue.

Squatting, Nick leveled his gaze with Joey's. "I think we got this command down. Let's move on to the sit command. We will train Gunther to sit before you feed him."

Joey nodded.

"You measure out Gunther's food." Like a prizefighter varying his punch, Nick perused the kitchen. "I see Gunther's dish. I will bring it to you, Joey."

"Remember, Joey, one cup of food." Jeannie draped the dishcloth over the sink.

"Okay, Mom." Joey reached into the bin, pulled out a large plastic scoop, and gauged the required amount.

Yip-yip. Thrusting his front paws on Joey, Gunther hopped on his back legs.

A string of saliva swung from the puppy's jowls.

Setting the dish on a counter, Nick steadied it.

"Joey, pour the food into the dish."

As the dry food dropped into the bowl, the puppy pawed Joey's legs.

Lowering to Joey's level, Nick moved his mouth close to Joey's ear and whispered.

Joey nodded. He pointed an index finger and gazed into Gunther's eyes. Then he aimed the finger down. "Sit."

The puppy jumped and danced around Joey. *Yip.*

"Let's give him a bit of help," Nick said. "Hold his collar so his head stays up. Now push down on his backside and say, 'Gunther, sit.' "

With Joey's maneuvering, Gunther sat.

"Tell him, 'Gunther, good boy,' and pet his head."

"Gunther, good boy." Joey smoothed the fur between Gunther's perky ears.

"I'll hang on to his collar so he remains seated until you put the bowl on the floor in front of him." Nick grasped Gunther's collar.

With both hands, Joey placed the food dish.

Once the dish was on the floor, Nick released Gunther.

"Good job, Joey. From now on, each time you feed Gunther, direct him to sit and stay."

Jeannie wiped her hands on a towel and clapped. "Well done." She gazed at Nick.

The smile on his face exposed a boyish thrill. Dimples crested through his rust-colored beard. A hank of hair draped over his brow.

Heat mushroomed in her cheeks. She opened the window over the sink.

A musky, woodsy odor flowed through the room.

She stooped to pull a colander from the bottom

cupboard. "Hey, want to stay for dinner? Stew, tossed salad, fruit cocktail."

"You don't have to ask twice." Nick grinned. "Need assistance?"

"You're already helping." Jeannie nudged her nose toward the center of the room.

Joey sprawled on the carpet.

Gunther laid his snout over Joey's back and huffed a sigh.

Raising his head, Joey turned and gazed at Nick. "Gee, that was so cool. Can we teach him more tricks, Nick? I want Gunther to fetch sticks and roll over and play hide-and-seek…"

Nick laughed. "Sounds like you've got big plans for your puppy. Sure, Gunther can learn how to do all those things." The trainer squatted and patted Joey's head. "Gunther's happy to do what you tell him. He'll be your best friend."

Jeannie turned off the stove burner. She carried a large salad bowl and two containers of salad dressing to a multi-windowed room. "Dinner's ready. I'll fix the plates. We'll eat here, in the dining room." She returned to the kitchen, heaped stew on a plate, and offered the dish to Nick. She filled a plate with a smaller amount. "Nick, would you mind carrying Joey's plate?"

"Not at all."

"Joey, please wash up."

"Yes, Mom."

Water ran in the bathroom sink.

"Happy Birthday…" Joey sang.

"Singing that song is a trick to get him to wash his hands long enough to clear the germs." Jeannie smiled.

"Ah, good one!" Nick grinned.

Jeannie flipped a wall switch.

A rustic chandelier lit and imbued a charming light over a glossy, maple dining table.

Joey scrambled into a child seat strapped onto a chair.

Jeannie smoothed the back of her skirt and sat.

Nick bent his knees and lowered himself into a chair.

"Nick, do you know the Johnny Appleseed song? Mom and I sing that grace before dinner." Joey twined his fingers together.

"I sure do. I learned it at Scout camp—years ago."

A baritone, a soprano, and a tenor chanted praise to apple seeds and earth.

Nick stuffed his hands in his back pockets and teetered on the soles of his feet. "Sure smells delicious, like something you could cook over a campfire."

"It's one of those investment dishes. You know, you make a big pot and reap the rewards all week." Jeannie smiled. "Take some salad, Joey. Then, you can have a biscuit."

"Okay, Mom." Joey furrowed his brows and, with the salad serving spoon, scooped a mass of greens onto his dinner plate.

Jeannie leaned toward Nick. "He's on his best behavior," she whispered. "You're a good influence."

"Do you know a lot about dogs, Nick?" Joey drummed his fingers on the tabletop.

"I love dogs, and I have friends who study wolves. And guess who Gunther is a cousin to?"

"Wolves?" Joey blinked his eyes.

"You got that right, partner. Did you know wolves have lived in Michigan a long, long time? According to some of our early peoples, the Ojibwa, the wolf has the same significance in the world's beginning as Adam and Eve. The Ojibwa believe the original man on earth and his brother, *ma'lingun*, our friend the wolf, traveled the world together naming all the other animals, plants, and places on earth."

"I like that story, Nick." Joey smeared butter on a biscuit and stuffed it in his mouth.

"This summer, I studied animals on Isle Royale, right in the middle of Lake Superior. Three wolf packs live on Isle Royale. Each pack is a family, and there are about eight wolves in each family. There is a mom and a dad, some teenagers, and some cubs. They all look a lot like Gunther. But wolves grow bigger than German Shepherds. They have bigger feet. Their tracks are about this big." Nick held his hands four inches apart. "Wolves move a lot. They travel about thirty miles every day."

"That many miles is how far it is to the zoo," Jeannie interjected.

"Wow, that's a long way." Joey pushed his hair off his forehead.

"Both wolves and dogs are pack animals. That means dogs like being with other dogs, and wolves like being with other wolves. I betcha Gunther would be happy if you arranged play dates with other dogs. I could bring my Golden Retriever over to play with Gunther."

Jeannie lifted a napkin and wiped her lips. "What do you think about that, son?"

Joey swayed his head from one shoulder to the other. "I'd like that. Gunther should have a friend."

The clock over the kitchen sink chimed seven.

"Goodness, Joey. It's time to get ready for bed." Jeannie turned toward Nick. "We start to wind down pretty early here."

Nick sipped water from a large iced tumbler and nodded.

"Honey, let Gunther out in the backyard, and then go upstairs and get into your pajamas. Then brush your teeth and pick out a bedtime story. I will come upstairs and read."

Nick crumbled his napkin and placed the wadded paper on the table next to his plate. He stood. "Well, Joey, it was great seeing you and meeting Gunther." The mammalogist crouched and looked Joey in the eye. He scratched Gunther's ears and shook Joey's hand. "Gunther's a lucky puppy. I know you're going to be a wonderful trainer, Joey."

"Goodnight, Nick. I'll see ya." Joey led Gunther toward the back door.

Nick turned to Jeannie.

She held a salt shaker in one hand and a pepper mill in the other. "Nick, thanks so much for giving Joey and me pointers on puppy behavior and working with Gunther. I'm sure your tips will make a big difference."

He followed her into the kitchen.

She opened a cupboard door and stowed the condiments.

"Jeannie, thanks for dinner. It's the first home-cooked meal I've had in a long while. You've got a fine boy and a wonderful canine companion."

"You mean wolf cousin, right?" Jeannie winked.

Nick laughed. "All in the family." He picked a wet dishcloth off the faucet and wiped food spills off the counter in lingering, circular moves.

The tips of his fingers were square and thick. Jeannie stared. She swallowed. Her throat tightened.

Nick draped the dishrag over the faucet. He wiped his hands on the front of his jeans. "I'll let Gunther in, and then I'll be on my way. Thanks again for a fun evening, Jeannie."

The door creaked open.

A puppy bounced across the floor.

The door closed.

A boy called his mother.

Jeannie climbed two stairs. She stalled her hand on the sleek wood banister, turned, and stared at the door.

Outside, a German-made car engine fired up its hallmark buzzing and puttering racket.

The clamor shattered the evening quiet and filled Jeannie's heart with a growing disquiet.

****

Oncoming headlights blazed as Nick continued north on Harrison Road. He tapped the dim headlights button on the left of the brake pedal and squeezed the steering wheel. On either side of the road, corn crops maintained as laboratories for the university's agricultural students stretched to Farm Lane. The fields attracted deer and several genera of nocturnal mammals, any one of which could spontaneously decide to cross the pitch-black asphalt path. Nick stretched his eyelids and fanned his head right and left like a nighttime guard wielding a flashlight. In his memory, flashes of Jeannie's inner world played out.

Less than three hours ago, he distinguished the scrabbly bark red pines announcing the driveway to Jeannie's home. Standing on a porch framed by thick square columns and fronting a stucco-and-brick

110

bungalow, Jeannie raised her arms and crossed them with a fervor that swelled his heart. She was barefoot, and her long hair fell from a tousled bandana tied around the rim of her face. She bounced the floorboards as he approached. One bare foot tested the first step down, and then she retreated. She crossed her arms and paused, all the time observing him as he parked the car and shut the door.

Remembering the eagerness in her wave and the tentativeness in her footstep, Nick gripped the steering wheel tighter. *Oh, boy. Did I detect a mutual attraction? Whoa, Nick. It's fine if you find her appealing, but you can't toy with her emotions. Are you sure you're just helping a colleague out or what's going on here, buddy?*

Inside, the house was just as inviting. Dark wood wainscoting and moldings, built-in cabinets, shelves, and seating adorned soft-white walls and ceilings. An open floor configuration encompassed a living room, a dining room, and a French country kitchen.

Coordinating blue-and-white ceramic canisters sized for flour, sugar, coffee, and tea rested in descending height, starting to the left of the sink. A blue-and-yellow print in a quilted fabric covered a toaster shape on the counter opposite the refrigerator. Ruffled-edged curtains framed the windows over the sink and the French door leading into the dining area. A small nook held a built-in desk topped by a telephone, a writing tablet, and a cup full of neatly sharpened pencils. An open bookshelf mounted above the desk, and Nick noticed all the books were covered in a variety of blue-and-yellow fabric sleeves. Everything was neat, tidy, organized, and covered in fabric. *How could anyone with a full-time career, an energetic child, and an errant puppy have time or energy to devote to such orderliness? Could she be some kind of neurotic with a cleaning obsession? Yikes.*

After a delectable home-cooked dinner, Jeannie cleared the table and busied herself at the sink.

He walked the living area's perimeter and paused at the wall where a silver-framed military picture hung. On a nearby shelf, a simply framed, triangular-folded American flag rested. He turned and locked gazes with a sober-faced Jeannie.

"Frank was killed in Vietnam."

The desire that originated from his first view of her on the porch had stilled. His heart ached. He tried hard to think of something to say. He failed. Silence had enveloped them. *Jeannie and Joey are casualties, too.*

The rural side of campus faded.

The vast stretches of darkness opened into the neon brightness of fast-food joints and the high beams of campus security lighting.

The pulse of rock-and-roll music and the reek of marijuana streamed through the open car windows.

Only three more blocks and he would be home in his sterile condo.

Sam anticipated a walk.

Elizabeth expected a call.

Nick shook his head.

Miss Harcourt possessed the deadly impatience of a world-flattening pandemic.

He shuddered.

Despite the consequences, Elizabeth would have to wait until tomorrow.

Chapter 11

Car doors slammed.

In the midst of evening shadows, welcoming lights shone over the First Presbyterian Church entrance.

Jeannie shivered. *Wish I wore a hat. Guess I better get our winter clothes out. Only two more weeks and it will be November. Brrr.* She scurried to the entrance.

Jim held the door. A couplet of uneven buttonholes and mismatched buttons created a gap at the highest point of Jim's portly belly.

"Just the farmer I wanted to see." Jeannie grinned. "Looks like you've got at least one free hand." Jeannie extended a pint-sized glass jar topped with a metal lid.

"What's this?" Jim raised his eyebrows.

"Just a minor payback. I hope you like homemade peach jam."

"That wasn't necessary."

"I had to get rid of all those peaches somewhere." Jeannie winked.

Jim held up the jar. "I'll tell you what. Tomorrow morning, I'll crack this open and spread it atop marbled rye toast. *Ummm, ummm.* Thanks, Jeannie."

I hope the ladies are just as pleased with what I have to give them tonight. She gummed her lips and smiled.

Jim followed her into the cool basement conference room.

Murmurs and footsteps echoed in the hallway.

"Guess we should take a seat." Jeannie laid her purse atop a table and shrugged off a jacket. *On second thought, I think I'll keep this on for a while, at least until it warms up in here.*

Jim pulled out a metal chair. "I ought to keep my gentleman skills intact." He winked.

"Oh, thanks." Jeannie settled into the seat and pulled a notebook from her purse. "I'm looking forward to tonight's discussion. How about you, Jim?"

"The boys helped me with this one." He grinned.

"Hello, all. Water's hot and Verna brought cookies tonight." Sharon rolled a chalkboard to the front of the room. She picked a piece of chalk from a metal tray underneath the board, raised an arm, and pressed the white marker to the green board.

Screech.

"Sorry." Sharon adjusted the chalk. "I'm kinda rusty at this." She spat on the marker and moved the tip across the board's surface. She wrote *Honor the Memory* in capital letters. Setting the chalk back in the tray, she brushed her palms together and turned. "Do we have new folks tonight?" Sharon asked.

Jeannie fanned her head left and then right. *Nope, no new folks.*

"Okay, then. Your homework was to share ways you remember your spouse. Who's first?" Sharon retrieved the chalk.

"I'll go." Bunny rose and walked to Sharon. She grasped the chalk and wrote *Story Book.* "I'm writing a story book for my grandchildren featuring their papa when he was a boy. Of course, I'll include tales about his hunting dog, Clemmie, and the time they met a porcupine on his way to school. I hope to both inspire them and caution them about Grandpa's science fair project that never went to school because the explosion blew out the garage door and foisted him on the hot seat with his parents." Bunny giggled.

"Well, your husband turned out to be a chemical engineer, right?" Sharon pointed an index finger.

"He sure did." Bunny nodded.

Sharon smiled. "Can't wait to read it, Bunny. I'm sure your writing will be a family classic."

"I have a ten-year-old granddaughter who loves to draw. I'm hiring her to be the illustrator." Bunny laced her fingers together and smiled the smile of a proud grandmother.

"Great idea, Bunny." Marie clapped.

"Anyone else?"

Jim cleared his throat. "It's not all my idea. But I think it's worth sharing."

"C'mon, up." Sharon retied a loose bow at her collar.

"Twenty years ago, when my father died, only a month remained before his birthday. We decided to celebrate his birthday, anyway. Nancy, my wife—bless her heart—made a cake. Then all of us—kids, grandkids included—surprised my mom. She was so grateful we hadn't forgotten the day and that we were willing to celebrate. We've done that every year since. I'm hoping our kids want to do that for Nancy. I'd really like that."

"How sweet. Did everyone understand that it was Nancy's idea?" Marjorie rubbed her cheeks.

Jim fiddled with his pen.

"So, you're carrying on a tradition Nancy started,

115

and now, that custom will also honor her." Bunny sighed. "Wow. What kind of cake will you make for Nancy's birthday, Jim?"

Jim snorted. "Well, I'm no baker, but like you, Bunny, I have a talented grandchild. This one enjoys baking. I'll have Martin make a German chocolate cake with lots of toasted coconut."

"I hope we're all invited to the party! Don't forget the vanilla ice cream," Verna called.

Jim drew a flaming candle on the board, waved, and returned to his seat.

"Who's next? By the way, you are taking notes, right, Jeannie?"

"I can see her pen moving from here." Marie stood and tugged on her hip-hugging stretch top. She moved to the board. With the chalk, she drew a circle. Marie toyed with a gold chain that hung around her neck. She held up the object that rolled along its length. "I still wear Paul's wedding ring, just not on my ring finger. From time to time, I pull it from its place next to my heart and press it to my lips." Demonstrating, Marie kissed the platinum band. "*Je t'aime. Pour toujours.*"

Verna cleared her throat. "I get that wanting to wear something that belonged to your spouse. I might be weird, but I find it very comforting to wear Henry's bathrobe. I just like to put it on, rub the fabric over my skin, and smell him. It's something I do without really planning." Verna chafed her arms. "And p.s., I have never washed it."

Marie nodded. She returned to her seat next to Jennifer. "I know you have good ideas, too. Go ahead, *Cheri.*"

Jennifer rose, wrapped her sweater tighter, and

walked past Marie. She pinched the chalk between her right index finger and her right thumb. She drew an American flag and a basket on the chalkboard. "The kids have gotten into the habit of decorating Bill's gravesite. They put small flags and red, white, and blue ribbons during the Fourth of July. They even ignited sparklers and sang 'God bless America' at dusk. On Easter, they left a basket with his favorite candy–black jelly beans—and those awful sugar-crusted marshmallow things that dry harder than boot rawhide. For our anniversary, my daughter organized a treasure hunt with clues that were written as love messages from Bill to me. The hunt ended at the cemetery. A dozen red roses, and a card to me from him rested on Bill's grave. Of course, I cried and cried. That was so sweet of her." Jennifer huffed.

Sharon ripped a tissue from a box and held it with the end of her fingers.

Jennifer claimed the offering and dabbed her cheeks. She coughed. "Our wedding anniversary is the worst day of the year for me." She formed a fist and drummed her chest.

Hums of agreement whispered through the room.

Verna raised a hand.

Sharon nodded. "Verna, what about you?"

"I'll just stay in my seat. What I want to add is that the cookies I baked and brought tonight were Henry's favorite. Kind of a cute story goes along with this." Verna smiled.

Oh, my goodness, she's blushing. Jeannie grinned and shifted in her seat.

"Henry and I were newlyweds, and we had our first fight. I still remember how dang mad I was. I mean, I was ready to pack my suitcase and go home to Vicksburg." Verna shook her head. Her neck wobbled.

Bunny giggled.

"Why, that man insulted me. Well, what he did was ignore the efforts I took to make myself prettier." Verna bobbed her chin.

Jim slapped his thigh.

"One morning after Henry left for work, I applied one of those home permanents. I tell you, when I put that solution on my head, the whole house stunk." Verna pinched her nose. "But by the time Henry walked through the door that night, the aroma of roast beef, onions, and carrots filled the place. I had set the table with his grandmother's china, filled a vase with apple-blossom sprigs and set those spring flowers right by his place at the end of the table. That helped cover up that stinky permanent solution smell, too."

Sharon snickered.

"Even though the garage was one hundred feet from the house, I heard his truck. That old jalopy was missing a muffler, and that truck was loud. I mean it sounded like thunder rolling. When I heard a backfire, I scurried into the washroom, applied scarlet lipstick, primped my beautiful new hairstyle, whipped off my apron, and threw it into a laundry basket. Then, I ran back to the stove, grabbed a potholder, and pretended to be all casual-like." Verna drew a deep breath. *Phew.* "Henry walked through the door. I called, 'Hi, honey. I'll have dinner on the table in just a minute. Go ahead and get washed up.' I filled a platter with the roast beef and vegetables. I heard the water running, and then his chair scraping against the floor. So, I grabbed the platter and walked into the dining room. I set the beef in front of him, then I sat. Henry closed his eyes and folded his hands. We said the grace together. Then, he reached for the carving knife and fork beside the roast."

Everyone is bracing on the edge of their seats. Jeannie grinned.

"Henry ate his whole dinner and didn't say a dang thing about my hair. I was so mad I wished he choked on a piece of the beef, but he didn't." Verna's neck quivered. "The next morning, after he left for work, I sat down and bawled. This leaving and bawling routine went on for two days. At day's end, he'd come home and ignore my new do. On the third morning, Henry's mother stopped by. She took one look at my red eyes and my red hair, and she asked, 'What's wrong?' She coddled my hand and said, 'Honey, menfolk, they don't so much notice these things. But I'll tell you what they do notice. They notice food. I've got an idea.' So then, she scribbled some directions on a piece of paper. That night, when I opened the door for Henry, he sniffed the air. 'Honey, is that my momma's gingersnap cookie recipe?' 'It sure is,' I said. Then, I went straight to the kitchen and brought him a still-warm cookie. The smile on his face melted my new bride haughtiness. 'Oh, honey, that was so sweet. You are the most beautiful girl in the world.' He pulled me to his chest, and we kissed like our first kiss. So, if anybody wants the recipe for these cookies, just ask me for the cookies my family calls the kiss-and-make-up cookie." Verna smiled.

Clapping filled the room.

Verna wiped a tear from her cheek.

"Bravo. Bravo." Jim whistled.

"And so every time you serve these cookies, you

remember that kiss-and-make-up with Henry, right?" Sharon asked.

"Absolutely." Verna grinned.

"I don't have a great kiss-and-make-up story like Verna, but I do have something to share." Jeannie walked to the board and picked up the chalk. She drew a few circles and sat. "I'm making a collage of Frank's high school varsity letters, merit badges he earned in Scouting, ribbons he won in Future Farmers of America, and the medals awarded him for outstanding service to his country." Jeannie cleared her throat. "I'll have the project framed and give it to Joey when he's older. Joey and I talk about Frank as if his father were here, as a part of our family. We pray for him every night, and we kiss his picture before we go to sleep." She sighed.

"What a meaningful way to preserve special belongings of a loved one." Marjorie pleated a paper into accordion folds.

Sharon stood by the blackboard and pointed to the dusty-white symbols. "Thanks for sharing, everyone. You all have touched on some wonderful ways to remember your spouses, to keep in touch with them and to keep their memory present for you, your children, and your grandchildren. Are there any announcements before we close?"

Jeannie held up her right hand.

"Jeannie?"

Waving a newspaper clipping, Jeannie turned her head right and left. "What do you think of this, ladies? Jacobson's Department Store is offering free makeovers in their salon. That means makeup and hair. They include complimentary fashion consultation—

foundation fittings and wardrobe suggestions. We all deserve some pampering, and I've heard it's good for the soul, too. Who wants to go?"

Marjorie elevated her hand. "Me!"

Jennifer leaned into Marie. She whispered into her friend's time-lapsed hairdo.

Marie pulled away and raised her brows. Then, she nodded.

"Two over here." Jennifer grinned.

She looks like she just won a contest. Could it be that Marie has consented to updating her look? Kudos to Jennifer! Jeannie bent sideways and retrieved her purse from under her seat. She unzipped the front pocket and fished out an envelope bearing a return address of Jacobson's Department Store. Jeannie held aloft the packet. "C'mon up here and grab a brochure."

With a rolling walk, Verna advanced. "It's been a very long time since I had a change."

"Now, Verna, if you get a makeover, do we automatically get cookies?" Jim guffawed.

"Has anyone told you lately, Jim, that you are a stinker?" Verna shook her fist.

"No, but teasing feels rather good, thank you. Guess I'm out of here, ladies. See you next week. Any homework, Sharon?"

"Thanks for bringing that up, Jim. Next week we'll talk about happiness guilt. Try to question yourself if you are allowing yourself guilt-free happiness. I'm warning you. This might be tricky. I wish you all a good week." Sharon gathered her teacup and folder.

"So, ladies, I will call Jacobson's salon and ask about making a group appointment for Verna, Marjorie, Jennifer, Marie, and myself. Anyone else?" Jeannie scanned the room. "Okay, reservation for five. I'll have information for everyone next week. But just so you know, I will be out of town the week after next. I am attending a conference in Chicago, so I will look for an early November date.

"Fine with me, Jeannie." Marjorie snapped her purse shut and pushed her chair back under the table.

"Sure," Verna called.

"Okay with us, as well." Jennifer waved. "Wow, we'll have a new look in time for the holidays!"

"Hey, Jeannie." Sharon touched Jeannie's shoulder and gazed into her eyes. "Regarding next session's assignment. You, dear are my inspiration for discussing happiness and guilt. Prepare to come with an open heart."

Why me? The question and the earnestness in Sharon's eyes plagued Jeannie all the way home.

Chapter 12

Nick leaned back, stretched, and pulled the lever on his recliner chair. He crumbled the Sunday newspaper lying across his lap and tossed the chronicle into the recycling bin. *Goodbye, November 1,1970.*

Creak.

He lifted the muslin curtains next to the lamp and peered outside.

Under the streetlights illuminating Nick's garage, his neighbor dragged a garbage can to the street edge. *His breath clouded into vapor. Yup. He sure looks cold. I'm glad I put flannel sheets on the bed. And that's where I'm going.*

Spasmodic snoring sounds drifted from the kitchen.

Nick grinned. *Good night, Sam.* He opened the refrigerator, grabbed a carton of skim milk, and downed a swig. After bending and tousling Sam's fur, he turned off the living room lamps and ascended the stairs. He snatched his pajamas from the end of his bed.

The phone rang.

Nick moved to the bed stand, grasped the receiver, and unfastened the top button on his shirt. "Hello?" He moved his fingers to the next button.

"Oh, God, you're home."

"Jeannie?"

"Nick, it's Gunther. I don't know what to do. He's really, really sick."

"Details. Give me details." Nick's heart bounced to his throat. He gripped the phone and stamped the receiver against his ear.

"He's been throwing up. He's panting, and he won't stand. God, Nick, I am so scared. What do I do?"

"Stay with him. Don't move him. Call someone to stay with Joey. I'm leaving now. And, leave the front door unlocked." Nick smashed the receiver into the cradle. He registered the heightened sensation of tremors hiking the length of his spine. His breathing cinched.

Reaching into his back pocket, he grabbed his address book. With shaking hands, he thumbed his way to the *R*s. He picked up the phone and dialed.

"Dr. Matt Richter here."

Thank God. Nick breathed. "Matt, geez, I know it's late."

"Sorry, I can't take your call now. Please leave a message."

Oh, no. Nick's heart sank. The momentary sense of relief plummeted to a weighty sense of gloom. "Matt, Matt, for the love of Pete, pick up," Nick shouted.

Sam appeared in the bedroom doorway, padded toward Nick, and nudged his wet nose under Nick's elbow.

"Hello?"

"Matt, Nick Randall. I've got a sick German Shepherd puppy—profuse vomiting, lethargy, and mobility loss. Can you see him?"

"Get him here as soon as you can. I'll be ready."

Click.

Nick clambered down the stairs and grabbed his jacket and keys from the front closet. "Bye, Sam."

Charged with adrenaline, Nick stumbled to the garage, thrust open the overhead door, and yanked open the car door.

Animal bite? Allergy? Distemper? Poison? Nick thrust the key in the ignition, shifted into Reverse, and peeled backward. He looked in the rearview mirror, shifted into Drive, and zoomed out the driveway. *Minutes count. She's terrified.*

****

Nick breached the door. "Jeannie?"

"In here," she called.

Picking his way through an unfinished floor puzzle and a string of toy cars, Nick followed Jeannie's voice.

Gunther lay on his side. Frothy, odorous puke veiled his muzzle.

Nick knelt on the floor and gently lifted his head.

The puppy briefly opened his glazed eyes and then shut them. He whimpered and flopped his tail.

"Hey, boy. Looks like you're hurting." Nick stroked Gunther's head. *Gotta hurry.* Nick's chest heaved.

Dressed in a pair of blue jeans and a pajama top, Jeannie hovered over Nick's shoulders. "Please, Lord, don't let anything happen to this precious puppy," she prayed.

"Jeannie, get me a sturdy blanket," Nick directed.

She darted down the hallway and returned with a coverlet.

A clattering noise erupted at the front door.

"I'm here."

"Dee, thank you. Thank you. Joey's upstairs. Can you stay with him?" Jeannie's high-pitched voice trembled.

"As long as you need." Dee grabbed the banister and climbed the stairs.

Nick turned to Jeannie. "Lay the blanket down between you and me. We'll create a gurney to transport Gunther."

Jeannie unfolded the blanket and pushed the cover close to Gunther.

"Jeannie, Nick, I think you better see this." Dee hung her head over the stair railing.

Nick lunged up the stairs.

Jeannie jumped two steps at a time simultaneously behind him.

Dee held a finger to her lips. "Shhh. Over there." She pointed to the spare bedroom.

Six empty chocolate bar wrappers, a half-empty packet of graham crackers, and a bag of jumbo marshmallows lay scattered on a braided rug. Discernable bite marks marred the foil liners of the candy.

"Chocolate. It's poison to dogs." With his heartbeat kicking into staccato, Nick ran downstairs. *Be strong.*

Moaning, Jeannie followed.

Nick grabbed one end of the blanket. "Time is of the essence. Hold the blanket, and I'll shimmy Gunther onto it. Roll your side up, as close to Gunther as possible. I'll roll mine. Now we're going to hoist him. Jeannie, lift from your knees."

Jeannie gathered the coverlet ends and squatted. Then, she furrowed her brows. Grunting, she raised her forearms and tugged.

"Anything I can do?" Dee moved down the stairs.

"Get the door for us." Nick staggered and righted his stance.

"Coming." Dee scrambled to the foyer.

"Dee, grab my jacket and throw it over my shoulders," Jeannie pleaded.

"I'm putting the chocolate wrappers into your pocket," Dee called.

Nick held the blanket edge closest to Gunther's head and walked backward. "We'll get him into the backseat. You sit with him. My friend Matt is on standby. He's the best vet I know."

Jeannie clenched her teeth and gripped the opposite end. "Oomph," she snorted. *Please, God.* She squeezed her eyes shut. In the seconds before she opened them, a vision of wiping Joey's tears before a Gunther-sized grave propelled a chilling grip from her head to her heels.

****

Nick drove like a crazy man, playing roulette with each stoplight and careening around corners.

In the backseat, Jeannie held Gunther's head in her lap.

"Warm enough back there?" Nick glanced in the rearview mirror.

"Don't think about me." Jeannie's teeth chattered.

Nick narrowed his eyes.

A lone beacon of hope gleamed from an entryway light.

Nick pressed the horn pad.

Beep.

A disheveled man appeared on the porch deck and held the door open.

Nick threw the truck in Park, jumped from the front seat, yanked open the cab door, and hoisted Gunther over his shoulder. Against the still of the frosty night, the noise of boot-crunching gravel assaulted his ears. The huff of Jeannie's breath assured him she was close behind.

Matt ushered them into a brightly lit, windowless room, paneled in white beadboard and wallpapered in a motif of multi-breed dogs.

Shelves filled with gleaming metal tops crowning glass canisters that contained cotton swabs, tongue depressors, and dog treats lined one wall. Both muzzles and nail clippers, sized from small to ridiculously large, hung from a pegboard. An autoclave, surrounded by an otoscope, a refractometer resembling a train whistle, and, of all things, a Frick speculum rested on a counter. *I didn't know Matt treated bovines.*

A paper-covered examination table dominated the middle of the linoleum floor. The smell of alcohol permeated the room. Nick rolled Gunther onto the assessment table.

Matt pulled a miniature flashlight from his pocket and shined a beam into Gunther's eyes. Then, he retraced the puppy's gums and scowled.

Gulping, Nick struggled to breathe. "Matt, this is Jeannie. And this is Gunther. Appreciate this." Nick stuck his hands in his back pockets. "We think he might have ingested chocolate."

Jeannie held up six candy bar wrappers. "Pretty sure these are Gunther's bite marks here. I should have been paying more attention." She frowned and placed the paper evidence in Matt's hand. She expelled a mournful sigh and hunched her shoulders.

Matt knit his brows and blew out a deep breath. "Damn. Nick, get him on the scale."

Cradling the puppy in his arms, Nick stepped on a

medical scale on the floor beside the office entrance. "Two hundred and forty-six pounds." He passed the puppy to Matt. He recalibrated the scale. "Minus two hundred and twenty-two pounds. Gunther weighs in at twenty-four pounds."

"Nick, help me out here." Clutching a thermometer, Matt transferred the instrument to Nick. Then, Matt snatched the handle of a drawer and yanked out plastic tubing and a roll of white tape.

"We've got a temperature of one hundred and six degrees." Nick ground his teeth. "Six degrees above normal."

Matt turned and faced Nick, holding Gunther on the examination table. He ripped a short length of tape, stuck it to his shirt, held a tubing end to the puppy's nose, and laid it against the puppy's left side. Noting where Gunther's ribs ended, he tore the tape from his shirt and, at the mark, wrapped the adhesive around the tube. With his unyielding gaze never leaving Gunther, Matt made a quarter turn, stretched his arm over the sink, and flung open a cabinet door. He clamped his hand over a syringe and narrow intravenous tubing. "I'm starting an IV and then flushing Gunther's stomach." In a brief flash, Matt met first Nick's, then Jeannie's gaze. "This process isn't pleasant. We need all hands on deck."

Jeannie petted Gunther's head. Her face clouded.

Nick's heart swelled in his throat.

"Nick, there's lubricant in the middle drawer. Coat one end of the orogastric tube. Jeannie, you'll find a funnel and a big green bucket in that closet," Matt directed. With the thumb and forefinger of his left hand, Matt squeezed and raised a track of loose skin on

Gunther's spine. With his right hand, he poised a syringe and plunged the needle through Gunther's fur. "That's gonna make this more comfortable, fella." Matt rubbed gently on the penetrated spot.

"Here you go, Doc." Nick handed off the prepared tube.

Placing Gunther on his belly and motioning Nick to hold the puppy still, Matt inserted an intravenous catheter into the puppy's right front limb. Then, he gazed at Jeannie. "Your job is to hold his jaws open."

Jeannie's eyes flickered dark in the blazing luminescence of the white walls, the fluorescent lighting, and the reflective, stainless steel instruments. Her pallor matched the blinging opaqueness. Nick swallowed a bile intrusion. *She's petrified.*

Jeannie clamped her lips in a hard line and curled her fists around each side of Gunther's mouth.

Bending low, Matt threaded the transparent tube across Gunther's tongue and beyond. He palpated Gunther's stomach as the tape marker leveled with the puppy's front teeth. "Nick, grab a syringe. Fill it with five milliliters of saline. You'll find everything in that top cupboard." Taking the syringe from Nick, Matt plunged the stopper, compelling the solution into the tubing. "Test run to make sure we're in the stomach." The wild-eyed veterinarian furrowed his brows and scanned his watch.

Gunther blinked. He flopped his tail.

"Good—great. No coughing or choking. We're in the right place. Funnel."

Jeannie grasped the *Y*-shaped instrument and placed it in Matt's hand.

"Nick, position the bucket by my feet. Then, fill

that canister with lukewarm water. You're pouring." Matt positioned the end of the funnel into the orogastric tube. "Eight ounces, then get the hell out of the way."

Jeannie heaved a broken sigh.

Gunther moaned.

Stomach contents colored grassy green and smelled odorous splashed into the bucket and splattered Matt's pants.

Nick gagged.

"Again," Matt called.

Measuring eight ounces of tepid water, Nick paired the lip of the canister with the tubing edge, tipped the canister, and stepped back.

Retching once again, Gunther rolled his eyes and squeezed them shut.

The men administered eight more flushings.

"Good boy, Gunther. Almost done, fella." Matt turned to Jeannie. "You can step away from Gunther for a moment." The veterinarian jutted his chin toward the wall of cabinets. "Middle cupboard. Grab a package of activated charcoal."

Jeannie flung open the center door, stood on tiptoe, and scanned the space. She grabbed a plastic bag, brought it to Matt, and resumed her post at Gunther's mouth.

Matt ripped open the package, measured an amount of the binder, and poured it into the funnel. "That will trap any residual toxins. Okay, team, hold on. I'm checking if the gag reflex has returned." Matt held his stethoscope against Gunther's lungs. "Sounding good. Tube's coming out. IV is staying in so I can administer fluids and additional meds, if needed during recovery."

Nick's legs buckled. "Whew."

Matt lifted a still-sedated puppy into his arms. "Nick, follow me."

Entering a warm, darkened room, Nick adjusted his vision.

"Open the door on that pen closest to the door," Matt said softly. Transferring Gunther into the bottom-padded cage butt first, he slid his arm from under the puppy's belly and released his body. Matt secured the IV tube outside of the enclosure.

Trailing behind, Jeannie tented her hands over her mouth.

Gone was the harsh bravado of a white-coated, spitfire action figure. In the veterinarian's place, a limp-muscled, heart-on-his-sleeve animal advocate slumped on a stool. Nick raked his bottom teeth over his top lip.

Matt ran a palm over his face and his slack bottom lip, reached into his pocket, and extracted the chocolate bar wrapper. He made eye contact with both adults. "From the label, one chocolate bar is slightly over an ounce and a half. I can discern that Gunther ingested approximately ten ounces of milk chocolate. The way the equation works for chocolate poisoning is this—one ounce of milk chocolate per one pound of puppy is considered lethal. We've got a few factors on our side. You got here immediately. The lighter the chocolate, the less lethal it is for dogs. So, white chocolate is almost no threat. Dark chocolate is the worst. Gunther is a young dog. Chocolate poisoning in older dogs is more severe. I'll keep him overnight. I'll be upfront with you, Jeannie: this could take a wrong turn, even though we've got a lot of good things on our side."

Jeannie moved to the tranquilized puppy and stroked his paws. "Hang in there, please. I love you.

Joey loves you. You're the best puppy ever."

Nick gripped her shoulder. A wad of anxiety lodged in his throat. *She doesn't deserve this.*

"So, listen, you two. Why don't you go home, get some sleep, and try not to worry." Matt set his jaw. "I'll get a strong cup of java and stay here. In a few hours, my staff will arrive, and I'll give you a call. Now go on." Matt motioned toward the door.

Nick held out his right hand.

Matt clasped it. Then he pressed Jeannie's shoulder.

On the way home, Jeannie sat in the front seat. "Why did I name him Gunther? Wasn't that just tempting fate? The worst fate? Gunther was Frank's Army dog. Why didn't we name the puppy Lucky or Bo or Rocky? Why didn't I pay more attention when Joey said, 'Hey, Mom, Gunther and I are playing camping?' I was too engrossed in my research paper to check in on them and see that playing camping was making and eating s'mores. I'm a terrible mother." Jeannie sagged against the car door and wept.

Nick slowed the car. He pulled into the back of a convenience store parking lot. He turned in his seat and gently folded her against his still-heaving chest. She smelled of puke and dog poop and rubbing alcohol. Nick didn't pull away.

"I was so scared. I didn't know who else to call. I'm so sorry I bothered you."

The words babbled out of her mouth like salmon propelling against the raging forces of an ice-melting mountain stream.

"Nick, he just has to be okay. Losing Gunther would crush Joey."

133

And you, too. Nick ran a palm over her head and smoothed her hair. His gut ached.

She pulled away and sat up. She lowered her eyes.

"Jeannie, Matt's the best. He trained right here at Great Lakes University Vet School. He's worked on wolves in reserves around the world. He's a great guy and a good friend. He's got a top-notch laboratory. He's treated hundreds of pets. I trust him with Sam. And that says it all."

Jeannie pulled a tissue from her pocket and wiped her upper lip. "What do I tell Joey about the reason Gunther is sick? I just can't lay that guilt on him."

Nick gazed out the window. He shook his head. "You'll tell Joey Gunther got a bad tummy ache. You'll tell him Gunther's sickness was no one's fault and that puppy's tummies are different from little boy's. You'll tell him that from now on we make sure Gunther eats only pet food, the kind that comes in a bag and is labeled for dogs."

Jeannie expelled a deep breath.

Nick wiped the condensation off the inside of the windshield. "That means no table scraps, campfire food, and nothing in the garbage can. And, just so we all know, grapes, onions, and chocolate are hazardous to dogs."

"I'm such a horrible mother. I should know what's going on every single minute." Jeannie tugged her cheeks.

"Aren't you being too hard on yourself? Trust me. In my opinion, you're the champion of mothers."

"I sure don't feel that way tonight."

"Someday, I'll tell you a story of comparison." Nick set his jaw in a hard line.

"Someday, I'll be glad to listen." She reached and squeezed his wrist.

Positioning his hands atop the steering wheel, Nick gazed at her. "Ready to go home and redeem yourself?" He winked.

Jeannie snorted. "Yes. Yes, I am."

"Nick, I don't know how I could have managed this alone. I really appreciate this." Her voice lowered to a whisper. "More than I can say."

He patted her knee.

She rested her hand atop his. "Gunther did look better when we left him, didn't he?" Jeannie's voice trailed.

"Yes, he did." *What you couldn't see was the way Matt Richter checked your bootie as we left the examining room.* Nick gazed in the rearview mirror. *Hindsight, gah.*

Chapter 13

"Honey, don't be sad. Please." Moving her suitcase aside, Jeannie knelt beside her son on the cement pad that lined the railroad tracks. Cold seeped through her neck, and traffic vibrations crept through her knees. A sliver of sunshine broke bravely through gloomy-gray clouds. "Think of how happy you are that Gunther is home and his belly is all better."

"Yeah, Mom. Gunther is all better." Joey scratched his nose.

What would we have done without Nick's quick actions? I wouldn't be here on my way to Chicago to present my doctoral research. For a brief moment, Jeannie squeezed shut her eyes. "And my goodness, you will have so much fun while I'm gone." Nodding to her best friend, Jeannie wrapped an arm over Joey's shoulders. "Dee planned a trip to the movies and the planetarium. I'll call you every night before you go to sleep, and I'll be home before you miss me." She pulled higher the zipper tab on his jacket. "Gotta keep you warm. *Brrr.*"

A train whistle blew.

Jeannie rose and gripped her luggage with one hand and Joey's hand with the other.

A stream of vapor burst from the engine car and enveloped the people, travel gear, cars, and vegetation within twenty feet of each side of the rails.

Joey squeezed her hand.

A tear rolled down his cheek. He bit his lip.

The bite ripped a chunk from Jeannie's heart.

Dee hovered on the sidewalk.

"I've got a secret." Jeannie gazed down at her son.

Wiping his face, Joey tilted up his chin. "What, Momma?"

"Dee has a surprise for you. Once you get back into the car, you can open it." Jeannie winked at Dee.

"Okay, Joey. Let's go." Dee clapped her mittens together. "Look! Tiny snowflakes are in the air. How about hot cocoa when we get home?"

Joey tilted his head and sniffed the air. "Can we build a snowman?"

"We'll see, honey." Dee grinned.

Thank you, Jeannie mouthed. "See you both on Sunday night."

The porter helped her stow her baggage.

Jeannie carried her briefcase and chose a seat on the side facing the depot.

Outside, Dee waved in fast arcs.

Joey's smile turned upside down as the train doors closed and the engine chugged forward.

"Be safe. Be good," Jeannie whispered, spreading a palm against the window. She froze a smile on her face and locked her gaze with him. As the train wheels advanced, her heart rocked to her throat.

My sweet boy.

College students dressed in school colors milled around the station.

Gray-haired parents clasped them to their breasts.

Parents' week. Jeannie turned away. *Things to come. Oh, Frank.* Sighing, she opened her briefcase and

137

reviewed the conference agenda.

Annual Meeting of the American Costume and Textiles Society

Thursday evening: Cocktails and Conversation Celebrating the Grand Opening of the Costumes of Famous Female Folk Musicians Exhibit. Location: Rotunda of the Doris Zetta Textiles Museum.

Friday morning: nine a.m. Tour of Heart, Shakespeare, and Lark. Meet in the hotel lobby. Bus transportation is provided.

Friday afternoon: Business Meeting

Saturday Presentations. She ran a fingertip over her name. *Jeannie Parks, Doctoral Candidate, The History of the Yale Woolen Mill, Yale, Michigan 1881-1963. Abstract. A brief survey of woolen manufacturing in the state of Michigan and a case study of one Michigan woolen mill were undertaken to compare technological operations, building changes, management techniques, and working conditions over time, and if possible, to relate those changes to the political, social, and technological environments of the manufacturing community.*

A search of primary documents, business records, and interviews of former management and employees yielded information that was analyzed for historical accuracy and for its relationship with concurrent events in Michigan history. Based on the findings of this study, the operations of a woolen mill reflected most particularly the economic situation of Michigan and, on a broader scale, the nation.

Saturday Evening: Formal Banquet Lakefront Hall

Jeannie tucked the heel of her shoes into the metal rungs under her seat. She leaned back.

The seat popped into a reclining position.

The gentle thrumming of the iron wheels induced a welcome calm.

"Dang, I don't feel one bit sorry for those war-mongering guys returning home with limps and missing parts. Shit."

Through a sleepy haze, Jeannie registered a slurred voice thick with vitriol coming from the seat behind.

"Yeah, if they had courage, they'd have called themselves conscientious objectors. Man, it takes balls to up and move to Canada."

The second speaker spit out the word *balls* like a cat chucking a hairball.

Jeannie sat upright. She widened her eyes.

"They just wanted to get a gun and shoot people—women, children, dogs…hell, they didn't care."

Curving her spine into a ball, Jeannie warded off a knee-jerk sucker punch to her gut.

"What if all those assholes had refused to play war? There wouldn't be no war. Simple as that, man."

"Hell, yeah. You and me should run the world."

The sound of hand slapping rang.

The odor of skunk wafted Jeannie's nose. *I know better than to mistake that as skunk, boys. You stink of marijuana. And you just plain stink.* She cringed. *I could really use a hug.* Closing her eyes, she conjured a hero surrounded by sterilized brightness whose quick movements had saved Frank's namesake dog.

****

At eight thirty a.m. Friday, with a takeout coffee in one hand and a leather-tooled handbag in the other, Jeannie boarded a rumbling bus parked in the hotel's circular driveway. A seated woman bedecked in a flawlessly matched violet-red-and-purple plaid, Bertha-collared coat motioned her to sit beside her. The wide neckpiece embellished with scalloped red fur framed her face like a portrait in a Victorian gallery. Bending her knees, Jeannie slid into the row.

The woman grabbed a pair of maroon-colored gloves from the empty seat. "I was so fascinated with the suit you wore to the reception last night. I've been dying to ask you about it."

A glowing sensation coursed through Jeannie. "Thank you so much for that. The fabric has personal significance. My father designed the pattern. Our family's woolen mill manufactured the fabric. The weave is one of a kind. It is my very own tartan. I guess you could say." Jeannie blushed. She held out her right hand. "I'm Jeannie Parks from Great Lakes University and I'm presenting tomorrow."

"Isn't that just the dearest thing?" The woman gushed. "I am so eager to hear your talk. So, the Yale Woolen Mill belonged to your family?"

"Yes, my family, the Andreaes, owned and operated the mill for its entire duration." Jeannie sighed.

"Well, you come by your interest in textiles naturally. By the way, I'm Claire from the University of Wisconsin."

"You'll learn of historical links between the Yale Woolen Mill and the woolen mill in Appleton, Wisconsin, tomorrow." Jeannie nodded.

Claire patted Jeannie's arm. "I'm on pins and needles."

Jeannie giggled. "Claire, we textile people own that expression."

"Yes, we sure do." Her seatmate winked. "Oh, look. There's the aquarium. It's so cool the ocean fish inside can swim along the shore of freshwater Lake Michigan. Glaring at their cousins—trout, walleye, perch—making fish faces at each other."

"Stop." Jeannie laughed.

"What?" Claire sucked in her cheeks and made her eyes wide. Then, she chuckled.

"I appreciate your humor, Claire. Laughter releases good things into the body."

Claire winked.

The bus threaded a traffic crush as it headed east on Lake Drive.

Landscaping crews, costumed in reflective-taped vests, hung from swinging aerial buckets and strung lights on naked oaks.

It's beginning to look. The familiar carol resonated in Jeannie's head. *Without Nick's help with Gunther, this would be a sad Christmas. Thank you, Nick.*

Castle-like buildings eclipsed a smattering of striped-awning expensive-looking boutique shops and bay-windowed bookstores.

The bus rolled gently to a halt.

Conference attendees disembarked.

As Jeannie alit, a gust of wind whipped the tail of her French braid.

"Chicago definitely deserves its nickname—the Windy City." Claire came alongside her. "I don't know about you but I plan to do holiday shopping." She stepped back and gazed at the thick glass doors framed in bronze. "Heart, Shakespeare, and Lark, here we are. I am so excited about this field trip."

"Me, too." Jeannie tugged on the door and allowed

her seatmate to enter first.

A young man outfitted in a wool suit, silk tie four-squared at his neck, and a tailored shirt secured at the wrists with peridot cufflinks parked inside. He ushered the incoming group to form a circle around him.

As Jeannie passed him, a delicious concoction of star lilies and pungent oriental spices filled her nostrils. She paused and inhaled. *Ah.*

The greeter sported an immaculately manicured and crisply cut hairstyle.

This young man is a far cry from the unkempt students I see daily. Jeannie sighed.

"Members of the American Textiles and Costume Society, I am immensely pleased to share with you the story of this remarkable company. My name is Marc, and I will be your tour guide today." Marc turned his right hand palm side up and glided it away from his body. "Please join me in the Shakespeare Auditorium."

"Oh, my goodness. Look at the carpeting." Claire touched Jeannie's elbow.

"And the wallpaper. The pattern has to be a William Morris—just lovely," Jeannie gushed.

Snapping sounds echoed as conferees lowered retracted upholstered seats.

Jeannie sat next to Claire.

Marc dominated the stage and centered himself behind a lectern.

A low grinding noise preceded an immense opaque screen that lowered from the ceiling and shadowed Marc.

Stage lights illuminated his face. "Let's start with some history. Usually, at this declaration, I look in the audience and see listless and soon-to-be shut eyes."

Marc swiped a hand over his brows.

Claire giggled.

"But not with this group. You all love history."

Laughter and tittering sounds filled the cavernous space.

"Heart, Shakespeare, and Lark, founded in 1887, has become an iconic American brand and a recognized fashion leader in men's wear. Heart, Shakespeare, and Lark is a proud member of the Chicago business empire. We now have thirty-eight factories and two hundred and fifty retail stores. We are a major employer in the city."

Clapping rung in the room.

Marc bowed. "Thank you. Thank you. I want to point out one of the most recent company plus points. The ensemble I am wearing today is a collaboration between Heart, Shakespeare, and Lark and one of the world's top fashion houses–the House of Pierre, specifically the fashion empire established by Michel Pierre. I'm sure as fashion historians you recognize Michelle as one of the most influential fashion designers of our time. Though Mr. Pierre is no longer living, having passed away in 1953, his design legacy continues. Heart, Shakespeare, and Lark is thrilled to continue his legacy in their men's clothing. The next slide is of our founders—each a German immigrant."

Just like the Yale Woolen Mill founders. Jeannie clasped her hands in her lap.

Click.

Marc advanced the next slide. "In 1917, the company began the first fabric testing laboratory operated by a clothing manufacturer in the United States. Being textile experts, you would recognize the importance of being able to conduct analyses such as tensile strength, abrasion resistance, wearability, flammability, air permeability, wicking properties, and color fastness."

Claire leaned sideways. "We are so fortunate to be employed at universities that allow us to continue this work."

Jeannie nodded.

"In 1936, the company caused quite a stir in the fashion industry. Does anyone know what they introduced to men's retail clothing?" Marc scanned the audience.

A member in a cashmere sweater set and cat's-eye glasses raised her hand. "The zipper," she blurted.

Click.

The image of a twelve-inch black zipper appeared as a six-foot tower on the screen.

Laughter and snorts rippled through the auditorium.

"*Voila!*" Marc fisted the air. "Yes, the zipper!"

Marc read from his notes. "Again, we attribute French fashion designers for instigating the concept of zippers in men's trousers. *Gentlemen's Fashion* magazine declared the zipper the 'Newest Tailoring Idea for Men.' Among the zippered fly's many virtues was that this marvelous new invention would exclude 'the possibility of unintentional and embarrassing disarray.' " Marc straightened. Scanning the crowd, he enacted a dramatic pause. Gripping either side of the podium and leaning against the top edge, he jutted his chin. "Obviously, the new zippered-trouser owners had not yet discovered the experience of forgetting to zip up. Or worse yet, zipping over."

Jeannie squeezed the bridge of her nose.

Giggling and snorting erupted.

"Do I see a question?" Marc pointed to a woman flagging her hand.

"A comment of comparison, not a question. When you think of all the contraptions women endured in the name of fashion throughout history, the zipper doesn't seem that disastrous."

"Yeah, there were sixteen-inch cinching corsets, and heavy skirts that trailed in muck, and shoes that crippled, and hairstyles that ignited," a woman called from the back of the auditorium.

"There's more," another woman chimed. "Stiff shrink-wrapping girdles that encased the body from neckline to ankle, and high heels that get caught in the crack of a sidewalk."

"Thank technology for the inventions of liberating spandex," claimed another.

A rumble of tittering filled the air.

People in the row ahead of her paired into whispering twosomes.

"Isn't this fun? Oh, my, the outlandish history of fashion." Marc moved his head back and forth in short ping-pong bursts.

Jeannie smiled.

"So, moving on to the next slide." Marc turned sideways. He flipped through a dozen more black-and-white images capturing the interior of a men's haberdashery in the 1930s, 1940s, and 1950s.

Claire pressed her elbow on the edge of their shared seat divider. "Hats. Every man wore hats then." She crinkled her nose. "Give me a man in a fedora."

Jeannie grinned. "I'll take mine in a slouchy

beanie." *Nick.*

"And lastly, I want to bring your attention to yet another historical milestone in men's clothing manufacturing. In 1953, Heart, Shakespeare, and Lark introduced the initial polyester- and-wool-blend suit, making care easier and costs lower by incorporating a synthetic. Thank you for being so attentive. Thank you for all the entertaining comments." Marc clapped. "The bus returns for you in an hour. I hope you enjoy your time viewing the exhibits. I'm sure you'll understand our policy of respecting the artifacts since all of you are conservationists, but at the end of the tour, you are welcome to examine our showroom samples to your heart's content."

Clapping and shuffling sounds ensued.

Meandering through the Heart, Shakespeare, and Lark garments, Jeannie extracted a memo pad from her purse, scribbled notes, and sketched exhibit ideas. *What a great lighting idea to showcase our Nightlife Exhibit.*

"Ohs" and "ahs" and murmurings of "damask," "tremendous drapability," "silk faille," "dobby weave"—jargon of people knowing how to judge textile quality reverberated in her ears. *My language. My world. My family's culture.* Jeannie smiled. She wandered through the racks of jackets and trousers. She raised the bottom edge of a jacket and crushed the fabric in her palm. *Hmmm. Warm to the touch.* Her memory eased into the Yale Woolen Mill's showroom.

Father had placed a scrap of woolen cloth in her ten-year-old palm, closed her fingers around it, and then encompassed her fist in his broad football-receiver hands. He grinned. "Warm or cold?"

"Warm, Daddy."

"Okay, let's try this one." He held another swatch of fabric. "I'll trade ya."

She repeated the movements, handling the new swatch.

"What about that one?" Dad cocked his head.

"It feels cooler." She pursed her lips.

"Good job! You just determined a basic difference between a natural fiber and a synthetic fiber. Natural fibers...remember what they are? There are only four of them." The worn floorboards creaked as he shifted his weight from one foot to another.

The noise echoed in a mournful sound.

"I know the answer, Daddy. The four natural fibers are cotton, linen, silk and, of course, wool."

"Yes. Natural fibers are warm to the touch, and synthetic fabrics feel cool." He squeezed her shoulder. "That's my girl. You're so smart." Then he had looked wistfully at the floor emptied of looms and spinning machines.

Oh, Dad, I could hear your heart crack. The echo skittered through the ghostly room. Jeannie shut her eyes. She put her hand over her heart and sighed. She reached for the sleeve hem of a herringbone weave jacket and clamped her hand over the fabric. *Warm. Love you, Dad.* She moved onto another rack of jackets. From its hooked top, she lifted a broad wooden hanger from the industrial pole. *I miss taking care of a man. I miss doing laundry with man-size socks and plaid boxers and finding screws and bolts and nuts in jacket pockets. I miss smelling a man's sweat. I miss scrubbing the collar of his shirts and sewing missing buttons back on. I would love to choose clothes for Nick, pick out his shirts, and match his ties. But by the cut of your cloth, Nick, it's obvious someone else matches your ties.* Jeannie dropped the jacket sleeve.

****

Back in her hotel room, Jeannie kicked off her shoes and languished in the full-size bed empty of a puppy and a kindergartener. Laying her head back in a stack of pillows, she squeezed shut her eyes. *What I'd really like now, even more than a foot massage, is a robust conversation about everything conference. Who can I call that shares the same depth of interest in museum work? Who would offer an honest critique of my impressions?* Dee. No good. Dee's world doesn't include intellectualism and the arrogance of research outcomes. No, conversations with her were better with parenting or relationship discussions.

She thought of her mother-in-law. Virginia would be encouraging but clueless about the impact. No, conversations with Virginia were better if Jeannie sought an answer to, 'How many pounds of potatoes do I need to make a potato salad for twelve people?' She thought of Cal, but by now, he'd be snoring in his lumpy recliner chair beside Loretta, who'd be engrossed in a paint-by-number landscape.

Nick. He'd be attentive, and he freely shared his opinions. He'd said they were friends, and friends could share a casual long-distance phone call, right? Jeannie picked up the receiver and punched in the first three numbers. She slammed down the handset. She covered her mouth and stared at the phone as if the cord were a coiled snake. Wrapping her arms around her midsection, she paced the perimeter of her room.

Outside, the city lights of Chicago twinkled. Some of the world's tallest buildings graced the sky.

Jeannie glanced at the one-inch-tall numbers on the desk clock. *Ten minutes have gone by. Either I'm going to call, or I'm going to bed.* She grasped the receiver, tapped in one and then eight more digits, and didn't hang up.

One ring. Two rings. Three rings.

Her resolve faded.

****

"Randall here." Nick rubbed his eyes. He glanced at the wall clock hanging between framed acid rock albums and his college diplomas. In the corner, Sam whistled in his sleep. *Kind of late. Pretty sure it's not Elizabeth since she's at some fancy spa.*

"Hi, Nick. Jeannie Parks. I hope I'm not bothering you."

He shot upright. "Everyone okay? Gunther? Joey?"

She chuckled. "Yes, everyone is just fine. Actually, I'm not with either Gunther or Joey. I'm in Chicago at the annual American Textiles and Costume Society Conference."

"Oh, yeah." Nick expelled a pent breath and slumped in his recliner. "I remember you talked about that at our last museum meeting."

"You said I could call as a friend, and I found an occasion to."

She's got that self-deprecating, apologetic tone in her voice. Nick shook his head. *Jeannie, don't do this to yourself.* "Jeannie, you don't need an occasion. How's the conference going?" The excitement in her voice crackled across the line.

"My presentation generated hearty applause. I've been asked to give guest lectures at Oregon State and the Helen Louise Allen Textile Collection Symposium in Madison, Wisconsin."

"No kidding? That's great, Jeannie." He pictured her with a flushed face and animated motions. He smiled. "What questions did they ask?"

"The audience showed a lot of interest in working conditions at the mill and the formation of the Textile Workers of America Union. A business researcher from Washington is compiling a chronological study of the unionization of textile workers and garment makers. She was particularly intrigued and grateful for the research I have already done."

"Hey, that's a great feeling, isn't it?" *Sounding more like the chatty Jeannie I know.* He grinned.

"You would love their exhibit in the Natural History Museum this month."

"Oh, yeah? What's going on there?"

"A collection of horned mammals from each continent. There's even a red hartebeest like the one in Mac's house. Remember, the one mounted next to the African mask?"

"I remember." *I remember your breasts silhouetted against the fire. I remember the curve of your neck, the shape of your tiny ears, the smell of roses in your hair.* He grew hard.

"Have you been to Chicago, Nick?"

He dipped his head to his chest and slumped in his easy chair. "I, ah...I well, yes, I've been to Chicago a few times. Big city." He crossed his ankles and flexed his toes. *Good grief, yes, Jeannie, I have been to Chicago.* He coughed. *Damn.*

"Cool. Could you recommend a restaurant with authentic German food? I'd love a dish of wiener schnitzel, and what I would do for a big fat slice of Black Forest cake. Ummm…sour cherries, whipped cream, kirsch liqueur."

"Sounds like you've worked up an appetite." His chuckle thrummed in his throat.

"I suppose I have. We've walked a thousand miles in this museum system." She giggled.

"In that case, I would suggest *Mein Zuhause*. That's German for my house. They serve huge portions. The atmosphere is intimate, and the restauranteur claims she makes everything from scratch. And for a beverage, I suggest you imbibe in a *Starkbier*."

"*Vas ist das*?" Jeannie laughed.

"A stout beer."

"Not much of a beer drinker. I'm more of a lemonade or soda pop kind of girl."

He sighed. "I can admire that." *Not like Elizabeth on that score*. Nick settled his backside in his recliner.

Jeannie continued recounting her experience.

"Stop it. Stop it. I'm gonna bust a gut here." He laughed. "That Marc sounds like an interesting individual. I mean, you even described his floral scent. Could he be Cal's cousin? Cal would be the wildflower." Nick chuckled. "Perhaps they could collaborate on the Michigan Mammals Exhibit. Cal could costume the otters and the beavers in custom-made men's wear…you know, like a depiction of a real suburban neighborhood."

Girlish giggles rippled through the phone line.

Nick sunk lower in his easy chair, cranked the foot recliner into position, and strung his sock-covered feet over the end. He listened, enjoying the sound of happiness in her voice. *God, I'd do whatever I could to make her voice always sound like that.*

"To be well dressed, the otters and beavers would need to be costumed by Marc's workplace—Heart, Shakespeare, and Lark." Jeannie laughed.

Heart, Shakespeare, and Lark? Why did that title sound familiar? Nick rolled out of his chair, grabbed the phone, and walked to his closet. *Glad I've got a long cord.* He pulled a jacket from a hanger and folded back the lapels. Sewn inside the neckline, a gold threaded label verified its origin. Nick dropped the jacket to the floor. *Oh my God.*

Blood pulsed through his face and heated his cheeks. *How long can I keep up this charade? Heart, Shakespeare, and Lark—Elizabeth's preferred shopping source for my clothing.* He tiptoed from the closet.

"Are you all right? I heard a crash."

"Yes, fine. Just got tangled up there."

"I should probably hang up. I know you have better things to do than indulge me by listening to my boring textile adventures. Your research takes you to much more exciting locales—the Bering Strait, the isolated Isle Royale, fishing for bathing suit bottoms in Capitol Lake."

Nick guffawed. "Listen, Jeannie, I am captivated by your Chicago visit."

"Captivated?"

"Okay, I'm interested. I enjoy hearing *your voice.*"

"What?"

"I enjoy you sharing your research. The information relates to the Michigan Nightlife Exhibit we're planning for the spring. Also, I am learning a whole new sphere of knowledge. Before I met you, I would have associated a leg of mutton sleeve with a side of mint jelly. And I would have imagined a portrait collar had something to do with a photographer's uniform. Nick coiled the phone cord around an index finger. So, changing subjects, I bet you miss Joey."

"I do, but the nice thing is we're getting a break from each other. He's having a great time staying with Dee, and I've got an opportunity to enjoy what I want on TV and take a leisurely bubble bath."

Nick squeezed shut his eyes. Lust gripped his body.

Silence hung like a hundred-pound barbell between them.

Finally, in a voice thick with desire, Nick broke the stillness. "Not sure where to go with that, Jeannie."

"Ah…Well." She fumbled her words. "Nick, sorry about that. I'd better let you go. I've held you phone captive for the better part of a half-hour."

Nick lowered his chin. He scratched the back of his neck. *Damn. What kind of a pickle am I in here? Suppressing information that I'm practically engaged. And, oh, yeah, conveniently forgetting to ask Jeannie if it would be okay for Matt Richter to call her. He's gonna hit me up to see if I asked her. Damn, damn.*

"Good night, Nick. Will I see you at the museum meeting this week?"

"Ah, yeah." Nick narrowed his eyes. "Good night, Jeannie." Now fully aroused, Nick clenched the phone and placed the connection to Jeannie in its cradle. *Damn.*

Chapter 14

Jeannie rested a hand on the thick oak door and peered inside. She shivered. The museum's basement level was always cool, and November, the month of ushering in bleak skies and winter disruptions, had arrived. Jeannie had another reason to quaver. She needed advice on a personal matter from a pal she could trust. Flexing her fingers, she smoothed her palm over her rumbling stomach.

Cal perched on his backless stool. Wire-rimmed spectacles rested a scant quarter-of-an-inch from the end of his nose.

Strains of Shostakovich's *Waltz Two* rolled off a thirty-three rpm album spinning on a record player nestled on an adjacent table. Jeannie smiled. *I could swoon. The swell of the violin swishes is so romantic.*

Contorted paint tubes, squared carpenter pencils, soft and hard lead drawing pencils, and a treasure trove of modeling tools scattered atop the blemished work table fronting the chief preparator and chief confidante.

Antique farm equipment, replicas of tractors, and Cal's personal favorite–plows—splayed on industrial-grade shelves on two sides of the room. Silver-framed photos of Loretta and his two adult daughters shared the space with toy harrow plows, seven-bottom chisel plows, horse-drawn plows, and walking-beam plows. The vintage teeth plow Jeannie gifted him last

Christmas smiled menacingly next to a photo of Cal in his military uniform. *What a wicked sense of humor.* She grinned.

The man in the photo glanced up from the balsa wood sculpture evolving in his hands.

"Knock, knock." Jeannie made the pretense of thumping the door. "Good morning. I thought I'd stop in before today's Campus Collections meeting." She gestured to the work in progress. "Is this part of the Michigan Nightlife Exhibit?"

"Yes. Can you speculate what it is? I'll give you a hint." Cal held up the figure and turned the object three-hundred-and-sixty degrees. "This is Bob the birdman's idea."

"Great horned owl, maybe?"

"That's right." Cal mimicked a jack-o'-lantern grin. "Scoops up bitty field mice, bops 'em on the head, and eats 'em whole," Cal sing-songed.

He showcased the gap in his front teeth, the perfect repository for the ever-present, dual-use toothpick. Jeannie had observed him on more than one occasion extracting the pick, poking indentations in his figurines, and returning the ubiquitous tool to the convenient parking spot in his mouth.

Jeannie cleared her throat. She swallowed. Cal's opinion mattered greatly. If ever a sage existed—it was Cal. This wizened elf of a man was her mentor, colleague, and her friend. Cal honed his carving skills by restoring the broken faces of his fellow soldiers on the fields of foreign soil during World War II. In the process, he experienced many of the same emotions Jeannie felt in the past five years. She and Cal shared a mutual don't-ever-take-it-for-granted gratefulness for living. "Speaking of the Nightlife Exhibit, what do you think of Mac giving the lead to Nick? How do you like working with him?"

Cal peered over the teetering glasses and studied her. "He's a comfortable guy. I likes 'im."

Jeannie smiled at his pirate parody.

"He's a good leader. Knows his stuff. Not too big for his britches. Know what I mean?"

Jeannie nodded. Cal's reference to Nick's britches unknowingly created an uneasy mental vision. In the span of time required for Cal to shape a left horn on the front of his owl, Jeannie's memory flashed a fashion runway of Nick in khakis—Nick in sharply creased wool trousers—Nick in soft-blue denim jeans with a hole at the left knee—Nick in wet bathing trunks—Nick in clingy running shorts. She tore her thoughts away. "I took Loretta's advice and went to that anniversary sale at McMillan's. I found a small sofa that's just perfect for my den. Now I have to figure out how to get the piece to my house. McMillan's wants to charge me a seventy-five dollar delivery expense and can't tell me what time they'll show up. That would mean I'd have to take a whole day off work."

Cal plucked the toothpick from his mouth. Pinching his thumb and forefinger in the middle of the tool, he dragged the point through the owl's body and fashioned overlapping feathers. He held the sculpture at arm's length and squinted his eyes. "Loretta's always been pleased with the furniture we've bought there. We've had the same couch since the twins were born."

The Russian composer's *Waltz Two* shifted into the percussion segment. Bells, double bass, and snare drum clangs echoed through the basement.

"Anybody home?" a male voice asked.

Gah. We were just talking about him. Jeannie widened her eyes. *Why is my heart racing?*

Cal looked up. "Hello there, Nick."

"I don't mean to interrupt." Nick lurked outside the door.

"C'mon in."

Moving his arms, legs, head, and neck like a wooden toy soldier, Nick glided into the room in syncopation with the symphony. He wore a blue oxford shirt, open at the neck, a navy-blue wool jacket, waist-pleated, tailored pants and shouldered a distressed leather briefcase. He looked like a corporate attorney, a far cry from his role as a field mammalogist. Jeannie giggled.

"We were just finishing. What can I do for you?" Cal croaked.

"I wanted to see when you have time to discuss the dioramas we'll need for the Nightlife Exhibit. Hello there, Jeannie."

"Hi, Nick. I need to see you about my costume ideas for that display." Jeannie dragged her top teeth over her bottom lip.

Cal held the owl figurine aloft. "This fellow will be part of the exhibit."

"Can't have a scene of nocturnal happenings without a wise old owl preying on hapless woodland creatures." Nick raised his eyebrows.

"That's nightlife." Cal grinned his toothy smirk. "Say, Nick, I remember you saying you have a pickup truck."

"Sure, what do you need to be moved? The abandoned beaver dam from Rose Lake?"

"No dams. It's Jeannie here who needs something moved."

Jeannie's face flushed hot. *What a conniver.* She set her teeth, narrowed her eyes, and glanced at Cal. "What are you doing?" she stammered. "No. I can arrange for the store to send their delivery truck."

"You just told me they charge a seventy-five-dollar delivery fee and can't guarantee you a delivery time, which means you would have to interrupt your work to stay home and be held hostage to their schedule," Cal drawled.

"Jeannie, that is no problem for me. What day do you need help?" Nick knitted his eyebrows.

"Well, I was planning on this weekend. Are you sure assisting me won't interfere with your plans?" Jeannie warped her lips as if she held a cigar between them.

"Not at all." Nick shrugged.

Cal beamed.

I could swipe that toothpick marker out of your mouth and jab you. Jeannie seethed.

"Just tell me when and where." Nick jingled some coins in his pocket.

"Okay. You will retrieve a love seat on Saturday at McMillan's on First Street."

At this, Cal's impish smile threatened to implode into thigh-slapping laughter. *Is he tickled he pushed Nick and me together?* Jeannie raised her eyebrows and gave Cal a side-eye.

"Saturday works for my schedule," Nick said.

"Guess that's settled." Jeannie scratched her nose. "I'll call McMillan's and tell them you're coming. It's already paid for."

Holding aloft the figurine, the preparator pulled a shaping tool from his chest pocket. "I have a beak and eight toes to finish. See you both upstairs in about an hour. I hear Mac has a big announcement."

Cal leered like an owl glimpsing a mouse. Jeannie puffed her cheeks. *What the heck is Mac's news?*

****

Dismissing the elevator and opting for the marble staircase, Jeannie traipsed the polished steps to the second level of Morris Hall. A raucous dissonance sounded from the other side of the sole open door on the floor. *Hmmm…that's Bob imitating a blue jay gurgle*. She stepped over the door threshold with a grin on her face.

Around the conference table, fellow faculty and museum colleagues sprawled in their saddle-shaped wooden chairs.

Jeannie grasped the back of an empty seat and sat next to Cal. A faint hint of cinnamon hung in the air. She turned. "Aha! Between the time I saw you this morning and now, you stopped in Capitol Dairy and sampled the apple crullers, didn't you?"

Hastily wiping his cheeks, Cal grimaced.

"Cal, I can see traces of glaze all over your mustache. Loretta's gonna kill you."

The chief preparator put a finger to his mouth. "Shhh…" Cal leaned over Jeannie's shoulder. "Whatcha got there?"

Lifting a glossy photo with the tip of a fingernail, Jeannie met Cal's gaze. She raised her brows. "What I have here are Halloween pictures. Joey said to give you and Loretta one."

"Oh, my. A robot. Did our boy get lots of candy?"

"Between our generous neighbors and my Chicago shopping, I would say Joey's sweet drawer is stocked at least until Christmas."

Cal smiled. He squeezed her shoulder. "I'm glad you got away for a while. And I'm also pleased that I found you a strong man to save you seventy-five dollars."

"Mmmm." Jeannie shook her head and scowled.

"Tee-hee. I think I'll sit by Mac's chair. I wanna be up close and personal when he makes his revelation. I want all the details."

"Just go. You are full of yourself today. *Tsk*." Jeannie rotated her head from shoulder to shoulder.

"Love you." Cal gripped the table edge.

"Love you, too." Jeannie smiled. She scanned the windowless meeting room. A welling in Jeannie's heart clotted her throat. *These folks are my family. They encourage me, confide in me, subject me to stupid jokes and pranks, and force fattening food on me.* Jeannie fixated on a shabbily dressed man seated on a chair in the corner. *Dear Hector, predisposed to a lifetime in Paleontology and a wardrobe of wool cardigans and plaid bow ties. One of the most brilliant, yet most socially inept, men I have ever met.*

Ignoring his colleagues, Hector jimmied a block wood puzzle and arched his brows.

"I'm excited about Show and Tell." Jeannie grinned. *Peg's chattering like a first-grader.* The museum gift shop manager wore her short gray hair in a classic bob, accented by a simple jeweled bobby pin above her right temple. Skillfully applied, her makeup made the most of her high cheekbones, petite nose, and green quartz eyes. She ran the store with the same panache, buying trinkets and baubles from around the world and turning them into respectable revenue.

The door swung open.

Mac McIvor filled the entrance. "Good afternoon, all." He carried a sheaf of papers and a battered briefcase.

Contained by a rubber band, Mac's silver-white ponytail graced the back of his tattersall-patterned long-sleeved shirt. A braided bolo tie cinched with a silver-trimmed turquoise stone hung square on his chest. *He's a dapper-looking cowboy today.* Jeannie nodded.

"Let's start with old business. I'm turning the meeting over to Steve, the Bug Man."

Snickers sounded.

"Nothing new to add to the flyer you have all received. And everything is fine in Entomology. Our collections were appraised at a replacement value of a cool five hundred thousand dollars. Please note"—Steve looked down his nose—"that amount includes the cost of one silver-head-pin-mount per specimen."

Nick whistled.

"I'm sure they will discuss that at the Provost meeting." Mac tilted his head. "Jeannie, how about announcements?"

"A reminder that free admission day is two weeks from this Saturday. So encourage all your friends and family to visit the public exhibits. Planning continues on the Michigan Nightlife Exhibit. I think Mammalogy, Entomology, and Botany are working together?"

"Yeah. Steve and Martha and me." Nick slapped the table.

Martha pointed a finger and twirled a circular path. "Yippee."

"It's a threesome, all right." Steve grinned.

Mac nodded toward Peg. "Guess what? Time for Show and Tell. Ta-da!"

"Our surprise bestseller has been a crochet ball."

Hector scratched his head. "You're kidding."

Peg held up a drawstring bag and pulled. After creating a large opening, she turned the bag upside down. "The kids just love them."

Six beanbag toys dropped onto the table, each no larger than three inches in circumference.

"The textiles are so cool. The designs mimic weavings by our indigenous folk, right, Peg?" Jeannie stood and leaned over the table. "Can I feel one?"

Peg tossed a red, black, and green cloth object.

Nick curled, unfurled, and flipped his fingers into a shovel-shape. "Gimme."

"Oh, you wanna play, too? Looks like I have two toy testers here." Peg grinned and scooted a bag across the table to Nick.

"I can vouch for Peg, at least from the witnessed point of view of Alaskan children. Wherever children gather in our forty-ninth state, you'll see these toys. The kids love kicking and hurling them and smacking each other in the head with them."

Peg beamed.

Nick tossed the toy.

It landed in Jeannie's lap.

"Hey!" Jeannie bent her head over her chest.

Mac cleared his throat. "Thanks, Peg. Anybody else with updates?"

"Me." Jeannie raised a hand.

"Okay, Jeannie." Mac fingered a filigree bolo tie aiguillette.

"Thanks to my new best friend Marc, the Michigan Nighttime Exhibit will be especially dashing."

"Dashing?" Peg opened wide her eyes.

"Probably none of you know this, but our Textiles Collection has no male mannequins." Jeannie pouted. "Mannequins are very expensive, but to achieve my vision for the costumes in this exhibit, we need two male mannequins."

Mac scratched his chin.

"When I was in Chicago last week, I toured the headquarters of Heart, Shakespeare, and Lark. For those who don't know, this company is known for classically tailored men's wear."

Nick frowned.

What's that about? Jeannie opened a folder on the table and pulled out some photographs. "Marc, the company's public relations manager, is lending us two of their mannequins for our use. Pass these around. I snapped photos of their exhibit on the history of their menswear evolutions." Jeannie grinned.

"Hey, Jeannie. That's wonderful. And free. Way to go." Cal drummed his palms on the tabletop.

"Don't forget to add their company's name to our sponsors list on the program. Nice job." Mac nodded. He picked up the stack of papers on the table before him and tapped the ends on the wooden top. He set the pile down, and with the butt of a fist, he spun the papers like the spokes of a wheel.

The shushing noise spouted like a gunshot.

Mac compressed his hands and spread them over the stack of papers. He looked up. "You might have heard a rumor rumbling down the museum corridors. I'm very keen on this. We have scored a huge donation." Mac placed his elbows on the table and laced his gnarled fingers together. "This gift will have a huge and lasting impact on this university."

Jeannie gulped.

"Great Lakes University has been named the benefactor of a private collection in Copper Harbor. According to the attorney representing the Eriksson estate, the collection is extraordinary. Specifically, the vertebrate specimens from Isak Eriksson and the Americana textile acquisitions of Mrs. Eriksson. That necessitates sending a team to conduct an immediate assessment of artifact conditions, perform urgent preservation techniques if required, pack the items, and transport them here."

Within seconds, the room became suffocatingly quiet.

"Jeannie, I'd like you to go. Nick, the mammal collection might be all you need to complete the Michigan Nightlife Exhibit. You're the best man to oversee the taxidermy specimens. The two of you better chalk off a week. One day to get there, a day to get back, and five days to assess and pack." Mac sat back in his chair. "I know this is a big endeavor."

Nick and me. Alone for a week. Jeannie registered small, shallow breaths and a disconnection with her hands and feet.

"You'll have assistance." Mac pursed his lips. "Volunteers from the Copper Harbor Historical Society will coordinate on the ground. The foundation will cover all travel expenses. See Marie in Human Ecology and do your paperwork before you leave. Wanda will give each of you a detailed copy from the attorney so you know what to expect and what archival packing materials you'll need. You two get together and let me know when you're going."

Jeannie straightened. "Mac, just how pressing is this? I mean, how soon do we need to go?" *What about Joey?* Heat crept up her collarless neck and bloomed on her cheeks. *Traveling alone with Nick?*

"I wouldn't delay too long. I know the holidays are approaching, but so is Old Man Winter. If winter came early, we'd have to send a dog sled and Paul Bunyan's blue ox to bring you back."

Jeannie grazed the tips of her fingers over the crown of her cheeks. She caught Nick's gaze.

He jutted his jaw and steeled his eyes.

Yearning flooded her. Urgency consumed her, too, but not because of a vague weather threat. Instead, her desire to be alone with Nick Randall was building into a storm of a different kind.

"Guess that wraps things up. See you next month." Mac stuffed a pen into a plastic shield in his shirt's breast pocket.

Nick came alongside Jeannie. "I'll see you Saturday morning. No need for you to go to McMillan's." Nick shifted his weight. "I'll deliver your little couch between eleven and noon. Hey, possibly we can discuss plans for our work in Copper Harbor. I don't mind driving." He ran the palm of his hand over the tabletop in smoothing motions.

Why is he nervous? Jeannie quelled an impulse to touch his arm.

He looked up.

Oh my gosh. He's blushing.

Chapter 15

Like bread boxes neatly lined on a hardware store shelf, empty school buses paused in the school district's transportation yard. *Today's Saturday.* Stretching his right arm along the top of the double seat, Nick glanced again in the rearview mirror.

A blue tarp lashed over a large object in the bed of his truck billowed as he rumbled down Jeannie's cedar-lined driveway.

From behind the curtainless front windows of the rock-paneled bungalow, Gunther bounded and circled.

You look great, Gunther—nice, healthy pup. Nick drove close to the door, secured the truck, and hopped onto the porch. He knocked at the back door leading into the kitchen.

Holding a lunging Gunther by the collar, Jeannie opened the door. "Gunther, quiet," she commanded.

The now thirty-pound puppy scaled his voice to a growl.

"Hey, there, boy." Nick knelt on the threshold, extended his right hand, and allowed the dog to sniff him. "He should remember me," Nick said. "The dog family has incredible olfactory capacity. Wolves can smell up to six miles and have pretty good memory. There, you go, boy. Good job calming down." Rewarding the dog's behavior with a rough petting, Nick rose to his full height and entered the kitchen.

Smells good in here. She smells good, too. Careful, Nick.

Despite frost on the ground, Jeannie walked barefoot. Her hair, always confined and sequestered in a prim bun or braid at work, hung loose and shrouded the side of her face.

"So, that's your truck?" Jeannie eyed the vehicle in her driveway.

"Yup. That's Katie."

"Katie?" Jeannie questioned.

"Name of an old girlfriend." Nick leered. "My revenge."

"I'm writing myself a memo to remember not to get on your bad side." Jeannie smiled. "Well, Katie sure has charisma."

"Yes, she does. Thank goodness for self-service car washes. I had to muck out her bed this morning."

Tossing a jacket over her shoulders, Jeannie trailed Nick to the truck.

Bowed native grasses, desiccated hydrangeas, and ninebark shrubs verified the colorless landscape of the oncoming winter season.

Gunther scuttled down the front steps and bounded across the yard. He halted, clamped his jaws around a tattered ball, ran toward the truck, and dropped his toy at Nick's feet.

Nick bent, picked up, and lobbed the ball. "Go get it, boy."

With his ears slicked back and his tail tucked, Gunther charged after the saliva-coated glob.

Again and again and again, he and Gunther volleyed the ball.

"I thought I'd see Joey by now. Is he sleeping

late?" Nick raised an arm and hurled the toy.

"Oh, he's at his grandparents' house this weekend." Jeannie pulled on shoes and a jacket. "My in-laws are hosting a cousins' weekend. They are taking all the kids to a tractor pull. Joey started packing a week ago. He included his cowboy hat and his cowboy boots. He jumped out the door the minute Grandpa and Grandma arrived."

"Sounds like fun." Nick grinned and walked to the back of the truck. He dropped the tailgate, hopped into the truck bed, and loosened the rope tied over the tarp. "I brought a furniture dolly and some planks."

"How can I help?" Jeannie gripped the tailgate.

"Come on up." Nick held out his hand.

Jeannie grasped his wrist.

Nick bent his knees, tugged, and catapulted Jeannie onto the truck bed floor. He grunted. "I can tell you right now, you are lighter than this baby sofa."

Jeannie staggered.

"Whoa." Nick tucked an arm under her armpits, drew her close to his side, and righted her. *Randall, is that really necessary? Jeannie Parks is a self-sufficient person by any measure.* "If you wedge your foot against one wheel of the dolly, I think that will stabilize the wheels enough so I can transfer the furniture." Nick maintained his grasp on the dolly and extended his right arm.

Jeannie stepped between the mover's cart and Nick's body. She gripped the handle next to his hand.

Nick stepped away. With his back to her, Nick squatted and grasped the ends of two planks. The waistband of his jeans sunk lower and cinched just short of his butt crack. He passed gas. *Not much I can do about that now.* "Whoops, excuse me."

Coughing, Jeannie sidled quickly beside him, grabbed the planks, and set one edge on the tailgate. Then, she aligned the opposite ends of the planks on the ground. "Should be good to go."

Nick rolled the love seat-occupied dolly to the yard.

"I'll get the door." Jeannie jumped from the truck bed and ran ahead.

Wagging his tail and lolling his tongue, Gunther trailed her.

Reaching the bottom of the porch steps, Nick turned the dolly in a half circle. With his back to the house, Nick stepped up and dragged the dolly after him. He grunted.

"What can I do?" Jeannie called from the door.

"Just let me know when I've got a proper foothold." Nick blew out a deep breath.

Coming alongside, Jeannie coached him. "Almost there."

Nick slid his boot until the dolly wheels connected with the riser.

"Got it. Good job," Jeannie exclaimed.

Nick winced. "Gah." He curled his head to his chest, raised his shoulders, and tugged.

Bump.

"Three more, and you're home free."

"Thanks, cheerleader." Nick grunted and gazed over his shoulder.

Scrambling to the door, Jeannie twined her fingers through the tongue and pulled. She gripped the metal trim edging and held open the door.

Nick rolled the dolly. Reaching the doorway, he

paused. He scratched his head. "I think it will go easier if I remove the storm door. Jeannie, can you get the toolbox from the truck cab?" He pulled a red bandana from his back pocket and swiped the sweat off his brow and the back of his neck.

"Sure." Jeannie started down the steps.

"Look behind the front seat on the passenger side. Oh, you gotta go through the driver's side. Katie's kinda one-sided." *And as you go, girl, I can view your backside.* Nick draped his arms over the dolly and stared.

****

Katie's kinda seen better days. Jeannie strode to the truck. She pulled open the door.

Squeak.

Wow. It didn't fall off. She hopped up in the driver's place and looked behind the seat. She found easily the latched metal box and turned to slide across the bench. Tucked in the left-hand corner of the cracked windshield, a faded photograph cast a shadow. Jeannie leaned inward and contracted her eyes.

A naked-from-the waist adolescent boy cleaved to a honed, naked-from-the-waist brawn of a man. They fronted a large, blue body of water. Sun bronzed their mussed, wet hair, and grains of sand dusted their tanned skin. The boy draped a skinny-by-comparison arm over the man's muscular shoulders. Each flexed their outside arms in a prizefighter's stance and mugged for the picture taker. Jeannie jutted her chin. She cataloged the details—square-shaped fingernails, dominant noses, jaunty smiles, blue-green eyes squinting in the sun matched like cards in a child's memory game. *Father and son.* Jeannie's breaths shortened. *Nick's waiting.*

With the handle of the worn toolbox biting her palm, Jeannie climbed from the truck cab and slammed shut the door. Back on the porch, she set down the tools and held the storm door.

Nick opened the toolbox and selected a twelve-inch crowbar and a flathead screwdriver. Inserting the screwdriver into the screws pinning the door's hinges, he twisted the metal pegs.

"Here, I'll hold the screws." Jeannie offered the palm of her right hand.

Nick dropped the rivets into her outstretched hand. Then, using the crowbar, he pried off the door and set it aside. Grasping the furniture dolly, he wheeled the love seat over the threshold. Nick blew out a breath. "Just point the way."

"It's going into my little office. Follow me. You'll appreciate the interior doorways are uncharacteristically wide." Jeannie kicked a pile of clothes and a headless stuffed animal out of the path. "Gunther destroys his toys with a vengeance." She chuckled.

Once over the threshold, Nick removed his boots and coat. He raised his eyebrows.

"Centered, under the window, where I'll have good light to read." Jeannie clapped.

Nick wheeled the dolly to a patch of light flooding the floor. "Grab the top, and I'll get the bottom." Rounding his shoulders like a wrestler, Nick thrust the mini couch into position. He stepped back. "Good?"

"Perfect!" Jeannie flopped back into the plump, cushioned seat. She bounced her butt and removed her shoes, socks, and jacket. "This will make reading endless reports a lot more enjoyable. Thanks, Nick."

"Is that coffee I smell?" Nick stretched his neck.

"Yes. How about a cup? And how about lunch? It's the least I can do." Jeannie leaned against the sofa back and fluttered her legs.

"I'd love a cup of coffee, and yeah, I am hungry." Nick patted his stomach.

"How's a grilled cheese sandwich and tomato soup sound?" Placing her hands on her thighs, Jeannie bent her knees and planted her feet on the floor.

"My kind of meal." Nick parked the dolly at the front door.

Jeannie moved to the still neatly organized kitchen and knelt before the oven. She slid out the bottom drawer. She pulled out a frying pan and a two-quart-cooking vessel.

Opening a cupboard door, Nick reached inside and pulled out a ceramic mug. He poured the umber-colored liquid into his cup and swallowed a sip. "Anything I can do?"

Jeannie handed Nick the pot. "There's a can opener in the second drawer down on the left." She pointed. "And in the panty over there, you'll find a can of tomato soup."

"Gotcha." Nick grinned.

"I'll make the sandwiches." Jeannie opened the refrigerator and bent to find Swiss cheese slices. She sucked a deep breath. "I couldn't help but notice the picture on the left side of the windshield."

"My dad and I. The summer before he died."

"Oh, Nick, I'm so sorry." Jeannie stood and closed the refrigerator door.

"He was a good man. The best, I miss him every day of my life. He was the kind of dad who taught instead of shouted and hugged instead of spanked. The model for the kind of dad I want to be someday." Nick set the soup container on the counter, separated the handles on the can opener, and sunk the opener's blade into the top of the tin cylinder.

Crunch.

"To have had a son like you, he must have been a wonderful man. I'm so sorry, Nick."

"Thanks, Jeannie."

"And your mother?"

Nick's face hardened. He squeezed the can opener levers and turned his gaze out the window. "How about we save that story for another day?"

From across the kitchen, Gunther slunk to Nick's feet.

"Hey there, boy." Nick gathered the puppy's snout. He smoothed the fur from Gunther's nose to the back of his head.

The puppy leveled sad eyes into Nick's gaze.

"Sure." A lump formed in Jeannie's throat. Silence hung in the air like a soggy lifejacket.

Gunther shut his eyes, and he dropped his head onto Nick's knee.

Nick stroked the puppy's ears and face.

Jeannie extracted four slices of bread from a wrapper. She reached for a butter dish on the counter and pulled a knife from the silverware drawer. She slathered both sides of the bread slices and added the cheese squares between two bread pieces. Setting the frying pan on the stove, she turned. "I found a spot for you. C'mon over." She sidestepped and fronted the right side of the stove.

Nick dumped the soup into the pot, filled the empty can with water from the kitchen sink, added it to the contents, and set the vessel on a left-side burner.

Jeannie gave him a large spoon and grasped a spatula. She hummed.

Nick laughed. "I know that tune." He shuffled his feet into a Texas two-step. Manipulating the spoon as a microphone, he warbled in a country twang. "*Hey, good lookin'.*"

Tapping the spatula on the metal stove top in the beat of the chorus line, Jeannie grinned.

"*How's 'bout cooking?*" Nick crooned and executed a grapevine step.

The soup bubbled.

The cheese melted.

"I'll grab some plates and bowls and spoons. Want pickles on your sandwich?" Jeannie grabbed the refrigerator handle and stalled.

"Not a sandwich without pickles." Nick made his eyes big.

"Totally agree." Jeannie opened the refrigerator, selected a jar of dill spears, and set the condiments on the table. Then, she ladled out the soup and flipped the sandwiches onto the plates. "Come and get yours, Nick."

He washed at the sink, tore off a paper towel from a towel bar, and dried his hands. He gathered a plate, a bowl, and a spoon and walked to the table. He hooked his foot around a chair rung and yanked the chair from the table. After he set his lunch on the table, he sat.

Jeannie followed.

Gunther lapped water from his bowl and curled up on a throw rug by a broom closet.

"Nick, you helped me so much today. I mean, moving the furniture here is one thing, but tiring

Gunther out with all the ball throwing and lulling him to sleep is also welcome. That saves me from giving him a long walk. I can get a lot of work done this afternoon. Thanks again."

"No bother. I'm pleased Cal clued me in." Nick grinned. "Now, there is a character."

"I'll say." Jeannie nodded. "He and Loretta are surrogate parents to me and grandparents to Joey. My parents are both very elderly and live on the other side of the country. And I am an only child."

"It's obvious Cal has your back." Nick bit into his sandwich.

Jeannie dragged her spoon through the chunky soup, raised it to her lips, and sipped the liquid from the utensil's bowl. She closed her eyes. The warm, salty, and traditional concoction grounded her anxiety. "Mmm…Dr. Nick Bailey, you make a good tomato soup." Jeannie opened her eyes and winked.

"The can opener is my favorite tool." He grinned.

A trail of melted cheese hung from his lower lip and wobbled as he spoke. He stuck out his tongue and manipulated the glob into his mouth. He bit into a pickle spear. Brine ran down his chin. He backhanded the juice.

Jeannie fidgeted in her chair. Heat flushed her face.

"I needed that." Nick sat back in his chair and patted his belly. "I bet you want to take advantage of Joey's absence and dig into that stack of paperwork I couldn't miss on the edge of your desk." He carried his dishes toward the sink.

"I need one tiny favor."

Nick turned and met her gaze.

She shrank her shoulders. "In addition to

paperwork, I've got a colossal stack of laundry. My washing machine is off balance. All it needs is a shim underneath, but I can't lift it myself."

"Sure, happy to. I'll grab my toolbox." He smiled.

Registering the privacy-shrouding gray clouds looming outside the kitchen window, the sleekness of the tile floor under her naked feet, the crumpled napkin whisked over Nick's lips, and the lingering odor of his manly sweat, Jeannie trembled.

****

Jeannie led the way to the basement laundry room.

"Ouch." Nick bumped his head as he stepped down. He lowered his head. *This stairway was designed for short folk.* A musty odor permeated the open space. Like a cloud of mist, a coolness encircled him.

Bins, cabinets, and shelves were organized and labeled. *Good grief, the woman labeled the laundry bins—Whites need Bleach, Fragile Whites, Darks, Lights, Presoak.*

Jeannie waited in the dim basement light.

Nick blinked as his eyes adjusted to the muted illumination. Unlike her workplace appearance, Jeannie wore no makeup. She wore a light-blue, scoop-neck, long-sleeved T-shirt that fit her like a second skin and left no imagination to the small shape and rigid peaks of her breasts. Embroidered peace symbols embellished the back pockets of her rolled-at-the-ankle, faded blue jeans. Tiny silver hoops hung from a single piercing in each ear. A medallion seashell ensconced in a waxed linen macramé cord hung from her neck and lay on the pink skin above the edge of the T-shirt neckline. Sometime after lunch, she had pulled her long, silky hair in a casual ponytail that hung to the middle of her back. Despite the chill, Jeannie forewent the slippers that were parked at the door to the basement.

She moved to the laundry appliances and waved, palms up. "I view laundry as a science. My friends know me as a stain removal expert. Just call me when you get a mustard spot on your silk tie. I can help you out!"

Nick grinned. *Anyone this much involved with their laundry was giving up something more important.*

She pursed her lips. "I know I've got something that can work as a shim. Just give me a minute." Sauntering to a shelf-lined wall, she popped open a plastic container.

Clatter- clatter.

"Nope. Nothing in here." Jeannie opened four more containers. "I bet I'll find something on the top shelf." Rising on tiptoe, she strained against a shelf mounted inches higher than her five-foot, four-inch frame.

Nick smiled. Her movements were graceful, as if hunting for tools in the basement was a choreographed ballet. *But her feet.* The bottoms showed pink in the high spots and asphalt black in the low places. Nick chuckled. "Anybody ever tell you that you have rabbit feet?"

Clunk.

"Oh, dang." She knelt and picked up spilled gadgets. She brushed errant hair from her face and sat back on her haunches. "What do you mean I have rabbit feet?"

Doubled over with a belly laugh, Nick eased his hands on his thighs. "Long and skinny."

Harumph. "Do you ever stop thinking like a mammalogist, Nick Randall?"

He swished his foot along the floor and squatted. He picked up a paint scraper. "You missed something." He tossed a wingnut into the bin at Jeannie's feet.

"Thanks." She set the top back on the container.

"Maybe I can look, too?" Nick gripped himself through his back pockets and rocked on the balls of his feet.

"No, no. I know it's here, really." She turned back to the boxes and bins. "How are your classes going?"

A wall of loaded shelves muffled her voice. Nick craned his neck. "Part of my teaching load includes field biology. We've set up a perimeter at Rose Lake to observe the habits of the Eastern Gray Squirrel. Remember my teaching assistant, Walter Ling?"

"The kickball maverick?" Jeannie ran her palms down her thighs and opened another container.

"The very same. Walter's doctoral dissertation zeroes in on the Eastern Gray. So, Walter manages the on-site student research. This past week, we initiated live trapping. Now, that was a blast." Nick grinned. "We're getting late into the season for disturbing the squirrels. It's only polite to give them privacy between December and February."

Jeannie turned and raised her eyebrows.

"That period is one of their mating seasons." Nick smirked.

"One? How many do they have?"

"Squirrels mate twice a year, also in June and July."

"Is that usual for mammals in general? My high school biology teacher steered clear of discussing mating schedules." Jeannie chuckled.

"Well, that varies." Nick clamped the bridge of his

nose. "From the sixteen species on Isle Royale, wolves, moose, otters, fox mate once a year. However, during that one mating season, they might copulate many times. Like I said, squirrels and chipmunks have two mating seasons a year. And then there are rabbits."

"Yes, then there are those rascal rabbits." Jeannie laughed. "Hey, look what I found!" She thrust a filmy-looking, foot-long glob in the air. "A whole pack of shims, shrink-wrapped by the hardware store. These should work."

Nick reached for the slim wooden slats. His face shed his smile. "Compared to the other mammals in this world, we humans sure are a lusty bunch, aren't we? Our mating urges aren't regulated by the sea's ebb and flow, winter receding, spring beginning, or the lunar calendar." Nick dropped his voice to a husky whisper.

She looked away.

"Jeannie."

Perchance, it was the good-natured bantering they had exchanged. Feasibly, it was the recognition they both had endured losing a loved one. Conceivably, it was sharing what was usually a lonely meal and a task done alone. Imaginably, it was the darkened intimacy of the basement or the opportunity to observe her body bending and straining. Nick didn't know, and he didn't care. Everything but tasting her had been dismissed from his mind.

He clasped her wrist with one hand, and with the other, he tilted her chin. Holding her at arm's length, he twined his fingers through hers. "Humans have urges—natural urges. At least this human does."

Jeannie gulped. She gazed into his eyes. She closed the gap between them by transplanting her dirty-soled feet atop his booted ones.

A sweet floral scent aired as he dropped his chin onto the top of her head. He inhaled deeply. He recognized his knees buckling.

She wrapped her arms around his waist and righted their joined bodies.

Pressing both hands on the peace sign appliqués decorating the back pockets of her blue jeans, he pulled her tight.

She buried her head into his shoulder.

Nick's throat constricted. "We've gotta make up for the gap in our heights." He growled, thrust his hands under her armpits, hoisted up her body, and sat her atop the washing machine.

Bam.

The machine's aluminum lid dipped.

Jeannie giggled and smoothed her butt over the bump.

Nick smiled with his eyes and moved his lips to one of her palms.

She stroked his head and cupped his chin.

Taking small nips, Nick moved his lips along her forearm from her wrist to the bend in her elbow.

Jeannie moaned. She brought her untouched hand to the top of his ears and stroked them from top to bottom. Gently pinching, she traced the lobe of his ear with her fingers.

Damn. I'm bursting. Planting his boots on the cement floor, Nick pressed the whole of his weight against the front of the washing machine.

Screech.

The machine jolted backward and crashed against the wall.

"Is this your idea of a shim?" Jeannie curled her fingers over the edge of the machine. She doubled over. Laughter bubbled from her chest. "Oh, my God." Her shoulders shook. She gasped for air. "Oh, Nick, I am so sorry. Oh, God, I can't stop laughing."

Nick stepped back and held his arms up in a motion of surrender. Then, he bowed over his knees and laughed. "No. No. This is not my idea of fixing an unbalanced washing machine. But I think I fixed it!"

Jeannie eased off the washing machine and padded the short distance to him. "How about a cold drink? Soda? Juice? Ice water?"

"Great idea, but I should go." Nick squeezed her shoulder and bent his head. He gazed into her eyes. *If I don't leave now, I might fall prey to my baser instincts.* He shuddered.

She smiled, wrapped her arms over her chest, and caressed her upper arms. "I appreciate all your help today."

Nick recovered his toolbox, set his jaw, waved a curt good-bye, and vaulted up the basement steps. *Cold shower, cold shower.*

****

Following Nick's departure, Jeannie scoured the kitchen sink, vacuumed the stairs, treated the coffeepot to a vinegar rinse, and dedicated the rest of the daylight tackling a mound of paperwork. Now, following dusk, the kitchen sink gleamed white. Dog hair and lint filled the vacuum bag, and the glass carafe in the coffee machine sparkled. Paperwork netted less success. Thoughts of standing on the precipice of hot desire and failure to launch into sex plagued Jeannie's concentration.

"Let's go for a walk, boy." Jeannie clipped a six-foot leash to Gunther's collar. She zipped her winter jacket and shrugged a tight-fitting striped cap over her hair. She opened the kitchen door and let Gunther lead them onto the front porch.

Muddy purple clouds scudded the horizon.

Frost welled Nick's tire tracks.

Phantom imprints from Nick's kisses surged along her neck.

Smoke poured from Fernandez's chimney and filled her senses with a welcome woodsy odor.

Jeannie inhaled deeply as Gunther's tugging compelled her down the porch steps. *Love that smell.* She shut her eyes and tipped her nose in the air. *I love Nick's scent, too.* She opened her eyes. *How would I describe the smell? Umph. Bay leaves, sandalwood, bergamot orange, rum. Wouldn't it be heavenly to roll it into an incense stick and release the scent into the air?*

Following his first burst of running frantically from tree to tree and circling three times before he relieved himself, Gunther settled into a stroll.

Jeannie let the leash lag, and her thoughts meandered. *Am I relieved or disappointed our foray into affection ended abruptly?*

Shots fired deep in the woods.

Gunther bolted.

His leash tightened.

The movement whipped Jeannie to the ground.

She scrambled to right herself and calm Gunther.

Hunting season. Squirrels scrabbling and rabbits with long, skinny feet zigzagging. Nick. Which sensation registered louder—awkwardness or carnality? Part of me wished desperately to rewind the clock to my waking hours. I regret passing up a shower and utilizing a sweet-smelling, skin-smoothing body lotion. I would have worn a cute, push-up bra and a pair of lacy panties instead of the faded cotton, waist-high, baggy step-ins I scrounged from my pile of reserved-for-camping clothing.

Remembering, Jeannie blushed. And though she had cast an exterior indifference, on the inside, she quaked from the explosion of long-dormant pleasure sensors. And then, guilt pummeled her psyche–the self-reproach of measuring Nick's physicality against Frank's. Thickly muscled, Nick owned an igniting, raw, and ever-so-sensual touch. Jeannie closed her eyes. Breaths cinched in her chest. Still, the man very much in the flesh and the man locked in her memory dangled side by side on a revolving carousel. 'Pick me. Pick me.' A compelling, revolting sensation started in her mind and moved to her gut. The bitter taste of bile roiled upward.

Automatic lights flared over the bus garage.

The remaining sun melted into the inky horizon.

Gunther turned his head toward her.

"You're right, Boy. Time to head back."

Jeannie followed Gunther to a dark house, where no man waited to eat dinner, stand at the sink and dry the dishes, or turn back a quilt, and share a bed. The events of the day foretold the possibility of an intimate relationship.

Awkwardness be damned.

Guilt, you are damned, too.

Chapter 16

Morning sunlight shone on the bare-leaved canopy of steady oaks, graceful maples, thin-gray barked beeches, and vertically ridged hickories casting their shadows onto the Main Street shop windows facing campus. Globes of gold, hot pink, and orange mums rooted in brass patina urns lined the walkway.

Last weekend of the Big Ten football season, and today, the game is away. That explains why downtown is so quiet on a Saturday morning. Jeannie clutched her purse and patted her bulky jacket pocket. *Coupons. Good.* She crossed the street and meandered along Grand River Avenue, passing antique shops, shoe stores, and a vegetarian restaurant.

A bearded, bespectacled man wearing a woolen, plaid Scottish tam and a thick, cable-stitched sweater exited the eatery. He carried a large paper sack that diffused the scents of jasmine tea and cumin.

Reaching the portico of Jacobson's Department Store, Jeannie clasped the rounded vertical handle.

Standing in a huddle fronting the lighted fine jewelry cases, Marie waved. *"Bon jour."*

Not a hair dared escape the hard-shelled, high-piled bouffant atop Marie's head. *I wonder if Marie's experience today will include any hairstyle changes.* Jeannie grinned. "Good morning, ladies. Let's head upstairs to the salon."

Verna struck her three-pronged cane on the tiled floor.

Clack.

The cane carrier wore a sad shade of lavender, polyester-pilled pants, a saggy cotton cardigan, thick-soled tennis shoes, and an exuberant smile.

Jeannie's heart thrummed. *Sweet woman.*

"I might come back down here and buy myself a turquoise necklace." Marjorie tented her eyebrows.

"Me, I'm looking for new underpinnings. I've lost so much weight I'm sure I need a new bra size." Jennifer sighed.

"We are all making progress today." Marie came alongside Verna on the opposite side of her cane. She touched lightly Verna's elbow.

Soft, sexy, jazzy music poured out of the salon door.

After observing the widows move inside, Jeannie approached the receptionist. "I made a reservation for five in my name, Jeannie Parks. We are here for the works." She turned toward her friends and winked.

"Come right this way," a pert twenty-something greeter said. "We'll first take an instant photo of each of you, and then I will set it aside. At the end of your sessions, you can see the before-and-after versions."

Tittering and guffaws filled the floral-scented space.

Following five flashbulb bursts and five photos developing at the receptionist's desk, their host led them past brightly painted walls decorated with glass shelves holding a myriad of lotions, hair gels, hair sprays, detangler solutions, essential oils, shampoos, and conditioners.

Five aproned beauticians smiled and beckoned.

"Have fun, ladies. Hair and makeup first. Personal shoppers next. Can't wait to see the transformations."

The young concierge smiled like a high school cheerleader celebrating her team's touchdown. Jeannie shook her head and grinned. "Thank you. I know we're in good hands."

Four hours later, the women emerged from behind mud masks, dryer hoods, and a team of nodding stylists.

"Verna, my word. You look twenty years younger." Jennifer covered her mouth.

Leaning on her walking stick, Verna conquered a slow turn before a wall of full-length mirrors. A short, sassy haircut replaced her dated self-administered perm. Pearl-gray hair fluffed over her ears and forehead. Verna's ruddy facial skin lay beneath an artfully applied foundation and the barest hint of rouge. A glistening pale-pink lip color crested her exuberant smile.

Gone was Marie's severely pasted hairdo. Chin-length, loosely curled tresses highlighted and low-lighted to complement the almond cast of Marie's skin hijacked their place. Three undulating shades of gray shadow and rich, black liner had been applied to magnify her eyes. Her lips shone with a coat of peach lip gloss. The personal shopper completed the new look with a midriff-minimizing, wired-cup bra topped with a sage-green *V*-necked sweater. In the vee, Marie sported a chunky necklace in shades of green and brown.

"Do you think this will rev Mike's engine?" Marie formed her lips in a moue.

"*Vrrrrroooooom.*" Jeannie wriggled a dance move.

Marjorie stuck two fingers in her mouth and

whistled.

"Jennifer, that blouse and pant set is so flattering," Marjorie gushed.

"I never would have thought to try something so feminine. I mean, the neckline and wrist ruffles and the wide-leg, flowy pants." Jennifer twirled. Sienna-brown eyeshadow stretched over her eyelids. She fluttered her lashes.

Marjorie fronted the mirrors. She turned her head from side to side. "I just can't believe this. I look so happy. And if I do say so, I look too young to have a thirty-three-year-old son."

"Blue is your happy color. You look lovely," Jeannie praised.

Scrunching her eyes, Marjorie clasped her hands. Slowly, she opened her eyes and drew a deep breath. "My first love, Bruce, favored me in blue." She turned. "Thanks so much, Jeannie. Arranging makeovers was such a great idea and look at you…"

Jeannie came alongside Marjorie. She stared at her reflection. *Oh, my goodness.* A tiny current rushed through her limbs. A weightless bubble filled her throat. For the past five years, the applications of soap and water, comb, brush, and a ponytail band sufficed as her beauty regime. Her face had been a blank canvas devoid of color, hiding behind shadows of sadness. But today, her scrubbed complexion, rouged cheeks, brushed brows, shadowed eyelids, rolled eyelashes, and penciled lips reflected *joie de vivre*. Vibrant from the combined efforts of a low-light color treatment and a light coat of glossy hair pomade styled into an elegant French braid, Jeannie's hair hung to the middle of her back. Lips outlined with a scarlet pencil and filled in with a rich rose color glimmered brighter than the pastel look Jeannie had adopted since accepting the position at Great Lakes University. She turned and gazed at the other renewed women.

Tears glimmered in Marie's eyes.

Jeannie squeezed the dean's assistant's right hand. *So glad we did this.*

"Let's go shopping. I need a new pair of earrings!" Jennifer looped her purse handle over the shoulder of her new stylist-chosen, jaunty-jean jacket.

"Shoes, jewelry, here we come." Marjorie led the way down the circular staircase.

"Don't forget lingerie," Marie hooted.

They spent the rest of the afternoon helping each other select clothing.

Marie encouraged each woman to choose something more figure-forming. For Jeannie, she selected a classic black dress in a wool jersey.

"I love, love the construction details, Marie." Jeannie fingered the boat neckline, dolman sleeves, and the straight chemise ending just above her knees.

United group persuasion channeled Marie from the leopard, cheetah, and zebra motifs. Smooth talking and concerted cajoling convinced her to try sedate paisley and floral prints. A psalm of "oohs" and "ahs" trickled as Marie sashayed before a three-way mirror. Outlined in black, orange peaches and golden pears festooned a bishop-sleeved silk blouse paired with an ebony pencil skirt.

"I feel like a model, straight out of a glossy fashion magazine." Marie rotated slowly in a complete circle and curtsied.

"*Oui, oui,*" Jennifer chorused.

"Jeannie, where are you going this afternoon, all dressed up and looking beautiful?" Verna grinned.

"I hate to waste all this effort on an ordinary visit to the veterinarian, but my dog, Gunther, has had this appointment for weeks. You know how you have to keep up with vaccinations. After that, a quiet evening at home with a good romance novel. I have the whole weekend to myself since Joey is staying with his grandparents."

"Quiet time is nice, too." Verna patted Jeannie's hand.

"What about you, Verna?"

"I'm supposed to have supper and play cards with a bunch of old ladies. But now, I'm thinking of going bowling."

"Bowling?" Jeannie raised her eyebrows.

"Yeah, you know. Where there are men and beer." Verna chuckled. "I think I can get there in time for happy hour." She gripped a pretend bowling ball and drew her right arm back.

"I would wish you a strike but since men are involved, I will wish you get a turkey." Jeannie smiled.

Verna choked and gripped her cane. Giggles erupted from her throat. "Great bowling pun, Jeannie."

Joey's gone. Stanley Turrentine is playing at the Jazz Club. Earthy, soul-searing music. Leather booths with slippery surfaces and space to stretch out. Jeannie's lungs swelled. Her breathing shortened. *I could call Nick.*

****

A wallpaper border of puppies sporting colorful bandanas and kittens trailing in unraveled balls of yarn plastered the perimeter of Matt's veterinarian practice.

Folding chairs spaced to allow sitting pets or small kennels lined adjacent partitions. Framed photos of patients, a miniature poodle, a border collie, an English bulldog, a Persian cat, and various indeterminate breeds dotted the walls. A bulletin board plastered with child-drawn artwork hung next to the door leading into the patient examination rooms.

Behind the counter, a receptionist in a set of bright-blue scrubs and a thick yellow ponytail managed a bustling office.

A dissonance of purrs, barks, screeches, and rattling cages competed with human communication. The odor of disinfectant fought with the base scents of dog breath, dog excrement, and dog food samples. Jeannie gagged. "We have a four o'clock appointment with Dr. Richter." She shouted as she leaned across the counter.

"Oh, yes, Gunther's here for a checkup. You can wait in Exam Room Four. Doctor should be with you within the next ten minutes."

The receptionist offered a teeth-gritting smile and a practiced wave. Jeannie maneuvered an excited Gunther past a mammoth fish tank, a pair of nervous chihuahuas straining against their sequined collars while baring their piranha-sharp teeth and a young woman wearing dreadlocks in her hair and a tabby cat with a nasty eye infection on her shoulder. Once inside Exam Room Four, Jeannie dropped into the lone metal chair, gummed her lips and shook her head. *I'm highlighted, perfumed, perfectly coiffed and irritatingly, sexually alert, with nobody to appreciate it or indulge in it.*

****

Bang.

The exam room door flew open.

Garbed in a short white coat and a pair of perfectly pressed blue jeans, Dr. Matt released the doorknob and tapped a wall outlet.

Dim lighting flared into blazing fluorescent lights. Jeannie squinted.

"Well, hello there." Matt folded his arms over his chest.

Jeannie's throat thickened. Her nerves tingled. *I'm hearing undisguised attraction. What the heck?*

The slack in Gunther's leash lengthened as he skulked beside Jeannie's knees.

"So good to see both of you." Matt pulled a stethoscope from his pocket and stretched the ends around his neck. Positioning himself behind the dog, Matt encircled Gunther's abdomen and hindquarters. "Has he been awake as many hours as usual?" Matt palpated Gunther's abdomen. He then held the dog's muzzle, pulled and stretched the skin surrounding the puppy's eyes, and peered into their dark depths. He raised the stethoscope that dangled on the surface of his lab coat, placed the apparatus on Gunther's chest, and listened intently during several breath cycles. He pulled the instrument's prongs from his ears.

Jeannie buttressed her arms to her chest and shifted her weight from one leg to another. "His alertness is back to normal. He slept almost twenty-four hours straight the first day after the emergency."

"Hey, Gunther." Matt ruffled the dog's head and neck fur. "You sure look better than the last time I saw you."

The dog flapped his tail against the table leg.

Whomp-whomp.

Matt positioned his hands on his hips and smiled. "And, Jeannie, I hope you don't mind me saying this." He scanned her up and down. "You look better, too."

"Considering that when you last saw me, I was a nervous wreck, and this time, I am fresh from a total Jacobson's makeover." Jeannie smiled a smile of abandon, the kind of expression one wore when they traversed in a convertible with the top down, and the temperature was a comfortable eighty degrees, and the route traveled wound through and around full-blossomed, intoxicating fruit trees backlit by rosy dusk.

"Well, you look fabulous. I bet that was fun." Matt shook his head and combed a hand through his thick, auburn hair.

"The pampering was cathartic. I belong to a widow support group. The makeover event was a shared group experience. It was emotional." Jeannie sighed. She scrunched shut her eyes.

The noise of rubber-soled shoes smacking and dog nails striking on a tile floor reverberated behind the closed door.

Jeannie opened her eyes and gazed at Gunther's head. She stroked his ears.

"I bet the experience was life-changing for some." Matt stepped behind Jeannie, removed the tin cover of a glass canister, and extracted a tongue depressor.

"I believe it was. Our oldest member, Verna, started this morning looking dowdy and depressed. By this afternoon, she literally sparkled, and she declared herself ready to ditch her old lady pinochle group in lieu of a bowling alley with barbeque chicken wings, beer, and men."

"Ah, Jeannie, that's great." Matt grinned. "How's Gunther's appetite?"

"We're following the prescribed diet and are vigilant about keeping all dog toxins out of sight. And Gunther readily eats whenever he is served." Jeannie puffed her cheeks and blew out a breath.

"Sounds good on all accounts." Matt bent his knees, extended his arms under Gunther's chest, and plopped the dog on the examining table. Beginning with Gunther's eyes, Matt performed a complete examination. "The only thing left here is to send in my assistant to administer Gunther's vaccinations and send you home with flea and tick preventative suggestions." Matt removed his stethoscope. He folded the tubes and shoved the instrument into his breast pocket. "So, how about you, Jeannie? Want to go bowling tonight?"

"Uh." Jeannie reached for the corner of the exam table. She curled her fingers on the cool surface. Matt's face blurred. The smell of disinfectant clouded her nostrils.

"Or maybe a movie? *Little Big Man* is playing in the Campus Theater." Matt lifted Gunther and set him on the floor. He gazed at Jeannie. "Maybe some back story, first." He sighed. "I am single. Like you, I've been through the loss of someone I loved very much. My fiancée, Lora, succumbed to breast cancer two years ago." He rubbed his forehead and raised his eyebrows. "I'm rusty at this."

Jeannie gathered Gunther's leash. "Matt, I totally get it. I appreciate the courage required to move from the grips of grief."

"Yeah, well, thanks for listening. Make sure you set up your next appointment with the front desk before you leave." Matt rubbed Gunther's head. "Glad to see you, Boy." Matt straightened and lopped his stethoscope over his shoulders. "Good-bye, Jeannie." He opened the door.

"Matt, hold on." Jeannie smoothed her cheeks and covered her mouth. Dropping her hands to her chin, she stepped toward him. She gripped his elbow. "I've been wanting to see *Little Big Man*." Her chest filled with an expansive air. Like a match to a pilot light, Matt's smile kindled Jeannie's heart. "I'll take Gunther home, feed and exercise him, and meet you at the Campus for the last show."

"Hey, that's great. I'll catch up with you there." Matt squeezed her shoulder and opened the door.

With a trembling hand and a fluttering heart, Jeannie threaded her hand through the handle of Gunther's leash and maneuvered her dog past a sterile office and a man offering a fruitful evening.

Chapter 17

Nick teetered on his haunches and buried his nose in Sam's fur. Against a dimming sky in his backyard, he gazed absently at the mist created by his breath.

Damn holidays.

Sam broke away, ran in a frenzied zigzag pattern and pawed at the frosty ground. The dog locked his jaw around a ragged tennis ball, sprinted back, and dropped the ball at Nick's feet.

Scooping the orb into his gloves, Nick rolled the ball in his palm. "Want it? Want it?"

Sam jumped.

Saliva dangled from his jowls.

Nick whipped the ball. He scowled. *Two days with Elizabeth. Turkey and all the trimmings. Vodka, whiskey, rum, wine, beer, aperitifs, cordials, and all the slurring and innuendoes. She'll expect me to impress her father and to heat her bed.* He gulped.

A slobbery tennis ball dropped at his feet.

"C'mon, Boy, let's get back inside." With Sam at his heels, Nick opened the door. Settling into his recliner, Nick picked up a recent *Michigan Wildlife* magazine and gazed at the phone beside the chair. He hovered his hand over the receiver. *Damn.* He dialed.

Jeannie picked up on the seventh ring.

"Hi. Did I catch you at a bad time?" Nick ran a hand through his hair and tossed the magazine into a basket next to the TV stand.

"No. Joey's just arriving home from a visit with his grandparents, and twenty minutes ago, they drove out the driveway."

Jeannie's voice buzzed with a lightness he hadn't detected before.

"Joey's playing with Gunther, so I can offer a few minutes. What's up?"

"I was looking at Mac's calendar regarding our trip to Copper Harbor. I tried to reach you last night."

"Oh. I was out." Jeannie sucked a few breaths. "I went to a movie."

"Good for you." Nick drummed his fingers on the arm of his easy chair.

"Let me grab my date book. Just a second."

Clunk.

Would she go to a movie by herself? She didn't say anything about who she went with. She just moved quickly off that topic. Hmmm... Breaths puffed through the phone line.

"Thanksgiving week is out, of course. I think Joey's grandparents could stay on after the holiday. What about leaving November thirtieth?" Jeannie asked.

"I think that's the best idea. We'll be taking our chances with the weather, but we can't postpone until spring, so..."

"You said you can drive?"

Why did she sound so no-nonsense? "I can. I have a hitch. That will allow us to pull a campus-owned, enclosed trailer to transport artifacts." Nick doodled snowflakes on a pad of paper. He puffed out his chest. "Washing machine working okay?"

"Y-y-yes. Which reminds me, I need to do a load of Joey's school clothes. Nick, I really need to go. Maybe I'll see you at work this week?"

"Probably not. The only time I'll be on campus is for lectures and office hours. I'll be at Rose Lake, finishing the squirrel trapping with Walter and his lab students."

"Well, okay. Hey, have a nice Thanksgiving."

"Yeah, you, too."

What do you expect, Randall? An answer to your niggling dilemma with Elizabeth?

****

"Nick, darling. So glad you're here." Clad in a snug black jumpsuit and skinny black flats, Elizabeth threaded her arms under his elbows and pressed her body against his.

She smelled of big-ticket perfume. Nick sneezed, backed away, and bumped into a potted fiddle-leaf fig tree.

Wall sconces cast a warm glow on the granite backdrop of the foyer. Clattering sounds emanated from the kitchen. Bedecked with orange bittersweet foliage and illuminated with a roaring fire, the lakefront hearth heralded a welcome message.

Elizabeth ran a hand through her billowy, blonde hair and laughed. "I'll have to recondition you. You've once again, I believe, become accustomed to the odors of the wild." She pointed a finger and wagged the slender digit before his nose. "What will I do with you? A man who spends days touching foul little animals."

Nick curled his fingers over her upper arms and kissed her forehead. "How about allowing me time to decompress? The drive was long." He stretched his neck and rotated his head.

"Of course. I'll have Paul bring your luggage up, and I'll see you at cocktail hour." Elizabeth checked the jeweled timepiece on her wrist. "In about an hour and a half."

Following a hot shower and a close shave, Nick crawled atop the pillowed bed and burrowed into the downy comforter. He shut his eyelids and drifted off. In a misty memory, Jeannie slid off the top of a washing machine. Her tiny toes recoiled as they hit the cold cement floor. Her breath came in tiny, chuffing giggles.

His manhood grew as it had then. Nick struggled awake. *It's time to join the party downstairs.*

Holding a sweating old-fashioned tumbler in his hand, Douglas Harcourt saluted Nick as he entered the living room overlooking Lake Michigan. "Nick, did the university receive my check for your Michigan Nightlife Exhibit?"

"Yes, sir, and your donation is much appreciated. Oh, I was supposed to ask. How would you like your name on the program? Is Harcourt Industries all right?"

Doug waved dismissively. "Sure, sure."

Elizabeth reached for Nick's forearm and tightened her grip. "Daddy?"

The silver-haired millionaire turned. "Yes?"

"What about listing the donor as *Douglas Harcourt and daughter, Elizabeth Harcourt*?"

"Fine, fine, darling." Doug nodded and strode to the hors d'oeuvres table.

Elizabeth purred. "That way, everyone at Great Lakes University will know my never-ending love and support of your work."

Ah Geez. Nick choked, ran a hand over his mouth,

and followed Elizabeth to the dining room. He pulled her chair and waited for her to sit. Then, he sat beside her.

Servants dispensed crisp Caesar salad topped with aromatic croutons into glossy wooden salad bowls at each place setting. Turkey with savory chestnut stuffing premiered as the star course. Bowls steaming with gravy, acorn squash, garlic mashed potatoes, and corn pudding proceeded to the table via maids. Alongside gold-rimmed china dinner plates, walnuts and cherries floated in sparkling gelatin inside footed crystal goblets.

With a snapping fire in a closed-hearth fireplace as a backdrop, Elizabeth's blonde hair, porcelain skin, and beige cashmere sweater met the criteria for a locker pin-up poster.

Nick removed a silver band from a rolled linen napkin and smoothed the square on his lap.

A tinkling sound came from the head of the table.

Doug tapped his fork against a long-stemmed flute. "Historians disagree on the date of the first Thanksgiving. Some say a harvest celebration in 1621. Others say it was a church-type celebration at the end of the 1623 drought. Whatever the origins, Thanksgiving is a day to bow our heads and be grateful. Cheers to all. Let's hope this damn war ends soon." He raised his glass.

Clinks broadcast around the table, succeeded by rattling forks and scraping knives.

A server paused at Nick's shoulder. "Roll?"

"Please."

Using an engraved silver tong, the maid moved the linen aside, collected a golden-brown crescent-shaped roll, and set the pastry on an empty bread plate fronting

Nick's dinner plate.

Nick picked a butter pat from a small dish and spread butter on the roll. Melted butter slid down the juncture of Nick's forefinger and thumb. He wiped the liquid with his napkin and popped the bread into his mouth. *Yum—salty, light as popcorn.*

Elizabeth shaped her lips into a sultry smile. "I just love watching you eat." Sliding a hand under the table, she squeezed Nick's thigh. Then, she licked her lips and shoved a turkey leg into her mouth. She bit the flesh from the bone, met Nick's gaze, and raised her eyebrows.

Nick slithered in his chair. *Damn.*

"Don't get too full, darling. Save room for later." Elizabeth raised her glass of Chardonnay and downed the liquid. She held up the empty glass.

A maid refilled Elizabeth's goblet glass for at least the third time since Doug said the grace.

Counting, Nick compressed his lips together and frowned.

The candles in the table's cornucopia centerpiece accumulated a thick overflow of molten wax.

Chairs scraped against the floor. Guests dropped soiled napkins atop the table and excused themselves.

Elizabeth sipped a cordial and swiveled her fork through the crumbs of a pumpkin pie slice.

Nick patted his stomach. "What a great meal."

Elizabeth leaned against him and brought her mouth close to his ear. "We don't have to keep pleasant company much longer. The real feast begins in the lake house, just you and me."

Better get her out of here. She's slurring her words. Nick traipsed behind her, giving polite greetings along the way. "Good night. Yes, wonderful to see you, too. Fabulous dinner. Thank you so much."

With each step, Nick's lungs cinched. His mouth turned dry.

Once inside the waterfront dwelling, Elizabeth shrugged off her shoes, padded down a hallway, and twisted a brass doorknob.

The bedroom door fell open.

Tumbling over deep-pile fur rug, Elizabeth pulled Nick. She loosened the silk moire print tie encasing his neck and flung the restrictive neck decoration over a tufted chaise lounge.

He kicked off his shoes and peeled off his socks.

An olive-green plaid, pleated wool skirt, a cascade-collared, maroon-colored silk blouse, a full-length black acetate slip, a nude-colored push-up bra, size thirty-eight C, a scanty pair of panties, a Heart, Shakespeare, and Lark labeled wool sport coat, a black leather belt stamped with the number thirty-four, a pair of wool tweed trousers, and an elastic-waisted pair of briefs scattered around the bed like palm fronds in the wake of a hurricane.

They made love.

Nick went through the motions as if he were a paid actor.

Softly snoring, Elizabeth shifted a foot atop his ankle.

He retracted his foot, turned to the wall, burrowed his head into the goose-down pillow, and faced a restless night. Pink toenails, appliqued peace symbols, and a long brunette ponytail haunted his dreams.

Chapter 18

The night-light plugged into the wall close to Joey's bed gave off a soft, diffusing glow.

The 1970 puppy-themed calendar on the wall displayed a basket of rusty-and-white colored Springer Spaniels for the current month of November. Tomorrow night, Joey could turn the page to December. *That's something else he can look forward to—a photo of puppies cavorting in the snow.*

The sweet smell of baby shampoo clung to her son's damp hair. Jeannie swept the just bathed mane away from his face as she knelt beside his bed.

"Mommy, will you be gone a long, long time?"

Gathering her son against her chest, Jeannie cataloged the lisp in Joey's voice, the soft cuticles of his fingers, the dusty pink coloration of his gums, and the gap in the uppers from a recently lost baby tooth. "Seven days and seven nights, sweetheart."

"Gramma and Grampa will stay with me the whole time?" Joey reached for a strand of Jeannie's hair and twined the filaments around his finger.

"Yes, and Grampa promised to read you the fuzzy caterpillar story. Gramma will need help baking cookies. She'll be surprised you are an expert egg cracker." Kissing the soft skin on Joey's temple, Jeannie lowered her eyelids. *We've never been apart this long. You'll be well loved in my absence, and this trip will benefit my career.* She opened her eyes and held her son at arm's length. "I will be gone when you wake up. Gramma said she will make you apple pancakes for breakfast."

"Will you sing me the cherry song, Mommy?" Joey squeezed his favorite blanket. "C'mon, Gunther."

Tap-tap-tap sounds echoed as Gunther's nails traversed the floor. Lying next to Jeannie's slippered feet, Gunther sighed.

"My favorite thing to do." Jeannie cleared her throat. "*I gave my love…*" Singing the last strains of Joey's favorite song, Jeannie's voice quivered. *This time tomorrow, I will be far away. Nick and I will be alone.*

****

"Are you snug enough?" Nick turned his head. "The sun will be up in another hour, and then it will feel warmer."

Clapping her mittened hands together, Jeannie grinned. "Getting there."

The muted glow cast from the recessed dashboard instruments provided an intimate predawn setting.

Fiddling with the radio, Nick settled on the lilting lyrics of an old-time country crooner. "Stopped loving her today…" He sang in a contrived drawl. Then, he hummed in tune with the melancholy song.

Rocking and swaying movements generated by the truck tires' rotation and the push-pull kinesis of the joined trailer lulled Jeannie to a dreamy state.

Gravel hit the undercarriage. *Ping-ping.*

A myriad of sensual memories cascaded—Matt's arm wrapped around her shoulders in the dim Campus Theater, Frank's fervent embrace on the tarmac, Nick's touch on her cheek as he shooed a bee, Nick's taste as he kissed her in the dank basement, Nick's butt tensing in a pair of gray shorts, Nick's hairy knuckles changing the radio station.

"Are you a coffee drinker?" Nick's baritone voice interrupted her reveries.

"I love that antioxidant morning picker-upper. Morning Jo is my favorite luxury," Jeannie murmured.

"You will find a thermos underneath your feet. You could pour yourself a healthy cup." Nick swung the driver-side visor down.

Dawn flooded the horizon. An ensemble of crows zoomed over emaciated corn fields.

Jeannie thrust her right hand under the bench seat, grasped the metal thermos, and lifted the container to her knees. She twisted off the top and poured the dark liquid into the cap.

The scent of morning manna permeated the truck cab's interior.

Fitting the canister between her knees, Jeannie breathed deeply and sipped a mild roast brew from the thermos cup. "Ah…heaven."

Nick chuckled. "My sentiments, too. We're making good time. The roads are clear. We should make Copper Harbor by late afternoon when we still have some daylight."

"That sun is coming on strong." Jeannie folded down the visor on her side. She giggled.

"What's funny?" Nick turned his face toward her and raised his eyebrows.

"Last week, I communicated with Hannah, one of our historical society contacts in Copper Harbor. She informed me about a contest they have in their local newspaper each fall. You have to guess the first day of winter that records two feet of snow at the harbor. You enter your name and your estimated date in a drawing. If you win, you get a snow blower. Guess what the winning day was last year?" Jeannie gripped the cup and set the lid atop the open thermos.

"November thirtieth?"

"No. And please. Don't jinx us!" Jeannie cast him a stink eye.

"December seventh?" Nick raised his eyebrows.

"No." Flexing her toes and rolling her ankles, Jeannie pressed her lips in a tight line.

With a voice inflection of shot-in-the-dark guessing, Nick blurted. "December thirty-first?"

"You're finally getter warmer, or should I say colder?" Bending from the waist, Jeannie retrieved carefully the fragrant liquid. She savored a leisurely sip. *Nice and hot and glad I added cream and sugar.* "Actually, the date was December fifteenth."

Nick slapped the steering wheel. "So we've got lots of time. We'll get there, sort and pack, and return with at least two weeks to spare. Hmmm, I sure could use a snowblower." He whistled low. "Is it too late to make a guess and enter the contest?"

"Sorry about that. The contest closed October first."

"I'll enter next year and have twelve months of data." Nick laughed. "Listen, you need to be prepared for some teasing. Are you familiar with the terms *Yooper* and *troll*?

"You mean Yooper, as in residents of Michigan's Upper Peninsula, and troll, as in that children's story where a grumpy, hairy beast lurks under the bridge?"

Jeannie chuckled.

"Back in Michigan's Lower Peninsula, you and I are respected professionals. But once we cross the Mackinac Bridge later today, expect heckling.

"What? No one mentioned potential verbal abuse in taking on this project." Jeannie pouted.

"You're catching on. In the fairy tale, the troll is an unrefined, lacking-in-social-mores-and-proper-hygiene despot." Nick stuck out his tongue.

"So the people who live in the Upper Peninsula, who call themselves Yoopers, really feel that way about us? What?" Jeannie slapped her thighs. "According to the last mileage marker, we're only forty miles to our moment of smackdown."

"The Yoopers are pretty serious. We are the intruders." Nick tilted his head.

"Well, what if they used another children's story? You know, something benign and sweet like the story of the kittens and their mittens. I mean, we are from the mitten peninsula." Jeannie shrugged.

"Hah, hah, hah." Nick burst into laughter. "Nah, I don't think that's gonna happen, but nice try."

On either side of the highway, rich, nutmeg-brown coloring in big bluestem grasses, dull cinnamon-tan pallor of foot-tall, tightly furled switch grass, and gold-blushed cones on the low-lying sweet gale grasses washed the landscape in a seasonal palette of holiday cooking spices. Jeannie threaded the thermos top to the container's neck and tucked the canister under her seat. She stretched her legs and drew a deep breath. "It's such a beautiful day."

Strains of guitar picking and twanging psalms permeated the cab.

Jeanie drummed the dashboard in cadence with the beat.

"Hey." Nick turned and drawled in a southwestern U.S. accent, "Are you a country girl?"

Pinching a pretend cowgirl hat off her head, Jeannie simpered. "My momma always tuned into the *Grand Ole Opry*."

"And here I had you pegged as an opera fan."

"Nope. Either campfire classics or country for me."

"Well, if it's campfire songs, how about a round of 'Bingo'?" Nick turned the radio volume to low.

"*There was a farmer*." Jeannie belted out the first line.

Nick joined in.

After completing all five rounds of B-I-N-G-O and amping the volume and giddiness with each successive letter, Jeannie fell silent. *Oh, how I've missed this. It feels so good.*

They sped past billboards publicizing insurance agencies, berry farms, car dealerships, ferry services, and pastoral wineries.

Nick extended his right arm and crossed his hand before Jeannie's face. "See those rows and rows of aligned red pines?"

"Um hmm…" Jeannie's gaze followed the point of his finger.

"That tree collection is one of the products of the Civilian Conservation Corps' efforts during the 1930s. Through the CCC, the federal government put unemployed people to work. They deployed men to perform tasks like reforestation."

"I'm familiar with the story. In the Historic Costumes Collection, we have dolls made by similarly employed people. The history is fascinating."

"Do you mind me asking about your husband?"

Jeannie widened her eyes and gummed her lips. *What is Nick thinking to ask about Frank?* She sighed. "No, talking about Frank is always a joy and an honor. He's my hero and never far from my thoughts. Where should I start?"

"We've got at least four more hours yet, so start at the beginning." Nick tugged his chin.

"Frank grew up in a tiny town almost at the tip of Michigan's thumb." Jeannie held up her left hand and pointed to the right side of her thumbnail. "See right here: Port Hope, a friendly pocket-sized town on Lake Huron."

Nick cast her a quick gaze and then returned his focus to the road.

"His parents farmed navy beans and dairy cows. They were hard-working folks, as good as they come. I'm happy they now enjoy leisure time, high-stepping at polka dances, and cheering Tiger baseball games whenever possible. Pete and Virginia are dear people. Frank wanted to be a history teacher, and he got a football scholarship to Western Michigan University in Kalamazoo. Oh, that Class D town of Port Hope sure was proud of him. Still are," she added softly. "Frank and I met because we both loved history and needed a humanities credit. He told me later that he fell in love with me the first day he walked into that class and saw me sitting alone in the center of the front row." Jeannie smiled.

Nick ventured a sideways glance. "Oh, yeah?" He grinned.

She returned a faltering smile. "I can't say the

sentiment was the same for me. I thought Frank looked like a bum, like somebody who slept on the beach or in the back of his car. And he had some unlovable habits, like always running out of gas, talking during movies, and eating stinky kielbasa." She laughed. "Oh, he could be a real humdinger."

"The kind of person everyone remembers," Nick interjected.

"The kind of person no one forgets," Jeannie added. "Frank kept after me, and I did fall in love with him."

"Despite the nasty kielbasa." Nick laughed.

Laced with tenderness and an attempt to boost levity, Nick's message and delivery restored the mood of elation inside the truck cab. "We were married June 10, 1960. Frank got a teaching job in Harbor Beach, just down the lake from Port Hope. He was the football coach, too, and the talk of the Thumb. We bought a modest house by Bathing Suit Beach and settled into small-town life. On Friday nights in the fall, everyone filled the football stadium bleachers. In the winter, everyone wore blue-and-white T-shirts, chewed gum, and yelled epitaphs like *all day long* and *you call that travel*? *Where's the suitcase?* at the Blue Star's basketball games. When spring came, everyone donned ball caps and hung out at the town's baseball diamond. Every Fourth of July, the town holds a huge parade, featuring every imaginable rolling farm implement."

"Real Americana." Nick stuck his fingers in his mouth and emitted a parade whistle.

"Frank, his dad, and cousins all rode their fleet of tractors. The town kids decorated their bikes and road them in the parade. However, if a town kid is a Scout or an aspiring farmer, they hold banners and march."

"It sounds like a perfect life, Jeannie."

"Yes, I thought so." She sighed and gazed out the window. *It was perfect. Now for the sad segment.*

"And then, Frank's cousin, Glen, received a draft letter. So, Frank, and Glen's brother, Bobby, decided to enlist. The three registered together and then shipped to Fort Benning, Georgia, for their basic training. As boys, they were inseparable. As men, they guarded each other's backs. They all ended up as Military Policemen. Frank was good with animals, so he volunteered to attend dog school. He trained a German Shepherd." Jeannie's voice cracked. "He loved that dog. Knowing Gunther went with him to 'Nam gives me solace."

"Gunther?" Nick questioned.

"Yes. The Gunther that you saved is a namesake." Jeannie blew a deep breath. "The last time I saw Frank, he was home on leave in August 1962. I got pregnant." She scrunched shut her eyes.

Tire rumblings exploded through the silence.

Opening her eyes, Jeannie wrung her hands and sucked a deep breath. "He never saw his baby son." Jeannie's words, spoken in a torrent, tumbled and fell between them.

Reaching with his right hand, Nick pressed his palm on her left hand.

"The worst day of my life was October 8, 1962." Jeannie's voice faltered. "A knock sounded on the door. I recognized the gentleman standing outside: Mick Lemanski, Port Hope's fire chief and a member of the National Guard. Mick wore his Marine uniform. And I knew from the lifeless look in his eyes. My husband, my hero, died for his country."

"Jeannie, I'm just so sorry. Frank's a hero in my book." Nick wiped a tear from his face.

Jeannie compressed her lips and blew out a gust of air. "Thanks."

"I gotta ask. What happened to Glen and Bobby?" Nick tautened his right arm and pressed the palm against the steering wheel.

Jeannie turned to Nick. "Thank you for asking. That's very thoughtful. Glen and Bobby came home, and they're both married now with children. Every time I visit the east side of the state, we make a point of getting together. They dote on Joey."

"It's gotta be tough, being a single mom." Nick rolled his lower lip under his top teeth.

"The two of us are making it with the help of Gunther Jr., who is better behaved these days, thanks to your training tips. I really do appreciate your help with training, Nick."

"By now, you know I'm a sucker for an animal in need. Heck, I'm just a sucker for any mammal."

Giggling, Jeannie held up her hands. "Oh, yeah, I did notice that about you. So, enough about me. Your turn. What is your life story up until today?"

Nick shook his head. "Hmm…"

"According to the last road sign, the next rest stop is twelve miles. So, you have twenty minutes to spill all the goods." Jeannie lifted her left arm and gazed at her watch. "Go!"

Nick bobbed his head to his chest and snapped it back up. "Okay, gotta talk fast."

Jeannie laughed.

"I was the boy always late for supper, engrossed in climbing trees, sailing paper boats, exploring creeks, caves, ditches, and bringing strays home." Nick scratched the back of his head.

"I'm getting the picture of you, loud and clear." Jeannie smirked. *I picture a regular zoo of squirrels, feral cats, birds with broken wings, and a few rabbit kits.*

"I was a bookworm, too. When I was about ten, I couldn't wait for my mom to come home from grocery shopping. She always bought a candy treat like bridge mix or root beer barrels. But what really excited me was the weekly edition of a children's encyclopedia. From the first book, *A through BL*, I was hooked. That book included aardvarks, alpacas, anteaters, badgers, Bengal tigers, and big-horned sheep."

"Ha, ha…" Jeannie slapped her knee. "I loved to read, too, but I had my nose stuck in craft books and mysteries."

"My favorite story of all time is *Call of the Wild* by Jack London." Nick tapped his palm on the steering wheel. "Buck stole my heart."

"Mine, too." Jeannie nodded.

"I can see a direct catapult from reading that story to my career today. Wolves are such magnificent, strong animals."

"I remember being impressed when you shared a comparison between German Shepherds and wolves with Joey," Jeannie interjected.

"The Isle Royale study has been going on for thirty years. The research is a unique opportunity to study a prey-predator relationship because wolves are the moose predators on Isle Royale. Bears and coyotes no longer live on the island."

"Why do you think wolves have a bad reputation in

some cultures?" Jeannie leaned her elbow on the armrest.

Nick furrowed his brow. He rolled his lips. "For one thing, wolves are covert creatures. They stay away."

"Will you be revisiting Isle Royale next year?" Jeannie asked.

"Definitely. And I'm excited to see a wolf study colleague who lives year 'round in Copper Harbor."

"Geesh, we're coming up on the rest stop, and I haven't heard anything about your romantic history." Jeannie picked sweater fuzz off her sleeve.

"Romantic history?" Nick sucked his cheeks.

"Nick, you know what I mean. Do you have a girlfriend? A past wife?"

"Oops, pulling in now." Nick rotated the steering wheel, edged between two cars, and thrust the shifter into Park. "Meet you back here." Then, he jumped from the cab, slammed shut the door, and sprinted to the welcome center.

Hoisting her purse strap over her shoulder, Jeannie followed. *Nick, are you in a hurry to stretch your legs, use the bathroom, or avoid a personal question—like are you involved in a romantic relationship?*

****

Better 'fess up, Randall. He fronted the automatic dryer in the public restroom and heaved a sigh. Blasts of warm air drifted over his hands and midsection. Staring at his reflection in the overhead illuminated mirror, he frowned. His heart boomed inside his chest. He gripped the edges of a porcelain sink. Cold seeped through his fingers and palms.

Chattering and foot-shuffling noises echoed from

just beyond the lavatories.

No way to avoid this. Jeannie deserves to know. Nick tucked his head on his chest and his hands in his pockets and walked outside.

Jeannie dawdled outside the truck.

Her hair gyrated around her head like a desiccated dandelion crown.

"I'm getting hungry. How about you?" She grinned.

"Next fast-food spot, let's stop." Nick grasped the truck door handle and pulled open the door.

Jeannie clambered onto her seat.

Nick jammed the key into the ignition, backed up the truck, and turned up the radio volume. Back on the highway, Nick glanced in the rearview mirror and cleared his throat. "There is a woman. Her name is Elizabeth. She lives outside of Chicago, and I spent Thanksgiving with her." He stared at the road ahead.

They passed a long trailer. Vented sides revealed a hay-strewn floor and rows of pink-skinned hogs.

"Ew…" Jeannie sputtered.

Bluegrass strains of a love gone bad filled the cab. Nick clenched his jaw. He gripped and regripped the steering wheel.

"Sounds kinda serious."

Jeannie's voice measured like a gavel dropping. Nick lifted a hand and smoothed the palm over his nose and his mouth. "Elizabeth considers us engaged." He exhaled a large breath.

"And you?" Jeannie raked her top teeth over her bottom lip.

"I am reconsidering."

"Why?"

"I met you." He turned his face.

The color drained from her cheeks. She tented her eyebrows.

"Hey, let's get some grub. How does a hamburger and fries sound?" Nick pointed toward a road sign.

"Famished. Just no pork today, please."

Nick laughed. Following lunch, he traversed the Mackinac Bridge and drove east on Highway 2 a route that provided a road-hugging view of Lake Michigan.

Jeannie shut her eyes. Mild snoring ensued.

Nick shook his head and grinned. By late afternoon, Nick woke Jeannie. "Hey, we're in Copper Harbor."

She yawned, rubbed her eyes, and stretched. "Yay."

Log cabin structures, some touting fish, fresh and smoked, some numbered rental cottages, and one with neon open and beer signs tacked on peeling siding lined the street they turned on.

Vistas of a calm, endless Lake Michigan blitzed them in all directions. "There it is, the Pines Resort." Nick pulled into the parking lot of a one-story rustic building. "Let's check in and then get some dinner. I hope you like German food." He gazed down his nose, put the truck in Park, and extracted the key.

"You mean schnitzel and big, fat pretzels dipped in mustard?" Jeannie chuckled.

"Yah! Sauerkraut and bratwurst. Oh, yuck, any kind of wurst–liver, curry, brat..." Nick slid out of the cab.

"*Jawohl.*" Jeannie grabbed her purse and jumped to the ground. "Gah. It's about twenty degrees colder here."

"Sure hope you brought long underwear!" Nick slammed the truck door, walked ahead, and opened the door to the resort.

****

Following a sunset-view dinner of sausages, hot potato salad, and a shared thick slice of Black Forest cake, Jeannie closed her fingers around the grip of a German stein. She sipped a stout lager, noting the faint taste of chocolate, and leaned back in her chair. "Nick, I hate the thought of interfering with another woman's happiness." She licked her lips. "Geez, just the combination of the two words, other and woman, makes me cringe." She shifted her elbows to the tabletop and dropped her chin into her palms.

Nick drew circles on the table with the bottom of a beer mug.

Shush-shush-shush.

Nick drooped his head.

Shush-shush-shush.

He lifted his chin and gazed at Jeannie. Taking a deep breath, he shuddered. "Believe me, I don't want anyone to be hurt." He brought the mug close to his chest and stared inside. He looked up and renewed his gaze with Jeannie. "But, damn it, I can't deny my feelings for you." He set his brew on the table and reached for her left hand. "Any chance you might be thinking of me in a fond way?"

Jeannie squeezed shut her eyes. She laced her fingers with Nick's. Blindly, she registered the thick knuckles, the long fingers, and the dense fingertips.

The warmth from his hands spread through her body and initiated a liquid fire. She opened her eyes and gazed into his. "Yes."

Chapter 19

"Hey, Yoopers, alert! Troll invasion!" A strapping, copper-headed, camouflage-jacket-wearing woman announced Jeannie and Nick's arrival. She rose from a crouched position on the floor of a huge warehouse, brushed her hands on her denim jeans, and stuck out her right hand. "I'm Hannah."

Her smile was as wide as Lake Superior's horizon and minimized the chill of the concrete-floored, aluminum-sided structure. Jeannie grinned and connected her right hand with the offered one. Hannah's handshake suggested an ancestral connection with Paul Bunyan, the iconic strongman of Michigan Upper Peninsula lore.

Nick shot Jeannie a glance. *I told you so.*

"Hannah, great to meet you. Thanks for your easy-to-follow directions and your recommendations for accommodations and restaurants." Jeannie smiled.

"You're welcome. Dr. Nick Randall, I presume?" Reaching around Jeannie, Hannah offered Nick her right hand.

"You're right, but I want to clarify: I am not a true troll. I qualify as part Yooper since I spend research time in Isle Royale." Nick crossed his arms over his chest and teetered on his work boots.

Hannah pursed her lips. She nodded. "Nick, you might have to prove yourself. We Yoopers are a pretty tight group."

"Gotcha. Challenge accepted." Nick pointed his index finger like a smoking gun.

"Hey, either of you trolls drink coffee? We have all that sissy stuff—like cream and sugar."

A lanky, bearded man wearing a pilled turtleneck sweater and wide-wale corduroy pants approached. He carried a clipboard.

"I take mine black." Nick grasped the man's hand. "Are you Arnie?"

"I am. Chief High Low Truck Driver and Packer, at your service." Arnie flipped a salute.

"So, you've had a promotion since we last talked." Nick chuckled.

"Looks like this is an upgrade for you, too, Nick. Last time I heard, you were picking through squirrel scat with a toothpick." Arnie finger-combed the graying hair on his head.

Unzipping her jacket, Jeannie giggled. She strode to a table against the wall topped with a spurting coffeemaker, disposable cups, plastic stirrers, a bowl with sugar packets, and a paper carton of creamer. She poured herself a cup of morning brew, selected a sugar envelope, tore off a paper end, and shook dry contents into the black steaming liquid. Then, she dribbled creamer into the cup and stirred the concoction with a red-and-white-striped spoon substitute.

Nick approached with an athletically honed, clean-shaven man wearing a youthful grin. "Jeannie, allow me to introduce you to Martin, fellow wolf aficionado and quasi-Yooper."

Martin smiled. He swept a hand in a square pattern. "As you can see, the Eriksson donation is massive. This assemblage represents over fifty years of collecting Michigan biological specimens and native crafts. And lucky for your university, both the Erikssons were loyal alumni."

"We have full backing from the president to honor this gift." Nick clasped Martin's hand.

Jeannie's heart gravitated to her throat. *Nick is so gracious.*

Martin cupped his hands into a makeshift megaphone. "How about everyone round up over here?"

People emerged from behind large plastic-swathed packages, carrying scissors, pencils, and clipboards, and fronted Martin.

Hannah zigzagged throughout a stack of wood pallets and came alongside Jeannie.

Sliding a pencil behind his ear, Arnie jogged toward them.

"Okay. This is the team. Hannah, the Historical Society of Copper Harbor President and owner of Hannah's Woodworks, will be invaluable in assisting with artifact description and cataloging. Hannah also manages the packing details, sourcing boxes, bubble wrap, and tape to negotiating hauling and shipping." Martin clapped.

Hannah flipped off her ball cap and upended the hat.

The copper-haired, bullish-handshaking volunteer's gesture suggested a request for tips. Jeannie grinned.

Nick winked and mimicked removing his wallet from his back pocket.

"Dr. Nick Randall, Great Lakes University, will

lead the cataloging and wrapping of Dr. Eriksson's mammal and bird specimens and his botany specimens. And Jeannie, also from Great Lakes U, will do the same with the textile artifacts. The remaining volunteers stand by with tags, pencils, and packing materials. Dr. Olmstead—Arnie, to all of us—is the official photographer, and yours truly, heads up security and preserving the fun factor." Martin set his clipboard next to the condiments and thrust his hands on his hips. "So, don't expect much."

Laughter and guffaws echoed.

"I'd like to invite everyone to the weekly fish fry at the Moose Lodge downtown, tomorrow night. If you plan to be there, get there by six. The place fills fast." Hannah tugged her ball cap over her unruly hair.

"Mary and I will be there with our dancing shoes." Martin grinned.

A chorus of "yup," "be there," and "sure thing" ensued.

Hannah tapped Jeannie's shoulder. "Let me take you to your workplace. I've selected veteran volunteers for you."

Two women joined them.

"Both Shirley…" Hannah squeezed the shoulder of a plump, gray-haired polyester-pantsuit wearer. "And Patty"—Hannah threw an arm around a buxom, frizzy-haired brunette—"have studied proper preservation techniques for textiles. They work fast, too."

"Lucky me." Jeannie rubbed her palms together.

"The quilts are going to wow you, Jeannie. They are treasures." Shirley adjusted the sidebars of her glasses. "We've prepared the examining tables with freshly laundered cotton table covers. We ensured the absence of active insect infestation and determined that mold is nonexistent."

Slipping back to her professional scientist modus operandi, Jeannie knitted her eyebrows and formed a tight line with her lips.

Holding up two pairs of white cotton gloves, Patty winked. "We didn't forget these. And I double-checked Shirley. Both of us left ink pens at home."

"Fantastic." Jeannie grinned. "How about we start with the quilts? Could you gather them and then bring one to the tables? I'm going to grab my preparation bag. I'll be right back."

At the other end of the room, Nick bent his knees, squatted, and lifted a four-foot-tall, plastic-wrapped object.

Could his thighs be any sexier? Heat surged in Jeannie's face. She wandered to the circle of volunteers congregating around Nick.

A middle-aged man in overalls and steel-toed work boots clambered to Nick's side and shored up the object. "Pretty sure this is the bald eagle."

As the men unwrapped the covering, a thick wooden base topped with rocks jutted out.

Nick and his helper, stepping slowly, moved the artifact to a waist-high work table.

Crinkling sounds enveloped the silent onlookers.

"Ohh…" Jeannie stared, transfixed. A memory of kneeling in church, gazing at a looming statue of the swathed-in-blinding-light Blessed Virgin, pervaded her psyche. *I can't wait to see your reaction, Dr. Randall.* She held her breath.

"God bless America." Patty clapped Nick's back.

"Wow!" Nick spread and tilted his arms like an

eagle swooping treetops. He twirled in a circle and shared smiles with his fellow archivists as they came into his radius.

Nick. I see you. His gaze and expression of awe pierced Jeannie's heart. She put a hand over her breast, and then fisted her hand and stuck up a thumb. *I bet Nick can't wait to bring this back to Bob. What an excellent specimen for Ornithology.* Jeannie walked to the entryway, retrieved her packet of preservation tools, and returned to the textile work area. "Oh, a LeMoyne Star pattern," Jeannie murmured. "Notice the eight-pointed stars." She pointed to a cluster of multicolored cotton blocks. "Each of the outside angles is forty-five degrees."

Patty formed a backward *L* with her right thumb and forefinger and shored her chin. "Hmm, how do you know the name of the pattern?"

"Good question. I've seen one in the Smithsonian Quilt Collection. That is the easy answer. There are several historical theories. The one I like best honors the French brothers, Pierre and Jean Baptiste LeMoyne. Those men founded the Louisiana city of New Orleans in 1718. This particular star pattern was part of Jean Baptiste's coat of arms." Jeannie shrugged.

"That's so cool." Patty grasped a quilt corner and tilted her head.

"Shirley, would you mind recording?" Jeannie held a clipboard against her hip.

"Not at all." Shirley extracted a pencil from her pocket and accepted the clipboard.

"Patty, let's get the measurements. First, we do width, and then length." Jeannie extracted a cloth tape measure from her kit. "Eighty inches by ninety-four inches." Then, holding a magnifying glass, Jeannie moved the glass close to the quilt's surface. "Shirley, please note seaming is, on average, twelve stitches an inch by hand."

"Not exactly fine sewing," Patty remarked.

"Great job on this hanging system." Jeannie folded the quilt in half and moved toward a rectangular plastic tube structure mounted to a wooden base with casters. Basted stitches moored a muslin backing to the arrangement.

"Hannah, our woodworking queen, rigged this up." Patty lifted a box of dressmaker pins in one hand and the opposite quilt corner in the other.

"I'll let Arnie know we are ready for photography." Shirley walked away.

Once Arnie shot full-size and close-ups, Shirley and Patty removed the quilt from the frame and rolled the textile onto an acid-free cardboard tube. Then, they covered the quilt in a muslin bag, added a tag with the quilt's pattern name, origin, the day's date, and put the artifact aside for Hannah's packing.

They processed the remaining dozen quilts.

"It's four thirty. You have thirty minutes to finish up what you are doing. At five o'clock, I will lock up. Doors will be unlocked at nine a.m. tomorrow. A continental breakfast will be ready." Martin's voice blared through his megaphone.

Feeling a tap on her shoulder, Jeannie jumped.

"Sorry, I didn't mean to startle you. Martin invited us to dinner at his home tonight. Is that okay?" Nick teetered on his heels.

"I'd love to get a shower before we do. I'm pretty dusty." Jeannie puffed a loose lock of hair sticking to her lips.

"Sounds good. I'm checking my boots when I take them off." Nick shuddered. "Good thing Martin brought auto chambers. We're leaving a few specimens in there overnight. One of the volunteers found insect eggs in the nasal cavity of a bobcat mount."

"Yuck!" *How disgusting.* Jeannie shuddered. "The worst we found today was deteriorating silk on a crazy quilt. Unfortunately, in the past century, artisans added metallic salts to silk production to lower the cost of silk fabric. No method exists to preserve these fibers. They evaporate." Jeannie frowned and shook her head.

"Meet you at the door when Martin sounds the close of day." Nick grinned. "I gotta check for a few last-minute things."

"Okay." Jeannie stepped toward Shirley and Patty. Then she turned.

Nick froze.

Their gazes met.

A current of magnetism rocked through Jeannie. *God help me.* She lowered her gaze and jogged to her work site.

****

"Man, that hit the spot." Nick leaned back in a cushioned kitchen chair and stretched his bulbed-at-the-toe stockinged feet along the hardwood floor. Barnwood framed photos of Isle Royale lichen and wildflowers stacked vertically on a wall leading into the living area. *Martin is also a talented photographer.* A collection of rocks settled on the top of a bookcase. Nick ticked off the rock names, all of them found in Michigan—*pudding stone, shale, sandstone, Petoskey.* Turning his gaze to Jeannie, who sat across the table,

Nick grinned. *Looks like Jeannie worked up an appetite, too.*

Pink and rosy-skinned from what had to have been as quick-and-hot-as-she-could-stand-it shower, Jeannie glowed.

An oily dribble extracted from Martin's homemade meatloaf glistened on her lower lip.

Nick picked a paper napkin from a wire basket on a lazy Susan in the table's center and tossed it in her lap.

Blushing, she wiped her face with his offering.

Martin rose and cleared the table. "Glad you liked the meal. I have a limited cooking repertoire. Had Mary been home, you would have been treated to more gourmet faire."

From the evidence of that cookbook assemblage lining the knotty pine opposite wall, I am not surprised. Nick piled his silverware atop ketchup, coating his plate.

"Everything was filling and delicious. I'd request the meatloaf again," Jeannie said.

"Perfect compliment." Martin grinned. "I'll brew some decaf coffee. How about some dessert? Mary left us a tin of brunscrackers—traditional Swedish cookies, very buttery and oh, so good."

Nick nodded and pounded a few drum licks on the tabletop.

"So, Jeannie, how much do you know about the moose-wolf study on Isle Royale?" Martin placed a plate of light-brown, trapezoid-shaped cookies next to Jeannie's water glass.

"I have gleaned a smidgeon of the history via Nick, but I'd like to learn more." She picked up a cookie, bit into it, and shoved a hand under her chin as crumbs fell.

Martin stretched his legs and crossed his ankles. "Some new perspective to the study is fascinating. In the course of studying hundreds of skeletal moose remains, evidence of osteoarthritis has been observed. Now, archaeologists are making comparisons to human skeletal remains. They are establishing hypotheses of the origins of this crippling disease. This study presents great opportunities to advance human history and medicine, particularly in the realm of nutrition."

"Such good news." Nick gummed his lips together and downed a swig of coffee.

"When's the last time you saw Doug Harcourt, and how do you think he will react to those findings?" Martin steepled his fingers.

Nick choked. Coffee spurted from his mouth. "Oh, damn, excuse me."

Jeannie reached into the tin basket and extracted a napkin.

"Thanks." Nick accepted the paper towel and scrubbed the paper over his face.

Martin frowned.

Outside, wind chimes tinkled. Inside, a fire crackled in an open hearth.

"Thanksgiving. I saw Doug at Thanksgiving." Nick averted his gaze.

Jeannie put her right hand over her left and pressed the joined hands over her heart. She curled her bottom lip and sunk her upper teeth into the puffy, pink flesh.

"I figured this news would work into his enthusiasm regarding government funding projects. That guy has so much political influence. I always want to stay on his good side, if you know what I mean." Martin tipped his chin and looked down his nose.

Nick steepled his fingers. "Yeah, I know." The muscles in the back of his calves constricted.

An onerous chime tolled. Nine times, clock weights reverberated.

"Grandfather says it's bedtime." Nick pushed back from the table and stood. "Martin, it's been an extraordinary day. Thanks for hosting us tonight." The mammalogist extended his right hand.

Martin shook the offered hand and clasped Nick's elbow with his other hand.

"A grandfather clock." Jeannie yawned and rolled her shoulders.

Her earlier pink flush had melted into puffy pools below her eyes.

"As always, my friend, the conversation proved stimulating. I appreciate your candor." Nick sucked in a breath.

Repeating the earlier gesture of bending his head and looking down his nose, Martin met Nick's gaze. "I got you, buddy."

Thanks for reading between the lines, old friend. I might need you.

Chapter 20

The high-ceilinged warehouse could substitute as a meat locker. Jeannie pulled the sleeve hems of her Icelandic-patterned, red-and-white woolen sweater as she shrugged out of her down parka. Snugging the garment to her wrists, she brought both hands upward and blew warmth on them.

"Once those propane heaters kick on, you delicate trolls should be able to work." Hannah, wearing a lightweight flannel shirt and a pair of canvas overalls, smirked.

The above-the-bridge, below-the-bridge bantering continued throughout the day.

"Arnie told me we're knocking off early. He wants to ensure we all get seats at the Legion tonight." Shirley hummed a polka beat. "They have an all-you-can-eat fish menu and a live band—local guys, The Pierogi Pied Pipers."

"My cousin is their accordion player. He's good." Patty grinned. "You're in for a treat, Jeannie. Do you know how to polka?"

"Not really." Jeannie gritted her teeth.

"Ah heck, Shirley and I can teach you. And Martin, he's a skyscraping stepper. You just gotta watch his bolting elbows." Giggling, Patty looked up from the handwoven tapestry she measured. "What's up with Hannah? She hasn't moved from that spot in over an hour."

Jeannie set aside a blue-and-white linsey-woolsey coverlet, removed her gloves, and placed them on the exam table. She stretched her shoulders and brushed her hands against her slacks. "I think I'll check."

Stooped on a no-frills camp chair, Hannah pored over a thin notebook. Holding the book nimbly between her fingers, she stirred her head back and forth, chomped on her lower lip, and turned the stained pages.

"Whatcha got there? Looks pretty absorbing." Jeannie put her hands on her hips and bent her head.

Gazing up, Hannah widened her eyes.

"I just opened a box labeled Viola Smith, Camp Cook and discovered a mess of stuff in here—recipes, news clippings, dried leaves, and letters."

Jeannie lowered to a haunch.

Holding a tattered newspaper, Hannah scanned the type. "Bean soup for large groups." She moved the paper under Jeannie's nose. "Here on the edge, there's a penciled note. Soak overnight in leftover potato water. Substitute sorghum if sugar is not available. Yummy." Hannah grunted.

"Why don't you whip some up for the squad?" Jeannie chuckled. Touching the paper as if it were the Declaration of Independence with fifty-six original signatures, Hannah laid the page into an acid-free box.

"I am really curious to see what the letters reveal. Have a go at it, Jeannie." Hannah passed the tin.

Jeannie sneezed. "Holy moly, is it my imagination, or is *eau de* bean soup packed into this tin?"

Hannah guffawed. "I detected cigarette smoke, too. Yuck."

Jeannie dug out a packet of letters held together by

a cracked rubber band. She extracted one from the pile, carefully pulled out the folded letter from the opened envelope, and read aloud.

"August 13, 1935

Dearest Mother,

Yesterday, I left Camp Hiawatha, along with eighteen other Juniors and our Captain, Edward Thomas. After a five-hour journey on beautiful calm waters, the good men of Company 2699 arrived on Isle Royale. We were obliged to leave the boat and wade into shore at a spot named Siskiwit Bay. Isle Royale is a land untamed, no man lives here, only wild animals. We set to work clearing a living area so that when the rest of the company arrives later this month, we will be in good stead. Each man has rations for a month and his bedroll and tarp. Last night, we enjoyed bathing in Lake Superior and frying lake trout. It was delicious but not as tasty as the stuffed catfish Mother cooks. Yes, I miss home cooking. And I miss sitting in our kitchen, with a tea kettle hissing on the stove, and Puss purring at my feet. I wonder if she has brought any rabbits and laid them at the door lately. I wonder how Julie, Kathleen, Sarah, and Kate are. They'll soon be back in school. I hope the money I'm sending helps the girls get by. I know life is hard since Father died, but as you say, God will provide.

It's time for lights out."

Hannah captured the letter from Jeannie, refolded it, and stuck the missive in its original envelope. "Here's one from the other pile. Let's see what this one has to say." She passed a faded blue sheet to Jeannie.

Taking the letter, Jeannie smoothed the edges. She squinted her eyes and brought the page closer to her face. "The handwriting is so tiny, but here goes.

My dearest Bruce,

Last night, Beth and I listened to Gang Busters *on the radio. It's the first of its kind program.* Gang Busters *features authentic police case histories. My goodness. Beth and I find it humorous how people can be so stupid. After that show, we heard Bing Crosby sing the song "Red Sails in the Sunset." It made me think of you and being on that island. It also made me miss you more, Bruce.*

Mother and Father had a huge argument the other night after we listened to a special broadcast by President Roosevelt. Father rolled his newspaper and whacked it against his fist. 'Government stealing my money,' he kept shouting. 'You mean from every dollar I earn in that hot-as-Hades factory, Uncle Sam will tax the hell out of me. Tax me for working?' Father's face got as red as the pickled beets in the cellar. 'Now, Fred, calm down,' Mother said. 'Think of how Social Security can save people from utter ruin and the clutches of the poorhouse. Look at our neighbors. Where are Millie and her children now? Living in a county poorhouse! It's a crying shame.' Father shook his fists and snapped his suspenders. 'I wouldn't trust the government with a five-spot, let alone pick away at my paycheck. The paycheck I earn.'

Mother kept trying to placate him by repeating the president's words. 'Social Security Tax doesn't go into effect until 1937—two whole years from now.'

Well, on to other things. I am sewing a new dress. I think it will turn out real snazzy. I'm using a Butterick pattern and Mother's sewing machine. The dress is blue, your favorite color.

Granma Bess, Mother, and I have spent the last three days canning tomatoes. Corn is coming in, too, and we've eaten boiled corn almost every night for dinner. Bobby ate six ears in one sitting. Mother doesn't mind. He's a growing boy, after all. Tomorrow after church, we're going to Aunt Barb's for dinner. I miss you, Bruce.

Your Margie"

Jeannie reached for an acid-free cardboard box from the supply table. Carefully, she laid the letters in a stack. "Hannah, I'd love to see more. But I better get back to the trunks of clothing. This trove of memoirs is very significant. I know you appreciate that. We should copy and share these artifacts with the Copper Harbor Historical Society."

"Just what I was thinking." Hannah puffed her freckled cheeks and blew out a gusty breath.

Nick will be excited about these letters, too, since he is so familiar with the terrain and history of Isle Royale. I wonder how he'll react to the contents of Viola's tin.

****

Patriotic red, white, and blue paint spelled the words *American Legion, Post 291* on a roof-mounted neon sign hanging above the entry to a flat-topped, one-story, faded-brown building. Outside the door, a canister overflowed with cigarette butts. A super-sized snow shovel leaned against the doorframe.

Jeannie inhaled lake vapors, pine scent, and an overwhelming odor of deep-fried fish. She stepped into a pothole and tripped.

"Whoa, there." Nick grabbed her elbow and righted her.

"Thank you, kind sir," Jeannie said. Holding her arm fast to his waist, Nick guided her between mud-encrusted, big-wheeled trucks and time-worn, weather-beaten sedans packed together like fresh-packed cucumbers in a ball jar.

He shoved against the peeling wood-paneled entry.

A line of beer-mug-thrusting arms saluted them.

"It's the trolls!" A chorus of greetings rang out.

Jeannie grinned and waved.

"Geesh, the whole darn town knows now," Nick muttered with a chuckle.

Martin sprang up and pulled two empty chairs from the table surrounded by their work team.

Sidling into one, Jeannie slipped off her jacket and draped the garment over the back of the steel-framed chair.

Sweeping his right hand toward a petite, silver-haired woman, Martin grinned. "This is my wife, Mary."

"Nick, I like your new look." Mary winked.

"Hmmm?" Nick tilted his head and jutted his brows.

"You look more carefree. Must be something agreeable about your job at Great Lakes University." Mary turned. "Happy to meet you, Jeannie."

A light feeling like flour sprinkled onto a rolling pin swathed Jeannie. "Martin makes a mean meatloaf, but your cookies were out of the ballpark." Her voice dinged like a timer alarm.

"What do you want to drink?" Nick asked.

Windswept hair and a lazy smile interspersed his face. *Mary's right. I like this never-care look, too.* Warmth radiated from the center of her chest. "A root

233

beer, easy on the foam."

Hannah nudged her shoulder. "Chips—all you can eat. Fish is on the way." She tugged on the tip of her ball cap. "Everyone here has a crush on that man." She gripped the neck of a beer bottle, nodded toward Nick's back, and lipped the bottle's mouth. "Geez, speaking of a crush, I unearthed some scandalous activities in those letters found in Viola the Camp Cook's treasure box."

"What?" Jeannie tented her brows.

Taking another swig, Hannah clanked the bottle on the table. "Yeah. I unearthed a letter from Margie telling Bruce he is a daddy. She basically rips him one. 'Why, oh why, haven't you written me'?"

"Seriously?" Jeannie smacked a palm over her mouth.

"What's weird is that I found this particular letter sealed in an envelope inside another envelope and not with either of the rubber-banded piles." Hannah shook her head.

Shirley leaned across the table. "Here's something else you trolls might find weird. Jeannie, do you know of our snow goddess, Heikki Luunta? Every year, the snow lovers pay homage to her, the mythical Finnish Queen of Snow. They light huge bonfires and dance and howl to get Heikki Luunta's attention. My neighbor bakes himself in his outdoor sauna, then runs naked across the backyard yelling *Heikki Luuuuuuuuunta.* Oh, yeah, it's a crazy thing up here! Well, naked works!"

Jeannie burst out laughing. Then, she quieted. *Whatever happened to poor Margie? And her baby?*

"What's this about naked neighbors?" Nick set a chilled root beer before Jeannie.

"Those crazy Yoopers." Jeannie giggled. "They are

snow-demented."

"I'll testify to that," Patty shouted.

Across the table, Arnie freed space by rearranging the myriad of beer bottles atop the table and settled his elbows in the clearing. "If you want to know a scientist's rationale, it's the marriage of winds crossing over the wide expanse of Lake Superior—as you know, the largest body of freshwater in the entire world—and the relatively mild air temperatures on this peninsula. And voila! An average snowfall of two hundred and fifty inches a year. I think the record is three hundred and ninety inches."

Hannah held up her arms like a football goalpost. "Yay!"

Beer-bottle bottoms clunked on the tabletop.

Arnie fisted his fingers and beat them on his chest. "Now that's when *Heikki Luunta* throws a party! My friends, the Keweenaw Peninsula—the very place where you now sit, casually enjoying your beer—averages more snowfall than anywhere east of the Great Mississippi River. Lake effect snow can cause blinding whiteouts in just minutes. Some storms last days."

A wax-mustached man wearing a cowboy hat seated beside Shirley raised a hand. "If you like skiing, you gotta experience Mt. Bohemia. It has the highest vertical drop in the Midwest."

"Yeah!" Arnie fisted the air.

A server, dressed in a long-sleeved black T-shirt and a blue-and-white bandana, deposited a wax-paper-lined wicker basket overflowing with battered fish on the table.

More servers followed and dispersed large ceramic dishes.

They ate family-style, passing bowls of crisped white fish, brook trout, and walleye as well as hot, vinegary German potato salad and a bowl of what Jeannie would have called goulash, but the Yoopers all referred to the concoction as hot dish.

The Yoopers imbibed with gusto. They chewed with their mouths open, talked with their mouths full, and tossed food into their mouths at a speed that vied with popping corn kernels in flashing oil. Jeannie cinched her eyebrows together. *Where in that Red Cross Safety manual are instructions for saving a choking victim?* Images of quickly turning black-and-white pages illustrated with line drawings of endangered body parts flashed through her mind. *And God forbid, what about fishbones lodged inside throats?*

Sighing, Jeannie turned her focus from fishbones to the well-grooved puncheon floor. *Did Bruce or any of the legions of young men assigned to the Upper Peninsula's Civilian Conservation Corps have a part in getting this lumber into this surface?* Leaning into Nick, Jeannie tapped his arm.

He turned and gazed into her eyes.

"I didn't have the chance to tell you about Hannah's very cool discovery."

"Did I hear my name?" Hannah asked.

"I'm telling Nick about the memoirs you found. He should be interested. A young man in the Civilian Conservation Corps stationed on Isle Royale wrote some of the letters. Sure was a primitive site then."

"Oh, yeah, what time frame are we talking about?" Nick steepled his hands.

"Nineteen thirty-five." Hannah chewed on the end

of a straw. "Hey, I'll tell you who knows a lot of the CCC history—Shirley's husband, Otto." Hannah stood, walked past Shirley, and tapped the shoulder of the waxed mustache wearer. "Come with me and educate the trolls. They are interested in CCC history."

Grabbing an empty seat from the table behind them, Otto turned the chair to face him, straddled the apron, and pressed his chest against the backrest. "Most people believe the CCC was one of Roosevelt's greatest accomplishments. The initiative put unemployed, impoverished men to work at a time in our nation when jobs were hard to come by. For some guys, joining the CCC meant the difference between worrying about where their next meal came from and where they could earn some money to help their families." He scratched his nose and tugged on one end of his mustache.

Jeannie frowned.

"The men had to apply to their local CCC boards, and they had to pass some physical requirements. They had to be at least five feet tall, and they couldn't be over six feet five inches." Otto chuckled. "I saw you walk in." He gazed down his nose at Nick. "You might not have made the cut. How tall are you anyway?"

"I would have had to take my shoes off. I'm six foot three." Nick shook his head.

Otto pointed his right index finger and stabbed the air. "Let's talk about weight. To qualify, a man had to weigh at least one hundred and seven pounds."

Arnie laughed and patted his stomach. "No problem here."

"Well, get this requirement." Otto drew a breath. "A man had to have at least three teeth on the top and the bottom."

Jeannie shrunk her shoulders. She gasped. "No."
Oh, the poor, poor souls.

"My God," Nick muttered.

Shirley set her elbows on the table and dropped her chin into her right fist.

Under his tartan tam, Martin furrowed his eyebrows and absently scraped one of his fingernails against the label glued onto his beer bottle.

Otto wiped a palm over his mouth and wiped his hand on his pants. "They had to agree to send at least twenty-two dollars of the thirty dollars a month they earned back home to help their families."

Hannah jumped and set the table on edge.

An empty bottle tipped over. *Clink.*

The Copper Harbor Historical Society president bent to retrieve the rolling hops-smelling container. "Oops. Hey, there's my cousin. Get ready for some polka, folks!" Hannah brandished a hand.

Waving back, a squat, square-faced man, sporting a silvery-edged accordion similar to a warrior breastplate grinned. He thumped the instrument's keys like a guitarist executing a riff. *He's got the same reddish hair and whole-face smile.* Jeannie grinned.

"Let me finish this up before things get really wild." Otto ran a hand over the crest of his hairline. "It is my humble opinion that, as a nation, we owe a debt of gratitude to President Franklin Delano Roosevelt and those young men in the CCC. Those men built our national park system into what we enjoy today."

Nick raised his beer mug. "Cheers to the CCC."

A chorus of "Hear yees" and glass clinking followed.

Other band members strained as they lugged guitar,

violin, harmonica cases, speakers, and long hanks of electrical wires.

Bright lights flooded a dim and empty wall.

"Don't forget to add the part about Isle Royale, Otto." Hannah bounced her shoulders.

"You bet. Isle Royale was established as a national park in 1931. You know Isle Royale is Michigan's only national park, right?"

Nick nodded.

Jeannie held up an index finger.

"If you two get the chance, stop and visit the CCC museum at the North Higgins Lake Camp Ground north of Roscommon."

"We go by there on our way back south. Maybe we can stop and take a tour." Nick turned to Jeannie.

"I'd like that. We could stretch our legs a bit, and I could take pictures of the grounds." Jeannie nodded. A lightness filled her chest. *I like him asking my opinion. I like making plans with him.*

"Thanks so much, Otto." Nick clasped Otto's hand.

"Get your fill of fish?" Brushing an arm against hers, Nick grinned.

Jeannie crossed her eyes and made a fish mouth.

Nick slapped his thigh. "I'll take that as a *yes*. Can I get you another root beer, or do you want the real thing?" He eyed the four-foot-high kegs lining a wall adjacent to the bar.

"How about making the order a float? I'd love something sweet."

"I noticed a familiar tin in Mary's purse." Nick raised his eyebrows. "If we are due for good karma, it's brunscrackers, and they are for us."

"She did say she had the recipe for me. I think

you're right. In the meantime, yes, I would like another root beer. Thank you."

"Be right back." Nick sidestepped through a gelling crowd.

Disco lights flashed.

Hannah's cousin's accordion wheezed.

Nick disappeared in the pack.

Martin lifted Mary's right wrist to his mouth and kissed the space between her sweatshirt cuff and the flesh. Still gripping her hand, Martin led his wife to the dance floor.

Sliding off his chair, Otto moved behind Shirley, grasped the back of her chair, and pulled slowly.

Shirley rose, grabbed Otto's upper arm, and led him to the band.

"Let's go!" Escorting the reluctant left-behinds, Hannah emptied everyone's table except Jeannie's.

Raucous reverberations thrummed against Jeannie's skin.

The over-the-Mighty Mac dwellers danced like they feasted—like heathens. Jeannie giggled.

"We've got the table all to ourselves." Nick set the non-foamy root beer on the tabletop, sat, and edged his chair closer. He levered one long blue-jean-clad leg on Martin's empty chair. Nick leaned back in a chair dwarfed by his frame, tipped his beer bottle to his lips, and gulped.

Tendons bulged underneath his chin and throat.

Sucking noises pulsed in Jeannie's ears. She slid her fingers through the mug's handle and grated the frosty bottom over the tabletop.

The liquid content sloshed.

"Having fun?" Nick asked.

Squeezing the mug grip like a life ring, Jeannie squirmed. She lifted her cheeks in a crowning smile. "A blast."

Nick gulped another sip of beer and set the bottle on the table. "I'm glad. You deserve some lightheartedness in your responsibility-laden life."

Jeannie sighed. *He's studying me with the practiced patience of a man trained to analyze every tiny nuance.* "Thank you for that." She scanned the dance floor, the tables littered with grease-stained paper plates, and the dusty elk, deer, and moose racks hanging on the wall behind the nimble-fingered musicians.

The polka band music switched from three-instrument arrangements.

Accordion rasping claimed the limelight.

The dancing crowd quickened their steps.

Hannah's cousin pumped the accordion buttons.

Chairs emptied.

The dance floor filled.

From either end of the lit-in-dangling-Christmas-lights bar, taps on wooden kegs flipped to the up position just long enough to prime their pumps.

"C'mon, you two." Hannah rushed the table and grabbed Nick's hand.

Coming from behind Hannah, Patty, red-faced and giggling, clasped Jeannie's elbow. The Copper Harbor textile preservationist waited for the troll preservationist to slide from her chair and then pushed Jeannie into the wiggling, frolicking throng. With one hand, Patty gripped Jeannie's waist. She wove the fingers of her other hand through the digits in Jeannie's left hand. Patty pushed their clasped hands down and hopped on one foot. Then, she stalled and locked her gaze with

Jeannie's. "Polka is an easy dance in two-four time. The movements are steps and hops. Left foot forward, right foot forward, left foot forward, hop on your right. Ready?"

Jeannie blinked her eyes and gummed her lips. She pressed a palm against Patty's sweating palm.

Patty jolted ahead and traced the step pattern.

Jeannie stumbled through the choreography.

"Good, good. Let's try the pattern in reverse: right foot forward, left foot forward, right foot forward, and hop on your left." Patty's breath blew in huffy chunks.

"Oops, 'scuse us." Hannah chuckled as she backed into Jeannie. "I'm trying to wrangle this guy into this Polish courtship dance." She inhaled, stopped, and threw up her hands. "And this big *galute* has progressed from sweet wooing into a full-fledged engagement. For crying in the beer cheese soup!"

Peering over the top of Hannah's head, Nick winked. "I've been on the polka circuit since grade school. Lots of Polish weddings in my past."

Hannah dropped Nick's hand and bent over her knees. "I'm trading." She grabbed Patty's waist and pushed Nick toward Jeannie.

"How about slowing it down, folks?" the band's vocalist asked. "Rob is jumping in on the concertina, and Sophie is adding the clarinet. Enjoy."

The music swapped tempo to a lyric three-quarter beat.

Nick wrapped his right arm over his stomach and stretched his left across his back. He bowed. "Madam."

Jeannie placed her right hand into his left hand. She lifted the hem of her pretend ball gown with her free hand. "Sir."

Drawing her close, Nick glided over the outside perimeter of the dance area.

Beneath her crushed breasts, her eager heart beat in staccato.

As he reached the corners of the dance floor, Nick raised their joined hands and executed a smooth turn. "Oompa." He hummed in her ear, digging his chin into her head.

She breathed in the tangled scent of woodsmoke, cooking oil, piney hops, and man sweat.

"Hey, you're a quick learner. You sure you never danced the polka?" Nick leaned back and gazed into her eyes.

You might think I'm steady on my feet, but truth be told, I'm falling.

Chapter 21

On Thursday morning, the crew finished packing.

With all the artifacts condensed into tagged boxes and no reason to turn up the temperature, the temporary sorting and packing building for the Eriksson collection transformed into a cold, empty cave.

Nick gathered his tools. *If we leave by noon, we should be home by midnight.*

The *joie de vivre* of the past days had evaporated.

Furrowed brows, tight lips, and accelerated taping, stacking, and transferring motions gained momentum as the coffeepots emptied and the Great Lakes University trailer grew fuller.

I'm really gonna miss this. What great folks. Nick rotated his shoulders and stretched his neck.

At the other end of the room, Jeannie, too, wore a look of dogged determination. If he had to guess, she regretted their visit end.

"One last box. Jeannie, Nick, I need both of you," Patty shouted.

All four flaps sagged loosely.

Nick hung back until Jeannie neared the cardboard container Patty held tightly at chest level.

Jeannie reached Patty and peered inside the container. "Oh, my goodness," she squealed. Then, she clapped her hands to her cheeks.

Patty set the box atop an empty table.

Tiny mewling sounds rent the chill air.

Nick's breath seized. His chest tightened.

In slow motion, Jeannie tunneled into the box and extracted a smoky-gray, weeks-old kitten.

Nick froze.

Jeannie tucked the kitten's limbs and tail into a ball and stroked its tiny, white-striped head. "Nick, come and look."

From a persona split from his past, Nick allowed himself to place a finger pad on the space between the kitten's ears and stroke its downy fur. He touched gently the wet nose and the wee clenched jaw. His heart jumped and knocked against his rib cage. Transferring the baby cat as if she handled a valuable, ancient pottery artifact, Jeannie placed the kitten into the folds of Nick's arms.

"These poor babies have a feral as a mom. I found them in my barn three weeks ago. I can't keep all of them. So, I'm hoping I will find some homes." Patty hovered over the box. "I know both of you love animals, so I thought I'd give you the first shot."

Gripping the edges of the moving box, Jeannie peered inside. "They are all so different. I see an orange-and-white tabby, a black, a calico, and the gray one Nick is holding. The gray one reminds me of a miniature wolf."

Wolf. Nick grasped tenderly one front paw and extended the kitten's leg. Claws so tiny and transparent they appeared non-threatening, jutted like talons.

The kitten mewed and opened its eyes.

Blue. Blue eyes. Hello, Wolf.

"Could we share custody?" Jeannie laid a hand on Nick's arm.

Nick grinned. "I'm game."

"Joey would be thrilled. I'm not sure about Gunther, but he can adjust."

"I'm not sure about Sam, but I think Wolf could be a pal while I'm gone."

"Wolf, is it?" Jeannie squeezed Nick's arm. "What a perfect name. Hey, Patty, we'll take this one."

"Congratulations and thank you. I prepared some take-home boxes. Your new kitty has a travel container with a food dish, a water dish, a blanket, and a litter container." Patty walked through the room. "Kittens, kittens, who wants a kitten?"

"Some lucky kitty gets a new home." Hannah petted the tiny kitten in Nick's arms. She handed Jeannie an envelope.

Moving her hands like a smoky campfire storyteller, Hannah exhibited flabbergasted excitement. Nick stared, his hackles rising on the back of his neck.

Jeannie nodded and stuffed the envelope into her pocket.

Huddled with their backs to him, the ladies traded words and earnest gazes.

Wonder what that's all about? Nick narrowed his eyes.

Hannah stuck her fingers in her mouth and whistled. "Last box secure. Great job, everyone."

"Don't forget you were born a Yooper. No sissy meowing. No sissy pouncing. Roar and kill!" Patty lifted Wolf from Nick's arms, kissed him on the head, and lowered him into the take-home container. She passed the box to Jeannie.

Steve slapped Nick on the back. He squeezed Jeannie's shoulder.

Then, the Upper Peninsula residents passed Lower Peninsula citizens around the room for more slaps and hugs.

"Good-bye, trolls," Hannah called.

Nick swallowed. He cleared his throat and the wad of melancholy that clumped there. "Good-bye, Yoopers. Hope you sissies make it through the winter." The mammalogist waved and stepped outside.

Cackles and hoots echoed as Jeannie followed.

A slight whisper trailed through the tall pines—the sole interloper to a great silence.

Turning, Nick registered the somber expression on Jeannie's face. *Now that we've confessed our attraction to each other, life is forever changed.*

****

"Thanks for warming the truck." Jeannie removed her mittens and set them atop her lap.

Nick checked his side-view mirror and nodded.

"Would you like me to read you some of the letters from the CCC artifacts?" Jeannie asked.

"That would be an entertaining way to while the time, especially since we won't have good radio reception for another forty miles."

Sighing, Jeannie turned and peered through the triangular vent window. "Those delicate, wispy, high-flying clouds remind me of the Battenburg lace on Mrs. Eriksson's wedding gown."

"You really should catalog those clouds as cirrus lace." Nick beat the palm of his left hand against the dashboard.

"Trying to infiltrate the world of a textile curator, are you?" Jeannie smiled.

Turning his head from side to side, Nick smiled. "I

am happy in the domain of skins and scats."

"Speaking of scats, let me check our cat." Jeannie peeked into the box at her feet. "Curled up and sleeping." She reached for her briefcase stowed beneath her seat. She plunked the case onto her lap, snapped open the hinge, withdrew a pair of cotton gloves, and threaded them over her fingers and thumb. Then, she extracted the letters. She cleared her throat. She turned to Nick. Against a dove-gray sky, Nick's profile evoked a mysteriously sensuous guise. A five-day reprieve from a razor allowed the growth of a soft, auburn beard. Saliva pooled in Jeannie's mouth. She swallowed. "First, I think I need to give you some backstory."

Gripping the steering wheel, Nick nodded.

"Hannah and I sorted this out. A young man named Bruce Kline kept a diary. Then, there are two piles of letters. One originates from Bruce. He wrote letters to both his mother and to a woman named Margie, apparently his sweetheart. The other group of letters originated from Margie and were addressed to Bruce."

"So, the entire collection was retained by a later married couple?"

"No."

"What the heck?" Nick frowned.

"The letters from Margie were all opened and, by their appearances, handled. Some of Margie's letters reveal obvious grease stains and evidence of a dark liquid spillage. There are no return letters from Bruce's mother." Jeannie expelled a shuddering breath. "*Pffft.* Bruce's letters to Margie, even though sealed and stamped, bear no postmark."

"Wow, now I'm intrigued. Tell me more."

"Yeah, well, hold your pants until I read you the

bomb letter."

"What?" Nick smacked the dashboard.

Whump.

"Before we left this morning, Hannah gave me one of the letters she found hidden within the flap of a bound Bible in the same box. As a result of what she learned, Hannah is determined to remedy a thirty-year wrong. And I agreed to help."

"Humph?" Nick tented his eyebrows.

"So, Hannah and Patty went through the letters and put them in date order. Here is the first one." Jeannie straightened her spine and held the paper.

"Dearest Margie,

Our days are pretty predictable. Its reveille at six a.m. Captain Murphy leads us in calisthenics, and then we have breakfast. Mostly, it's oatmeal and salt pork. Then, we have chores of cleaning the camp. By eight a.m., we are off to the work site. We are building a trail from Senter Point to Lake Desor. Lumber companies left a lot of trash wood, so we have to clear mounds of timber slashings. Captain says we will build a ski-patrol cabin and a dock real close to our camp. I am itching to build things again, so I will like that detail."

"Oh yeah, Lake Desor is between Minong Ridge on the west side and Greenstone Ridge in the center." Nick scratched his thigh. "I think one of the things I enjoy the most about Isle Royale is its pristine, unspoiled beauty. There are no cars. It's hard for me to imagine Isle Royale without wolves, but those predators were not there when Bruce the letter writer and his comrades worked on the Isle." He whistled low. "In the 1940s, a minor pack of wolves crossed ice-encrusted Lake Superior and landed on Isle Royale."

"I have been pondering the existing wolf persona. Historically, wolves are portrayed as monsters and bloodthirsty marauders. Think of fairy tales—the big bad wolf is pretty prevalent." Jeannie sighed. "Wolves have been given a bad rap for centuries. Is that fair?"

"I like your way of thinking." Nick patted Jeannie's left hand. He lowered his shoulders and head and stared out the windshield. "I know we wanted to stop in Roscommon to view the CCC grounds, but I think we should save that excursion for another time and stick to getting home." He formed his lips in a straight line.

"I agree." *Those clouds look pretty scary.*

"But there is one thing we don't need to save."

"Hmmm?"

"Mary's brunscrackers. I saw that tin she snuck you the other night. Where did you hide the cookies?" He turned and batted his eyelashes.

She reached under the seat, grabbed the round container, pried off the lid, and extracted a flaky cookie. Jeannie took a deep breath. "Wow, these smell like a Polish bakery."

Nick held out his right hand.

"Enjoy your treat." Jeannie deposited the cookies into Nick's open palm. "Meanwhile, back to Bruce's letter and the wonders he found."

"The island overflows with beautiful trees and vegetation. We were happy to find thimbleberry shrubs for two reasons. Because it is now late summer, the berries are red and ripe. They are rather tart. Sure wish I had some sugar to add. But the best use we have found for this plant is its leaves. Thimbleberry leaves are large, about the size of maple leaves. They are soft

and fuzzy. They make perfect toilet paper. All of us in the company have harvested a personal collection of the leaves and stored them in our pockets. We will be glad we did."

"My goodness, the riches of Isle Royale." Jeannie giggled.

"What, didn't you know about the secondary use of thimbleberry leaves?" Nick smirked. "I take it you have no primitive camping experience."

"Hey, you should know I have used a pit toilet or two," Jeannie retorted.

"Really?" Nick bounced the seat.

"I do admit rolls of toilet paper strung from wall pegs."

He snickered.

"Hey, Nick. Mind if I close my eyes for a while? This radiant sunshine makes me sleepy. I promise to take a turn driving after a teeny nap."

"Sure." He rotated the radio dial and, after sampling a few stations, settled on the one with the least static, and licked buttery remains off his fingers.

"Zzzzzz…"

Great—static and snores. Nick glanced at Jeannie. Her lashes trembled against her skin. Her mouth parted just enough to view the soft flesh on the underside of her lip. *If only two bees would pilot that beautiful face. I'd have an excuse to run my fingers through her hair, over her ears, and stroke her cheeks.*

From the corner of his eye, the cirrus clouds plummeted and rolled in a southwest direction. Wispy white moments ago, the puffs curdled into clumps of stone gray.

A flock of seagulls winged low over a field of

summer crop remnants.

Inside the truck, the internal temperature dropped ten degrees.

Nick shivered. *Snow and from what I see—a potential blizzard. Damn.*

****

Whap-whap-whap.

"What?" Jeannie stretched and yawned.

Moving in a tandem arc, the windshield wipers swiped the truck window.

Ping-ping-ping.

Icy crystals rushed the windshield and melted.

Jeannie wrapped her arms around her chest and turned her head toward Nick. The skin over his knuckles stretched tight against the bones underneath. His eyes reflected the steely hue of obsidian. "Nick?" Her voice withered.

"Watch for an exit sign. We've got a serious whiteout going. The last municipal sign I saw was the town of Delaware."

Jeannie clasped her hands, buried them in the warmth of her knees, and rooted her head to a forty-five-degree turn.

Despite the abundance of historical trivia dropped on her this past week, the commonplace name Delaware set off an internal alarm bell. In telling the story of Heikki Luunta, historian Arnie credited the town of Delaware as the goddess's home away from Finland. Delaware also had the meteorological distinction of snow capital of the Midwest. Once a mining town and eight hundred feet above sea level, Delaware possessed perfect conditions to morph into a naturally created snow monument. Long since neglected, Delaware's ghostly inhabitants bore no interest in plowing snow from her pathways.

A wad of anxiety thickened in Jeannie's throat. Delaware was a mere fourteen miles south of Copper Harbor. They had over three hundred miles to reach home and wouldn't get there tonight.

Snowflakes as wide as dragonflies pelted the windshield at a dizzying speed. Jeannie recognized a shifting-in-reverse sensation.

"Jeannie, it's too dangerous to drive." Nick's voice reverberated with take-charge confidence.

She closed her eyes shut and inhaled a deep breath. *I'm a partner here, not just an unwilling participant.* She opened her eyes, leaned forward to the brink of falling, and thrust her nose within inches of the windshield. Wiping condensation off the bottom edge of the glass, she peered outside.

"I'm pulling off the road as far as possible. Roll down your window and stick your head out. Let me know if you see any barriers. I'll go slowly."

Straining from her waist, Jeannie pumped hastily on the handle to turn the window. A blast of ice-greedy pellets blew up her nose and pricked her face. "As far as I can tell, you're good." Her voice jutted backward into the cab of the truck.

In excruciatingly measured motion, Nick veered the truck off the road.

The truck skidded. The trailer slid in the opposite direction.

Jeannie thrust her palms onto the dashboard as the freeform motion cinched her seatbelt tight against her chest.

Nick held fast to the steering wheel.

Screech.

Jeannie rotated the window gear into a closed position.

Pressing her thigh, Nick expelled a deep breath. "Are you okay?"

"Yes, fine." She brushed snow from her eyelids and her shoulders.

"Can you open the truck's glove compartment? An emergency flag should be in there."

"Got it." Jeannie passed a reflective cloth across the seat.

Nick pulled the collar of his coat around his ears. He yanked a knit hat over his head and gloves over his hands. "Open your luggage and drag out warm clothing. Stack layers on. I'll check the trailer and attach this flag."

"Be careful, Nick." She stiffened her spine.

Mother-honed adrenaline coursed her veins.

Thrusting his shoulder against the door, Nick jumped from the cab and slammed it shut. Immediately, his form disappeared in an onslaught of swirling white flakes.

Jeannie stretched her turtleneck collar over her nose and shivered. *Joey will be so disappointed when I am not there to wake him up tomorrow.*

Whump-whump.

He's kicking the tires.

A blast of cold air surged into the cab. The truck door flapped back and forth.

"Yikes!" Nick catapulted onto the bench seat, conveyed a snowpack with him, and yanked shut the door. "We're off the highway by at least four feet. Thank God." He threw off his hat and gloves and swept melting snow from his jacket, eyelashes, and five-day-old beard. He shook his head and met Jeannie's gaze. "So, here's the plan. We bundle up. Every thirty minutes, I'll go out and clear the tailpipe. We'll run the heater when we can't stand the cold but try to conserve gas. We'll take turns sleeping. Jeannie, we need to be a team on this. We'll be okay, trust me."

Rolling her lower lip, Jeannie nodded.

"I'll take the first watch since I'm alert from the cold." He patted the layers of sweatshirts and sweaters and tucked them around her shoulders and chest.

"Okay." Jeannie pulled the knit cap over her ears and burrowed her head into her chest.

The winds buffeted the truck in a cradle-rocking rhythm.

The insulative warmth from wool fibers enveloped her. Her eyelids grew heavy.

Joey's baby cheeks heaved like an accordion. He gurgled and kicked his feet against her thighs. The doorbell rang. She fell to her knees. A tightly muscled butt clad in gray figure-hugging shorts appeared ahead. The cool, musty basement evoked a buried lust. A rough palm smoothed her hair.

"Jeannie, wake up." Nick brushed her cheeks.

She opened her eyes and rubbed her temples.

Two pairs of oncoming arcing lights bounced. They split and went on either side of the truck, the whine of their engines so loud the sound pierced the snow layers, the metal truck, and Jeannie's thick hat.

Two alien-like creatures brushed snow from the passenger front windows and peered in.

Nick waved and pushed against his door.

The wind howled. The engines revved.

One of the aliens stuck his helmeted head in the door. "You folks all right? We're from the Houghton County rescue team. How does a warm bed and a hot meal sound?"

"Too good to be true," Nick hollered. "We've got a trailer full of museum artifacts. Is it safe to leave?"

"Any open peanut butter in there?" The stranger held fast to the door handle, lifted his face shield, and revealed a handsome bearded face.

"No." Nick shook his head.

"Well, you're pretty much good to go. No bear's gonna bother breakin' in, and no thief is out in this storm."

"We'll take you up on that offer then."

"We have snowmobile outfits, protective headgear, and gloves. Put them on. Secure your vehicle. Then, we'll take you to Greenstone Cottages. Have either of you ridden a snowmobile?" Not delaying for an answer, the man continued. "Just hold onto the driver's waist and lean into the curves. That's about all. We should reach the destination within thirty minutes. We'll give you a few minutes to suit up and grab a small pack with essentials." Then, he shut the truck door.

Grabbing a small duffel bag, Nick fumbled through his backpack and removed some items. "If you want to add things like a toothbrush and paste and a change of clothes, use this. I'll do the same, and I will hang onto this during our snow ride. Give me Wolf. He can ride on my chest. Do you have a T-shirt we can wrap around him?"

Forget the makeup. Forget the hair products. Limit this to pajamas, a change of undies, socks, and T-shirts. Jeannie clenched her teeth and combed through her backpack. She culled the items, wadded them, and stuffed them inside Nick's bag. She set aside a T-shirt, levered Wolf from his travel nest, wrapped him in the shirt, and tendered the twitching kitten to Nick. Then, she tugged on the emergency snow apparel.

Zip.

From head to toe, Nick now presented as an extra-terrestrial. He glanced over. "Ready? I'll meet you at Greenstone Cottages." Then, he shoved his shoulder against the door and jumped outside.

A rescuer opened the front-seat passenger door from the outside.

A swirling mass of breath-sucking, ice-pelting wind rammed Jeannie and threw her off balance.

One of the aliens slammed shut the door, clamped a gloved hand over Jeannie's wrist, and guided her onto the backseat of his snow machine.

Clinging with gloves too large for her small hands to a stranger's waist, Jeannie tucked her head and braced her limbs.

Gasoline fumes tunneled through the helmet crevices. Machinery thrumming, jerks, and jolts rattled her body.

Ice spheroids pelted and seared the unprotected flesh around her eyes and latched to her eyelashes and brows.

Thirty minutes later, she and Nick huddled in the white-pine paneled office of Greenstone Lodge.

A mustached, dimple-anointed, beefy, middle-aged man stuck out his snowshoe-sized hand and pumped Nick's hand. "Hi, I'm Gerry Boom-Boom Nickles. You folks sure rode into a whale of a snowstorm." He dropped his overdeveloped arm on the shoulders of the brunette at his side. "This is my woman, Carol. She puts up with me. She's a really sexy babe, too." Playfully, he swatted her backside. "We've been married for twenty-nine short years. Can't see my life without her."

"Honey, stop. You're embarrassing these poor, wet, freezing people." Carol turned to Nick and Jeannie. "You folks okay sharing a cottage? With the dogsled races this weekend and this storm, there's only one cottage left for miles." In the silence that followed, the innkeeper looked from Nick to Jeannie.

Shock waves ricocheted Jeannie's body. *Alone. We'll be alone.*

Nick alternated his weight from his right foot to his left, withdrew a handkerchief from his pocket, pressed the cloth to his mouth, and rubbed his nose. Then, he wadded the fabric and stuck it into his back pocket. "Well, of course, we're grateful to be out of the storm and for the rescue."

"So, how about you two get out of these wet clothes, come into the dining room, and I'll feed you? In the meantime, Gerry will take your gear to your cabin and get a fire going." Carol turned.

"Gotta be honest. We have a tagalong." Nick unzipped his suit, reached inside, and withdrew Wolf.

"Oh, my." Carol reached for the kitten. "Oh, you poor thing, out in this crazy weather." With Wolf tucked under her arm, she pointed to a closet. "Gerry, we've got Ozzie's old dog carrier in there. That will work for a temporary kitty home." She fluttered a hand. "Gerry, make sure our bedroom door is closed. We'll let Ozzie out after we all get settled."

"That is so gracious." Jeannie bent, tugged off her

boots, unzipped the one-piece snowsuit, and stepped out. She folded the foul-weather gear and laid it on the floor. "I wonder if I could use your telephone? I'll be happy to reimburse you for the charge."

"Of course. You'll find a phone hanging on that wall." Carol pointed.

Following Carol's direction, Jeannie reached the phone, gripped the receiver, and dialed her home phone number.

Her father-in-law answered the call.

Explaining the situation and her estimated return date and receiving a good report on Joey's mood and behavior, Jeannie nodded. Then, she hung up the receiver. She met Nick's gaze, made a fist, and stuck up a thumb.

Gerry lugged the carrier to the kitchen floor.

After Carol lined the bottom with a dish towel, she placed Wolf inside the mesh-walled short-term shelter and set the carrier by a heat vent.

Nick shed his outer layer and placed the items next to Jeannie's. He stepped to the dining room table and withdrew a chair.

Jeannie slid into the maple-spooled chair. Nick's light touch against her back as he moved her chair close to the table sent shivers down her spine. She flinched. The savory aroma of dill weed and tomatoes sparked her appetite. The close presence of Nick's flannel-wrapped arm on the tabletop flamed her desire.

Carol placed a butter dish and a basket of thick-sliced, marbled rye bread on the table's center. After returning to the kitchen, she padded back with two bowls of steaming soup. Setting them on placements fronting them, she pulled two spoons from her apron pocket and dispensed them to Jeannie and Nick. "I'll be right back with ice water." She paused and winked. "Maybe you'd prefer hot tea?"

"Water is good," Jeannie answered.

"Me, too." Nick chuckled.

Silence enveloped them except for the *tick-tick-ticking* of the mantel clock resting above the hearth where a cheery fire licked hoary-skinned logs.

We'll be secluded in a cabin with a romantic fire. She nibbled on the hard-crusted roll and swallowed. Jeannie's throat tightened around the piece of bread lodged there. She coughed and reached for a glass of water.

Heat rushed her cheeks. She pressed her palms against the hot patches on her face and braved a glance at Nick. Matted on one side and spiky on the other, Nick's hair, coupled with the scrawny stubble on his face, rendered a mussed-up, mildly macho persona. Jeannie slumped in her chair.

The door pitched open.

Gerry Boom-Boom stomped snow-covered boots on the sisal mat inside the doorway. He removed a pair of fur mittens and rubbed his palms together. "Got a cozy fire going with plenty of firewood. Even turned down the sheets." He winked at Carol. "You two ready?"

Wiping her mouth with a paper napkin, Jeannie stepped out of her chair. She registered tremors streaming through her legs.

"Back you go into your snowsuits." Gerry offered a wry smile. "I suggest we hold hands. It's not a long walk, but you can't see anything recognizable outside."

"Watch your steps. A rock garden is buried out

there," Carol chimed.

Nick threaded his feet through the snowmobile pants. He hoisted the top of the suit and thrust his arms through the sleeves. Retrieving Wolf from the carrier, he pressed the kitten against his chest. He passed the carrier to Gerry. Then he pulled on a hat, tugged the snowmobile hood over his head, and zipped the garment from ankle to chin.

Jeannie's heart lurched into her throat. She gulped, and then donned her winter survival outfit. In only moments, she and Nick would traipse hand-in-hand through a world of disappearing white, in a world she had only fantasized about.

****

Nick wrapped his gloved hand over Jeannie's wrist.

Gerry commandeered Jeannie's other hand.

As Nick stepped from the porch of the Greenstone Lodge office, he watched his boot disappear under a foot of snow, visible by the lone lantern Gerry held at eye level.

Moving slowly between them, Jeannie tucked her head.

A chain attached to a flag pole swung and alternately banged against the iron, sounding a metallic clanging.

Inside Nick's snowmobile suit, the tiny kitten clung to his shirt and periodically stretched his claws against the top three buttons. With his free hand, Nick gently massaged the kitten's back through the puffy fabric.

Stopping abruptly, Gerry dropped Jeannie's wrist. He held his gloved hand at shoulder height, stepped a few feet forward, and dragged a large fallen tree limb from their path. Then, he captured Jeannie's hand, stepped ahead, and continued his lead.

The snow depth alternated from foot deep to knee deep, and for a perilous ten feet, the snow reached thigh level.

Raising the lantern above his head, Gerry slowed. He pointed.

A cabin lit from within came into view.

Underneath the soft kitten fur, Nick's heart agitated like an agate breaking ice.

Gerry tapped his foot against the cabin's entryway. Then, he dropped Jeannie's hand, tugged on the cabin door's latch, thrust his shoulder against the door, and pushed against the log construction. He set the kitten carrier inside the entrance.

Like a beacon, a crackling fire danced in the hearth and propelled Nick inside.

Pristine, knotty pine boards faced every wall and cathedral-ceilinged surface. Overstuffed easy chairs, split-log end tables, amber-colored lamps, and an oversized sofa rested upon a large braided rug.

A galley kitchen featured a full-size stove and refrigerator. A coffeemaker, toaster, dish drainer, and cutting board set on the kitchen counters.

Behind a curtained door, a four-poster bed with a turned-down chenille bedspread lingered.

Nick scoured four front teeth over his bottom lip. Every fiber in his body vibrated. Every muscle in his body stiffened.

Without removing any of his gear, Gerry pointed to a closed door. "That's the bathroom. It's nice and warm with the door closed. I put a box in there for the kitten with some food, water, and a stuffed toy. He should be happy. Carol serves breakfast at nine. And speaking of Carol, she sent along a bedtime snack." Gerry unzipped his suit, pulled out a paper bag, and gave it to Nick. Then he dropped keys into Nick's hand. "Storm's supposed to go all day tomorrow. I'd plan on spending another night. It'll take at least twenty-four hours for the county boys to clear the highways. In weather like this, it's best to travel during daylight. Well, have a good night."

Nick stepped to the door and gripped the handle on the top of Wolf's cage. "Thanks again, Gerry. We sure appreciate all your kindness."

Gerry closed the door behind him.

A delicate pine scent permeated the cabin.

Jeannie shrugged off her boots, hat, and snowsuit. She ran her hands through her long hair, bent from the waist, and shook her head. Standing upright, she smiled. "That felt good."

Breath stuck in Nick's throat. He set the carrier down, unzipped his suit, and passed Wolf to Jeannie. He removed his boots and slipped off the rest of his gear. "I'll get Wolf settled." Nuzzling the kitten to his face, Nick entered the bathroom and placed the transporter on the floor. He opened the hatch, pushed Wolf inside, secured the closure, and set the container next to a floor vent. His hands trembled. *How can I keep my hands off her? I don't want to rush this. I don't want to ruin this. I don't want Elizabeth again. That's over.*

"Do you mind if I use the bathroom?" Jeannie poked her head inside the door. She crouched next to the kitty carrier. "He looks like he has everything he needs." She put a finger through the carrier slats and petted Wolf. "Goodnight, baby howler. Sleep tight."

Nick stepped aside, allowed Jeannie to pass around him, and secured the door behind him. He crumpled his fingers into a fist. *I'm leaving the decision up to her.*

****

Jeannie gripped the small porcelain sink and confronted the bathroom mirror. She trembled. *Where are my cosmetic case and my electric curlers? Where are my perfume and my gardenia-smelling body lotion?* She raked her upper teeth over her bottom lip. She turned her head, stretched her neck to view the left side of her face, and then she reversed the turn. *Jeannie Parks, you deserve happiness. Jeannie Parks, you have been so lonely. Jeannie Parks, embrace this unexpected moment.* She turned on the faucet and ran cold water. She splashed her face, brushed her teeth with her index finger, finger-combed her hair, and opened the door.

Nick squatted before the fire and jammed an iron poker between two red-glazed logs.

"Cold, cold." Jeannie jumped on the cabin's tile floor.

Still gripping the tool, Nick turned. Forged by the fire, Nick's face steeled. In slow motion, he returned the poker to its stand on the hearth. He dropped his head on his chest. Nick turned and stretched to his full height. He stepped forward and closed the gap between them. Gently and at arm's length, Nick clasped Jeannie's triceps. He dipped his head to meet her gaze. "Jeannie, do you believe in destiny?"

She raised her chin to search his eyes and to observe his handsome face now sprinkled in whiskers and windburn. Her heart raced. Her lips quivered. She met his gaze with an unflinching assent.

"Jeannie, let's just take this gift. Let's not analyze the situation as we scientists do. Let's *carpe diem*. Seize the day."

"And what about the night, Nick? What about the night?" He answered her by squeezing her upper arms, bending his head to hers, and thrilling her with the taste of winter lust seasoned by a spring day introduction, a summer's day sail on Lake Lansing, and a fall field trip with kindergartners. His kiss was flavored with snowmobile exhaust, spearmint-flavored gum, and pinewood smoke.

Scooping an arm under her knees, he lifted her and carried her. With his free hand, he parted the curtained bedroom door.

Jeannie clung to his chest.

Nick set her butt atop the bed, knelt on the floor, and in fast succession, tugged off her socks, and stripped off her pants with both hands. He gripped the delicately rucked band and teased off her panties.

She stretched her toes and tensed her calves and thighs. "Nick…" She moaned and arched.

The weight of Nick's arms depressed the bedding on either side of her. He grasped her wrists and pushed them into the soft chenille bedspread. He held her like that as his mouth moved over her. Then, Nick sucked, nipped, explored, plundered, and stripped away every ounce of her resistance.

****

He nudged his chin into her mound. "Ah, you're so sweet—just as I imagined." Like a flash fire, warmth spread to his every muscle. He had wandered through the dense thickets of Isle Royale where sunlight struggled. A faint buzz caused him to stop, turn in a circle, and, there, in a luminesce of sunshine, a beehive dripping of golden honey hung. In any other territory, he would worry about a bear intrusion. But on the terrain of isolated Isle Royale, no bears lived. Standing twenty feet from the tree, Nick unzipped his backpack, extracted a canister of bee-repellent citronella, and slathered the substance on every bit of his naked skin. Then, he jumped the tree, dove two fingers into the warm, sticky queen wax and, in a moment of rapturous oneness with nature, took his fill. He had not expected to ever replicate the sensations of that intoxicating smell and texture but, here he was, taking his fill.

Jeannie shrieked. She erupted. She screamed and thrashed.

"You're beautiful, so beautiful," Nick murmured. He climbed atop the bed, pulled her to his chest and kissed her head. As he rocked in his arms, Nick smoothed her hair and tucked a strand behind her ears. "Sweet woman," he whispered into her ear.

Extending a hand, Jeannie caressed the denim waistband of his jeans. She poked her fingers along the inside of the band.

Nick groaned.

Jeannie flattened her hand and scratched her fingernails along the ridge of his fly.

"I'm dying." Nick's voice wavered.

"Oh, Nick. Let me save you." She unbuttoned the waistband and disengaged the zipper.

Nick wiggled out of his jeans and threw them on the floor.

Parting the fly on his cotton briefs, Jeannie grasped Nick's throbbing penis.

Nick skimmed his hands under her sweater, unhooked the back of her bra, slid the straps down her shoulders, and deftly plied them down her sleeves, over her hands, and shucked her from the tiny garment. He held the intimate apparel aloft in triumph like a primal warrior thrusting a scalp to his chief. Then he crossed his arms, reached for the hem of his T-shirt, pulled it over his head, and sent the garment the way of his jeans.

He rose on his knees and gazed down into Jeannie's wide-open eyes. "Only two to go." He grinned.

She held up her arms.

He pulled on the sleeves and divested her buttery-soft sweater. Hopping from the bed, he lengthened his spine and shrugged off his briefs.

Jeannie rolled under the covers and spread open the bed linens. "Come here." She growled. "Now."

He bent one knee and rolled onto the bed. He sprawled on his back and pulled her atop him.

Digging her toes into the bedding and grasping the pillow underneath his head, Jeannie leveraged her weight from the soles of her feet and ground her soft, warm body over Nick's tough and turgid body.

He wrapped his arms around her waist and compressed her body to his. Then, he fit his body into hers.

Outside, the wind rattled the cabin's timber shingles, jangled the paned windows, and whirled an opaque snowstorm that secreted the cabin.

Inside, the cries of delight and awe mingled with the hissing and crackling of seasoned maple limbs.

Flamed wood flashed and dropped tenderly as

spent embers.

Jeannie rolled off of Nick and nestled her head into his moist armpit. She kissed his bicep.

He ascended on one elbow, kissed her eyelids, and kissed her brow. He stuffed a pillow under her head. Then, he lay back and locked her body to his side between his neck and his calf. He grasped her left hand and kissed her palm.

"Oh, Nick—so good, so good." She breathed in deep, languishing breaths. "Thank you."

"My pleasure." He squeezed her open hand. "You're wonderful, so perfect. Before we both fall asleep, I'll check on Wolf." Nick pulled aside the covers, sat, and put his feet onto the braided wool rug. Then, he snugged the blankets over Jeannie and walked to the bathroom.

The air—denied heat as fire sparks palled—washed over his nakedness.

Goose bumps emerged on Nick's trunk.

Nick crossed his arms over his chest and crouched next to the kitten carrier. *Nobody's ever gonna harm you, little fella.* Turning his face back to the bed, he bit his bottom lip. *And that goes for you, too, Jeannie.*

"Hey, guy." Nick opened the gate and hooked two of his fingers under Wolf's tiny chest. He lifted the kitten and petted his head and his spine. Nick set him on the tile floor and tidied Wolf's enclosure. He refilled the water dish from the sink tap. Then, he sat cross-legged on the bedroom floor.

Wolf scampered over Nick's legs and feet.

Barefooted and wrapped in the bedspread, Jeannie padded to Nick and sank to her knees.

Sweet, sweet woman, the taste of you, the wild

abandonment of your lovemaking, the pinkness of your secret places. He shuddered.

She opened a fist and let a hair ribbon unfurl a few inches from Wolf's nose.

Wolf pounced.

Jeannie fluttered the ribbon in a corkscrew pattern.

Wolf swatted the air next to the dangling trim.

Yanking the ribbon before the kitten snagged it, Jeannie yawned.

To describe bliss I would use three words—ribbon, kitten, Jeannie. With lungs full of buoyancy he hadn't felt in a long time, Nick snatched the bedspread from Jeannie and pulled her onto his lap. He licked her neck, ears, and moist, puffy lips. Nick leaned over Jeannie and set Wolf back into his carrier. Then, he hoisted Jeannie from his lap, stood, and carried her to the bed. "Nighty-night time for you." He retrieved the coverlet from the floor and tucked blankets and the retrieved bedding around her naked form. He kissed her on the forehead, stared into her open eyes, crawled into the four-poster bed, and lay beside her. "See you in the morning."

She sighed, turned on her side, and nuzzled her pillow.

Nick lounged on his back and gazed at the cinnamon-brown knots embedded in the golden-white pine ceiling. Wintry air currents whistled in the chimney. A sweet applewood scent drifted.

As Nick's breathing slowed, a question popped into his head. *What about the day, Nick? What about the day?*

Chapter 22

"Do you like puzzles? They're a great way to pass the time during a winter storm." Standing in the Greenstone owner's kitchen, Carol hovered over Jeannie's shoulder with a fragrant carafe of caffeine. "How about a top-off?"

Cracked ice edged the external side of the above-the-sink kitchen windows. A thermometer capillary illumed against a whirling, opaque backdrop outside the window. In blood-red mercury, the gauge indicated a temperature of ten degrees below zero.

"Sure, I'll take a refill. I might have a trifling room left after that lumberjack breakfast. Thank you again." Jeannie grasped the handle of the handcrafted blue-and-brown glazed mug and leaned back in her chair. "I love your sweater. I've never seen a cardigan with a cable stitch like that."

Turning the disc cover, Carol poured the morning elixir into the cup. "Life for cottage owners in the winter allows solitary time. It's a nice change from the daily rush-rush of laundry stacks, grass cutting, bed making, raccoon trapping and rehoming, grill cleaning, oh, I could go on! So, when the snow lands, I peruse gardening catalogs and knit."

"Oh, don't tell me you made this sweater?" Jeannie leaned forward and splayed a hand over her chest. "Such a complicated pattern."

Blushing, Carol nodded.

A golden retriever curled on the rectangular deep-pile rug at Jeannie's feet. She bent to pet his head.

"Meet Ozzie," Carol said.

"Hello, Ozzie. I apologize for your confinement last night." Jeannie scrubbed the dog's velvety ears.

Ozzie flopped his feathery tail on the floor and licked her hand. Jeannie crossed her arms over her chest and shivered. Turning, she met Carol's gaze. She smiled. "I do like puzzles. My little boy, Joey, and I work on them frequently. He favors the floor-sized superhero scenes."

"C'mon over." Carol gestured. She pulled out a chair from the worn kitchen table and sat. "I've got a five-hundred-piece pure Michigan lighthouses puzzle started. The guys will be a while. There are six roofs to rake. You can tell me about Joey."

Jeannie moved to a seat beside Carol. She picked up a puzzle piece and the box top. "Wow, one hundred and twenty lighthouses in this state. Not surprised."

"Not if you consider we have over three thousand, two hundred miles of shoreline." Carol smiled.

"Here's where I grew up." Jeannie traced a finger over the paper thumb peninsula. "Ah, there it is—the Harbor Beach Lighthouse, just south of Port Hope."

"That is one beacon I haven't visited yet." Carol pursed her lips.

"Since that lighthouse is a spark-plug design, the only way you can tour it is to arrive by boat. This lake house is three stories high and a mile from shore. Seeing it brings back a lot of memories." Jeannie closed her eyes and sighed. *Frank.*

"Neat!" Carol fit a puzzle piece into Big Red, the

lighthouse in Holland, on the state's west coastline. "Ta-da!"

Jeannie opened her eyes.

Carol selected a spikey shape and rotated the piece in an attempt to connect the multi-pronged paper to adjoining pieces. She looked over the rim of her pink-framed reader glasses gripping the end of her nostrils. "Boom-Boom and I have three grown children. Every Fourth of July and Thanksgiving, they congregate here with their kids and pets. It's mass chaos." She sighed. "I love having them all with us."

"Joey is my only. He's in first grade. His father, my husband, Frank, was a military dog handler, and he died in Vietnam before Joey was born."

"No." Carol laid down the puzzle piece in her hand, placed her palm atop the back of Jeannie's hand, and squeezed. "I am so, so very sorry."

"And Nick? He seems like such an attentive man." Carol clenched her teeth and stared into Jeannie's eyes.

Jeannie bowed her head. She wrung her hands, then looked up. "He is."

Carol rocked forward in her chair. "Well, that's good." Then, she smiled, shoved her glasses to the bridge of her nose, and examined another puzzle piece. She chuckled. "I don't know if you are aware of this, but you and Nick are twins."

"Huh?" Jeannie straightened her shoulders.

"You both scrape your top teeth over your bottom lips when you're nervous." Carol grinned. "You were nervous when you arrived and nervous when Gerry led you out the door to your cabin."

"Oh, goodness. That's embarrassing." Jeannie tented her eyebrows.

"I personally find it adorable." Carol puffed out her cheeks.

Boot-shuffling noises sounded outside.

The door creaked on its hinges.

A blast of cold air and a smattering of snowflakes blew inside.

"About two feet of snow atop the cabins." Gerry's voice boomed. "We might need to do another raking before nightfall." He removed his outerwear.

Nick stomped inside behind Gerry and remained at the entrance.

Carol rose, gathered her husband's outer clothing, and hung the garments on a peg outside the bathroom.

"We should get back to Wolf." Nick rubbed his hands together.

Jeannie stood from her chair. Nick's ruddy cheeks, his tousled hair, and the soft expression in his eyes pierced her very core. She grew moist.

"Let me pack some cheese and crackers, egg salad sandwiches, fig cookies, and sodas." Carol bustled about the kitchen. She gripped the refrigerator handle. "I'll throw in a couple of women's magazines, a crossword puzzle book, and a recent newsletter on area fishing holes."

"Your hospitality is five-star." Nick saluted. "We really appreciate it."

"Sure glad for your help, Nick." Boom-Boom grasped Nick's extended hand.

Jeannie moved to the wall pegs, retrieved her snow gear, stepped into the suit, and tugged up the zipper. She stooped and pulled on her boots.

Passing the bag of food and reading materials to Nick, Carol gazed through the window above the sink.

"Best we all hunker down for a while. You two are welcome to share a pot of chili with us. We eat at six. Maybe we could play some games, too." She smiled.

"Thanks, Carol. That sounds wonderful." Jeannie yanked on her hat.

Nick reached for Jeannie's hand.

Carpe diem, Jeannie. She clasped his gloved mitt and stepped behind him into knee-high, sound-absorbing, secret-saving snow.

Cedar branches, thick with soft, cloud-like cover, hung heavy to the ground. Billows of fluffy white, disengaged from the roofs above, mounded the cabin foundations below.

Air so fresh it stung her warm nostrils flowed into her lungs. Grasping Nick's wrist, Jeannie trudged alongside.

Their love nest came into view.

Desire flooded her limbs.

Using his teeth, Nick extracted a glove, fumbled in his pocket, and pulled out a lanyard.

A tiny tinkling noise activated as metal keys dangled.

Nick unlocked the door, pushed it aside, and allowed Jeannie to move forward.

Jeannie breached the entry, knocked the snow from her boots, and shook the snow from her body.

After slamming the door behind them, Nick turned Jeannie to face him, and with his cold gloves, bookended her face and sucked her lips.

The breath left her body, effecting a vacuum of weightlessness and lust.

In quick succession, he shucked gloves, hat, boots, suit, every remaining manly body covering, and cascaded the items about the entrance. With mounting impatience, intermittent growling, and thick, calloused hands, Nick divested her of every shred of clothing. "I promise to warm you." He turned her to face him.

Stretching to the tips of her bare toes, Jeannie jumped and locked her supple legs around his waist. Against the hard muscles of his abdomen, she rubbed her thighs. "Nick, I want you so bad." She moaned.

He slid one arm underneath her butt, wrapped the other arm across her back, and bounced her.

Her body settled against his lower arm.

With his upper arm, Nick squeezed and crushed her to his chest. He rubbed his beard against her cheeks and teased her earlobe with the sawed edges of his teeth and his hot tongue.

With a cry, she arched her back.

Pulling aside the curtained doorway, Nick entered the bedroom. Leaving one hand on her backside, he used the other to jerk back the bed linens. Then, he placed her body crosswise on the sheets. He knelt, and with his strong, animal-trapping hands, he parted her legs.

Jeannie grasped the bedding on either side of her and balled the sheets into her clenched fists. She pointed her toes, arched her back, tightened her glute muscles, and opened her womanhood.

Nick's silky beard, bumpy tongue, swollen lips, and rigid teeth grazed over her engorged juncture.

Her breathing grew ragged. She twisted her wrists. She planted the soles of her feet on either side of Nick's face and ground her feet into the bed. She raised her butt.

Nick lifted his head. With one finger, he traced a

lazy path from the top of her nose to her belly button. He plunged gently into her navel and rotated his finger. He suckled her breast.

Jeannie screamed. She writhed and squeezed shut her eyes.

Rapid-fire skittering sounds echoed through the ceiling.

She shot open her eyelids.

Snow dumped outside the four-paned window above the headboard and left a gaping spot on a snowflake-frothed pine bough.

"I promised you warmth. Now the heat." Nick's voice pierced her core. His tongue pierced her craving womanhood.

Jeannie's voice trilled to the apex of the cathedral ceiling. Aligned with the crescendo of dried, seasoned wood fissuring and bursting in the fireplace's iron grate, and the heavy descent of the wet snow, Jeannie shuttered her eyes and joined the most primal of nature's callings.

Rising to his full height, Nick leaned over the bed.

Sighing, Jeannie gazed into Nick's flushed face.

"Ah, there you are." He ran his fingers through his hair and his beard. He grinned.

She scooched her butt into the center of the bed, reached for his engorged penis, and gripped his organ with both hands. "And here you are."

He smoothed one knee onto the bed.

She slid her hands up and down.

Groaning, he collapsed beside her.

Then, with her silky face, bumpy tongue, swollen lips, and rigid teeth, she brought him to the place he had taken her.

Jeannie kissed his brow and sank her head back into the pillow. *I am pushing all doubts aside and living in this moment. Destiny. Fate.*

Nick swallowed against her temple. "Wow." He sat up and pulled her tight to his side.

Her stomach rumbled. She laughed.

"You hungry?" He scratched his ear.

"Famished."

"I'll collect our clothes and bring them back here. Then, let's dig into Carol's snack pack." Nick rolled from the bed, turned, and walked from the room.

My imagination captured perfectly that gray-shorts-clad-jogging butt. Jeannie grinned.

****

"What's a seven-letter word for tease?" Nick looked up from the open paperback crossword puzzle book.

"Got any letters yet?" From her perch on the opposite end of the couch, Jeannie squashed her long, skinny feet between Nick's thighs.

"Hmm...there's a *T* at the beginning and a *T* at the end." Nick tapped the eraser end of his pencil in the fold of the book.

"Target?" Jeannie sucked in her cheeks. "No. That's only six letters."

"I got it!" Nick leaned and grabbed her knees. *I got you!* "Torment."

Jeannie blushed and covered her face. "Let's get Wolf."

"Good thinking. We should tire him out before we spend time with Boom-Boom and Carol."

****

Gerry gripped the domed top of a yellow game

piece, tapped the plastic piece on three successive game spaces, and knocked over Carol's green token. "Hah!"

"Meanie." Carol pouted.

Oregano, bay leaf, and onion odors permeated the air.

Ozzie rose from his spot under the table, on the rug and Nick's feet, and sauntered over to his water dish.

Water lapping sounds broke the game-strategizing silence.

Nick rubbed a rough foot along Jeannie's ankle.

Jeannie started, gazed into Nick's eyes, and flushed.

"I saw fox tracks this afternoon." Gerry looked up. "Deer, too."

"Did you secure the dumpster? I bet trash piled up. And those raccoons are relentless." Carol pressed her hands on the table and frowned.

"Yup." Gerry scratched behind his ear. "Wind has shifted. Temperatures are still below freezing. That bodes well for travel tomorrow. I'll drive you to your truck after breakfast."

"That sounds great. Thanks, Boom-Boom." Nick grinned. "Jeannie, before we were so rudely interrupted by a snowstorm, you told me a mysterious tale of unrequited letters."

"What?" Carol shuffled her elbows on the table and braided her fingers.

Jeannie shook her head. "It's really quite a discovery. While cataloging all the artifacts in the donation, my colleague came across a collection of personal letters written by a young man serving in the CCC on Isle Royale and a girl he left back home."

"How sweet. Sounds like a movie script." Carol

smoothed her palms over her cheeks.

"Well, not exactly sweet. From what we can tell, the letter writers never received the letters meant for them."

"What?" Carol jolted her head.

"My colleague, Hannah, from the Copper Harbor Historical Society, is determined to see that the letters, although over thirty years overdue, are delivered to the addressees." Jeannie shifted her eyes and made a moue with her mouth.

"Wow." Boom-Boom fist-bumped the table. "That is some sleuthing work."

"Handling artifacts often presents mysteries and moral dilemmas." Jeannie sighed.

"You two sure have interesting careers. We've known you for only a few days, and you feel like old friends. This has really been a gift." Carol pressed a palm over Jeannie's hand.

"You've both been wonderful. We'd love to give you a personal tour of the museum when you're down our way." Jeannie smiled.

"I bet they'd like to see the dermestid closet." Nick thumped the table.

"That is an emphatic no," Jeannie shouted. She gazed at Carol. She locked gazes with Gerry. "Flesh-eating beetles to prepare skeletal remains for taxidermy."

Carol shivered. "I'll take Jeannie's tour of all the cool costumes and quilts."

"Me, too," Gerry chimed.

"Now, how about some warm Michigan apple pie with a scoop of vanilla ice cream?" Carol rose from her chair.

Jeannie pushed away from the table. "Let me help." She trailed Carol to the kitchen.

After giving Jeannie four forks and four napkins, Carol looked over her shoulder. "That one is a keeper, Jeannie." She grasped a potholder, opened the oven door, and brought out a golden, lattice-woven crusted pie.

"I agree," Jeannie whispered. Inside her chest, her heart lifted like a released dove. Thick and sweet aromas of cinnamon and baked apple spiced the air. While sniffing deeply, Jeannie walked the utensils and fabric squares to the table and returned to the kitchen counter.

Carol shuffled pie pieces on dessert dishes and plopped ice cream balls atop the warm pastry.

Jeannie carried two plates and set them in front of Gerry and Nick.

Gerry folded the gameboard and put the cardboard in its box.

Leaning back in his chair, Nick patted his chest.

Carol brought the remaining desserts and settled one before herself and one in front of Jeannie.

"What kind of apple do you use?" Jeannie bit into the warm, chunky filling. "I'm guessing MacIntosh."

"Good guess." Carol smiled.

"My dad used to make a pie like this." Nick gummed his lips.

"Your dad?" Carol asked.

"He was the bomb." Nick stuck out his tongue and licked ice cream from a side edge of his lips. "My mom, not so much." He tented his eyebrows and pierced a fruit piece with his fork.

Jeannie cleared her throat. *Why would he say that*?

****

The door closed gently behind them.

Grasping Jeannie's mittened hand, Nick steered her toward a thick stand of conifers.

Pink clouds drifted between the cabin roof tiles and the snow-burdened boughs.

The sun—a cheery red orb—drifted lower.

Hoary speech bubbles lifted above Nick's head with each breath he expelled. Out of sight from the Greenstone Office, Nick gripped Jeannie's waist, led her to a break in the pines, and walked her to a place where a diminishing streak of sunlight ebbed over unbroken snow.

"Oh, it's charming." Jeannie clasped her face. "Nick."

With both hands, he levered her waist and leaned back.

Above them, an aromatic canopy of black-green spruce needles loomed.

"I feel like I'm in a cathedral." Jeannie's breath flowed like an otherworldly vapor.

Nick's inhalation lodged in his throat, competing in the space his heart occupied. "Maybe this is the right place to tell you I have feelings for you, Jeannie."

She turned and pressed her cold lips and nose against his. "Nick, please. Listen to me. We've had two days of lust, and maybe we should just leave it at that. I don't want to be responsible for someone else's heartache. God, I feel so guilty. Don't make me bear that, too, Nick. Please." She stared at their feet.

He drew a deep lungful of air and flexed his knees. *Girl, the last thing I want is to inflict shame on you.*

"You said it the night we arrived. This time was a

gift." Jeannie's voice shook. "A gift—a precious gift. But Nick, think. You have a committed relationship with Elizabeth."

A hollow convenience. No more. He dropped his head to his chest.

"And don't forget your life's work and the funding. It's all tied together with Elizabeth."

He seized her left hand. He tucked a wayward hair under her hat. He frowned, extracted a handkerchief from his jacket, and wiped her nose. He grinned. "That's better." Holding her at arm's length, he sighed. "First of all, I experience energy and hopefulness with you. And second of all…" He tipped up her chin to secure eye contact. He kissed her frosty eyelashes.

She sneezed.

Crumbling the paisley-print-bandana handkerchief, Nick clamped it over Jeannie's nostrils and scoured her upper lip. "The sex was pretty darn real, too." He nudged her toward their cabin. "Now, let's get inside before my hanky is all used up."

"Better hurry."

Her muffled voice signaled more comedic than urgent. He grinned. "Just one more sentiment before we leave this hallowed place." Nick knelt on the ground, looked up, and caught her gaze. He raised his arms to the sky and tipped back his head. He beat his chest. "*Heikki Luunta*, Goddess of Snow, thank you." *And while I'm at it, Goddess of Love, Aphrodite, smile on us. Keep Medusa and Elizabeth at bay.*

Chapter 23

Three pots of wilted poinsettias—their holiday luster as spent as the gaily colored wrappings and stepped-on boxes below Jeannie's needle-shedding Christmas tree—reposed behind the industrial-sized trash can in the church basement foyer. Lingering odors of sage and thyme infused the damp atmosphere.

Senior lunches served at noon. Jeannie brought her mug of peppermint tea close to her nose. *Ah.*

Shaking a sheaf of worn college-lined, loose-leaf papers, group member Jim scanned the faces of his fellow widowed friends.

Jeannie caught her breath.

Jim sighed so deeply the buttons down the front of his shirt strained against the edge-stitched holes cut in the overlapping flap.

Fluttering the pages, Jim jutted his chin. "These are Mary's notes from forty years of teaching middle-school-aged students Sunday school. I still hear from some of these kids. They just loved her." With his free hand, he reached for the pen in his breast pocket and plunged the end.

Click-click.

" 'Jim,' I says to myself, Mary went to all the trouble of writing these directions for someone. And that someone will be me if they'll have me." He sighed. "Teaching those kids will be the best way to remember my Mary."

"They'll be lucky to have you, Jim—along with Mary's wisdom and grace." Sharon nodded.

Jeannie clapped.

Soon, the room filled with the sounds of palms hitting together.

"I got one more." Jim buffed together his grooved palms. "Mary loved her flowers. She transplanted some roses to our property from her parents' homestead, and she nurtured them with the soul of a gardener. I'm going to keep them going." He scanned the room. "I'll take anyone's suggestions."

"Banana peels." Verna bobbed her head. "Bury them in the soil under the bushes."

"Jim, remember that granddaughter of yours who is getting married late this summer? Tuck one of her grandmother's roses into her bouquet. And while you're at it, stick one in your boutonniere." Jeannie pointed to her lapel.

"Great ideas, ladies. Thanks." Jim nodded, set the papers on the table fronting him, and shoved the pen into his breast pocket.

From across the table, Marie slid her right hand over her temple and behind her right ear.

Jeannie smiled. *That motion is so ingrained. Even though her hair is now loose and short, she still reacts as if the concrete beehive resides on her head.*

Marie cleared her throat. "I'm taking my grandsons to the Henry Ford Museum in Detroit to see the wonderful history of automobiles. Their grandfather would have shared his appreciation of cars with them. Also, I will take the boys to local car races since Paul enjoyed that, too. Every March twenty-second, we celebrate Paul's birthday. We don't mention the number of birthdays. We just put a few candles on. Everyone makes a wish, and we sing '*Bonne Anniversaire*,' '*Happy Birthday*' to him. I make his favorite cake—German chocolate with lots of coconut flakes."

"German chocolate. With nuts. Delicious." Jennifer gummed her lips.

Verna stuck a hand in a paper bag that lay on the table.

Crackle.

She extracted a plaid camp-style shirt with short cuffed sleeves and a frayed collar. Then, she pulled a blue chambray shirt mottled with stains and held the garment by the shoulder seams. "I'm using Mike's shirts to make quilts for our children. I'll embroider his name, his birthplace, and the names, dates of births, and marriages of each of our children and grandchildren."

"Oh, I love that idea," Sharon said.

"You might want to add his special flower, or song or sports team, too," Marjorie suggested.

"Yeah, even better." Verna refolded the shirts.

Sharon rested her elbows atop the table, twined her fingers, and pressed her palms together. "These are all such wonderful ways to celebrate your spouses. Has anyone found conflicts with experiencing simultaneous happiness and pangs of guilt?"

The tinny sound of a metal chair flexing rent the succeeding silence.

Scanning the room, Sharon nodded. "Guilt—the elephant in the room."

Jeannie shrunk her shoulders. She swallowed. "I've been wrestling with this one." She chewed her bottom lip. "Living in the moment and appreciating cheerfulness is a good way to move forward. I remind myself Frank dedicated his life to protecting my happiness, and I honor his memory by choosing joy over remorse."

"That's lovely, Jeannie." Jennifer offered a somber gaze.

Jeannie clenched her teeth and wrung her hands. *Frank, no matter what, we won't forget you. I promise.*

****

Winter break remained in effect.

The corridors of the Great Lakes University Museum were so quiet the sound of dermestid jaws could be heard—divesting flesh from the bones of a zoo-donation, snow leopard cadaver in the east-end laboratory. Nick flexed his fingers, opened his briefcase, dropped a stapled packet of papers inside, and shut the clasp.

Air billowing from a floor radiator flailed a crayoned illustration of a stick-figure Santa against the wall. Nick puffed his cheeks.

Joey signed his artwork with finger-spaced, uneven letters. *Merry Christmas, Nick.*

Did I just feel my heart grow three sizes? Nick feigned work fatigue and the flu to avoid spending Christmas with Elizabeth.

She sent him a combination *Get Well, Merry Christmas, I Love You, Sexy* card scored with hearts and flowers and scented with her expensive bottled aroma.

He sent her a box of pears. Nick completed most of his Christmas shopping during a trip through the local sporting store. He bought a four-seater toboggan and snowshoes in Joey's size. Two days before Christmas, he and Sam joined Jeannie, Joey, Gunther, and Wolf for a romp in the snow and a meatloaf and mashed potato dinner. His heart beat ardently, remembering the day.

"Again!" Joey had shouted more times than Nick bothered to tally, as the red-cheeked boy positioned the long sled atop a hoary precipice. Jogging alongside or jumping on behind, Nick partnered with Joey on each downhill run. Each finale culminated in a tangle of white-peppered feet, legs, arms, faces, snow-snorted chuckles and the refrain "again!"

Later, in the cozy French country kitchen, seated at the round, maple table, Nick tucked thick-socked feet under a chair rung, reached across a handwoven placemat, and ruffled Joey's sweaty head. The softness of the boy's feather-fine hair, coupled with a front-teeth-missing grin, had melted Nick's heart as fastidiously as the snowy remains puddling at the threshold of Jeannie's house. Typing taps detonated from an open office door.

Floor polish, applied over the holiday break, tinged the hallway.

In moments he would see her. He registered muscle-tensing sensations in his back, his legs, and his jaw. Nick entered the conference room, dropped his briefcase on the table, and sat beside Jeannie. Peering over her shoulder, he ran his index finger across her penciled list. "Dish soap, garbanzo beans, mayonnaise, kitty litter." He set his elbow atop the table, leaned his face into his palm, and gazed dreamily at Jeannie. "How is our shared progeny?"

Jeannie squinted. "You better come and get him. He's ruining my wardrobe. Yesterday, he levered himself on top of the refrigerator and then pounced on the ironing board—an action that caused me to drop the iron on an expensive blouse." Curling her fingers into a catlike grip, Jeannie bared her teeth and hissed. "And just like that, the blouse has a big old singe mark and is now relegated to layered outfits—hidden under a vest."

"Yikes." Nick lifted his eyebrows.

Just arriving at the monthly Exhibits meeting, Peg gazed her bright-blue eyes at Jeannie. "What?"

Nick thrust back his chair and crossed his right leg over his left. "Jeannie and I divide custodial rights of Michigan's smartest, most adorable kitten."

"Hah, sassiest, most vexing, did I mention wool-sweater-chewing kitten in Michigan?" Jeannie clasped a pencil at both ends and mimicked snapping the instrument in two.

"Wolf, the kitten in question, was an unexpected collectible from Copper Harbor." Nick flashed an impish grin.

Peg shook her head.

Bending her neck and lowering her chin, Jeannie gazed at Nick. "Your turn this weekend."

Nick extracted a pen from his pocket. *Click.* Gripping the writing tool, Nick wrote on Jeannie's list. *I miss you.* Then, he unbuckled his briefcase, withdrew the inventory list of the Erikkson donation, and fought hard to resist kissing her head. Desire hardened his body.

Picking up her pencil, Jeannie added *Me, too* under Nick's message.

He contorted his butt in his chair.

"Geez, Nick. That bald eagle mount from the Eriksson collection is magnificent." Bob sauntered into the conference room, adjusted his bow tie, set a clipboard and pencil on the table, pulled out a chair, and sat.

Nick stuck up his thumb from a rolled fist.

Shuffling in on his ten-minute-after-the-start-of-the-meeting schedule, with his upper lip and mustache glazed in remnants of an indistinguishable pastry and his hands stuffed inside his white lab coat pockets, Cal scanned the room right and then left. Then, he lowered his head, stuck out his tongue, and smoothed the glistening facial hair.

Bet you got more than toothpicks in those pockets. Nick grinned.

Wanda trailed Mac into the room.

Mac filled the doorway and cleared his throat. "Good morning, all. I hope your holidays were memorable. We'll dispense with our usual round of Show and Tell and concentrate on finalizing details for the Michigan Nightlife Exhibit Opening. Only a few weeks to go."

"And I do mean details," Wanda interjected. "Concrete numbers regarding the number of easels desired, amount of electrical access, placement of and timing of light and sound systems, and polished descriptions and titles for the programs."

"Eight easels with spotlights for the indigenous plant artworks." Martha shook her long, gray, wavy hair.

"I contacted the student radio station, and we've got some students familiar with sound engineering to orchestrate the bird sounds." Birdman Bob waved his pencil toward Wanda. "I'll have them speak to you, too."

"The hospitality committee decided on the food and drink offerings." Peg brandished a printed list. "We are using various ethnic caterers to highlight the diversity of Michigan's cultures and indigenous foods. So, just a few to mention—Native American fried bread, Polish *pierogies*, German brats, Lake Superior white fish, and cherry wine.

"We're also showcasing indigenous Michigan flora in decorations," Martha added. "Native wildflowers, ornamental grasses, and cone-bearing boughs—colorful and fragrant."

"Excellent," Mac exclaimed. "Invitation responses are pouring in. We'll have a full house."

Jeannie nudged Nick's elbow. She tugged a phone message slip from the grip of her clipboard. Biting her lip, and connecting her gaze with Nick's, she traced the script with a fingertip. *Call me soon. I've got news regarding our CCC lovers. Hannah.*

Nick squeezed Jeannie's elbow. "Wow."

Gazing at the note, Jeannie inhaled deeply. "I know. Wow," she whispered on her exhaled breath.

"Nick and I have some tricky specialty lighting for the mammal exhibit, but campus electricians have come through. We're testing the effects next week after closing hours." Cal drummed his palms on the tabletop.

"Anything else?" Mac scanned the room. "All right then, our next get-together is Saturday, February twenty-second. I expect to see everyone in their best looks for opening night. Keep up the good work, all."

Gathering her purse and paperwork, Jeannie gazed into Nick's eyes. "Joey and I are having a pizza dinner. We'd love you to join us."

"Extra cheese?" Nick grinned.

"Absolutely." Jeannie rose. "See you tonight. I'm making phone calls. I'll keep you updated."

"Great."

What could Hannah be reporting? Jeannie's stack of phone messages included more than the missive from the Copper Harbor Historical Society. Underneath that standard office form, written in Marie's distinctive European flair, a request for a return phone call from veterinarian friend Matt lolled like an ill-fitting puzzle piece.

****

"Jeannie, you'll find this hard to believe." Hannah spoke in a rushed voice. "I found Bruce."

"Oh my gosh!" At her work desk in the bowels of the Costume Collections, Jeannie gripped the phone receiver.

"He lives outside of Marquette. Bruce retired from the Department of Natural Resources as a Fish and Wild Game Officer and owns a bait and fishing store."

"And?" Jeannie shut her eyes and held her breath.

"And he's a widower. Get this. His wife's name was Viola."

"No." Opening her eyes, Jeannie stared out the window. Bare oak limbs stretched over the cement walkway to the Student Union.

Walkers, their heads bowed as they trekked into a north wind, passed underneath the undressed canopy.

"Yes. Viola, confirmed as the camp cook. Hey, just a second, Jeannie, I gotta let the dog out."

The phone dropped.

Jeannie massaged her forehead. Shuffling noises reverberated through the phoneline.

"I'm back," Hannah said.

"I was about to ask you if you've been able to find anything about Margie?" Jeannie asked.

"That one is harder to track. For one thing, Margie's surname might have changed. I've already searched the Eaton Rapids, Michigan, directories of the 1930s. With Margie's return address, I could identify her father and his occupation. What a coincidence. Margie's father was a weaver."

Jeannie gasped. *Margie? Marjorie? The widow Marjorie I know?*

"I wonder if your woolen mill-owning family ever crossed paths with those folks," Hannah said. "Jeannie, do you think we should contact Bruce now or first exhaust all resources trying to find Margie?"

"I think the latter. Maybe Bruce and Margie have already reconnected." Jeannie doodled on a pad of paper. "I will dedicate time to finding Margie, too."

"Agreed. Now, how is Nick? How is Wolf?"

Smiling, Jeannie wound the phone cord around her fingers. "They are both chasing their tails. Nick's coming over for a pizza dinner. And he's leaving with Wolf—part of our shared custody agreement."

From her Copper Harbor office, Hannah laughed. "Tell them both I said *hi*. Keep in touch."

Tapping a finger on the message to return Matt's phone call, Jeannie sighed. *He's so thoughtful. The terror of heartbreak is a shortcut between us. That makes it so comfortable to be with him.*

Click-click.

"Jeannie?"

The sound of Marie's heels and her French accent disconnected Jeannie's reverie.

"Marjorie from our Widowed Group dropped a package off while you were up north. She said you might want the contents for the Collections. Did Tina tell you?" Marie adjusted her glasses.

"No." Jeannie pushed away from her desk. "But maybe she already put the donations in the decontamination cabinet." She walked toward the unit, jerked on the handle, and pulled open the door.

Inside, a neatly wrapped paper parcel lay on the top metal rack.

In Tina's identifiable scrawl, *December 12, 1970,* recorded the entry day.

"This was her last day of work before finals. No harm done to the donation." Jeannie pulled out the package, walked to the muslin-topped examining table, tugged on white cotton gloves, and extracted the contents from the bag. Three pieces of intricately woven woolens stamped on the selvages with *Horner Woolen Mill, Eaton Rapids,* slid atop her gloves.

Marie came alongside Jeannie. "She said her father worked as a weaver."

"Oh, my God." Jeannie stared at the dobby, twill, and jacquard woolens. *Marjorie.*

Chapter 24

Overhead, the moon shone as a shimmering pearl in a sea of midnight blue. Thousands of minuscule lights threaded the bare trees and bushes, flanking the quartz-based, Lake Superior-quarried sandstone steps and the open, Georgian-pediment-styled entrance of the Great Lakes University Exhibits Museum.

Lilting harp music and buzzing voice murmurs floated out to the chilly campus night.

Jeannie slowed her hurried walk. *Opening night. I want to savor it all.*

Strolling arm-in-arm couples passed her.

An intense wave of melancholy penetrated her gut. *All the behind the scene tinkering, anguished decision-making, artifact hunting and preparation is now on full display. If I had a Cinderella moment here, I'd wish to be swept across the floor by Prince Preserved Poop Inspector.* She giggled. Taking a breath, she scrunched shut her eyes, tipped her head back, and opened them. *I've got this.*

Graduate assistants Dermestid Donita and Kickball-King Walter flanked the main entrance and doled out programs.

Raising the hem of her floor-length skirt, Jeannie picked her way up the steps.

"Mrs. Parks, looking fab." Donita flaunted her beautiful, gapped-front-teeth smile.

"Looking dapper, all of you." Jeannie smiled.

A tuxedo-wearing, tie-strangled Cal fronted a row of black iron easels. He shook his head and pointed a paint-stained finger.

Loretta leaned her ear next to his.

Joining them, Jeannie gasped. "The student artwork is absolutely lovely. They're so realistic I can smell them."

Cal revolved. "Wowser!" He kissed Jeannie's forehead. "You're even prettier than all these depictions of night-blooming, native Michigan flowers."

"And you smell good, too." Loretta brushed her cheek against Jeannie's.

"What's your favorite?" Cal rotated his shoulders in his too-big jacket.

"I'll go first." Loretta swirled her cocktail glass and guzzled a sip. She sidestepped to a poster illustrating a larger-than-life plant composed of heart-shaped, shiny green leaves and clusters of tiny white flowers. "The smooth hydrangea. It's so romantic. Think of sundown garden strolls with these gleaming white bloomers leading like lanterns."

"And that's my beautiful, night-blooming poetic wife," Cal gushed.

I adore these two. Jeannie sidled to the last-in-the-row easel. "Hands down the foamflower for me."

Standing just behind the artwork, a ringlet-haired student dressed in a tiered patchwork skirt and a tie-dyed sweater grinned. "So glad you think so. My favorite, too."

"You did this?" Loretta clasped her cheeks and blinked.

The student nodded.

"The rendition is so enchanting. I always thought the blooms resembled a bottle brush. Can we buy prints?" Jeannie bent her knees and peered at the art.

"Yes, you can. You'll find them in the gift shop. All the proceeds go toward student scholarships." The colorful student artist beamed.

"Exceptional work. Thank you for contributing to this exhibit." Cal shook the student's hand. "I'm buying your print, and I'd like you to autograph it. Someday, you'll be a famous artist, and I'll have a notable work of fine art." He winked.

"Thank you. Thank you so much." The student blushed and tented her hands over her mouth.

Cal cupped Jeannie's elbow and steered her toward a white-skirted table. "Let's get you a beverage."

A garnet-lipped, mirror image of Marilyn Monroe, a platinum-blonde goddess, threw back her head. Sultry, deep-throated laughter gusted from her fully open mouth. She lifted her right hand to her spread orifice and slung down a glassful of burgundy-colored liquid. Then, she extended her empty glass.

A bow-tied bartender refilled the container.

A crisp, tuxedo-wearing athletic man gazed at the floor-trailing sequined train of the blonde and backed clumsily away. In his apparent panicked retreat, the fancy dresser narrowly missed colliding with a waiter balancing a chock-full tray of a northern Michigan specialty—pasties.

Jeannie's heart jumped to her throat and blocked oxygen consumption. She froze. *Nick.*

Still moving, Cal bumped her side.

On the opposite side of the catered bar, fellow museum directors lined up like cowboys in a Western saloon.

His white hair shining like a Southern moonflower, Mac held a crystal glass aloft. "A toast. To our great state of Michigan, its unique nature and creatures, and those who preserve it."

Glasses *clinked*. Heads nodded. Smiles exchanged.

"Jeannie." Marie reached for the curator's wrist. "The band is setting up. The models are cued. You've got fifteen minutes." The dean's assistant turned and disappeared into the crowd.

"Troll Two!" Tugging Nick's hand, Hannah rushed Jeannie.

"You made it!" Jeannie wrapped her arms around her freckle-faced friend.

"Definitely more classy than the Copper Harbor Legion." Hannah smirked. Grasping Jeannie and Nick by the wrists, she formed a trio of north-country allies. She leaned her head against Jeannie's temple. "I had to rescue this guy. Thank me later," she whispered.

Every sound in the room stilled. Every other person blurred. Every observation, every scent, and every remembered taste and sound of Nick remained.

Her heart thrummed in her chest and revved every nerve in her body. Jeannie met Nick's gaze. Heat and desire slammed her core. Gone was the Yooper beard. Gone were the casual jeans, flannel, and cleated boots apparel. *He's beautiful*.

Nick's Adam's apple protruded against the formfitting collar of his pin-tucked white shirt. His muscled arms shone in the glossy cover of a silky black athletic cut jacket. A sober gaze heightened his sexuality.

"Did you tell him I found Bruce?" Hannah tugged

Jeannie's wrist.

Jeannie nodded. "And the most incredible thing is I know Marjorie."

"What?" Hannah's eyes widened.

"Are you free tomorrow morning? We can discuss our plans then." Jeannie craned her neck.

Grad assistant Tina stepped on tiptoe and waved frantically.

"Gotta go." Jeannie fled. *To all the gods in the universe, please trigger the next minutes to befall as treasured memories.*

****

"We can't miss this." Nick grasped Hannah's elbow. He turned and motioned to the blonde.

Rustling tambourine backbeats of a soulful Motown melody surged. Melodic strains of a bass guitar electrified the echoing space.

Nick swung Hannah in a circle, dropped his left hand from her waist, moved in front of her, and executed a loose grapevine step—working his feet in a horizontal line twelve marble tiles wide.

A thunderous mezzo-soprano voice belted a popular phrase "R-E-S-P-E-C-T."

Cheers and claps rang.

Female models donned in hot pants and go-go boots, paired with male models in blue jeans and loud print, open-front shirts zigzagged through the crowd.

Following them, dancers in tuxedos and sequined sheaths injected funky dance moves.

"Nighttime in Michigan." Jeannie's voice spouted through the sound system. "Brought to you by Great Lakes University Historic Costumes and Textiles Collection staff and students."

Nick stared open-mouthed. She wore a shimmery blue dress that fit her like a silk cocoon. *Oh, to shed her of it.* Stockings concocted of a sheer misty fiber accented the curve of her calves and her delicate ankles. Stiletto heels, dangerously steep, caused her to teeter as she struggled to maintain connection with a metallic pocketbook and a tri-pod-based microphone stand. Nick held his breath. *Easy, girl.*

Food service staff deployed through the museum offered palates of Michigan-grown delicacies and treats—cherry tarts, chilled asparagus stalks in dill sauce, apple blintzes, ginger ale culled from a Civil War era beverage formulated in an oak cask barrel, cookies topped with fine sugar gleaned from the acres of sugar beets grown in Michigan-thumb-peninsula cities like Croswell and Sandusky.

"Please enjoy our Quilt Exhibit as well. Sweet dreams!" Jeannie rolled a thumb over the microphone button and set the instrument into its stand.

A student violinist shuffled the bow across her instrument and conjured a lilting lullaby.

Mobbed by well-wishers, Jeannie shot a gaze at Nick.

He smiled and upheld a fist. Registering his heart pumping in Michigan-Motown accelerated beats, he opened his left hand, placed it over his chest, met Jeannie's gaze, and tapped the palm over his lapel. *The pink in her cheeks matches the pink under her panties. The sparkle in her eyes corresponds with her utter abandonment in the sheets. God.*

A combined scent of a grossly familiar perfume, dill, and merlot floated.

Nick choked. *Elizabeth. Damn.*

****

Approaching Nick, Elizabeth gnawed an asparagus sprig. She sidled beside him and caressed his right bicep. "There's Daddy. Why don't you show him the mammal exhibit he funded?"

Nick shrugged off her hand, stiffened his arm and retracted his shoulder. "Sure."

Elizabeth tilted on her black patent leather heels and stared at Nick's advancing back. *Jeannie Parks, Textile Curator. Just one of the museum folks, my ass.* Turning, Elizabeth calculated the round-trip distance between the surveillance spot she held and the bar. Beginning in her lower lumbar region, one vertebra at a time, she straightened her back. Then, she squinted her eyes and paraded her show-stopping silhouette to the source of fortification.

With the body language of a man familiarized with seduction, the bartender lowered his chin and winked.

Elizabeth purred. In a sweeping motion, she waved her hand. "Strongest libation you got. I'm feeling fiery tonight."

"Comin' right up." Licking his lips, the bartender broadened his eyes and reached for a crystal decanter. Then, with a pair of long-legged tongs, he levered ice cubes into an old-fashioned tumbler. Finally, he uncapped the decanter and poured straight bourbon over the rocks. He lifted the glass. "For the lady."

For the tramp. Elizabeth downed the liquid. *Clank.*

Retrieving the discarded drink, the bartender nodded. "Have a good night."

Elizabeth raised one eyebrow and threaded her hair behind one ear. She formed a tight line with her lips, nodded, and gyrated.

The crowd shielding Jeannie dissipated into two people.

A pair of withered old ladies. Ugh.

Jeannie hugged one of the women. Then she hugged the other. "I think Dr. Randall did you both proud with his dance moves tonight. That was a special surprise for both of you."

The women chuckled and waved their goodbyes.

Tucking her head and her evening bag to her chest, Jeannie walked down a corridor. Overhead, a sign denoted *Restrooms*.

Maintaining a distance, Elizabeth followed Jeannie into the ladies' room. She positioned herself before the sink, opened her purse, and extracted a compact and lipstick.

Toilets flushed. Air dryers blew.

Doors swung open and shut.

Jeannie walked to a sink, set down her embroidered bag, and washed her hands.

"You're Jeannie, the textile curator, right?" Elizabeth gazed into the mirror, caught Jeannie's startled stare in the reflection, formed her mouth into a moue, and with steely precision, applied scarlet red lipstick. Without pausing for a response, Elizabeth tapped her lips together. "Elizabeth Harcourt—Nick's fiancée." She held up her left hand, splayed the fingers, and wiggled the digits. "No ring. We just haven't found the right one yet. I am pretty particular." She sucked in a deep breath and ran a hand over her never-stretched-by-pregnancy abdomen.

"Nick is a wonderful addition here." With widened eyes, Jeannie grabbed a paper towel and whisked the disposable item over her wrists and fingers.

Got the reaction I wanted. She looks shocked as hell. "Don't get used to having him around. Once we're married, I will team up with my father to secure my husband a position with the Worldwide Wolf Alliance. That's Nick's dream job."

With trembling fingers, Jeannie opened her bag and pulled out a lipstick case. She fumbled the cap. Stepping back from the sink, she brushed the smooth compound over her lips.

"That's a charming pink. Nick prefers deep red." Elizabeth tapped her lips together.

Jeannie squinted into the mirror.

"I know I'll have my hands full. Nick is a wild one." Elizabeth rocked her shoulders and smiled. *Tramp.*

Chapter 25

Crude, handwoven hemp sacks, stamped in black ink with the Spanish word *café* hung from beams overhanging the meeting place Jeannie and Hannah had agreed on the night prior.

Pitted wooden flooring creaked as incoming customers approached the domed glass pastry case, the chalkboards festooned in a rainbow of pastel colors announcing assorted tea flavors of the day—jasmine, chai, organic mother's herbal, chamomile, peppermint, and orange pekoe.

The combined tea fragrances melded with aromatic cinnamon and allspice scents of warm fruit pastries circulated from the bustling kitchen.

Sitting in a sunny nook of the energetic bistro across from Hannah, Jeannie grinned. "Glad you could make it."

Hannah rotated an earthenware saucer on the rough-hewn tabletop. "That was quite the opening night. Congratulations." Scanning the room, Hannah blew on the tea, forming a wake and corresponding ripples in the liquid. "This brew shop is pretty cool, too."

Coffee sloshed over the rim of a white ceramic mug as a waiter set down the cup in front of Jeannie. Grabbing a rag from her back pocket, the server wiped the liquid off the table.

Jeannie leaned back against her hardwood chair, held up her hands, and smiled.

Hannah turned her head to the right and scanned deliberately the café interior. She threaded her fingers, knotted them on the tabletop, and repeated the scanning action toward the left. Then, she applied pressure on her tangled fingers and jutted her upper body across the table. Hannah cleared her throat and frowned. "Before we get to the business of reuniting two duped lovers…" Hannah stretched her neck and gazed into Jeannie's eyes. "Who the hell was that blonde clawing Nick?"

Jeannie folded her bottom lip under her top teeth and brushed her palms on the tabletop. "Elizabeth Harcourt."

"And?" Hannah tented her eyebrows.

"Ever hear of Harcourt and White?" Jeannie slunk in her seat and widened her eyes.

"You mean, toothpaste, cereal, razors, shampoo, bandages, and toilet paper Harcourt and White?"

"Bingo." Jeannie aimed a pointed index finger toward Hannah's nostrils.

"So Elizabeth is an heiress. Well, I gotta say, she knows how to upstage an otter exhibit." Hannah snorted. "I noticed Miss Razor Blade while I took in the Michigan Mammal Exhibits. Some of the onlookers dropped their jaws as readily as a beaver gnawing lodge joists."

Spittle piloted across the table. Jeannie clapped a hand over her mouth. "Oh, geez, Louise." Bending her head low, Jeannie struggled to abort an onset of giggles. Her breath expelled in spastic hiccups as she gazed up at Hannah. "I needed that."

"Yah, well, sometimes a troll needs a friend."

Hannah leaned back in her seat, spread her arms, and rested their lengths along the top of the bench.

Jeannie lifted a hip and pulled a handkerchief out of a back pocket. She blew her nose, scrunched the hanky into a ball, and stuffed it into her purse. "Miss Razor Blade and Nick were almost engaged."

"Good grief. And here I thought you and I were working to reunite a pair of lovers. Rather ironic, isn't it?" Hannah swiped her cheek.

"The absurdity has not escaped me. I had no intention of interfering with a duo of *amants*. That's French for lovers. Stuff just happened." Jeannie clamped her lips. "And frankly, I have no more assurance of how Nick and my friendship develops than I do of the risky rekindling of our ill-fated friends via artifacts—Bruce and Marjorie."

Pressing her elbows on the table, Hannah plunked her forehead into her palms. She shut her eyes. Then, she spread her fingers apart and gazed through them. "Speaking of the letter people, what if we're tampering with fate? What if this news creates a tsunami of personal catastrophe?"

After inhaling the calming elixir of a Sumatra brew, Jeannie set a hand atop Hannah's. "What if we are bringing together two lost souls? What if we are instrumental in dismissing thirty years of grief?" She squeezed Hannah's hand. "The way I see it, those letters fell into our laps for a reason."

Hannah formed a fist and banged the table. "Geez, I wish we had a crystal ball."

"I have a personal stake in this, too. For the past year, through a widow support group I belong to, I have become friends, with believe it or not, *the* Margie. Or as

305

she goes by now, Marjorie."

"What?" Hannah blinked her eyes.

"She's lovely, and she's lonely. Marjorie married and has two children. Her husband died a year ago."

Dishes clattered in the background. Sputtering noises and bursts of steam rose from metal carafe warmers lined on a cracked linoleum countertop.

"Holy crap." Hannah shook her head.

"Anything else today, ladies?" A server with a single long braid and wearing a black T-shirt and jeans waited at Jeannie's right elbow.

Reading Hannah's headshake as a 'no,' Jeannie reached for her wallet inside her handbag. "No, we're set. Just the bill, please." She gazed into Hannah's eyes. "As much as I'd like to relay this whole scenario to Marjorie, as I know her, don't you think this is all in Bruce's court? As Viola's spouse, he is the legal owner of the tin and all its contents." Jeannie toyed with her spoon.

Hannah scratched her head.

Lifting the pink-lipstick-stained ceramic mug over her nose, Jeannie tipped the cup back and downed the last of the earthy-flavored, campfire-smelling coffee.

"I brought the tin with me. How about we call Bruce today? And I'll arrange to drop all Viola's mementos on my way back to Copper Harbor."

"Agreed. And I'll keep in touch with Marjorie if she needs someone to talk to. Let's call Bruce." Jeannie wiped the lip of her cup clean with a napkin. "My office is just across the street. We can phone from there."

"Let's do it!" Hannah grabbed her jacket.

Jeannie checked the tab, extracted a ten-dollar bill, and laid it on the table. Then she shrugged a shawl over her shoulders and followed Hannah to the exit.

Yah, let's do it before I lose my courage, which took a wallop in the ladies' room last night.

****

Nick pulled open the floor-to-ceiling brass-trimmed door to the hotel lobby. He checked his watch. *9:54 a.m. Elizabeth is probably already here.* Inhaling a deep breath, Nick crossed the terrazzo-floored atrium in syncopation with the triplet swing of the jazz band drummer riffing behind eight-foot-high Erica palms. Ahead, wrought-iron railings abutted carpeted steps to a dining area below.

In velvet upholstered booths, smiling, silver-haired grandmothers tucked spit-and-polished Sunday-dressed grandchildren under their arms.

Grandfathers tweaked mini noses, shook hands with menfolk, and laughed with gusto.

Parents alternated their nonverbal messages between compressed eyebrows and straight-lined lips with relaxed shoulders and side-eye winks.

Glasses, filled with thick orange pulp and juice and coffee carafes, ivory in color and Doric column in design congregated on glass-topped tables amidst the breakfast clientele.

He ran a shaky hand through his hair. *Shit.*

Elizabeth lounged against a high-backed seat.

A bright-green scalloped leaf, a ribbed celery stick, and a tan bamboo skewer immersed in a tomato-red liquid blurred against the red of her lips.

A Bloody Mary. Her morning juice. Nick closed his eyes. He unzipped his jacket. He opened his eyes, bent his head, and covered the steps to the window seat with a view of the eighteenth hole. Bending at the knees,

Nick slid into the opposite seat. He steepled his hands atop the table. "Good morning."

Elizabeth smirked. She kicked her pointed, shoeless toes on his calf.

Retracting his leg, Nick squeezed together his hands. "Stop."

"Nick, we're so good together. I missed you last night." Elizabeth eddied the celery stalk.

Outside the window, a gloomy sky hung seamlessly over a mid-winter thaw.

Inside, the odors of sizzling bacon, maple syrup, and overripe cantaloupe swirled. Nick cleared his throat. He waved off a hovering attendant. "Elizabeth, I've rehearsed this a thousand times." He lifted his chin. "I find no easy way to say this."

"Shush." Elizabeth put a finger over her mouth.

Nick furrowed his brow.

"I met Jeannie Parks last night. Nick, she's not for you. Much too mousy."

Raising his shoulders, Nick fell backward on the cushioned backboard. *Damn. You better not have done anything to hurt Jeannie's feelings.* Under the table, Nick furled his hands into fists. *What gives you the right to make judgments for me?*

"I know you. The most important thing to you is saving the world's imperiled animals. Love is secondary." Elizabeth sucked the celery stick. She licked the salt off the rim of the cocktail glass. "So ditch this easily forgettable fling and walk back into your picture-perfect world. The Worldwide Wolf Alliance…" Gripping the table edge with her shellacked fingernails, Elizabeth glared. "Did I just say Worldwide Wolf Alliance? Oh, yes, the WWA

President offered Daddy a board seat."

With narrowed eyes, Nick gazed over her head into the sunless day of reckoning.

"I'll make your excuses to Daddy—a man who I wouldn't want to piss off, Nick." Elizabeth gathered her purse. "Tell the concierge to put your breakfast on my tab. I recommend the *Huevos Rancheros*—hot and spicy." She angled her tongue over her top lip and lashed slowly the hot-pink organ. "Just the way I know you like it, Nick." Walking away, she paused, turned her head, and shot him a steely glance. "Don't be stupid."

Stupid? Nick clenched his jaw and flared his nostrils. *More like furious and scared shitless.*

****

The phone rang nine times. Finally, the beeping ended, and a fumbling noise developed. Sitting beside Hannah at her work desk, with the phone on speaker, Jeannie held her breath.

"Hamilton's Bait and Tackle."

The voice identified male, outgoing, and flavored by a familiar hard-consonant, Lower Peninsula accent.

Angling the receiver with a gap between her ears, Hannah squinted. "Is this Bruce Hamilton?" She held a crossed index and center finger above her head.

"This is Bruce."

Jeannie clapped her hands over her mouth and widened her eyes.

Hannah curled her fingers inward and thrust the fist upward. She mimed a goofy face toward Jeannie. "My name's Hannah Kline, and I'm a member of the Copper Harbor Historical Society."

"Copper Harbor, so how are the fish biting at the

very top of Michigan?"

Hannah chuckled. "Well, as a matter of fact, the perch have been latching on well this season."

"I could live on fried perch," Bruce answered. "What can I do for you, Hannah Kline of Copper Harbor?"

"I think I have something that belongs to you, Bruce. Something that's over thirty years old. It was found in an estate donation."

"Well, hellfire, is it worth any money?"

"That's hard to answer. Did you work on Isle Royale in the Civilian Conservation Corps?"

Fisting her hands, Jeannie dug her thumbnails into her upper lip. *I can't stand the suspense.*

"Why yes, I did. Boy, I'm really curious now. Mmm...I did lose a penknife my father gave me. My initials were engraved on one side. There were four blades and a corkscrew. Did you find that?"

"No, we found some letters." Hannah made eye contact with Jeannie, pressed tightly her lips, and blinked her eyes.

Jeannie wrapped her arms around her breasts and swayed. *God, I'm so nervous. This man's life will never be the same.*

"Letters?"

Gazing into Hannah's eyes, Jeannie mouthed *Viola*.

"Yes. We went through a barn full of items bequeathed to the museums at Great Lakes University, and we found a tin box with the name of *Viola Smith* scratched on the top."

"That would be my wife. She died three years ago. Viola was the cook at the Isle Royale Camp. That's how we met. It's nice you tracked me down about this, but the things in that box belonged to her, and she can't read them now."

"Bruce, the letters in that tin box were addressed to you. A colleague and I took the liberty of investigating the documents."

Silence crackled and spat.

"Oh, my word."

"Bruce, there were two stacks of letters in the box. There were letters addressed to you, and there were letters addressed to Miss Margie Sheridan that were never mailed."

"Oh, my God."

Bonk.

Jeannie's eyes opened like an awakening barn owl. *Did Bruce suffer a heart attack? Did we kill him?*

"Bruce, are you there? Are you all right?" Hannah's voice squeaked.

Jeannie fidgeted with the pencils on her desk.

"Sorry, I dropped the phone, and I had to sit. I thought, I thought, back then that Margie didn't love me anymore. I thought she'd found another sweetheart while I was away. She never answered my letters."

Hannah frowned.

Jeannie stuck out her lower lip. *How tragic.*

"Viola was in charge of the camp mail…"

Erratic breathing punctuated by jerky huffs wavered through the phone.

"My God. Viola's the one who broke us up. How could she live with herself?" Bruce cried.

Jeannie drummed her knuckles on the tabletop. She slid to the edge of her family heirloom Windsor chair and wrapped her fingers over the well-worn arms. *How could anyone be so awful?*

"Say, Hannah Kline from Copper Harbor, you're not pulling my leg on any of this? You're not a crank phone caller, are you? You're not one of those stalker people, are you?" Bruce's voice turned gruff.

Sucking in a deep breath, Hannah readjusted the phone receiver. "No, Bruce, I've gotta tell you, if the shoe was on the other foot, and someone called me whom I didn't know, I'd be skeptical, too. Would you like the letters returned to you? I'll bring them myself, if you'd like."

"Is Margie in good health? Is she married? Is she happy? What must she have been thinking about me all these years?"

"Bruce, I think you'll have an opportunity to find out. I have her phone number. I can tell you Margie is a widow."

"Well, Hannah, I guess I'd like to get a hold of those letters."

"I'm going to Marquette on Friday. I could stop by your shop."

"I sure do appreciate this, Hannah."

"I'll get there about two p.m." Hannah returned the ear and voice piece to its cradle with the tenderness of tucking in a baby.

In less than a week, Marjorie's life will radically change. Please, God, let this news bring joy to this woman's world. Jeannie reached for Hannah's hand.

****

On Friday, Hannah drove Highway 2 to Marquette and found without difficulty the Hamilton Bait and Tackle Shop.

Gigantic buzzing coolers chock-full with darting

minnows and an ice cupboard parked outside the door.

Hannah crossed the threshold, and a small tinkling bell strung overhead announced her entrance. Pungent fish odor filled her nostrils. Squeezing her right thumb and forefinger over her nose, the Copper Harbor native moved farther into the shop. "Hello!"

"I'll bet you're Hannah." A short man with acrobat-muscled arms and profuse, dark hair sprouts on the backs of his hands enfolded her extended hand in both of his.

"That would be me." Looming over him, Hannah noted the brushed-over bald spot on the apex of his head.

Mechanical sputters and whirls burst from the floor-to-ceiling refrigeration units on three sides of the tightly crammed shop.

Hannah shivered.

A myriad of neon-hued plastic wriggly worms, inch-long, shiny-silver decoys, faux-haired fish attractions, rubber floaters, pronged metal hooks, and reels of transparent fishing line gobbled space on a pegboard-backed wall. Adjacent to the fish enticements, tack pins skewered into a stained corkboard held photographic memories of sun-bronzed people and their catch of the day.

She passed him the faded blue tin with the name *Viola* etched crudely into the top.

With shaky hands, Bruce grasped the container. Tears welled in his eyes. "I just can't believe this." Bruce wiped his face.

Hannah's heart clenched. "Listen, Bruce, I have to get going. Here's my business card. Would you do me a favor? Give me a call and let me know how things turn out."

Using his right knuckles, Bruce scrubbed his nose and upper lip. He nodded.

"Good luck, Bruce." Hannah gripped the doorknob. "I hope this turn of events goes well." She opened the door. As she exited, the overhead bell tinkled softly. *What will you do, Bruce?*

****

Bruce closed the shop, drove his faithful late-model truck home, and warmed up leftover goulash casserole his widow neighbor, Mrs. Pruitt, had brought over the previous night. He carried the plate to a TV tray beside his easy chair and swallowed his dinner, barely registering the savory onions and the choicest-cut burger Top Town Grocery offered. After setting his plate and fork aside, Bruce put on his reading glasses and pulled the Hannah-delivered tin from the floor beside his chair. Then, he organized by date the unmailed letters he had written to Margie. He did the same with the letters Margie sent.

Against the black-and-white backdrop of Miss Kitty, Chester, and Marshall Matt Dillon on the long-running television series *Gunsmoke*, Bruce scanned the letters one at a time.

Tears streamed down his face and clotted in his beard. *The loss of all these years. The heartache that could have been avoided—the joy that could have been shared.*

He suffered living with Viola and buried his yearning for Margie in the quicksand of memories.

Viola. She had been eager to please—to offer him the pleasures so greedily wanted by a lonely man.

Viola. She hypnotized him—a man ten years

younger, and then seduced him into a torrid affair.

Mrs. Pruitt's concoction roiled in his stomach.

Viola. Heat crept up his neck and infused his cheeks.

Shame flooded his psyche for the umpteenth time—humiliation for his weakness and his damn pride.

Viola's jealousy and hunger for attention only increased as the years passed. She questioned his every move. When he left for his lodge meetings, he suffered her harangues. 'How long will you be gone? Who are you meeting there?' "

And if he stayed later than what he committed, or if he'd had a few beers, or if his hair was mussed, he endured her accusations of infidelity that ripped through the night like bullets fired.

Viola grew fat and slovenly, and her smoking escalated to three packs a day.

Gray film darkened their entire home, like the suffocating apathy that exterminated their love life. Smoking, the cause of the mess, disgusted him and sickened her.

Viola died of lung cancer, hacking and sneaking cigarettes until the very end. She took the secret of these letters to her grave.

Damn. Clenching his fingers into fists, Bruce tipped back his head on the doily-covered headrest.

Static sounds reverberated from the rabbit-ear-antenna-topped television.

Bruce moved the chipped china plate pasted with congealed gravy from his lap to a tray beside his recliner. He retrieved the last letter Margie sent. His breath caught in his throat. Tears dropped and wet his faded shirt.

One word written in Margie's flowery penmanship jumped off the scallop-edged stationery and played on a loop.

Daddy.

Chapter 26

Beethoven's Fifth Symphony filtered through the high-ceilinged, museum-administrative-offices hallway.

A custodian shouldering a step ladder, a window-cleaning squeegee, and a bucket looked up and grinned.

I bet he's got a lot of fingerprints to erase. The Nightlife Exhibit has brought in hundreds of visitors in the three weeks since the opening. Jeannie waved.

The door to Cal's office rested ajar.

Jeannie thrust a wax-coated box through the entrance. "Breakfast, anyone?"

Turning from a shelf of tinctures, turpentine, and paints, Cal grinned. He dialed down the volume on the radio, accepted the package from Jeannie, and laid it on his desk. "Hey, thanks."

Wire armatures, tin snips, and needle-nosed pliers lay scattered over the surface of the room-centered work table. In contrast, a neatly piled one-inch slab of stapled papers heralding the campus logo aligned with the left-front table corner.

Pointing to the stack, Jeannie tented her brows. She sighed. "That time again, huh?"

"Yup. Evaluations. Goalsetting. Bureaucracy." Cal winced. He lifted the top of the box and extracted an almond-flaked cruller. "If Loretta were filling out the goals section for me, she would pencil in *substitute raw vegetables for pastries*. Winking, Cal chomped into the end of the baked good.

Jeannie laughed. "I'll be writing the same thing as last year. Complete my PhD."

"What about work goals?" Cal squinted through his glasses.

What gives with this grim look? Jeannie stilled. "More collaborative efforts. Look how great the Nightlife Exhibit was received—combining Botany, Ornithology, Textiles, Entomology, Mammalogy…"

"Working together on this last project has been a great experience. The key ingredient is the caliber and personal commitment of each colleague. Leadership weighs heavily in success." Cal looked away and blew out a breath. "Nick served us well in that score." The chief preparator shrugged. "I just hope it continues."

A chill spread through Jeannie's extremities. "What do you know that I don't?" She sucked in her cheeks.

"Word is Nick's been offered a position by the Department of the Interior. Big stuff." Cal blew out a low whistle. "Ever since the 1966 Endangered Species Preservation Act was established, mammalogists are in demand nationally. But, man, you really gotta know somebody to get an opportunity like that." Cal crinkled his nose. "Somebody like that Doug Harcourt fellow." He stowed the half-eaten cruller in the container and put his finger over his lips. "I'm not supposed to know this." He narrowed his eyes. "And neither are you."

Jeannie gripped the table edges. She nodded.

"We both know a nationwide spot is a premier position." Cal leveled his gaze to meet Jeannie's. "I believe the work would take him to Washington, D.C."

Jeannie pressed Cal's shoulder. "Thanks, Cal." She

faked a smile and pressed her finger against her lips.

With a cherry-lipped, rich-as-roses wife, his life would be perfect. Jeannie clamped her top teeth over her bottom lip.

****

Marjorie rolled a sharpened pencil between her palms. A blank pad of paper lay on her home desk. She slumped her shoulders and gazed outdoors.

Creamy-white, bell-shaped petals of the spring harbinger—snowdrop flowers—hung from the lime-green crowns poking above the thinning, early-March snow cover outside the floor-to-ceiling dining room windows.

On the kitchen wall, the phone emitted a jangling ring.

Grabbing the paper pad and a pencil, Marjorie padded across the linoleum and reached for the phone. *Yes, Mother. I'm ready for your grocery list.* She pressed the receiver to her ear and set the writing materials on the counter.

"Margie?"

She gripped the receiver, slipped off clip-on earrings, and repositioned the phone. *No way. My mind is playing tricks on me. I better call Dr. Fitzgerald for a cognitive test.*

"Margie Sheridan?"

With her free hand, she spread her fingers and pressed them against her forehead. *My God.* Her heart thrummed in her throat.

The dishwasher cycled into a raucous rinse sequence and, for several anxious moments, filled the space with sound that drowned out the voice on the phone.

Marjorie cleared her throat and swallowed. "You mean Margie Sheridan Howe?"

"Yes."

Marjorie widened her eyes and gasped. *Oh, my God.* "Bruce, is it you?"

"I have a lot to tell you, Margie."

With shaky hands, Marjorie pulled a chrome barstool away from the counter.

"I'd like to see you, Margie. Would that be all right?"

Am I hallucinating? Marjorie flattened her right thumb over her left wrist. She registered the pulse of her heart. "Y-y-yes."

"From your area code, it looks like you still live in the middle of the state." Bruce's voice wavered.

"Just down the road from my mother." Marjorie registered her knees buckling. Huffing small breaths, she dropped onto the vinyl-covered chair seat and anchored her feet on the rungs underneath.

"I live in Marquette. How about I make a trip down when the weather looks good?"

"Spring is in my backyard, Bruce. Come as soon as you can." *Get in your car and leave now.*

****

Arching his spine in a high-backed chair, Nick crossed his ankles under the twenty-foot-long board table in the Washington, D.C. Office of the Secretary of the Interior. He scanned the printed agenda lying atop the glossy table surface and turned his attention to the speaker.

"Take, for illustration, the trumpeter swan—North America's heaviest flying bird—with a wing span of six to eight feet. No, it wasn't predators such as wolves or foxes that brought the trumpeter swan to the brink of extinction." The spokesperson, one of the original authors of the United States 1956 Fish and Wildlife Act, leveled his gaze.

Inwardly, Nick raised his left fist in triumph. *One more voice shattering the undeserved nasty reputation of wolves.* He exhaled slowly. Back in Michigan, museum colleagues met for the first time since the Nightlife Grand Opening. *Wish I could be there to congratulate everyone on the overwhelming success and tell them how proud I am.*

Down the table's center and within reach of each participant, black metal trays held glass pitchers of ice water and four glasses.

As Nick poured himself a drink, ice thudded and splashed against the sides of his goblet.

Fronting each participant, a desktop microphone waited to amplify comments.

"As in many instances, the human being is responsible for the greatest decimation of the fish and mammals listed on the 1966 Endangered Species Act." The presenter lingered on the two-word culprit.

Well emphasized, sir. I wouldn't be surprised if a hat plastered in trumpeter swan feathers remains in a box somewhere in the Great Lakes University Historic Costumes Collection. Nick sighed. *Jeannie.*

"I'd like to hear from Dr. Cameron, an ichthyologist, regarding the plight of the pug nose minnow and the silver shiner," the moderator spoke into his microphone from the end of the table.

Tugging on his fish-motif tie, Dr. Cameron snapped the On button on his lavalier mic. "Biggest threats are habit degradation and water pollution. The latter is caused primarily by agricultural and industrial runoff. Again, we humans are the bullies."

"Let's turn to solution-driven action. Dr. Anderson will address this body on the ongoing discussion of genetic purity in regard to reintroducing species to geographic locations where they exist in peril." The moderator adjusted his spectacles.

The specialists droned on.

Nick yawned. He allowed his thoughts to wander from threatened habitats to a sweet, inspiring woman trying her darndest to make a purposeful life for her and her son. *Jeannie. Damn. What do I do? Could we have a future together?* If he could predict their potential for life everlasting by the response of his male parts, they would live in bliss for the remainder of their days on Earth. Under the table, Nick squared the Italian designer shoes he hadn't worn since his Great Lakes University interview. He rotated his butt. He slanted one shoulder forward, then cleared his throat.

From his vantage point in the stark conference room, Nick noted steely-gray file cabinets interspersed between neutral-colored-tweed-paneled dividers that provided workspace for the colony of gray-wool-flannelled government employees managing uniform black-and-white papers. Rows upon rows of fluorescent lighting hung overhead. Currents of air recycled by the lungs of the group blew from vents cut into the tiled ceiling.

A gavel slapped a wood block.

"There being no further business, this meeting is adjourned." The facilitator set the wooden, hammer-shaped portent on the table.

Paper shuffling, chair creaking, and murmuring

sounds ensued.

"Dr. Randall, we have a car outside. My name is Ursula. I'm to take you to the zoo for a visit with the preservation experts." A young woman stood a respectable bodyguard distance away with a peacoat draped over her forearm.

After a stop-and-go drive through the capital city, the driver pulled from the freeway into the nation's premier zoo and followed the signposts to the administration building. He pulled into a circular drive and let them out at the entrance to a modest-looking cement building.

Ursula pressed a doorbell to the right of the entrance.

Following a five-minute wait, a lab coat-wearing, ponytailed, thirty-something man flung open the door. "Hey." He thrust out the hand of a lumberjack lookalike. "Greg Peterson, at your service."

Grinning, Nick clasped the offered hand. "Nick Randall, accompanied by Ursula."

"Ursula, good to see you again. And Nick, my pleasure. My staff will show you our operations. I'm really interested in your feedback." Greg stepped aside and motioned them forward. "I've been following your work on Isle Royale—home to the gray wolf. I'm sure you're aware of the dismal plight of the red wolf."

Nick turned and furrowed his brow. "Very disconcerting."

Greg pinched the top of his nose. "They're on the brink of extinction, with less than one hundred known genetically pure wolves in the United States. Because mates are scarce, the red wolf has interbred with the coyote in several areas of the country. I'm part of a national discussion group in the American Association of Zoos and Aquariums which is considering a breeding plan and a release strategy into designated historic areas. We hope to restore some measure of genetic purity to sustain the genus *Canis rufus*."

Nick crimped his fingers and made a fist. "A close relative to the genus *Canis lupus*."

Greg bumped his knuckles against Nick's.

I've met a kindred spirit. Warmth spread across Nick's chest. His heart pumped passionately in his chest. He followed Greg into a single-windowed office.

Ursula joined them.

Maps and charts plastered industrial beige walls. Stuffed animal wolves, bears, and otters sat in a tangled cluster in a large wicker hamper.

Dipping his head toward the toys, Greg smiled. "For the kids at heart."

A not-unpleasant odor of eucalyptus swirled with disinfectant permeated the space.

"Well, how about we start with the wolves, then?"

"Let's go!" Nick scarpered to the door, stepped outside, and squinted against the afternoon sun. He gripped the iron top of the gated enclosure. "My compliments on the habitat. I see slash pine, loblolly pine, and short-leafed pine."

"Thanks. They are all indigenous to the American Southeast, just like the red wolves."

"How big a pack?" Nick bounced on his toes.

"Pleased to say we're up to sixteen." Greg nodded. "And I guess that's saying something since the red wolf is one of the rarest animals in the world."

"Can't say that about his cousins. On a global scale, gray wolves are in no danger. Maybe because they are the heftiest?" Nick scrutinized the pen. "Afternoon. They must be napping. Come dusk, they'll be more active."

Greg stuck his fingers under the bottom of his ball cap and scratched his head. "And looking for food."

"I like to ask other animal preservationists this question." Nick gazed at Ursula. "You first. What is your favorite mammal?"

Ursula crossed her arms over her chest and tapped a finger to her chin. "I'm a total sucker for lemurs. Maybe it's their googly eyes, but I'm just captivated."

"I get that." Nick laughed. "And Greg, how about you?"

"That's easy. Wolves—every color, every shape. Ever since I was a kid. Wolves are loyal to their own. They're athletic. They're magnificent. What about you?"

Nick bent his head. "Same for me." *This is a guy I could work with.* Recognizing a lightness he had subdued since leaving daily fieldwork, Nick breathed in the ancient, fecund scent of the conifers and the odors of scat and fur. He brushed his palms on his pants, arched back his head, and laughed with gusto.

Greg grabbed the fence and squatted. "I even have a Schnauzer named Wolf."

Nick slapped his thigh. "Geez, I have a kitten named Wolf." *His mama will get a kick out of this coincidence.* He froze. *Damn.* His smile dissolved. *Jeannie, Joey, Gunther, Wolf and Sam.*

Scanning the sky, Greg looked over his right shoulder. "We better turn back. Otherwise, we might get drenched."

"What's your concept for the breeding program?"

325

Nick fell in step alongside Greg.

"We'll have field associates in the wild trap what appear to them as red wolves. Then, through comparative measurements, vocalization analyses, and skull X-rays, we'll cull the pure red wolves from the coyotes and coyote-red wolf hybrids."

"That is good stuff. I gotta tell you, I'm very enthusiastic about getting involved in this project." Nick pounded his chest. "Yeah, good stuff."

Greg shook his head and smiled. "I gotcha."

"And once you have narrowed the field to the pure genetics, you'll foster the right environment for breeding." Nick punched the air.

"That's right. After that, we reintroduce the red wolf to his natural habitats along the Gulf Coast and in Texas. And here's some great news. We've heard from almost thirty institutions who want to assist." Greg stuck his hands into his pockets.

"Wonderful." Nick beamed.

"Dr. Randall, we are hoping you'll come on board." Greg nodded.

School-age children, wearing large laminated name tags, jumped and skipped as they passed the exhibits.

A boy roughly Joey's age walked between a man and a woman. The joined trio advanced three steps and stopped.

The sound of their merriment lanced Nick's heart.

The adults swung the boy.

The boy kicked the air.

A happy family experiencing the wonderment of animals. Damn.

It would be summer, and Joey would be out of school. Jeannie would swing their interlocked hands as they tried to keep up with an excited Joey. When Joey reached the wolf enclosure, he would jump up and down, and like an encyclopedia, spout all the facts, and lore of wolf anatomy, hunting skills, and interactions with humans. Joey would freely educate soon-to-be astounded fellow zoo visitors. "Wolves aren't monsters. They won't attack you. Aren't they beautiful?"

Nick pictured Jeannie heightening her seasonal glow with a layer of beaming motherly pride, sharing a smile so bright the warmth would melt his heart again. At the end of the day, they would share a picnic dinner—grilled fish, a crisp green salad, watermelon slices, bug juice for Joey, and mojitos for the adults.

Jeannie, can you even fathom what I envision? He risked heartbreak—backing off his pursuit of Jeannie. Denying Elizabeth jeopardized a sure funding source for the work he loved.

Overhead, in the nation's capital, a robin flew. Nest fodder hung perilously from the bird's beak.

Springtime—everywhere. Mammals and birds choosing mates—building nests. What about you, Randall?

Chapter 27

Forty minutes. Marjorie bit her lip. *No, don't mess up your lipstick.* She shifted her gaze to the bumpy aloe vera plant on the windowsill above the sink to the slope-shouldered refrigerator. The kindergarten art of her granddaughter's fingerprints stuck by magnets on the appliance door. *Their granddaughter.*

A vinyl thirty-three rpm record of "Red Sails" lay atop the domed cover of a record player. Marjorie had considered setting the needle to its grooves the moment she saw Bruce's car enter her driveway. But that action, like donning the last dress—that still fit—he had seen her in had been discarded in favor of appearing current.

She made a few concessions to reminiscence. After receiving Bruce's confirmation as his visit date, Marjorie made a hair appointment for a fresh cut and color at Jacobson's salon and requested a style familiar to Bruce. Prior to returning home, she perused the clothing racks downstairs in the ladies' department, and settled on a forest green, formfitting pantsuit.

In the blue spruce outside the window, a yellow-bellied Kirtland Warbler perched—warbling a melodic series of *ch-ch-chattanooga-choo-choo* couplets.

In comparison, Bruce had been more close-mouthed. During the two phone conversations she and Bruce shared, Marjorie attempted to discern why Bruce called her, but he kept repeating that he wanted to tell her in person. The mystery escalated in Marjorie's mind. *Will our meeting cause joy, or anger, or despair?*

Reaching in the hall closet for her purse, Marjorie extracted a small perfume bottle. She uncapped the glass container and dotted the vintage 1934 Blue Grass scent on her inner wrists and behind her earlobes.

Twelve-year-old poodle Ruby, Marjorie's constant companion since the death of her husband a year ago, curled on the rag rug fronting the portal to the two-car attached garage.

Intermittent wheezing sounds synchronized with the slow rise and fall of Ruby's chest.

A knock sounded on the door.

Marjorie flinched.

Ruby thumped her pompom tail and fell back asleep.

With her heart in her throat, and with the weight of over ten thousand questioning nights, Marjorie staggered to her front door. Despite the leno-weave curtain, the fleur-de-lis pattern etched on the window pane, and the years tallied as a loss, she merged into Bruce's steadfast gaze. Pulling back the door, she stepped aside and unleashed a wellspring of stomach flutters. Heat flushed her face.

Bruce dropped his head on his chest and wiped his feet on the doormat.

Everything on this man is new to me—a revealed bald spot once you bent over, trifocal glasses, a jaunty leather coat. But those boots—those boots could be the ones I helped him pick out in Woodbury's Department Store before he joined the CCC. Marjorie grinned.

The cellophane wrap surrounding the bouquet of roses he held in his left fist squeaked.

Seeing Bruce thrust forward the spray, Marjorie reached for the sweet-smelling, red-thorned flowers. "Thank you, Bruce. Come inside." She held the crinkly wrapped flowers with both hands at her waistline. *Just like a bride.*

He held his right arm close to his jacket.

Marjorie squinted. *Hmm...a rusted-around the edges tin that has seen better days—tucked tightly under your arm. Did you bring me cookies?* She pursed her lips. *What can possibly be important enough to share after all these years?* She moved toward the double-sided sink. "Let me put these roses into water." She busied herself—opening cupboard doors, stooping and peering, raising and scrutinizing. Finally, she settled on a tall green-glass vase with a scalloped lip. With the flowers and vase in hand, she rotated and walked to the small kitchen table in a sunny alcove.

Bruce stood on the threshold. He looked up and froze. "My God, you're as lovely as the day I kissed you good-bye." He removed his hat and held the duck-bill emulating a newsboy style in both hands.

"I'll take your hat and coat." Marjorie held out her hands with the palms up.

Passing off the garments, Bruce leaned and petted Ruby's head. Then, he pulled a chair from the kitchen table and sat. Curling his stout fingers, he tapped the tips on the wooden top.

Returning from a small closet, Marjorie moved toward the kitchen counter. "Still a coffee drinker?"

"Yes. And still black."

Bruce spun a lazy Susan that rested at the center of the table. He rearranged the salt and pepper shakers and ketchup and mustard bottles threatened by centrifugal forces.

"You never could sit still." Marjorie returned with two mugs in her hands. She set one in front of him and one on the opposite side of the round table. His hands were thicker and bore the evidence of countless wrenching motions. *You were always a hard worker.* The shirt cuffs on his long-sleeve woolen shirt stretched taut over his wrists. Silver hair poked above the last fastened button on the front of his shirt. Her body spilled liquid. She closed briefly her eyes. *My God.* She returned to the counter and slipped her fingers through the grip of a glass carafe.

She padded back to the table and set the pot on a handwoven trivet. Marjorie sucked the end of her index finger and shook the limb. "Ouch."

Bruce widened his eyes.

"I burnt it on the stovetop this morning."

"Lemme see."

Moving to his side, Marjorie extended her right hand. The nearness of her hip to his shoulder sent shock waves through her body.

Taking her wrist in one hand, Bruce levitated his other hand over their joined ones. Slowly, he descended his fingers and pressed hers open and flat. Gently, he trailed his thumb over her palm.

She slid back to the vacated chair, slumped onto the seat, and closed her eyes.

"Better?"

His voice drifted like a dream. "Much." Marjorie opened her lids and plumbed the depth of his once bright-blue eyes.

"Tell me about your life, Margie." Bruce cast his gaze into the center of her palm, bent his head, and kissed lightly the calluses at the bottom of her fingers.

"I'll start from now and go backward." She reclaimed her hand and refilled both cups on the table.

"Makes sense." He leaned back in his chair, brought the mug to his lips, and swallowed.

"We have a granddaughter." She smiled.

Bruce put his elbows on the table and his head in his hands.

Marjorie peeled his fingers back from his forehead. "See for yourself. There are pictures on the refrigerator door."

He pushed back his chair, strode to the icebox, and gaped. "May I?" He turned to Marjorie.

"Sure, bring them here."

Bruce moved the photos from under the magnets and, with the edge of a fingernail, lifted the images from their background. Carefully stacking them, he returned to the table, sat, and lay the pictures on the surface.

"Her name is Claire." Marjorie tapped on a snapshot of a heart-shaped faced, pig-tailed brunette. A wide-brimmed sunbonnet shaded her round cheeks and her saw-toothed smile.

"Hello, Claire," Bruce whispered.

Pulling another picture from the pile, Marjorie squared the photograph before Bruce. Within her chest, Marjorie's heart expanded and blocked her ability to breathe. "And here is Claire with her daddy—our son, Bruce."

After picking up the picture with trembling hands, Bruce held the photo at arm's length, and stared. "You gave him my name?" He squeezed shut his eyes. His breathing grew rapid. Silent sobs wracked his chest.

Then, in the kitchen where Marjorie had turned the pages of decades of Michigan lakes-themed calendar pages—featuring photos of canoers traversing the Au Sable River, riders waving from the rails of a Mackinac Island ferry, and fishermen raising nets on Lake Huron, she viewed Bruce crying a watershed of tears.

Ruby shook herself, setting the metal tags dangling from her collar in motion.

Clink-clink.

Then the elderly dog walked to her water dish and lapped her tongue through the liquid.

Swish.

"They both have your eye color that fades from blue to green." Marjorie wiped her cheeks.

"I see that." Bruce gazed at Marjorie and back to the image. "They're wonderful. Absolutely wonderful." Bending from his left hip, Bruce reached for the tin he had placed on the floor next to his chair. He positioned the canister on the table and pushed it over the tablecloth to Marjorie. "Open it." Bruce folded his arms over his chest, clenched the folds in his shirt sleeves, and leaned back in the chair.

Marjorie removed her glasses, leaned over the tin, and squinted. "Viola Smith?" She planted the glasses back on the bridge of her nose, peered at Bruce, and tilted her head.

Beeps and gear-switching sounds advanced toward the house.

Ruby rose from her place under the kitchen table, padded to the door, and whined.

"She likes to greet the trash guys. They always throw her a stick and rub her head." Pressing the palms of her hands on the tabletop, Marjorie pushed herself upright. *Who's Viola? And why did Bruce bring this old tin?* With a frown crowding her forehead, Marjorie met Ruby at the entrance, opened the door, and allowed the dog to exit. Turning back to the table, Marjorie gazed at Bruce. "I'll give her a few minutes." Bruce's complexion faded from ruddy to Petoskey-stone gray. Marjorie curled the fingers of her left hand, moved them to her closed lips, and tasted the salty residue of sweat and tears. *Maybe I don't want to know what's in that tin. Maybe I want to run out the door with Ruby and ride away with the friendly men in the smelly, green truck.*

Bruce gummed his lips and breathed out a voluminous breath. "Open it, Margie."

Reclaiming her seat, Marjorie pried off the top of the container with her square-shaped, petal-pink-polished fingernails and set the lid on the pansy-appliqued runner that fashioned a bridge across the white oak table.

A musty odor wafted.

Marjorie crinkled her nose. Removing the uppermost bundled envelopes, she spiked her spine and shot up her eyebrows. "Bruce, I remember sitting at my desk in my attic bedroom and writing these letters." She pulled the envelopes loose—one by one and tossed them across the table as if she dealt a deck of fifty-two playing cards for a game of War. "Why didn't you answer them?" Marjorie stood abruptly, gritted her teeth, walked to the front door, and opened it.

Ruby dashed into the kitchen, turned in a circle, snorted, and curled her body in front of the dishwasher.

Wrapping her arms over her chest and keeping her back to Bruce, Marjorie stared out the window. *I asked myself that question a thousand times—when I wrote that I was pregnant, when I wrote and told you that Mother and Father were sending me to live with Aunt Mildred in Minnesota until the baby was born, when I wrote with my aunt's address.* Her heart thrummed and thickened in her throat.

A gulping sound preceded the *clank* of china as Bruce's cup met a saucer.

I'm about to find out. Stiffening her shoulders, Marjorie hooded her eyes and returned to her chair.

Sighing, Bruce lifted his right hand to his face and pointed his index finger toward the tin. "Pull out the next packet."

Marjorie grabbed the twine-wrapped plain, white packets. Bruce's familiar, wide, angular penmanship spelled out *Miss Margie Sheridan, P.O. Box 112, Eaton Rapids, Michigan,* on fourteen, opened, unstamped envelopes. She coughed as bile permeated her mouth.

"They're in date order—from the first unsent one to the last—all fourteen of 'em." Bruce rubbed his hands together. "Take your time. I'll pour myself another cup of coffee."

The furnace droned.

Warm air blew through wall vents and rattled a stack of newspapers.

Marjorie removed her glasses and brought the letters two inches from her eyes. Her lips moved as she read silently the long, overdue missives. With trembling hands, she folded and restuffed each letter back into its envelope. She threaded her fingers together, stationed her elbows on the tabletop, and pressed the thumbs to her lips. Marjorie squeezed shut her eyes. She registered the *whap-whap* sound of Ruby's tail bump and Bruce's soothing voice. "Attagirl." She opened her eyes and met Bruce's gaze. "What happened?"

"Viola." Bruce formed fists and ground the vein-topped knuckles into his cheeks.

Marjorie clenched the bottom of her chair and expelled a deep, crescendo breath.

"The biggest regret of my life. I am so ashamed— so embarrassed." Bruce licked his lips and laid his palms on the tabletop. He arched his back and ran his hands through his thinning hair. Bruce slid slowly his hands across the wooden gulf between them. He sighed, retreated his hands, and cleared his throat. "You should hate me." He scrunched shut his eyes, then opened the lids, and gazed steadfastly into Marjorie's soul. "Viola was the camp cook. She took a liking to me. She was in charge of the mail. I swear on all we hold dear, Margie, that I never saw your letters until a few weeks ago." He released a breathy sob.

Reaching her hands across the last obstacle separating them, Marjorie dropped her palms atop the backs of his hands. "And Viola saw to it that I never received your letters."

Bruce raised his right shoulder, twisted his neck, and wiped his nose across the top of his sleeve. He laughed. "I didn't want to lose your grip."

"I'll be right back." Marjorie scooted from her seat, walked down a hallway, and returned with a box of tissues. "We can share." She grabbed a tissue and dotted her cheeks. "What happened a few weeks ago?"

"A lady from the Copper Harbor Historical Society called and said she had something belonging to Viola." Bruce squeezed Marjorie's hands. "My deceased wife." He nudged his nose across the shoulder seam of his plaid shirt and inhaled a snort.

Marjorie lifted the tissue box and tapped it on the tabletop.

Chuckling, Bruce plucked a disposable wipe from the offered container. "Sorry, force of habit."

"I'll let you off this time." Marjorie grinned.

Next door, a car door slammed in the driveway. A succession of three friendly beeps sounded.

"Viola's secret got left behind on Isle Royale and fell into the hands of rich people who collected items of Michigan history. The couple donated the artifacts to Great Lakes University Museum. When the institution's team examined this tin, they determined to return the contents to the owner. That's when the call came into my bait and tackle shop."

Marjorie broke her right hand away, raised it to her mouth, and flattened her palm against her nose. "Oh, my God."

"The museum staff did better than that, Margie. They tracked you down and gave me your phone number." Bruce shook his head.

"What amazing folks—to do all that work for us." Marjorie filled her lungs with air and expelled slowly the oxygen.

Bruce ran the tips of his fingers over the snapshots lying on the table. "Do you think I could meet them?"

Grabbing a tissue with one hand and twining her remaining hand around Bruce's left hand, Marjorie offered a wobbly smile. "We'll make that happen."

Chapter 28

Tina's handwritten note lay across the desk blotter beside the examination table in the Collections Room. *We're making good progress cataloging the remainder of the Eriksson collection. Only one more box to go.*

Jeannie blew a breath bubble from deep in her chest. She opened the recording log, donned white cotton gloves, and reached for a sharpened pencil. Folding back the flaps Hannah and the Copper Harbor volunteer team taped shut, Jeannie withdrew a packet of light items enfolded in crinkling tissue paper. She laid the package on the muslin-wrapped tabletop. A white cotton pillowcase with crudely crafted hand embroidery covered a clumpy baby quilt. *Quilter used 100 percent cotton batting, evidenced by the unsmooth condition. Appliqued with gingham dog and calico cat motifs.* Jeannie recorded the descriptions in the acquisitions log. Tenderly, she examined a fine batiste bonnet comprised of strips of faggoting and tatted lace. Frayed silk ribbons hung from the two face edges. *This baby had to have been tiny.* A lump formed in Jeannie's throat as she fingered the soft adornments.

A curled-edged, sepia-toned photograph depicting a frightened baby lay at the bottom of the tissue wrapping. Propped by pillows on a high-backed wicker chair, the child made its eyes wide and held its hands as if reaching for its mother. *He or she looks terrified.*

Jeannie felt her heart sagging in her chest.

"Jeannie?" Marie's voice echoed from the entrance.

"In here, Marie." Jeannie sighed.

"Cherie, whatever is the matter?" Marie touched Jeannie's shoulder.

"It's so sad. It's just so sad." Jeannie's voice came in huffing breaths. She held the faded photograph.

Marie sat and folded her hands. She tented her eyebrows and gazed into Jeannie's eyes.

"Nothing is left of this family except these photographs, a baby bonnet, and an embroidered pillowcase," Jeannie whispered.

Settling into the stool next to Jeannie, Marie scooched the seat closer.

Floor-scraping noises pierced the quiet.

Gently, Marie ran her pointed fingernails over the photograph. She brought the artifact close and squinted. As if she listened to a French lullaby, Marie rocked her head. "I see the effort of a loving, creative mother. This baby is shiny clean and well-fed. Here's a happy moment, frozen in time. No one can take this away. It's stamped in the universe. Surely, this baby grew to be a confident person, surrounded by the care and love of his family. Love is passed to the next generation. So, something of great value remains. Love."

Jeannie gritted her teeth. "You're right, Marie." She smoothed the baby cap. "I don't know why I am so melancholy."

"*Cherie*, you are too young to be alone. You will always love Frank, but if it was you who had died, would you want your Frank to walk the rest of his earthly days all alone?"

"No, I would want him to have comfort and love and to enjoy his journey." *That would include allowing you to take on a new love with all the splendor of physical intimacy. Of course, I would want that for you, Frank.* Jeannie set her jaw.

Tears welled in her eyes.

"That is what true love is, don't you think?"

Marie's calming voice and plaintive plea swirled in Jeannie's psyche.

"Placing the joy of the other above your own? I think you should say *yes* the next time you are asked."

Jeannie nodded. *As long as there is no harassing heiress in the picture.*

****

Wandering to the *U*-shaped table formation, in the First Presbyterian Church basement, Jeannie shrugged her sweater from her shoulders and patted the inset pocket. *Widowed care homework.*

The folded letter inside crackled.

Sitting at the left top corner of the *U*, Jim rapped an envelope on the tabletop, rotated the edge, and drummed it again.

Tucked into an eave, a mobile rack held uniform choir robes. *That style hasn't changed in hundreds of years. The solid color, voluminous-sleeved gown serves as a recognizable rite of passage garment. In addition to identifying a choir's altos, sopranos, bass, and tenors, the style also signifies college graduates, faculty, and guest speakers.* Jeannie sighed.

Graduation ceremonies loomed on the university calendar. As a faculty member, Jeannie donned her college graduation robe, hood distinctive to the university she graduated from, and her mortarboard hat.

Then she marched shoulder to shoulder with colleagues as they preceded the excited and exhausted graduates into the auditorium. On university schedules, this time of year also signified a changing of the guard. Faculty retired. New faculty dotted the *I*'s and crossed the *T*'s to their fall semester onboarding.

Nick, what have you decided? Are you going to Washington and Elizabeth, or are you staying at the university with me?

"Good evening, everyone." Sharon set her elbows on the table and folded her hands in a praying position. "This is our graduation night. Congratulations."

"Ta-da!" Verna clapped. "I'm proud of all of us."

Jennifer thumped the palms of her hands on the tabletop. "Drum roll!"

Sharon leaned, pulled a metal mailbox from the floor, and set the receptacle on the table. "We'll spend the time sharing our letters. Again, if you do not want to read your letter aloud, just say *pass*. At the end of the evening, we will put our letters in this special mailbox, symbolic of getting our message to our loved one." She lifted the red plastic flag on the box's side. "Who wants to start?"

Marie tipped her head low, raised a ruled piece of paper before sequined glasses, and waved a hand. "I will."

I might be the only one at Great Lakes University privy to this side of Marie Denue. She's been through so much, and she's so courageous. Jeannie smiled.

"*Mon Cherie*, my Paul." Marie cleared her throat. "I'm finally taking your wish for me seriously. You wished me a happy life, a live with *amour*—with love. I will take a trip to Paris, buy an expensive *chapeau*, and

341

revisit the cafes where we spent hours, and I will allow myself to love again. *Je t'aimerai pour toujours.*" Marie refolded the letter and passed the mottled blue stationery to Sharon via Jennifer and Marjorie.

Sharon opened the mailbox and tossed in Marie's letter.

"Bert." Bunnie fanned her fingernails through her brow. "We had big plans, buddy." She expelled a sigh. "I'll remodel our bedroom. I'll paint the walls yellow so it'll look like sunshine. I'll take watercolor painting classes—something you always encouraged me to do. I'll volunteer at the Cancer Center. I think I can be a big help to other people going through what we did." The widow tucked the message into an envelope, licked the gummed triangular flap, ran a manicured finger over the edge, and passed the missive to Sharon.

"Dear Hank, the kids might not like it, but I'm gonna sell the cottage." Verna formed a moue with her mouth. "I don't like going there without you, and the upkeep is too much work. Let someone else worry about the taxes and mice and boarding it up in the winter. Hank, I'm going to forgive you and the cigarettes you smoked. After all, some people smoke their entire lives and live to be ninety. You didn't smoke so you could leave me. Who's to know?" She raised a gnarled finger and adjusted her glasses. "I'm gonna buy a short skirt, and I'm gonna surprise the man who is used to hearing the word *no* from me. The next time he asks, I'm heading to the Crooked River Lodge with him, sidle up to the bar, and buy him a beer. And just to make things clear—I'm buying that man whatever's on tap. I'm not blowing all the money you left me on thirsty guys, Hank."

Jeannie widened her eyes. *Verna?*

"Good for you, Verna! Pass that letter up here." Jennifer clapped.

Verna winked.

Jim wiped the front of his clenched hand over his nose and scratched the unruly hair fringing his balding head. He looked at his lap and coughed.

"Dear Mary, I've decided to take the money I was saving to give you a surprise visit to Hawaii and go there myself. I will visit Kolekole Pass, the Big Island, and the outer islands. I'll go to a luau and maybe even learn to hula. And when I get back, I'll take cooking lessons and start accepting invitations from our friends to their card parties. Love, your Jim."

"When I first knew about this final letter writing assignment, I had no idea the impact letters would have on my grief journey." Marjorie licked her lips and shook her head.

Jeannie held her breath and scrunched shut her eyes. *No kidding.* She opened her eyes and met Marjorie's gaze.

"Really, this story is just incredible." Marjorie held up a packet of letters.

Jim punched the top of his pen.

Click-click.

With a long-handled spoon, Sharon whisked her tea. Thin vapors swirled above the cup like a low-lying snow cloud.

"These letters are over thirty years old." Marjorie waved the papers in the air. "And they were never delivered." Marjorie stiffened her expression and every noticeable muscle in her body.

"What?" Jennifer cried.

"Hmmm?" Sharon suspended the motion of lifting her teacup.

Around the table, gasps and titters rose.

"My first love, Bruce Hamilton, joined the Civilian Conservation Corp in 1933. He was stationed on Isle Royale, over four hundred miles and one big Lake Superior away from me. We were so distraught to be apart, but the CCC offered him a good livelihood during the Depression. We promised to write to each other." Marjorie gripped the pile of letters, held them above her head, and shook them. Her face flushed. "And we did."

Jeannie's heart thrummed in her chest. Tears threatened to spill from Jeannie's eyes. *Oh, Marjorie.*

"These letters were intercepted by a woman who stole Bruce away."

A low moan escaped Marie's lips. "Terrible." She pulled her wrap sweater closer to her chest.

"This deception broke us up and, even sadder, kept our son Bruce and his father, Bruce, apart." Marjorie wrung her slender fingers. "Until recently, that is." She gazed at Jeannie. "A few months ago, our curator friend"—Marjorie pointed to Jeannie—"on a work trip to Copper Harbor to retrieve a trove of historical artifacts came across a camp cook's tin of recipes, news clippings, and letters."

Bunny swiped her forehead with the palm of her right hand. "Unbelievable."

"So, with that unfolding saga, here is my letter. Dear Marv, thank you for loving me with no restraint. Thank you for loving Bruce with no restraint. In our last moments together, you urged me to go on with my life. As it turns out, I'm going backward first. Bruce's father and I have been reunited. I promise to grab ahold of love and never take that miracle for granted. Oh, and I'm keeping the tomato competition going. I'll grow the biggest beefsteaks ever, and then, grill some burgers, top them with those juicy fruits, and remember you. Love you, Marjorie."

Jeannie ground her right elbow on the tabletop, cupped her right hand over her mouth, and shook her head. *What a love story for the ages. Marjorie, I am so happy for you.*

The newly unified lover dabbed her glasses on her shirt. After finding Jeannie's gaze, she offered a wobbly smile.

Reaching, Jennifer clasped Marjorie's shoulder and bumped her forehead against Marjorie's.

"I want everyone here to witness this letter disappear into Sharon's mailbox. No letters of mine are going into a camp cook tin again!" Marjorie stiffened her shoulders.

Sharon came around the table and grasped Marjorie's letter. Then, she walked to the mailbox, unfastened the door and, as if she were tossing a football, hurled the letter into the box, and slammed the lid.

Clapping sounds rent the basement air.

Marjorie's cheeks reddened. She fisted her left hand in jubilation.

"That gives me the courage to go next." Jeannie squeezed shut her eyes and fluttered them open.

The room grew quiet.

Lolling her tongue over her top teeth, Jeannie straightened the folds in a lined yellow paper. "Dear Frank, I wrote you thousands of letters—some on paper and most on my heart. As I put pen to paper, I see our last day together." She closed her eyes, drew a breath, and reopened her eyes. "The tea steaming from your cup smelled of lingering mornings and sun risings over Lake Huron. Your induction haircut had grown out. I threaded my fingers through your thick hair and tugged it so tightly the natural crimp straightened. You protested with a smile. Then you told me I was the prettiest girl on earth. I corrected you. 'I am the luckiest girl on earth.' My heart swelled and spilled into every crevice of my body."

The group of grievers passed a box of tissues down the table.

Marie nudged the supply of tear wipers against Jeannie's forearm.

"Since you left this earth, every sense in my body dulled. I buried myself in grief. Frank, it's time for me to emerge from a shell into a creature with wings and excitement for taking a breath and pursuing life. I need to do it for Joey, our son, and I'll do it for me, too." Slowly, Jeannie exhaled. "With the help of special friends"—Jeannie scanned the room and made eye contact with each of them—"I've found the courage to go on and build a full life for Joey and me. Frank, you are my forever love. Jeannie."

Chapter 29

Without knocking, Cal shuffled into Nick's ground-floor office in Morrill Hall. "I've got an opportunity for you, Dr. Randall." Cal leaned over Nick's shoulder, pulled a sheaf of papers from his paint-riddled pocket, and set them square in front of the mammalogist.

Cedar-scented, curlicue-sculpted wood shavings clung to the chief preparator's jacket. Dust motes danced in the deep afternoon sun that poured through the shoulder-height window. Dithering crocus buds, brave this morning and festooning the university octogenarian oaks, now recoiled at day's end, padlocked their petals, and cowered close to the brick walls, constructed in 1900—the first year of the century.

"What's this all about?" Nick ran a hand over glossy brochures scattered amidst his workspace, as if he were culling the fifty-two cards of a playing deck. On the strewn documents, oversized fonts vying for attention advertised Washington, D.C. real estate, car rentals, and community events.

For a brief moment, Cal shot Nick an X-ray gaze. "You need a volunteer project to check off on your faculty evaluation. I recommend this one."

Nick held the papers in one hand. "Looking for Scout leaders." He tilted his chin. "Huh?"

"It would be a perfect fit. You've got camping skills, a love of nature, a zany sense of humor, high tolerance for chaos, and according to Donita and Walter—your graduate students—you are a natural-born teacher."

You nailed it. Sure sounds like me. Nick chuckled and leaned back in his chair. He gazed at Cal. "You do know I might not be here next year."

Cal squinted, nodded, wrapped his arms around his chest, and swayed side to side. "I've heard rumblings."

"If I accept the Washington offer, I'd get to make a positive impact on preserving our country's most vulnerable mammals." Nick puffed his chest.

"Yeah, that would be the cat's meow." Cal scratched his chin.

"Ever been a Scout, Cal?" Nick asked.

"Nope. I just happen to know a little guy who's really interested. His mom told me he brought home a flyer in his backpack. She fished it out and asked him about it."

Nick sucked in a breath.

"The little guy tore up the paper and got real mad." Cal turned his attention to the pile of brochures. "He said all that business was just for kids who had dads. It got me thinking. Vulnerable mammals come in all shapes and sizes."

A trash can clattered in the hallway. The smell of disinfectant waffled through the door.

Cal glanced up at the uniform university wall clock. "The cleaning crew is here, and geez, look at the time. I gotta git home. Tonight's spaghetti night, and Loretta can cook Italian like she grew up in Tuscany."

Nick nodded.

Buttoning his jacket, Cal lumbered toward the door. He stopped and met Nick's gaze. "I love that boy and his momma, too." Leaving the door ajar, Cal let his voice trail. "You be careful."

Turning in his chair, Nick registered sawdust remnants flaking willy-nilly from Cal's back. The fragments fashioned a trail into the hallway—like a forked road imposing a decision.

****

Majestic white spruce and balsam fir rooted as watchmen on Isle Royale's backbone. Frothy spray misted Nick's face. Through his hand gripping the tiller, Nick experienced fifty-horsepower, outboard motor vibrations thrumming his body.

Gasoline dribbled on the water's surface, fashioned a modern art canvas of iridescent green-and-purple spatters, and floated a sweet smell that crammed his senses. Nick shut his eyes and tipped up his chin. He could think more clearly here.

The gravity of the decisions facing him bucked and battered as the skiff split Lake Superior chop. The albatross of time hung around his neck like the weight of the kapok filler in the life preserver encasing his neck.

Doc McIvor levered an ultimatum. When this Isle Royale trip ended in one week, Nick's resignation or commitment to continuation was due.

Martin had arrived ten days ago and set up camp on Lake Mason. Once Nick reached the site, they would catalog the skeletal remains of moose found in the spring thaw. Then, they would partner the report anticipated by the physicians and nutritionists working on the osteoarthritis study.

Looking forward to chewing the fat with you, friend. I might take you up on that promise you made in Copper Harbor. In the same breath you mentioned Doug Harcourt, you also said, 'I got you, buddy.' Nick chewed his lip.

Bubbles erupted in the wake of the propeller swirling.

Nick adjusted the engine's speed from a comfortable trolling to a four thousand rpm cruising speed. Going faster would burn gas quicker, but he'd left the dock with four gallons, a more than adequate amount to reach his port.

Below the surface of the Great Freshwater Sea, carp, herring, brook trout, lake sturgeon, rock bass, and at least forty more species of fish cycled through life stages of egg to larvae, fry, fingerlings, adults, spawning, and death. Along with the aquatic life dwelling beneath the inland ocean, sinister shadows lurked. Ghosts of the *Madeline, S. S. America*, the *Henry Steinbrenner*, the *Chester A*, and more than twenty other ships swam.

Two decades earlier, on the island's northwest side, the *Emperor*, a ten thousand-ton Canadian wheat packet, crashed into the Canyon Rocks and lost its propeller. Less than an hour following the loss of that critical component, the *Emperor* listed and sank, dumping thirty-six men into the frigid waters of Lake Superior. Eighteen sailors drowned.

Nick shivered. *I've read the accounts of the survivors. Damn lucky, they were. Many of the unlucky met their death due to suction caused by the boat's plummeting into the four-hundred-foot depths.*

A gust of air brushed Nick's brow and through the

hair sticking to his temple. He closed his eyes. *Dad, I feel you.* He chuckled. *Here you are, Dad, using your fish analogies to sort through life's dilemmas.*

They'd had a favorite fishing hole in Mullett Lake and frequented it whenever Nick's mother reverted to her bat-shit rantings. As he grew older, he and his father found more reasons to angle for blue gill, crappie, and perch—the mild, white-fleshed, pan-fried feasts of inland lakes.

Dad had sat, hollowed out a spot for his butt, stretched straight his long legs, threaded a worm on the hook, and cast his line. Nick repeated his father's preparations.

"See that, son, the unsuspecting fish is attracted to the cheap, shiny bauble. He forgets everything his dad ever told him about thinking first before you bite. Remember that when it comes to people. You might lose all sense when you see a shiny lure, too. Maybe it's that new bicycle in Green's Hardware, or maybe it's a woman all fancy and smelling nice. But take a step back. Think before you bite. Is that bicycle overpriced? Do you really need it? Will you use it for a long time or soon tire of it? The same with a woman. She might be all dolled up. But is she kind? Does she make you a better person?"

A backless, sequined, shiny lure smelling of raspberry liqueur—Elizabeth. Nick's stomach roiled.

Overlapping strangulated cries of seagulls pulsed from the craggy shoreline.

The Great Sea contracted and constricted like a giant lung.

A flotilla of bird plumages bobbed on the lake's surface.

Nick jerked the motor casing.

Too late.

Whipped forward to the rigid wooden bow, Nick thrust up his hands. He grappled for the gunwales.

The smell of burning oil stuffed his nose.

Metal grating shrieks rent the still air.

Smoke poured from the engine cowling.

Drifting on the current at a threatening angle to the island's perimeter, the runabout separated from the nautical circle of life—the propeller—and blew apart.

****

Jeannie bolted upright. Frantically, she swept a hand over the familiar cotton comforter topping her body. "Wolf? What the heck was that about?" She scooped the kitten to her chest and kissed his standing-on-end fur. "You scared the crap out of me, you crazy boy." She reached for the antique lamp on the bedstand and switched on the light. Squinting at the alarm clock setting at the base of the yellow-and-blue porcelain converted oil lamp, Jeannie rubbed a circular configuration on her cheeks. *It's only six a.m. Glad you jumped in my bed and not Joey's, Wolf.*

The kitten's eyes glowed eerily.

Goose bumps rose on Jeannie's arms.

Still clutching Wolf, Jeannie rose and threaded her arms into the sleeves of her chenille bathrobe. She slipped her feet into hard-soled slippers and crept down the stairs.

Screech.

Illuminated by a pink dawn, thin-as-needle branch tips brushed against the kitchen window.

Snubbed popcorn kernels flecked plastic bowls resting on the sink bottom.

Walking Wolf to his food and water bowls, Jeannie bent and lowered him to the floor. She yawned, placed her hands on her hips, leaned back her head, and arched her back. Then, she straightened, rolled her shoulders, and swiveled her head side to side. *Might as well get something done.* After putting the teakettle on a stove and turning the gas on under the burner, Jeannie padded into her makeshift office at the end of the dining room. Sighing, she extracted a thick bundle of yellow-highlighted pages from her briefcase and sat in the hard-backed chair fronting her desk.

Final edits were made. Once the university's graduate office signed off, her PhD. dissertation would be printed, bound, and dispersed to the university's collection of theses and dissertations and the U.S. Library of Congress.

Jeannie ran a hand through her bedhead hair. The heaviness of a steely rock crowded her stomach. Visions of Nick quizzing her before the oral defense of her dissertation flooded her mind. Celebrating the triumph of handling the black leather-bound, gold-imprinted ticket to the title of Dr. seemed hollow without him.

Tweet.

Jeannie jumped, strode to the stove, grabbed a potholder, and lifted the teakettle from the blazing red burner. She selected a mug from the shelf, dropped a tissue-paper-thin, peppermint-flavored tea bag into the cup, and poured steaming water over the herbs.

Ring.

Gunther slid across the kitchen floor.

His nails struck the surface like a match hitting flint. With her heart tingling in her throat, Jeannie squelched the grating ring by picking the receiver off the wall-mounted phone.

"Hello? Hannah?"

Jeannie clenched the phone. She grimaced. "Oh, my God." She grabbed a pad of paper and a pencil and scribbled a phone number. "Say it again. Got it." She nodded. "Please do." Slowly and with both hands, as if the dumbbell-shaped receiver was a landmine, she planted the receiver back in its cradle. She sidled to her chair and collapsed into the seat. *God, not again. Why me? First Frank. You can't do this to me, God.* Jeannie reached for the bottom of her cotton nightgown. She crumpled a section of the hem into her fist and moved the fabric to her mouth. Hyperventilating, she stuffed the wad through her teeth and clamped down.

Silent sobs wracked her chest.

Wolf scampered under the table and sprung into her lap.

Caressing the kitten, Jeannie folded like a Scout jackknife.

****

Directed by a baton-holding zoo employee, a trumpeter swan arched her bony wings, stretched her webbed feet on her folding chair, and squawked her symphonic call.

A red fox, lying prone in a thicket of neatly folded black wool-serge cuffed trousers, licked his mangled paw.

A bucket of barn kittens, their eyes not yet open, struggled as a gallon of cold water flushed away their faint mewlings.

Nick forced open his sand-abraded eyelids.

A canopy of leaving birch floated far above.

Waning sunlight filtered through the interstices of the fluttering sawtooth-edged foliage. Finely crushed rock nipped the back of his legs, arms, and skull.

From his prone position, he held his fingers close to his face. With each successful finger stretch, a bubble of hope filled his belly.

Pain so hot it registered as an electrocution shot through his lower right leg.

Son of a bitch. He groaned.

Lifting his head, he gazed the length of his body. The acknowledgment of a purple welt close to his ankle with the circumference of a plum elicited a consigned sigh. He planted his palms into the damp gravel and leveraged his spine into a sitting position. He grunted.

A broken shell bit into his right palm. Slowly, he lifted his right hand, picked the shell, and, with every ounce of desperation infusing his being, flung the casing.

He replanted the palm and leaned forward. *Gah.* He scrunched shut his eyes. *I gotta look. Damn.* Putting all his upper weight on his left hand, he raised his right hand and moved it along his thigh. *So far, so good.* Nick moved his fingers to his knee and opened his eyes.

The lower half of his leg angled out from his thigh. The kneecap hugged his leg like a wasp nest stuck to a roof eave. He lay back on the cold, wet beach. *Son of a bitch.* Nick lolled in that position for what he remembered as ten minutes. Then, he culled his memory for lifesaving nuggets from the *Survival Manual for Field Mammalogists.*

Step One. Take stock of your surroundings. *The engine clogged well after Mott Island. Depending on the current, I washed ashore on either the southern shore of the Moskey Basin or the southwest tip of Caribou Island.*

Step Two. Assess your tools. Nick fumbled the pockets of his cargo shorts. *Metal match, my old friend. Jackknife, sand in every crevice, but good. Shoelaces, soggy as hell, but good.* He scanned the beach. *Three wooden boat ribs—my life raft.*

Step Three. Assess your physical condition. *Well, shit.*

Step Four. Evaluate water and food sources. "Hah!" *An ocean of fresh water. Small pine saplings within my reach, full of sugar and vitamins. Peel the bark and chew.*

Step Five. Plan your rescue. *Once Martin figures I'm missing, he'll contact the Island Emergency Services. They'll deploy an aerial surveillance pilot. I need to build a fire.* Nick scanned the beach and a land radius to a steep incline. *Plenty of driftwood. By minimal crawling, I can pluck tree branches. But first, I gotta make it through the night.*

Darkness breached the sky.

Shadows melted into oblivion.

With sight diminished, Nick's senses of hearing and touch elevated.

Owooooo-Owooooo-Owooooo.

Nick scrunched shut his eyes.

The quickly repeated, high-pitched ending howls pierced the wolf-lover's psyche.

Just like me, you're lost and all alone, fella.

Step Six. Ditch all negative thoughts. *Fight like hell to survive.*

****

Jeannie selected a cardboard tube from the textile

collection supply closet, laid it on the examination table, and wrapped it in acid-free tissue paper. *Gotta keep my hands and my mind busy. Hannah, what is happening? Any news this morning? It's been two days. I have to know.*

Coming alongside, Tina donned a pair of white cotton gloves.

"You take that end." Jeannie laid a *Ghiordes*-hand-knotted Persian carpet on the table. Then, she set the tube at the top of the piece and pulled a few inches of the textile over the tube.

On the other side, Tina did the same. "Finals are next week. Ugh."

Together, they rolled and wrapped the rug over the cardboard and covered the tube with a muslin sheet.

"You're quiet today." Tina secured the fabric covering with a rubber band.

Jeannie swallowed. She stifled tears. "I'm expecting some important news, Tina, and I'm just trying to stay distracted."

Tina frowned. "We could tackle the shoe closet."

"Jeannie?" Marie appeared. "Hannah from the Copper Harbor Historical Society just called. She said for you to call as soon as possible."

Underneath her feet, the tile floor appeared as a boundless ocean topped by a razor-thin coat of ice. Even testing the surface with a toe could catapult Jeannie into a strangling darkness. Her heart beat as if the organ were a fish darting for a secretive labyrinth to escape predators. "Excuse me." Jeannie covered her mouth, ran to her desk, and dialed the phone. "Hannah?"

Tina lingered in the background.

Marie straddled the doorway.

"He's where?" Jeannie licked her lips. "In what hospital?" She opened a desk drawer and selected a pencil. With a shaking right hand, she scribbled on the desk blotter. "Thanks for keeping me in the loop. Yes, thank God for that." Jeannie set down the phone. She wiped tears from her face. She turned to the women displaying wide eyes and color-drained faces. "He's alive. Nick Randall is alive. He survived a boating accident in Lake Superior. He's been rescued and flown to a hospital in Chicago." The curator sucked a shuddering breath. "He's being treated for a leg injury and exposure."

Marie moved forward and squeezed Jeannie's shoulder.

"No wonder you were worried." Tina smoothed her hands down her jean-clad thighs.

Jeannie's heart plummeted to her heels. Hannah's words rang in her ears. *Flown to Chicago in a private plane chartered by Doug Harcourt.*

Chapter 30

A crew of fluorescent-vest, orange earmuff wearing university landscapers fortified with industrial mowers, weed whackers, and sidewalk edgers chewed, whirled, and snipped fresh paths flanking the entrance to the Great Lakes University Museum.

Nick leaned heavily against the side of the checkered cab. *It's been seven weeks since I left this place for Isle Royale.* He breathed in the fertile odors of root-exposed plants. Nick extracted his wallet from his back pocket, pulled out a twenty-dollar bill, and paid the driver. Leveraging both wooden crutches under his arms, the injured mammalogist resumed the now-familiar patterned motions of pole vault swing and elated weightlessness, followed by teeth-clenching braking. He made his way down the incline and through the ground-level entrance. *First things, first. I've gotta man up.* Nick turned right and followed a long hallway to the bowels of the museum artifact preparation work area.

"Well, as I live and breathe—it's Robinson Crusoe." Cal reached for a rag and wiped the square between his oily, black palms. "Just finishing up some signs for a summer exhibit." He stepped to the doorway and grasped Nick's right hand in both of his.

The recognizable and comforting scent of Eau de Cal, a concoction of turpentine, mothballs, and paint additives, mingled in Nick's strained respirations. The mammalogist smirked. Shoring a pair of crutches under his armpits, he leaned against the concrete-cubed wall of Cal's office. "What's going on over there?" Nick lifted a crutch and pointed the rubber-tipped end toward a small cluster of crude clay figurines.

Poking his fingers inside the deep-welled pockets of his lab coat, Cal sidestepped to a long table. "These, my friend, are first drafts of the Endangered Species of Michigan Exhibit, coming to a field museum near you. Someone I know, and have come to respect, initiated this idea." The errant hairs sprouting from Cal's ears glistened in the afternoon sun, funneling through the west-facing window.

Nick swallowed. "Could you give me an idea where I might find Jeannie?" The mammalogist curled his fingers over the cross bars on the crutches.

Cal dipped his chin to his chest. He peered down the end of his nose and met Nick's gaze. "Done being a knucklehead, are you?"

Nick cleared his throat. "Yeah, I'm done being a knucklehead."

"All right then." Cal withdrew a toothpick from his pocket. He nodded.

"This is just a hunch, but she mentioned today she hankered for Mose's burrito supreme. It's just after five o'clock, and it's Friday night. Remember what that means?" Cal raised his eyebrows.

Nick tapped his forehead. "Yup. Two-for-one burritos." He reached for Cal's hand. "Thanks, Cal. That sculpture on the end wouldn't be a red fox, would it?"

Cal winked. "Once I paint it, doubts will disappear.

Now get the heck out of here."

I think I just received the first round of approval. Nick bit his lower lip. *Round two, Jeannie.*

****

Along the main drag, mannequins in Jacobson's window dressed in lightweight summer frocks and garden party separates. And even though they looked ready to engage in a socially stimulating event, they, like her, had nowhere to go. Jeannie adjusted the watch face she had grown sick of viewing. *I hate weekends.* Sighing a shaky breath, she resumed her heavy-footed walk. Jeannie upstretched her right hand and fingered the stone pendant nestled in the groove between her breasts. She registered a tightness in her chest. A few days before last Christmas, following a rambunctious day of sledding and snowball throwing, Jeannie had served a winter-comfort meal of meat loaf and mashed potatoes for Joey, Nick and herself.

A tiny smile crept across her face.

Seated at the table, she and Nick had engaged in playful bantering and an intermittent under-the-table game of footsie.

Clunk.

Sleepy Joey dropped his face into his mashed potatoes.

Jeannie covered her mouth and giggled.

Nick pushed back his chair, put a finger to his lips, rose, and went to Joey. Gently, he pulled the boy from his seat and wiped the child's eyelashes, brow, and nose with a napkin. Then, the man hoisted the sleeping boy, and in tiptoe fashion, carried Joey upstairs. As Nick descended the creaking stairs, he reached into his back pocket. *That bulge did have me curious.* Reaching the table, Nick centered a small box in front of Jeannie.

On the lid, small, black-inked letters spelled out *Copper Harbor Rock Emporium.*

"For me?" she asked.

Nick smiled impishly, nodded, folded his arms over his chest, and rocked on the balls of his feet. "I did a little shopping between packing artifacts."

Ever since that evening, Jeannie had worn the cut and polished Petoskey stone pendant and treasured the words Nick spoke. "I know it's not a pretty gem, like a red ruby or a blue lapis, but this three hundred and fifty million year old ugly gray fossil, formed by glacial movements in this beautiful state of Michigan seems more fitting for you, my Michigan diamond."

She smoothed her fingertips over the delicate chain and the lacy filigree mount encasing the stone, older than a dinosaur and recently named Michigan's state rock. "I absolutely love it, Nick. It's perfect—from one preservationist to another. Thank you." Once he fastened the chain at the nape of her neck, cleared the dishes, petted both Gunther and Wolf, kissed her lips, and wished her a Merry Christmas, he had left.

Remembering the wishes she made watching the taillights of his truck fade into the crystal-clear December night, she gulped. *Sunday marks two months since Nick's accident. Two empty, despairing, heavy, physically draining, exhausting pages of a calendar.* And not one word from him. The chatter she'd heard today reinforced she was all alone. Tina had a movie date with her boyfriend. Cal and Loretta were heading down to Indiana to the Amish flea market for the weekend. She could call someone from her widowers' group, but she didn't have the emotional energy to cheer someone else up.

Tomorrow will be better. I'll be too busy to be melancholy. Tomorrow is graduation.

Frank's mother had called two weeks ago. Knowing how busy Jeannie would be, she'd offered to take Joey the weekend of graduation.

Jeannie sighed. *He's gonna be spoiled rotten.* She smiled. She walked idly past the storefronts of the campus bookstore, the campus sports store, a dance studio, an ice cream shop, and a used-book dealer.

Salsa music and the aroma of refried beans blasted out of the basement level *El Azteco* Restaurant in rhythm with the large framed door opening for the next bunch of jovial Friday night happy hour revelers. Going home alone was one thing. Heading home hungry and alone was another. She trucked down the outdoor stone steps, picked her way through the people exiting the restaurant, and squeezed through the door. She inched to the neon *Takeout Here* sign and stuck her nose in the menu.

"A booth for two, please." A male voice competed with the cacophony.

Jeannie spun around. She dropped the menu. Her lungs seized. "Nick!"

Leaning on crutches, Nick pointed to the hostess's clipboard. "Yup, there I am. Just two."

"Nick!" Wedging her way between two football-sized dudes, Jeannie thrust out her arms and wrapped them around Nick's waist. She pressed her face against his chest, registered the indentation of his manly breastbone, and inhaled the intoxicating odor of his cedar-scented cologne. Jeannie pressed her eyelids closed. *Oh, God.*

A stuffed paper bag smelling of onions and cumin brushed against her shoulder.

"Excuse me," a long-haired turtleneck-shirt wearer mumbled.

"Right this way, Dr. Randall," a server directed.

"Table for two, me and you. What do you say?" Nick whispered.

Moving across his body to stand by his side, Jeannie flicked open her eyes and skimmed a hand behind his back. "*Si, Senor.*"

Parting the crowd like the lead runner carrying the Olympic torch, the server led them to a secluded, high-walled booth and set two menus on either side of the table. "Drink orders?"

"How about two virgin margaritas?" Jeannie gazed at Nick and raised her eyebrows.

"*Si.*" Nick smiled. Handing off the crutches to Jeannie, he bent his left leg and scooched his butt across the wooden bench. He folded his arms and surged his weight on them as he set his elbows on the tabletop. "Ahhh…"

Jeannie leaned the crutches against the wall and slid into the opposite seat. "For all the adventures you've been through, you look great," she gushed. "Tell me everything."

"How about just the basics? I just want to look at you." He laid a warm, moist palm on the back of her right hand. He gazed into her eyes.

Within the confines of her chest, Jeannie's heart beat wildly. Her pulse thrummed and awakened nerve endings in her limbs and in her female responders. She laid her free hand atop his.

The server arrived, set cocktail napkins on the

tabletop, and moved two salt-rimmed glasses atop them.

Nick bowed his head and closed his eyes.

The sweet plucking of violin strings, chased by the mellow echoes of a marimba, flowed through the overhead speakers.

Nick opened his eyes. "I had the opportunity to review my life."

Plopping a straw into her drink, Jeannie squeezed her lips around the other end. She gazed up at Nick and sucked up the tangy flavors of lime, orange and lemon. She winced.

He ran his hand over his mouth and chin. "There were parts of my story I didn't like." He turned his head and set his gaze on the carefree crowd. "My biggest regret is callously using you." Nick withdrew his hand. He tented his fingers and blew into them.

Pffft. Sitting straight against the bench back, Jeannie expelled a deep breath. "Nick, your guilt is inflated. I benefitted from our affair, too." She leaned forward and pressed her breast on the table edge. "The sex was really good. I mean really, really good," she whispered. She stared into the bottom of her glass and swirled her straw. Raising her head, she met Nick's gaze. "You forced me out of a long-standing grief bubble." With a fingertip, she caressed the back of his hand. "I'm in a much better place. I've found the will to live and love again."

The server waited with pen and paper in hand.

Nick met Jeannie's gaze. "How about we order two supreme burrito dinners to go?"

"Perfect." She braided her fingers together.

"I'll put this order into the kitchen. Should be

ready in about fifteen minutes." The server pushed her pen over her ear and threaded her way back through the jammed tables.

He laid his warm palm atop her joined hands. "Can't believe we are here together."

"Say, how did you know to come here in the first place?" Jeannie squinted her eyes.

Nick drew his lips into a flat line. "A few months ago, I made a promise to a mutual friend."

Jeannie tilted up her face and met his gaze.

"Cal. It was Cal. He told me to stay away from you until I, well, he didn't say it quite like this, but the implication was to stay away until I got my shit straight."

"And?"

"He's the one who clued me in on your burrito craving today."

"That sugar-addicted interferer." She pushed back her hair and grinned. "Where did you park?" A warm sensation flooded her. *Cal.*

"I didn't. My car's at home. I arrived via taxi."

"Perfect again. While you stay for the food, I'll move my car to a takeout parking spot, and then, I'll come back, get you, and carry the food." Jeannie's limbs trembled.

Nick squeezed her left hand.

He's here. He's here. But will he stay? With her heart stuck in her throat, Jeannie fumbled through the El Azteco crowd and raced up the medieval-like steps.

****

During the entire way to Jeannie's house, Nick gripped her right thigh. "I like it when you drive."

"Until you get that cast off, I will be the

chauffeur." Jeannie cast him a quick glance.

They pulled into the driveway as the sun bloomed pink as a rose and flamed the backsides of black-green pines.

"I insist on helping you. No arguments." She parked snug to the bottom step leading to the house, shut off the ignition, and walked around to the passenger side. Jeannie opened the door to the backseat and pulled out Nick's crutches. "You get adjusted, and I'll run the food in."

Bark-bark.

Taking long strides to the porch, Jeannie unlocked the front door, reached inside, and kneaded a hand over Gunther's snout. "Hey, boy," Jeannie flung back the door. "Guess who's here?" She stepped back. "Just don't knock him down!" Nick's laugh filled her ears and her heart.

The dog lunged and circled and wagged his long tail.

You're just as happy as I am. Jeannie grinned.

Nick stuck the tip of one crutch between the screen door and the wooden front door.

While trudging across the kitchen, Nick whistled in low tones. He laid his crutches across a kitchen chair, gripped the table, and pulled out a chair. He slid his butt onto the cushioned seat and extended his casted leg.

The German Shepherd flopped on the floor, rolled to his back, and exposed his underside.

Nick leaned and roughed up his belly. "Good boy." Scanning the room, the recovering mammalogist stroked Gunther's chest, legs and head. *Sweet dog. It crossed my mind I might never see you again.* He tousled the fur surrounding Gunther's ears. "Where's your buddy, Wolf?"

"Hiding somewhere. He's stealthy." Jeannie set two plates, two forks, and the takeout bag on top of the table.

"C'mon here." Nick reached for Jeannie's hand. He grasped her right wrist and pulled her onto his lap. He pushed her long hair aside and brushed his lips against the back of her neck.

Gunther sauntered to his food bowl, sat, and cocked his head.

Nick chuckled. "Pets and children first."

Jeannie rose and looped her fingers in his. "I love how you prioritize. Pets and children first." She walked to the cupboard, opened the dog food bin, scooped the dry pellets, and dropped them into Gunther's bowl.

Crunch-crunch

Opening the refrigerator, Jeannie loitered between the lighted shelves and the opaque refrigerator door. "Root beer okay?"

"Please."

She grabbed two bottles and thrust her hip against the artwork-and-magnet-cluttered door. After setting the beverages on the table, she sprang a can opener off a hook on the wall and handed the tool to Nick.

"Happy to do the honors." Nick seized a bottle, applied the opener, and popped off the serrated-edged metal cap. He handed the long neck to Jeannie, opened the remaining bottle, and knocked it against hers. "Cheers."

Jeannie lipped the bottle. The sweet, woodsy taste of sassafras swirled through her mouth. Sticking out her tongue, she smoothed foam that remained from the swallow's aftermath.

Nick traced a finger over the outline of her lips. He licked the tip of the digit.

"What are we celebrating?" Jeannie rolled her bottom lip under her upper teeth.

"Us." Nick gripped the brown, thin-necked bottle with his thick hand and pressed the glass against the tabletop, as if he were sanding a bumpy spot. Keeping his fingers curled, he slid down his clutch on the root beer. His throat constricted with a sudden dryness. He tilted the beverage to his lips, gulped, and backhanded his quivering lips. He tipped his chin and gazed at Jeannie. "If you'll have me."

****

Jeannie clasped a hand over her mouth. She widened her eyes. "Nick?"

"If I didn't make myself clear enough, I'm asking you to marry me." He pushed the bottle away and extended his fingers.

"Really? Yes!" *I'm dreaming. I'm shaking.* Jeannie squeezed his hands. "Burritos later." She walked to the door and locked it. She held Nick's crutches and handed them to him as he rose. Putting an arm across his back, she slanted her head. "Stairs gonna be okay?"

"I can hop. I can crawl. I can fly. Nothing will keep me away from you."

"Please don't put those words in our vows." Jeannie smirked.

"Some things are meant to be private, future Mrs. Dr. Randall." Nick rested on his good foot, swung the crutches to the step above, and leapt. He panted.

"Last step, coming up," Jeannie announced.

Creak.

Jeannie kicked open her bedroom door. She sat on

369

the bottom of the bed and peeled off her socks. She stood, unbuttoned the waistband of her jeans, and unzipped the fly. She shucked off her jeans and stomped on them. Then, unabashedly, as she gazed into Nick's eyes, she slipped off her panties.

He groaned.

She gathered the crutches as if they were canoe paddles and positioned them in a corner of the room. Cinching her fingers into the belt loops of his pants, she guided him to move backward. Once the back of his legs hit the side of the bed, Jeannie pushed him into the down comforter strewn atop the mattress. Kneeling aside him, she tugged off his socks. Then she unclasped his buckle, pulled off the belt, and pressed her open, trembling palm against his crotch.

With both hands, Nick reached for the back of her bra and separated the hooks from the eyes. He filled his hands with her warm, nipple-rucked breasts.

Breathing with exertion, Jeannie pressed her calves against the edge of the mattress, clasped Nick's waistband, and shrugged his pants down to his knees.

Nick lifted his butt from the bed and grimaced. "Gah!"

"I don't want to hurt you." Jeannie grabbed the pant hems and tugged. "But, dang, I'm exhausted." She chuckled.

"Don't slow down now, please." Nick gasped.

"I'm trying. I'm trying. This cast thing is temporary, right?" She snorted. "Well, it's only one leg…"

"At least six more weeks." He panted.

"The best part is, you can't run away again," Jeannie taunted. "Not with a cement leg. I could set you on my porch and put a plant on you."

"Don't wanna," Nick grunted. "Wanna stay right here."

"Hang on. We're at the end here." She scrambled off the bed and stood next to Nick's long legs. Lifting his uncast leg first, she threaded the pant leg down his calf and around his foot. "Voila!" Then, she placed a pillow under Nick's still-dressed knee, and using both hands, she shrugged the remaining denim over the cast and his bare foot. She bent, massaged gently the toes, and slid a finger between each, separating the digits as she moved. The musky scent of his feet consumed her inhalations. Jeannie snatched Nick's jeans and flung them across the room. She sat at the bottom of the bed, and then, snaked her body to align with his prone position. Jeannie pressed her nose against his lips.

Nick opened his mouth and joined his tongue with hers.

The sweet, lingering taste of the sassafras root, the main ingredient of root beer, swirled in her mouth. She pulled aside the frayed elastic band holding the lone garment, separating her mouth from his rigid organ.

Nick brushed his palms over her back and gripped her shoulders.

His tight, muscular texture triggered liquid spills from her body. Bringing her face close to his heated body, she blew hot, panting breaths. Jeannie opened her mouth and clamped his throbbing manhood like a vise. She pressed down on his good knee and fluttered her fingers from his calf to his ankle. The future Mrs. Dr. Randall stirred her fingers over her soon-to-be husband's heel and kneaded the bottom of his foot.

Nick squeezed shut his eyes. His face flamed. His

breathing came in short huffs. He arched his back. He tensed his thighs. "Jeannie, Jeannie, oh, Jeannie." He growled.

Jeannie quickened her ministrations.

Nick shuddered. "Jeannie." His voice grew raspy and then stilled.

Sitting back on her haunches on the wool rug, Jeannie smoothed his brow. "Shhh…" She pressed her lips on his eyelids.

As if her kisses were a magic ointment, Nick fluttered open his eyes.

The furnace clicked on and blew warm air upward through the floor vents. The forced air currents initiated curtain billowing like spinnaker sails hoisted for a Sunday afternoon sailboat race on Capitol Lake.

Jeannie shivered.

Nick ran his index finger over the top of her ear. "Come here." He fanned his left hand over the bedding that had been shoved hastily away.

She rose, walked to the opposite side of the bed, and crawled on to the mattress. Curling beside his body and avoiding his casted leg, she lifted his shirt and smoothed her palms over his rippled chest.

Spreading his arm around her shoulders, Nick rolled toward her and pressed her abdomen against his pelvis. "Your pleasure means the world to me," he said in a strangled voice.

Meow-meow.

"There's our boy." Jeannie dangled an arm over the side of the bed.

Wolf padded on the footboard, pounced on Jeannie's foot, and landed on Nick's cast.

"Argh." Gently, Nick lifted the kitten and cradled

him in his hands. "Good news for you, Wolf. No more split households where your allegiance is confused. Your folks will make it easy for you—one big happy household."

Giggling, Jeannie tousled the kitten's fur. Turning, she lifted Nick's shirt and buried her face in his downy chest. "Tell me why you want to marry me."

He wound a strand of her hair and tugged. "Let's start with Wolf."

Jeannie's head rose and fell in tandem with Nick's breaths.

Stroking her hair with the same motion as petting Sam, Gunther, or Wolf, Nick pressed the tip of his chin against Jeannie's head. "Remember the day we claimed Wolf?"

"I do, and I remember sensing how conflicted you were." Jeannie ran her finger pads over Nick's arm, delighting in the honed musculature and the realization that this luxury of touch had no expiration date.

He kissed the top of her head. "If I didn't know yet that I loved you, I knew it that day."

Jeannie curved her neck and met his gaze.

"You were so aware of this creature's needs." Nick ran his index finger down the valley of Wolf's forehead to nose. "When I was eight years old, I was playing in our barn. I heard mewling sounds and discovered a nest of kittens. I don't remember being more excited than witnessing those teeny, eyes-closed creatures. For several days, I kept that secret, and as soon as I got home from school, I ran to the barn to check on them."

"Oh, that's sweet," Jeannie whispered.

Nick raised his arm and moved his hand to the top of his nose. He squeezed shut his eyes and clamped his hand over the bridge of his nose. "One day, the kittens were gone."

Jeannie raised her head. "Oh, no."

Nick took a deep breath and opened his eyes. "I searched every corner of the barn. I sifted hay mounds. I got on my hands and knees and crept under an old wagon and around plows and rusted car parts. I ran outside and scrambled around the outbuildings." Shaking his head, Nick drew a shallow breath. "And then, I saw it."

"What?" Jeannie laid a hand on his chest. She recorded the rise and fall of his skin. An icy sensation traveled her spine.

"By the chicken coop...an old metal bucket covered with a tarp." Nick shuddered. "I took the tarp off. The bucket was full of water." Nick swallowed. "And drowned kittens."

Jeannie gasped.

"I stumbled to the house. My mother swept the floor. She looked up, scowled, and sneered. 'What are those big crocodile tears for?' I sputtered, 'the kittens...' She continued swishing the bristles against the faded linoleum. 'You aren't a baby. There are too many cats on this property. I did what I had to do.' "

Suddenly, the mystery of Nick's shallow human connection and deep animal bond became as clear as the crystal waters of Capitol Lake. "Oh, Nick. I'm sorry. What a wound to carry. But you have used this sorrow to better the condition of other animals. I admire and support that." Blood rushed to her ears and pounded inside her head. Her stomach churned. *Oh, Nick, no, no*. Jeannie wrapped her arms around his neck and laid her cheek against his.

"Jeannie, I'm thirty years old. I've traveled the world. I've had all the girlfriends I've ever wanted and then some. I want to spend the rest of my life with a woman I love and raise a family. I love how you are such a miserable bowler, but you are a good sport. I love that you enjoy polkas more than salsas. I love that you would rather sleep in a tent than a five-star hotel. I love how you can make your voice into a sturdy woodsman, a crotchety old witch, or a scared little boy when you read Joey bedtime stories. And, Jeannie, I love Joey, too. If Joey is the only child we are blessed with, it will be more than enough."

Raising her head, Jeannie met his lips in a kiss. "Remember the day in my basement when you pointed out I have rabbit feet?"

Nick chuckled. He flicked the bed linens off Jeannie's lower extremities and stared. "Yup. There they are—all skinny and pink."

Jeannie kicked her legs and flexed her toes. "Rabbits are renowned for other mammalian qualities. Would you mind having a kit or two of our own?" She clenched her teeth and fashioned a goofy smirk.

"Let's start now, Mama Bunny." Nick folded her into his arms. He kissed her forehead. "That would be a dream come true."

Sighing, Jeannie closed her eyes and felt herself drifting into a worry-free slumber that had been denied for months.

Leaning against a pile of pillows propped against the headboard, Nick shifted the upper part of his body into an upright position. Gently, he traced a heart on one of Jeannie's cheeks.

She opened her eyelids.

"I do have something else to offer you." Staring earnestly into her eyes, Nick paused.

Wolf stretched his front paws and quivered.

"Would you consider bringing Joey and spending July and August on Isle Royale with me? You could polish your presentation for Oregon State University, and Joey could work alongside me in the field. We'd stay in primitive conditions, with no indoor plumbing but a rather charming log cabin cottage."

Sitting straight up in bed, Jeannie grinned. "Yes, yes, yes!"

"And c'mon. If you need more proof of my love, consider the great efforts required for a broken man like me to maneuver those dungeon steps at the El Azteco." Nick pouted.

Jeannie giggled. "That did it."

Chapter 31

They were married on the thirtieth of June in Our Lady of the Pines Catholic Church, just a day after the wedding of longtime loves Bruce Hamilton and Margie Kammer and one week after the mammalogist groom was cleared from physical therapy.

Nick suggested the venue.

Jeannie agreed the Upper Peninsula setting was the ideal place to formalize their love and for all the guests who would share the day.

Of Finnish-style construction and built entirely from Mandan logs and rocks from Keweenaw County, the church rested on the eastern edge of Copper Harbor, within view of the Legion Hall. Inside, their family and friends sat on handcrafted Michigan pine pews.

Dressed in a crisp, white cotton-pique, cocktail-length dress of her own making, Jeannie stood before Nick and voiced her vows. "Nick, you bring me peace. You bring me hope. You show me how generous and patient love can be. I vow to shelter you from life's disappointments and sorrows—just as I promise to share in your happiness. I will strive to be worthy of your love all the rest of my days."

Facing her and clasping her hands, Nick uttered his pledge. "Jeannie, you are my muse, my inspiration, and my ideal. Jeannie, you and Joey are my family. I will respect and honor your memories of Frank, and I will always be thankful for his sacrifice. Jeannie, memories of the past will guide our present and the futures of all who follow us. Jeannie, make memories with me. I love you."

With tears streaming her face, Jeannie accepted hugs from her family, friends, and colleagues.

Joey jumped on Nick's hip and circled an arm around his stepfather's neck.

Nick inched close to Jeannie.

Then, Joey linked them as a trio when he threw his other arm around Jeannie's neck.

Cameras clicked.

A local Polish-themed caterer hovered over banquet tables in the church's nave.

Rectangular metal dishes sat atop fuel cups, and their bottoms reflected the denatured alcohol's blue flames.

Jeannie dawdled beside her cast-free groom with a sturdy paper plate in her hand. Her eyes widened, and her empty stomach growled.

The aromas of grilled kielbasa, shimmering caraway-laced sauerkraut, ruby pickled beets, and a family honored favorite passed down through generations—Annie Erhardt's specialty baked beans laden with sweet potatoes—penetrated her nostrils and made her mouth pool with saliva.

Bubbly ale foamed into glasses and spilled over their edges as guests tapped the kegs of beer, standing as sentinels.

"Hey, Nick, I'm eating grow food!" With a wide front-tooth missing grin, Joey held up his plate.

Nick scraped his knuckles over the boy's hair. "I'm proud of you. You're getting strong muscles."

"I'll need them for digging up arctic facts, right, Nick?" The boy clenched his fist and muscled his upper arm.

Gripping lightly Joey's bicep, Nick chuckled. "You mean artifacts—like rocks and skeletons."

"Yup, things to be saved for history." Joey lisped the last word through the temporary space in his upper jaw. "See ya later. I'm sitting with Cal. He brought me a new tractor."

Jeannie smiled. She drew a deep breath, growing weepy again. *So many dear friends.* She turned.

"I'm right behind you, honey. I've got two sets of silverware," Nick said.

She walked out into a shaded, grassy section where bouquets of spruce boughs and lilacs festooned linen-covered picnic tables and filled the surrounding air with a blend of earthy fragrances.

Setting up their instruments under a white tent, The Pierogi Pied Pipers, Copper Harbor's own Polish band, announced the bride and groom's dinner arrival with a short blast of accordion, guitar, and clarinet sounds.

Cheering ensued.

Shirley sprang from her bench seat and tugged Otto's hand.

Stumbling, the historian allowed his wife to usher him onto the dancing field.

Martin draped an arm around Mary's neck and whispered in her ear.

Laughing, the brunscracker baker rose from her place at a live edge table, twined her fingers inside her husband's, and joined the jolly crowd.

Gallant Arnie extended a hand to best friend Dee.

Smiling, Dee tagged after Copper Harbor's best

artifact packer to the fringes of the dance arena.

Nick set down their plates on the head table and responded to the cheers with typical groom behavior. He slipped an arm around Jeannie's waist, tipped her shoulders, and planted a lusty kiss on her lips.

"Attaboy!" Widowed farmer Jim, who drove over three hundred miles to deliver hand-picked roses for Jeannie's wedding bouquet shouted from his chair under a grove of leafing birch trees.

Seated beside Jim, fellow grief group member Marie blew kisses in the direction of the bride.

Sunshine glazed the top of Nick's head and curly chest hair that sprang from the unbuttoned collar. Jeannie registered the gilded cheekbones, the spongy earlobes, and the full and flavorful lips. She reached a finger and wiped a tear from her husband's cheek. *You're mine—my handsome, adventurous, protective, funny husband.* Jeannie felt her heart swell anew.

Lake Superior, the world's largest freshwater lake, gleamed in the background.

Sixty miles out over unbroken waters, a magical congregation of four hundred plus islands jointly named Isle Royale, beckoned the new family of three and their passion for preservation.

Praise Comments for Past Preserve Us

"I loved learning about unfamiliar subjects through the lives of these likeable, authentic characters. Every page is filled with beautiful, descriptive writing."

~Barbara Teller, Retired Special Education Teacher

~*~

"An historically accurate view of Michigan with an ode to second chances and finding love. A deeply moving romance that keeps you rooting for the protagonist to open her heart again."

~Sally Steinborn, Writer

~*~

"The story develops with a sizzle of romantic longing by the main characters and a dive into Michigan history. I enjoyed the spicy romance but was completely enthralled with history of the region. Subplots add to the mystery including a tin of old letters. The beauty and history of Michigan's Upper Peninsula and Isle Royale wolves in interwoven throughout the novel. Great read."

~Cherie Logan, Retired Nurse

~*~

"Through the beautiful descriptions of all seasons in Michigan, a loving treatment of a career in textile preservation, and a full cast of characters that enhance the setting, Nickles has created a work that pays tribute to her own home state and the love of its history while giving us all the romance that we need to keep the spark of hope alive in our hearts."

~Karen Alley, Freelance Editor

A word about the author...

Carol Nickles is an historical romance novelist based in Ypsilanti, Michigan.

She has a Master's Degree in Clothing and Textiles from Michigan State University and has been a faculty member at both Utah and Michigan State Universities.

https://www.carolnicklesauthor.com

Other titles by this author

Beards, Brunscrackers, and Snowflake Kisses

Thumb Fire Desire

Thank you for purchasing
this publication of The Wild Rose Press, Inc.

For questions or more information
contact us at
info@thewildrosepress.com.

The Wild Rose Press, Inc.
www.thewildrosepress.com